BLOODLINE

BLOODLINE

THE HERITAGE TRILOGY:
BOOK ONE

ALAN GOLD
AND
MIKE JONES

ATRIA PAPERBACK

New York   London   Toronto   Sydney   New Delhi

Go beyond the pages of *Bloodline* and unlock hidden secrets
by scanning the QR codes throughout this book.

ATRIA PAPERBACK

A Division of Simon & Schuster, Inc.
1230 Avenue of the Americas
New York, NY 10020

Copyright © 2013 by Alan Gold and Mike Jones
Originally published in 2013 by Simon & Schuster (Australia) Pty Limited.

First Atria Paperback edition September 2014

ATRIA PAPERBACK and colophon are trademarks of Simon & Schuster, Inc.

For information about special discounts for bulk purchases,
please contact Simon & Schuster Special Sales at 1-866-506-1949
or business@simonandschuster.com.

The Simon & Schuster Speakers Bureau can bring authors
to your live event. For more information or to book an event,
contact the Simon & Schuster Speakers Bureau at 1-866-248-3049
or visit our website at www.simonspeakers.com.

Interior design by Leydiana Rodríguez-Ovalles
Cover design by James Perales
Cover photographs: Jerusalem old city, Israel © Jevgen Sosnytskyi/Shutterstock,
Vintage aged old paper © Maxx-Studio/Shutterstock

Manufactured in the United States of America

10 9 8 7 6 5 4 3 2 1

Library of Congress Cataloging-in-Publication Data

Gold, Alan, 1945–
  Bloodline : The Heritage Trilogy : Book One / Alan Gold and Mike Jones.—First Atria
Books trade paperback edition.
      pages cm.—(Heritage trilogy; Book one)
  1. Politics and government—Fiction. 2. Jerusalem—Fiction. 3. Political fiction.
I. Title.
PR9619.3.G5764B56 2014
823'.914—dc23
                                                              2013047461

ISBN 978-1-4767-5984-5
ISBN 978-1-4767-5985-2 (ebook)

Absolute faith corrupts as absolutely as absolute power.
The opposite of the religious fanatic isn't the fanatical atheist,
but the gentle cynic who doesn't care whether or not there is a god.

—ERIC HOFFER, MORAL PHILOSOPHER

The Middle East—Ancient and Modern

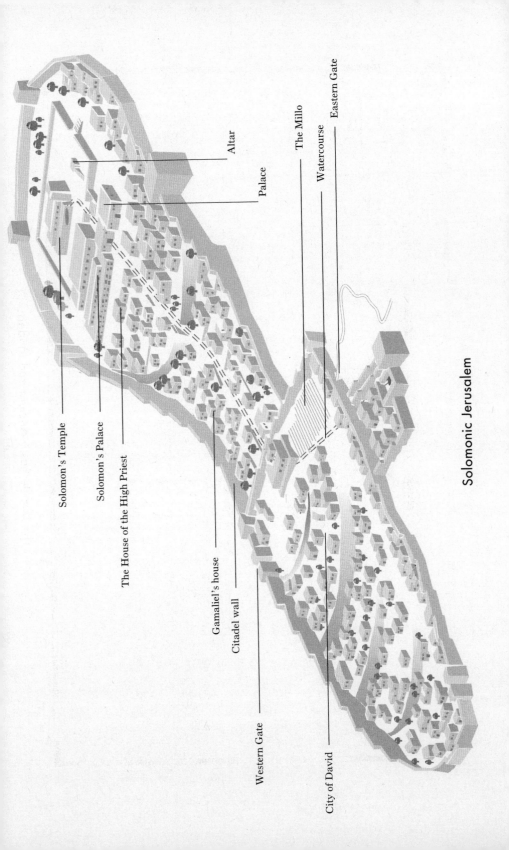

Solomonic Jerusalem

Altar

Palace

The Millo

Watercourse

Eastern Gate

Solomon's Temple

Solomon's Palace

The House of the High Priest

Gamaliel's house

Citadel wall

Western Gate

City of David

A TIMELINE OF THE EVENTS IN JERUSALEM

1000–970 BCE:	King David rules over a united Israel.
970–931 BCE:	King Solomon rules. During this time the First Temple is built in Jerusalem.
922 BCE:	Under the rule of Solomon's son, King Rehoboam, ten northern tribes of Israel secede from the two southern tribes of Judah and Benjamin.
722 BCE:	King Sargon II of Assyria conquers the northern kingdom and exiles inhabitants.
586 BCE:	King Nebuchadnezzar II of Babylonia conquers the southern kingdom of Judah, destroys Solomon's Temple, and exiles thousands of Jews to Babylon.
538 BCE:	King Cyrus of Persia conquers the Babylonian empire and allows Jews to go back to Israel.
516 BCE:	The Second Temple is built on the site of Solomon's Temple in Jerusalem.
332 BCE:	Alexander the Great conquers the Persian Empire. Israel is now under Greek domination; early synagogues spread throughout the Greek world.
167 BCE:	The Maccabees, the Jewish rebel army, rise up against the Syrian Greek overlords to rid the Second Temple of idols.
73–4 BCE:	The life of King Herod the Great. During his reign, he invites the Roman Empire to

	make Israel a client nation and rebuilds the Second Temple to be one of the major structures of the ancient world.
6 CE:	Because of unrest in Israel, Rome annexes Judea.
66 CE:	The beginning of the first great Jewish revolt against Rome, put down by General (later Emperor) Vespasian and his son, Titus.
70 CE:	The Romans destroy Jerusalem and the Second Temple.
132–135 CE:	The Jewish leader Simon bar Kokhba leads a second Jewish revolt. Emperor Hadrian crushes the rebellion. Jews are expelled from Jerusalem, but many remain in the rest of the land.

American National Broadcast Network

OPINION

Iran Holocaust Conference: Global Jewish Community Outrage

"Affront to Memory of Martyrs" says US President

NOTE: Opinion columns do not reflect the opinions of ANBN.

From ANBN Correspondent Ivan Grossman

0950 Atlantic Standard Time, Thursday, December 14, 2006

TEHRAN, IRAN – (Transcription from filed report)

Even by the Messianic standards of the ultra-religious Hassidic Jewish sect, Neturei Karta, this was a step into the unknown. In the past they'd formed strange bedfellows with anti-Semitic protesters at the UN Conference in Durban, South Africa; protested against Ehud Olmert's visit to the White House; and denied Israel's right to exist. Yet being honored guests of the Iranian president, Mahmoud Ahmadinejad, displayed an unprecedented step for the radical Jewish group.

Ahmadinejad had invited representatives of Neturei Karta, along with Ku Klux Klan leaders, white supremacists and anti-Semitic revisionist historians, to examine whether the Holocaust – perhaps the most documented and researched event in history – had actually happened.

Gathered in Tehran over the past two days, these 67 marginalized and peripheral representatives from 30 countries earnestly asked each other whether the Holocaust, which killed six million Jews, along with countless Slavs, Communists, handicapped and the mentally ill, had actually taken place.

To prove their case, discussion explored the half-life of Zyklon B, the poisonous chemical used in the Nazi gas chambers; the fact that no chimneys had been found, hence no gas chambers; and proposed that the concentration camps had been respite places for overcrowded Jews from the ghettos.

Holocaust denial conferences have been organized for many years by discredited historians, and anti-Semites masquerading as bona fide researchers, but the presence of ultra-Orthodox rabbis from Israel, the United Kingdom and the United States shaking hands with Ahmadinejad represented a new and quite bizarre level.

The leader of Neturei Karta from Jerusalem, Rabbi Shmuel Telushkin, told the conference on its opening day, "The Orthodox Jewish community views the Holocaust as significant, but it was a punishment from God for the creation of Zionism, the political philosophy to create Israel before the arrival of the Messiah; it is God's punishment for the arrogance and secularism of the Jews who have wandered off the path of Orthodoxy and Judaism, and who fail to put into practice the dictates of the Torah. Yet these very same Jews are using the Holocaust to legitimize the criminality and actions of Zionism."

Rabbi Telushkin's remarks were greeted with loud applause.

President Ahmadinejad has been a major accuser of Israel in its treatment of the Palestinians, and his policy positions have been given strange new legitimacy by the appearance beside him of the Neturei Karta. The front pages of Tehran's newspapers have been quick to carry the pictures of the rabbis standing side by side with the Iranian leader. In his state-controlled media, Ahmadinejad calls the Holocaust a myth created by Zionists as a propaganda tool to raise money and dominate the Middle East. He speaks of a glorious future for Arabia and Iran in which Israel ceases to exist. The implications for Iran's estimated 20,000 Jews, whose lives are already fraught, are unknown.

Hard as it is for the outside world – and a vast majority of Jews – to understand the rationale of Neturei Karta wanting the destruction of Israel, the sect believes that it is a sin before God for the secular Zionists to have created a Jewish state. The Torah says that God will create the state and Jews will live in exile by divine decree until the circumstances are right for the Messiah to return. And those circumstances? Upheaval, wars between nations, genocide and what they dub "the end times." The creation of Israel, they believe, has caused massive pain for Jews, and so the Holocaust itself was God's displeasure with the Zionists.

Shmuel Telushkin wore a Palestinian flag in his lapel and believes that his presence was intended to shake the Jewish community out of its complacency.

Ivan Grossman in Tehran, reporting for ANBN, the American National Broadcast Network

PART ONE

October 16, 2007

S LITTING THE MAN'S THROAT wasn't the problem. Bilal
waited, watching the Jew enemy shift position in his chair,
and fought to overcome his rising panic by remembering
the lessons he'd been taught. One hand over the man's mouth to
stop him screaming as the knife in the other hand sliced through
the soft tissue of the throat and all the blood vessels. Keep the
hand tightly over his mouth for at least a minute for the lifeblood
to drain away. He'd practiced the movement in his bedroom until
he was fluid as a dancer.

Bilal crouched and held his breath as the Jew, remembering
his duty, stood, scratched himself, walked around his position
glancing left and right, up and down, made certain that everything was in order, and then sat again. Bilal saw the man looking
directly upward to the white walls of the ancient city of Jerusalem and the golden mosque beyond—but what was he thinking?
And did it matter?

The panorama in front of Bilal made his heart beat in excitement. The massive walls of the Old City that surrounded the Temple of Solomon gleamed white in the glow of the arc lights. The moon was a thin crescent over the distant mountain ridge. In his rising panic, he tried to calm himself by remembering what his imam had taught him. That the great sultan Suleiman the Magnificent had built those walls and Bilal even remembered the date: about 1538. It was impossibly long ago. Bilal couldn't even understand how long. But it all seemed so grand and old.

Above the walls was the gray-blue dome of the third holiest site in Islam, the al-Aqsa Mosque. And beyond that, the gleaming golden cupola of the Masjid Qubbat As-Sakhrah, the Dome of the Rock, both mosques the symbol of Islam's ancient claim to the city of Jerusalem. Bilal found himself imagining pictures from the stories he'd been told since a child, of Mohammed tethering his wondrous horse al-Buraq, with its head of a woman, wings of an eagle, tail of a peacock, and hoofs reaching to the horizon, before ascending on his journey to heaven.

"Peace and blessings be upon him," Bilal murmured under his breath as a reverential reflex to using Mohammed's name. But Bilal's mission wasn't to pray. He prayed every Friday in his own mosque and lately, urged on by his imam so that he could familiarize himself with the terrain, he prayed in the al-Aqsa. No, today his mission was to begin taking back Jerusalem; to take revenge on the Jews who had dispossessed his family, destroyed his homeland, made his people into paupers, imprisoned his brother as a terrorist, and cast him as a refugee.

Jerusalem's night air was cold, but he felt comfort and warmth when he remembered being in the mosque of Bayt al Gizah, his village just across the valley, sitting at the feet of the imam a month ago, along with twenty other young men from his village. The imam sat cross-legged on a cushion, surrounded by Bilal and his friends on the carpet. His imam was smiling and talking with such ease and confidence about the splendors they would each experience in the afterlife; but then his face and voice became severe as he spoke of the way in which their people, the Palestinian people, were daily abused and murdered, tortured and brutalized, by the Jews. He asked each youth on his way home that night to glance over the valley toward the city of Jerusalem; to look at the glory of the mosques, one gold and the other silver, their subtlety and quiet beauty, and then to look at the gaudy, tawdry, and immoral modern city the infidels had built. One day it would be gone.

When they were leaving the mosque, the imam asked Bilal to wait. At first he thought the imam had made a mistake, confusing him with one of the older boys whom Bilal so looked up to. But from the moment he spoke, Bilal knew that his words were for him, and him alone. Barely able to breathe, the young man wondered why the imam had held him back. Was it because of the way he worshipped? Was it to ask him to do a job? Was it to say something now that he was approaching his eighteenth birthday? It was none of these.

"Allah has chosen you for a special purpose, Bilal."

The boy made no response but his heart thudded in his chest. Of all the prospects of hope and excitement that the sentence suggested, it was the sound of his own name from the imam's lips that filled him with the greatest pride and settled any doubt that his holy teacher spoke only to him. His shoes were worn near through, his family wasn't rich, and he'd long since stopped going to school. But there, staring up at the imam, he felt for a moment like a prince.

"You will be among the blessed. You, Bilal, will be a hero to our people, the pride of your mother and father. You will strike a blow from which the enemy will never recover. And I will ensure that your name is inscribed in the holiest of holy books and kept in pride of place in Mecca."

"Me? My name?" Bilal could barely speak.

The imam smiled and put his hand on the young man's

shoulder. "You, my son. Though I've only been your leader for a year, I have grown to love you and the other young men who have flocked to sit at my feet and listen to the words of Mohammed, peace and blessings be upon him. And in these past months, you, as well as a number of others, have impressed me, Bilal. You will lead the fight of our people against the Zionist enemy. Soon, I will inform you of a mission I wish you to undertake."

Close to tears of pride, Bilal whispered, "I won't let you down, Master. This I swear."

And during the month, the imam and the mosque's bomb maker had worked hard to ensure that Bilal's mission would be successful. His training done, his prayers said, his will written, his face and voice recorded for all the world to admire on the Internet, Bilal stood in the shadow of the wall with the imam's words still fresh in his ears. He smiled to himself as he waited and watched the Israeli guard shift his position protecting the entrance that led into the tunnel. He ached to strike a blow for the freedom of his oppressed people, to reclaim his land from the Jews. He lived a degraded life in a crowded village while just over the valley the Jews lived in luxury houses and had maids and manservants and wore gold jewelry and drove expensive foreign cars around a city that should have been his.

Bilal was a Palestinian but his culture told him he was born a refugee because of the 1948 war, and the war of 1967, and the war of 1972, and the other wars waged by fearless Arab armies to push the Jews back into the sea. Each war, each attempt to eliminate the Jewish presence from Palestine, had ended in failure and misery; but the Jews were few, and the Arabs were many and they could wait for a hundred, even a thousand years to win, but win they surely would, according to his imam.

And so Bilal waited patiently for the right time to kill the Jew. He hated waiting, but his imam had told him that patience and judging the moment were more important to his mission than rashly moving forward and exposing himself to the enemy.

The Jew guard seemed to relax; he moved his head in a circular direction as though massaging his neck muscles, put down his rifle from his shoulder to his lap, and reached down to a thermos; he poured himself a drink and Bilal saw the steam coming out of the cup. As the man lifted it to drink the coffee, Bilal slipped his knife from its scabbard, ran forward silently to cover the twenty meters between himself and the Jew enemy, and, before the man even knew that his life was in peril, put a hand over his mouth, pulled his head back, and sliced his throat in a gash of crimson from ear to ear.

Bilal kept his hand over the man's mouth so that he couldn't scream and embraced his body firmly against his own to prevent him from struggling. Even though the guard was seated, Bilal could barely constrain the tough body flailing against imminent death. He felt it through the shirt. It was a hard body, a strong body. Not a bodybuilder's physique with constructed muscles only good for posturing and lifting weights; no, this was the taut body of a man who'd done physical work all his life. Compact, tight, beautiful.

He put his face close to the Jew's, smelling his sweat and fear and blood. And in the moonlight, Bilal saw that he wasn't a Westerner but a Yemenite, a Moroccan or maybe even a black Ethiopian Jew—certainly a Jew with Arab blood, but difficult to tell without the daylight sun. Bilal felt a moment of empathy with the man. Killing an Arab Jew was different from killing one from Germany or Russia or America. As he held the man's increasingly limp body, he worried that he'd killed one of his own; but the man wore an Israeli Border Police uniform, and that made him the enemy, no matter where he'd been born.

With his hand still over the man's mouth, Bilal held him closely until he felt no more struggling. Just a body slumped in his chair, the stench of urine, coffee, blood mingling in the cold night air, making Bilal want to gag.

———

YES, SLITTING THE ENEMY'S THROAT was easy. As was concealing his body. He just pulled the dead Jew out of the seat and dragged him inside the fence where the excavations were being conducted to reveal the City of David at the base of the wall that encircled the Old City of Jerusalem.

And weaving his way through the digs, it was easy to ascend from deep in the valley at the base of the City of David, up the newly discovered tunnel, and out of sight into the Old City, where he'd create mayhem, headlines that would be read around the world.

Bilal stood at the base of the tunnel and switched on his flashlight. He remembered the feeling two days earlier when he pretended to be nothing more than a tourist, joining lines of people walking up through the tunnel. He was there to memorize the way, to plan every footstep, for when he came again to complete his mission, it would be dark.

On that day, the first time he'd been in the tunnel, he stood at the back of a group of American evangelical Christians, some black, some white, waiting for them to finish praying. Their leader, a tall, white-haired black preacher, was holding up the other tourists, but the man of the Christian god didn't care. He raised his arms and shouted to his congregation, "Brothers and sisters, let us ascend to the Temple of Solomon as the ancient Israelites did three thousand years ago, and raise our voices in praise of the Almighty . . ."

Every evangelist shouted, "Praise the Lord . . . Hallelujah . . . Praise be to God."

"Praise the Lord who has brought us to the Holy Land and enabled us to walk in the footsteps of our very Lord Jesus Christ himself, who came from the line of King David, who built this very tunnel three thousand years ago, my brothers and sisters . . ."

"Praise the Lord!" they all shouted as the guide for the City of David tried to round them up and usher them all into the tunnel.

Bilal hung around the group, and when the last few were

walking toward the tunnel, he attached himself to the rear, try-ing to hide himself in the crowd, avoiding the eyes of the guards and police and soldiers. And as they walked up the slope, which once was a waterway from the top of the city down to the Pool of Siloam, they began to sing "Onward, Christian Soldiers" at the tops of their voices as they slid and stumbled on the slippery floor and clung to the handrails in the dark. Had he been born across the valley, as a Jew Bilal might have known that this tunnel was used by King David to breach the defenses of the Jebusite city. But the intricacies of such history were unknown to him. All he knew of his people's history was filtered through devotion to the Koran. Yet, even so, Bilal knew that his beating the security in the tunnel would grant him accolades. It was history repeating itself. King David's captain had climbed the tunnel to open the gates, capture the city, and slay its people, and now Bilal, too, would climb the tunnel and kill the Jews who had usurped the holy city of Islam.

So Bilal sang along with the Christians, raising his voice for most of the song, mouthing the words he didn't know and qui-etly, under his breath, changing the word to "Muslim" when the evangelicals shouted out "Christian." He was a proud Muslim soldier marching onward, like the armies of Mohammed, peace and blessings be upon him.

And now that the Jew guard was dead, there was nothing to stop him carrying out his mission. Tonight he was climbing the tunnel again. There were no singing Christians this time, no throngs of tourists. This time his problem was the night-vision scopes of the Israeli soldiers who guarded the holy places around the clock. And despite what his imam had told him about the joy of being a martyr, a *shahid*, who would feel no pain as the bullets entered his body, there was a part of him that was afraid, a part that he knew he had to keep under control. Escaping after his attack on the Jews would also be difficult, but what did es-cape from enemy guns matter when he had the afterlife to look forward to, a green garden full of blue water and seventy-two virgins to attend to his every need for all eternity?

In his backpack were four bombs pieced together that afternoon by his mosque's bomb maker. Each had a timer, a detonator cap, and enough explosives to kill a cluster of Jews that would be praying at the Western Wall of the temple later that morning.

All he had to do was to get to the top of the tunnel and then continue along the path that led to the Western Wall, which the Jews called the Wailing Wall of King Herod's Temple. There he'd emerge, place his bombs, and hide in the shadows until early light, when the Jews would come to pray. That was the time he'd watch with pleasure as heads and arms and legs flew here and there and people screamed and men and women and children looked at the carnage in horror. In the mayhem, he'd dump his backpack and outer clothes and make his escape through the Dung Gate and down to his village of Bayt al Gizah.

———

943 BCE, the month of Sivan

MATANYAHU, SON OF NABOTH, son of Gamaliel, of the descent by God from the tribe of Judah, lay on his back, looking up in suspicion at the shard of stone that was poised to drop onto his throat. Like any good tunnel builder, he knew not to make a sudden move or to continue chipping at the stone until he was certain that such a move wouldn't bring a rockslide down on his head. The evil-looking shard, more like a dagger than a stone, was pointed like a needle, and could—no, *would*—do him great harm if it dropped and speared him.

Matanyahu's experience told him that if he hit the rock in the wrong way it would dislodge and fall, piercing his throat and probably killing him in the process. In the days of his father, Naboth, son of Gamaliel, a tunnel builder called Ezekiel of

10

blessed memory had been carried out from a tunnel when a similar shard had fallen from a roof and pierced his eye; he'd died in agony a week afterward, and Matanyahu, although only a boy at the time, could still remember the poor man's screams.

Blinking the dust from his eyes, he maneuvered himself so that if his next hammer blow dislodged the shard, it would land away from his body. He realized he was sweating despite the cool of the tunnel and the constant wetness from the underground river.

Matanyahu hammered a seam in the rock and clenched his eyes shut as the dust fell away into his face. He rolled over onto his shoulder, spat dust from his mouth, and then brought the hammer back, poised to strike again. But he hesitated. It was going to be a long day. He called out to the slaves nearby hauling rubble.

"Sing. Sing a song of King David, so that the Lord Almighty guides my hammer and my chisel, and the rock comes off without killing me."

Matanyahu continued to hit the rock, and eventually the shard dislodged and fell harmlessly a cubit away from him, breaking in two. He thanked the Lord Yahweh, then he thanked Solomon for giving him the job of building the tunnel that ran along an old water pathway from the top of the city of Jerusalem, all the way to the bottom, where it watered the crops of the farmers who fed the city.

Solomon! Solomon the Wise! Just two days earlier, King Solomon had made a surprise visit to the tunnel; Matanyahu had no idea he was visiting or he'd have prepared an offering. One moment the tunnel builder was on his back, covered in filth and debris and dust. The next moment he saw a man in rich garments lying beside him, asking him questions.

To his eternal shame, half-blinded by dust, Matanyahu snapped, "Fool of a man, this is dangerous work. Get out of here immediately or I'll tell King Solomon."

The fool of a man laughed, and said, "Then you'd better tell me now how stupid I am!"

Solomon continued laughing while Matanyahu stammered apologies. But the king waved him off and commended him on the excellent progress of his work.

In preparation for the building of the temple, Solomon had ordered the construction of a tunnel, expanding the watercourse that ran underneath his city of Jerusalem to the source of water at the top of the hill where the pagan building sat. And Matanyahu was just the man to build such a tunnel. He loved the dark and the damp. His wife said he was mad and ridiculed him to all the others, but when he came home after a day of chipping away at the rocks and ordering his slaves to carry out the debris and dump it into the valley—after being drenched in the ever-flowing water or sprayed by the drips that dropped from the roof of the tunnel—he walked into his house and he was cool, while his wife was pink from the heat. She might ridicule him, but she spent these summer days in exhaustion. Yes, he was dirty, but as a tunnel builder he could afford a plentiful supply of water from the well, and his servants knew to have clean towels to wash and wipe his face and body, his arms and legs. So when they sat for their meal he would be clean and cool, while his wife, she who ridiculed him, would still be pink and hot. And he would smile smugly to himself.

But those thoughts were for tonight. He still had a complete day of work to do. And that meant hacking away at the rocks on top and to the sides of the tunnel, which had been built by the Jebusites to fetch their water.

In years long past David, king of the north and south of Israel, had captured the city of Jebus from the Jebusites. His captain had secretly climbed this watercourse from the valley, under the impenetrable walls, and opened the gates. It was one of the last of the Jebusite cities to be conquered by the Israelites, but this was the important one, for it sat on the border separating the ten tribes of Israel in the north from the two tribes of Judah and Benjamin in the south, and David needed to show he was king of all Israel.

David himself had been forbidden by God from building a temple on top of the mountain called Moriah; this task fell to his son, Solomon, and it had become his driving mission to rid his land of the shrine to the child-eating gods Ba'al and Moloch. Yahweh had to replace them on the top of the sacred mountain.

The worshippers of those stone gods were long gone, but still their pagan building remained because the priests of the Israelites refused to allow any Jew to step onto land where pagan worship had been exercised. So the building remained, and Solomon's dream of a vast temple—a source of power and glory, of wealth and fame, built to the exaltation of Yahweh and himself—remained unfulfilled.

EVEN THOUGH HE HATED THEM as the enemy of King David, Matanyahu had to admit that the ancient tunnel builders had done a first-class job in extending what must have been a natural watercourse into somewhere that slaves could easily ascend and descend beyond the walls of the city to fetch their masters' water.

But the family of merchants who had been sanctioned by King Solomon to collect taxes to build his temple when the priests allowed it had also been told to raise money for the extension and widening of this tunnel. For King Solomon the Wise had determined that the people of the city of Jerusalem needed a secure source of water if the city was under siege, and so he had ordered Matanyahu and his slaves to improve what the ancient inhabitants of Jebus had done.

The work was filthy, dangerous, well paid, and he loved it. What Matanyahu enjoyed most was being in a place where he could see his work improve every single day. The more he banged and chiseled, the larger and more amenable the tunnel became. Where once he'd crouched, now he could stand. In the seven months he and a few other master stonemasons had been hacking away, they'd extended the tunnel remarkably, and the year they'd estimated it would take could actually be revised down to months. It wasn't pleasant work to be wet all the day long, but it certainly was better than being in the fields tending sheep, with ravenous foxes and wolves and lions constantly on the prowl, and a desert wind screaming in his ears, blowing sand into every opening God had made into a man's body.

At the beginning of his life, as a boy of seven, he'd been a shepherd, and all day, every day, he'd take his sheep from their pen beyond Jerusalem's walls, down into the valley where the thin but constant river that flowed from the Spring of Gihon ensured vegetation. He'd watch them drink, frolic, eat, and at the end of the day he'd round them up and put them back in their pen so that the guard ensured no wolves or foxes took one. And that was what he did the following day and the day after.

At the age of twelve, he'd been given by his father as a bonded apprentice to a metalworker in return for his food and lodging, and spent years building and lighting and tending the furnace so that his master could heat the iron, then beat it, then heat it—day in and day out.

So when his father, Naboth of blessed memory, died, he suddenly found himself free to pursue a profession he'd chosen himself. He would follow in his father's footsteps and become a tunnel builder. First he became a rock cutter, then a mason, and then after the death of King David, in the reign of the blessed King Solomon the Wise, he'd specialized in tunnels. Few wanted to do this work. Most were afraid of the dark and the damp. Some told fantastic stories of the collapse of the tunnels and men dying in the dark and cold, starving to death before they could be res-cued. But Matanyahu trusted his hands and his tools. The rock was familiar, like an old friend, and he had an instinct of when a rockfall might take place and knew how to avoid it.

And he had one other blessing that he knew would protect him from any harm. In his pocket was a seal, a precious stone that a scribe had faithfully inscribed—a seal that he carried with him at all times, and which, the moment he reached the top of the shaft, he'd place on a ledge so that God Almighty and all Is-raelites who passed to collect their water would know of his work and devotion, and he would be blessed in the afterlife. He'd done this on every tunnel and on top of every building he'd ever con-structed. It was Matanyahu's way of ensuring that Yahweh God knew of his work as a great builder when he died and ascended into the heavens for judgment.

Meanwhile, he had many cubits of rock to cut that day, and his slaves were waiting patiently, sitting in the cold tunnel below him, some with their feet in the stream of water, others resting before their backbreaking work began, and others still eating their rations. Lying on his back in the cramped area directly be-neath the roof, a cloth covering his face to protect him from the dust and debris, Matanyahu began to seek out a fault or an edge that he could use to begin chiseling. Provided he hit to his left or his right, then chips or lumps of rock or even boulders that were dislodged wouldn't fall on him. But that shard of rock pointing at his throat had frightened him.

———

October 16, 2007

THE PAIN IN HIS SHOULDER and his leg was excruciating. He gasped in shallow breaths because breathing hurt. It was like being hit repeatedly with a hammer. Bilal's eyes were nearly blinded by sweat, but he had to get out of the glare of the arc lights that were shining on him. He distantly heard voices screaming at him to stay still, not to move, throw down his backpack, put his arms on the back of his head.

His fury made him crawl toward the beginning of the shaft, away from the temple wall, out of the burning lights of the Jews. Another gunshot rang out beside his head, kicking up dust, which clung to his sweating cheeks.

"Stop right there!" shouted a voice in Arabic over a bullhorn. "Remain still, or the next shot will be at your head. Keep still! If you move, you will be shot dead. Stay still!"

But he crawled on, and soon his aching head and torso were already over the top of the tunnel. He heard more gunshots and felt a searing pain in his leg. His hands were too weak to grip the treads of the ladder, his arms gave way, and he tumbled down the well, screaming in agony.

Bilal landed in a crumpled heap at the foot of the steel ladder, the one that took visitors up to the base of the temple wall. The fall and the bullet wounds made him cry in pain. A part of his mind remembered his mission, and if he was going to die as a martyr, he would die blowing up the tunnel and the walls and bring the whole festering Jewish building down on top of him.

Somehow, despite the pain in his shoulder and arm and his leg, he managed to bring the backpack around to his front, and he took out one of the bombs. He smiled bitterly when he thought of the damage it would cause; he hoped that Jews would be up top, looking down, and they would die too.

Bilal tried to wipe the sweat from his eyes, but all he managed to do was to rub specks of dirt into them, causing him to blink furiously. It didn't matter. He'd soon be in paradise.

He held his breath and prayed once more to Allah, telling his God that he would be with him shortly. Then, thinking of his mother and father, he pressed the button on the ignition switch that would explode the bomb in the backpack. He smiled as he felt the button move. But then he suddenly remembered that the bomb was activated by a timer, and all he would do was set off the primer. His last words were a prayer for salvation.

The flash burned his back and the hair on his head. It made a huge noise, and some mud and dirt and rocks came falling down from the roof of the cave. It pushed him from a sitting position onto the filth of the ground. He grasped the stones that fell beside him. He looked up and wondered how that could have happened, how he could still feel stones in his hand. There should have been seventy-two virgins . . . and where were the green fields? Then he fainted.

———

BILAL LAY THERE SHIVERING, wet with sweat, his face a mask of terror. Like a fox, his eyes darting this way and that, never once meeting the eyes of the soldier, policewoman, or ambulance driver who'd brought him to the emergency room. Handcuffed to the bed, Bilal had wet himself, and the smell of urine rose above the aroma of antiseptic, making people who were close by stop, sniff the air, and turn toward him.

The young policewoman looked at him in disgust. She'd been the first to notice the yellow stain spreading outward from his crotch to dirty the thin white bedsheet that covered him. As he was carried out of the tunnel at the base of Herod's Temple, just moments after they'd challenged and then shot him, they'd covered him in a thermal body blanket to reflect his body warmth and treat him for his wounds so that he wouldn't die in the shadow of the monumental walls. It had been removed when he reached the hospital.

A doctor came running down the corridor with a sense of urgency and pulled aside the curtain. She looked exhausted. The policewoman, Dorit, assumed that she'd been on duty all night and probably most of the previous day. That was how they treated young doctors.

"My name's Yael. Who's this?" said the doctor.

"Says his name is Bilal. That's all he'll tell us, except to say that he's a Palestinian freedom fighter, blah blah blah, the usual bullshit. You know the rest."

"What happened?"

"He killed a guard, climbed up David's tunnel carrying four bombs in a backpack, and tried to enter the area of the Kotel. He was going to place the bombs at the base of the wall and blow up Haredi later this morning when they came to *shaharit* prayers. Stupid bastard. As if—"

"Wounds?"

"He wouldn't stop when he first emerged from the tunnel, so our snipers shot him in the arm."

The doctor carried out a cursory examination to determine the size and extent of his wounds, and saw that he'd sustained burns and abrasions to his back, his neck, and his head. None was life-threatening, but initial triage to stanch the bleeding and the pressure bandages applied to his wounds by the ambulance paramedics needed to be fixed properly.

"What happened here?" asked Yael, pointing to his neck and head. "And here?" she said, indicating his wounded leg.

"The shot to his arm didn't stop him, so our guys were forced to take him down again, this time in the leg; but he's a tough little bastard and somehow he managed to crawl back into the tunnel. He detonated one of the bombs but only the detonator cap exploded, which scorched his back and neck. Lots of smoke in the tunnel, and a bit of the rock work came down, but no real damage."

Yael nodded and turned her attention to the young man. She looked at his face, but he wouldn't meet her eyes. A sudden loathing suffused her and threatened to overwhelm her years of medical training: Ignore the person, treat the body.

But he was a kid who'd tried to kill a congregation of religious Jews, and now he'd spend the rest of his life in prison. If, of course, she managed to save his life. She asked him in Arabic, "Bilal, are you allergic to penicillin or any antibiotics? Before I prep you for surgery to remove the bullets, I have to give you an injection to stop any infection. Do you understand?"

Surprised that he heard his language coming out of the Jew doctor's mouth, he turned and looked at her. She was tall and slender and quite beautiful. She had big eyes and long, black hair.

Yael took a half step back. She'd experienced this kind of look before and expected him to spit in her face.

"Understand me, son. If I give you an injection and you suffer an allergic reaction, it could be very dangerous for you. Now, Bilal, for your own sake, tell me: Are you allergic to antibiotics? Yes or no?"

"Why bother?" asked Dorit in Arabic. "If it kills him, it kills him. Seventy-two virgins! *Inshallah!* Right, kid?"

Suddenly confused, Bilal turned to the policewoman, then to the doctor. And he could feel fear rise inside him. How had it all gone so wrong? The imam's plan had been meticulous. Before he set out, he'd been blessed. He'd been told that he was going to be a *shahid* and his rewards would be in the afterlife. But now he was in a Jew hospital surrounded by Jews speaking Arabic—his language—getting ready to use a knife. He'd been told they took organs to sell on the black market and used the blood of Arab children to make their bread. Or was it Christian blood? The morphine that the ambulance officer had given him had made him feel secure and happy until now. Suddenly fear was taking over.

"Fuck you!" he sneered at the two Jews in front of him.

Dorit shrugged and nodded to Yael. "I'll leave you to it. I'll be in the cafeteria. He's going nowhere. Here are the keys to the handcuffs; just make sure that he's properly anesthetized before you undo them." She slipped them into the doctor's gown pocket. Then she and the ambulance man left the cubicle.

Yael watched them go, then turned her attention to the kid.

"Okay, Bilal. As I said before, I'm Yael. I'm a trauma surgeon. You're going into the theater now, and I'll remove the bullets and stitch up the damage they've done. From the bleeding and your blood pressure, I think they've probably hit some minor arteries, but not major ones, so you're lucky. We'll take a blood sample, cross-match you for compatibility, and then tomorrow morning you'll wake up feeling drowsy."

Bilal turned his face away and clenched his eyes against the pain. Yael deftly inserted the needle and within moments his eyelids relaxed as he slipped back into unconsciousness. Yael continued to examine his wounds as the nurses swabbed and then inserted lines into his arm for the anesthetic and painkillers, and a tube into his penis to collect his urine. And as she looked carefully at the wound in his arm, Yael saw that Bilal's left hand was tightly clamped. Now that he had drifted into narcotized sleep, she forced his hand open, concerned that it might be hiding some form of explosive. But it was just full of dust and debris, presumably from the tunnel where he'd exploded the detonator cap.

Yael picked up a metal bedpan and brushed the stones and dust from his hand. As the debris fell, she heard the clank of something solid hitting the metal bowl. Sifting through the debris, she found that it wasn't a rock at all but some kind of colored stone, maybe marble, the size of a large pebble, with faded writing on it. She picked it up, dusted it, and held it close.

It was obviously old—very old. She blew on what she now observed was a semiprecious stone, possibly quartz or lapis. She took a bottle of distilled water and squeezed a thin jet of liquid over the face of the object, which revealed the glassy, iridescent original. The fluid exposed ancient words and symbols, but the comatose body of Bilal in front of her made her slip the stone into her pocket.

She noticed the theater nurse looking at her strangely. "What was that?" she asked.

Without consciously choosing to lie, Yael found herself answering, "What? Um, nothing."

The nurse gave her a curious look, but Yael quickly returned her attention to Bilal. She knew the theater nurse was a stickler for rules but hoped that she wouldn't question a senior surgeon.

As she set her hands to work checking Bilal's vitals and intravenous line, she felt her ire rise once more. This kid had tried to kill innocent people praying at the Western Wall. Those people would have been Orthodox Jews, devout and dedicated. In truth, she didn't have much time for ultra-Orthodox Jews, the Haredi, and she never prayed herself. God was a faraway and unprovable abstract idea to her scientific mind. Her culture and her country were Western and modern and she didn't like the direction in which the hard-line ultra-religious Jews were dragging Israel. But that was politics, not blood and murder, and she bit her lip and concentrated on saving Bilal's life.

Ensuring that he was now prepped for surgery, she readied herself for scrubbing up and entering the theater. But before she left the prep room, she glanced out the window. She saw in the distance the panorama of the Old City, resplendent and eternal within its ancient stone walls. There was the Muslim golden cupola of the Dome of the Rock, built on top of where once stood the Jewish temples of Solomon and of Herod; there the Tower of David and there the gray-blue dome of the Christians' Church of the Holy Sepulcher, beside the Via Dolorosa, route of the Jewish Christ's last agony. Three of the holiest sites to the three great monotheistic religions, dedicated to peace and harmony and the love of the Almighty; yet the site of some of the greatest crimes of humanity committed by fervent men in the name of a peace-loving god.

And she looked at Bilal, the latest fanatic in the army of madmen who believed in their absolute right to kill all those who disagreed with them. It was her job as a secular, nonreligious Jew—a doctor trained to the highest levels of professionalism in one of the world's greatest hospitals—to ensure that he didn't die. She felt aware of the strangeness and stupidity of it all as she felt in her pocket for the key to his handcuffs. And as she did, her fingers found the semiprecious stone she'd retrieved from Bilal's clenched fingers.

———

October 17, 2007

IN ANY OTHER CITY it would have caused people to turn and stare. But in Jerusalem it was part of the tapestry of Israel, a country where Jews of many different sects walked side by side with Christians of all colors and creeds representing a plethora of beliefs, watched by Muslims resolute in the belief that their version of the Prophet's heritage was the truth. And all of these zealous believers were ignored by thousands of irreligious men and women wearing the latest fashions, speaking on their iPhones, or engaged in heated discussions about politics or current events.

So when a middle-aged man wearing a business suit and a white shirt open at the neck sat on a park bench with another man dressed like the reincarnation of a seventeenth-century denizen of the backstreets of a Polish village, in the uniform of the ultra-religious Jews known as Haredi, few turned and stared. Those who did were hardly surprised by the elderly rabbi's clothes or by the other man's strip of white hair that ran from his crown to the back of his head, surrounded by graying hair on his temple, making him look as though he had a skunk sitting on his head.

The two men nodded as they spoke, their heads close together to the point of almost touching, and from a distance it looked as though they were whispering in each other's ears.

They were seated on a bench in the middle of Sacher Park, one of the most popular green spaces in Jerusalem. The park—a long and thin stretch of verdant sanctuary separating the suburbs of Nachlaot and Rechavia, and close to the center of government power in the Knesset and the Supreme Court—was a magnet for families, lovers, and workers on their lunchtime break.

But neither Eliahu Spitzer, dressed like a twenty-first-century business executive, nor Reb Shmuel Telushkin, in the black hat and frock coat of the ultra-religious Jew, was there because it was lunchtime, and certainly not because of any notion of passing the time of day. The two men, one in his late fifties and the elderly rabbi in his late seventies, were discussing the recent attempt to destroy the Western Wall, the Kotel of King Herod's Temple, and Bilal's failed attempt to kill a dozen Jews in particular.

"And?" asked the rabbi.

"Too early to say," said Spitzer, deputy director of the Arab Affairs department for Israel's internal security agency, Sherut haBitachon haKlali, or Shin Bet, as it was known to spy agencies throughout the world. Not many outside of Israel knew of Shin Bet, though its high-profile sister organization, Mossad, responsible for external security, was famous and feared by terrorists. But Israel had just as many people wanting to kill Jews inside the country and its territories as it did in the rest of the world.

Spitzer unscrewed the cap on his bottle of water and swallowed a mouthful. The elderly rabbi watched him with careful eyes.

"But do you think he could have got through?" asked the old man.

Eliahu shook his head. "He wasn't meant to. The police and the guards knew about him. The death of the guard was my miscalculation."

The old rabbi sighed. "The boy remains alive."

"True," said Eliahu. "I had a man there to finish the task, but there was no opportunity."

"This was not how it was meant to be." The rabbi waggled a reproachful finger at Spitzer.

"The boy knows nothing."

"But while he's alive, Eliahu, he remains a threat to us."

"It will be taken care of," Spitzer told the rabbi, who simply shrugged and got slowly to his feet.

They parted, the rabbi to get a taxi back to Mea Shearim, the ultra-Orthodox part of Jerusalem where he lived, Eliahu Spitzer to stroll back to his office ten blocks away.

He walked slower these days than before his massive heart attack three years earlier. Had he been less fit, there's no doubt that the infarction would have killed him. But as a Shin Bet field operative, he was strong, healthy, and muscular. His problem was the fatty meats he ate and the diet of cigarettes smoked during a stress-laden day secretly convincing Palestinian youths to become covert Israeli agents.

The heart attack had been caught before it was catastrophic and the quintuple bypass saved his life. Few outside his circle of friends and family would have known of his brush with death; the only outward sign had been the stripe of white hair on top of his head, where once it had been gray and black.

As he approached the Knesset building, he shook his head in sadness. He'd once so admired Israeli democracy that he'd brought his fourteen-year-old daughter, Shoshanna, there so that he could explain the Byzantine ways of Israel's parliament to her. As he walked past the building, the hideous memory train restarted. Kissing her good-bye at the bus stop, seeing her climb on board with her other excited friends contemplating a school trip to the Dead Sea and Masada, her angelic face in the window waving him and his wife good-bye, turning and heading toward their car to drive home, the massive explosion that had blown them off their feet and deafened them. The screams, feet pounding, parents hysterical, Eliahu trying to claw people out of the way to get to the bus—and the anger and hatred and sorrow and grief that became their lives forever after.

But it was a memory train that he had to drive, to control, or it would take control of him. So he did what his psychiatrist had

24

trained him to do: he forced himself to think of Shoshanna as a child in their garden, digging with him as he planted a vegetable patch, and sitting on his knee, hugging him as he read her Dr. Seuss. And the train slowed and came to a halt as he smiled at the warmth of his beloved Shoshanna and walked past the walls where great Jewish temples had once stood, back to his office.

———

942 BCE, the month of Elul

THE SHUFFLE OF SANDALS on the stone behind him told the king that somebody was approaching. He knew who it was. There was no need for him even to turn. The smell of incense on the man's tunic told him enough.

"Three years I've been waiting. Must I wait any longer?"

Azariah, the high priest, responded calmly, well used to such frustrated ranting from the king. "The king of Tyre has agreed to the supply of wood from Lebanon and craftsmen for the new temple, Your Majesty, but the old fox didn't make their time of arrival known."

Solomon's eyes remained fixed on the mountain before him.

"Only the men of Jerusalem know how to cut the stone. Massive stones for my temple. But such work needs timber and labor. And so I am kept waiting."

The king turned suddenly to face his priests. The lesser priest cast his eyes to the stone floor. The high priest looked steadily at Solomon.

"God and his temple are kept waiting for want of trees," Solomon sighed. Then he cursed under his breath. He looked out into the distance, away from the sight of the proposed temple. Watchmen had been standing on the tops of five mountains running into the distant northwest toward Lebanon, armed with polished discs of metal to reflect the sun's rays one to the other and send a warning, long in advance, of the arrival of the woodworkers from Sidon and Tyre, with their tools and implements and the vast amount of cedar he would need for the construction.

Solomon closed his eyes and imagined he could already hear the sounds of construction: of the cutting of the wood with saws and adzes; of the chipping of the stone blocks to ensure a precise fit, one abutting the other; of the polishing and sanding of the roughness so that it was perfect.

"The delay is costing me a fortune. Every day, every week, every year the temple remains unfinished means I am a lesser king in the eyes of those on our borders. We lose trade, respect, and money."

The high priest suppressed a sneer. "The temple is for the glory of our god, Yahweh, Solomon. It will be built when I say it will be built, and not a moment before or after. And when it is built, my king, it will be on land that is clean for Jews to stand upon, pristine for the use of the Lord. It will be perfect. We will fire clay into beautiful tiles and they will line the inner sanctum in which will reside the most holy of holies, the Aron Kodesh, the Ark of the Covenant, the agreement made between Father Moses and his people in the Sinai. All of these things, my king, will come to pass when I say that the time is right. But one thing I tell you, Solomon, and that is that no Israelite will set foot on that terrible place until the men of Lebanon have pulled down the hated temple and I have cleansed it with our sacred rituals. Not one Israelite, Majesty!"

Solomon looked at his high priest in anger but knew that if he were to move against him, Azariah would bring the entire priesthood crashing down on his head, and then the people would revolt. So, despite his power, he felt at that moment like the most powerless of kings.

But how could he wait longer for what he most desired? For years the Ark had been a site of veneration and worship, but in a temporary house; now, soon, it would have its own home. Then the Lord God of Israel would have His own dwelling place, His Shekinah, and He would be pleased. And Solomon would be pleased and more trade would begin, and Solomon's prestige would expand.

"I should just send my soldiers up to the mount and pull the foul thing down with ropes and iron," Solomon said in anger and weariness.

"My lord, I will curse any Israelite who steps onto that land. You know this cannot be so," said Azariah. "The sons of Zadok the Blessed have decreed the land profane. No Hebrew is to set foot on the mountain until strangers have destroyed its blasphemy—"

Solomon cut him off. "Stone by stone, pebble by pebble, until the mountain is again bare and naked before the eyes of the Lord. All I have to do is command, and it will be done!"

Azariah shook his head wearily. "That is not the way, my king. The ground must be cleansed. God has willed it so."

"And it seems you have the monopoly on God's will."

But despite his rebuke that bordered on blasphemy, Solomon knew that the high priest was right: for though he was beloved by his people and admired for his wisdom, all of the Hebrew people would obey the high priest. The power of the priesthood's curses for those who transgressed held more sway than all the whips and swords in Solomon's army.

He had waited with growing impatience for years, and his many wives kept chastising him, reminding Solomon that he was the king, that all knelt before him, and that it was his right to order the priests to obey his commands. And the most vociferous of all, the wife who complained long and loud in his ear, was his lesser wife, Naamah the Ammonite. He had been pressured into marrying her by her father, Harun, the king of Ammon, who wanted a political alliance, and in the many years they'd been married, she had proven herself time and again as a wildly seductive and adventurous woman. No matter how many women

27

were available to him, somehow Naamah was always close to his bed when it was time for him to retire.

And it was Naamah, more than any other, who had urged him to pull down the pagan temple and rebuild it as God's house, no matter what the cursed priests threatened. But Solomon was not that naïve.

Shaking off his thoughts, Solomon looked at the man who stood beside the high priest, a man named Ahimaaz. Why his daughter Basmath had married him, he couldn't understand: the man was short of stature, had a ridiculous giggle, and rarely said anything interesting. The king seemed as though he were about to renew the discussion but stayed his words and dismissed the two priests; he would win no arguments with them today, and diminutive priests like Ahimaaz were not worth the expenditure of breath. Instead he returned to his brooding over the pagan temple, starkly outlined by the cold but brilliant moon.

———

AHIMAAZ AND AZARIAH, the two priestly brothers, walked in silence through the streets of the sleeping city. Ahimaaz, as a junior priest, would return to his modest house low down on the hill on which the city of Jerusalem was built, and Azariah, as high priest, would be headed to a palace just below that of King Solomon. But for now they walked together.

Ahimaaz had grown up in awe of the seeming brilliance, knowledge, and worldliness of his older brother. But as they walked he found himself questioning the wisdom of Azariah's words.

He said softly, "Forgive me for saying this, Azariah, but I don't think you should have spoken to Solomon like that. He will become annoyed and it could go against us."

Azariah didn't bother looking at Ahimaaz before saying, "And how would you have spoken to him?"

"I would have explained to him the reasons we're not allowing anybody to build the temple until it's been cleansed."

"Is that not what I did? As I said to him two days ago, and last week, and two weeks before that. I have been telling him since I made the decree. It's not that he doesn't understand, brother; it's that he doesn't want to understand."

"But—"

"Our job as priests of the temple, by our descent from the line of Zadok, is to ensure that the worship of Yahweh is conducted properly, purely, and by all. Any deviation, any breaking of the rules, will weaken us."

Ahimaaz contemplated the words of his brother and couldn't help but wonder who Azariah meant by "us": the people or the priesthood?

———

October 17, 2007

YAEL RIPPED OFF her gloves and mask as she left the theater and threw her bloodied gown into a dump bin. Dressed only in surgical shoes and a light frock, she walked briskly to the doctors' changing room and showered. Now, dressed in modern street clothes and partly refreshed but tired after standing on her feet for four hours, she walked to the parking lot and drove the few miles from the Jerusalem Hospital in the direction of the center of the city until she reached the Israel Museum. She could have left it for a couple of days until she had more time, but she was anxious to see her grandfather again, and the object she'd taken from Bilal's hand gave her the perfect opportunity to go to the museum.

Even though she had lunch and dinner with her grandfather regularly, she missed his gentle ways, his wisdom, his knowledge. And especially his link to her grandmother. Judit had died when

Yael's own mother was a baby, killed by snipers when Israel was first declared a state in 1948. Yael loved hearing his stories of the old days in Russia and Germany, his work founding a kibbutz, and his training in archaeology.

She wondered what the precious stone was; she'd never have taken it to the museum had it not been for the inscription, which she recognized as ancient Hebrew writing. As she walked from the parking lot, she saw to her right the extraordinary building that housed the Dead Sea Scrolls, the roof of which was created in the shape of one of the ancient jars in which an Arab smuggler in the last days of the British mandate in 1947 had discovered the greatest treasury of biblical Jewish writings. There was a time when she would have loved little more than walking around the Shrine of the Book and the grounds of the museum. But that was a different Yael, a different life.

After passing through the metal detector and having her bag searched, Yael walked to the reception desk and announced, "I have an appointment with the director, Professor Shalman Etzion. My name is Yael Cohen."

The receptionist looked down at her list and saw Yael's name. She smiled and nodded, then phoned through to the director's office. "Do you know the way?" she asked, and Yael nodded. She knew the way very well, as she had visited her grandfather here on many occasions.

Walking down the corridors, up the stairs, and along passageways, she breathed in the perfumes of the ages. This wasn't public territory; the men and women who worked in these offices were working on stones and clothes, woods and metals, papers and parchments and all other types of things that hadn't seen the light of day for thousands of years. She felt strangely nostalgic but quickly dismissed it as whimsy.

As she walked purposefully down the upper corridor, she heard a deep baritone voice behind her.

"Ms. Cohen? Yael?"

She turned to see a short, gray-haired Palestinian in a dusty cardigan. For a moment Yael didn't recognize him, but distant memories from her youth enabled her to remember the man's name.

"Mustafa?"

The old man smiled and gave a short single nod of his head.

Mustafa was a museum expert on ancient Islamic arts and culture, respected throughout the world for his knowledge, and often appeared on television panel shows dealing with cultural issues. But to Yael in that moment he was an awkward and distant memory from childhood: a man her grandfather, Shalman, knew, a friend from times long gone, times of which her grandfather rarely spoke. They had visited Mustafa and his wife, Rabiya, when she was a child. She had played with their children. But that was a long time ago, and a lot of bullets and bombs separated that time from now. And Mustafa had told Yael, many years ago, about how Shalman had changed his life, about his sponsorship and encouragement of Mustafa's love of archaeology. How Shalman had fought to have Mustafa accepted into the university and how he'd become a top-grade student. But rarely did the two men talk about the old days, no matter how much she pressed them to do so.

Yael looked at Mustafa and thought that perhaps she should hug him, kiss him on the cheek as she might have done as a child. But she didn't. Childhood was her past, and the man before her was no longer a part of her present.

Instead Yael smiled and said, "It's been a long time. Are you well?"

Mustafa shrugged and said, "I'm old, like your grandfather. We have earned our right to complain."

Yael laughed. Grandfathers, it seemed, transcended culture.

"I have many grandchildren now, Allah be praised. But they grow up too fast. One moment you're cuddling them on your knee, the next moment they're helping you find your walking stick."

"But we love them for all their faults of growing up, don't we?" replied Yael. She struggled for what to say next, strangely awkward as she stood in front of the old Muslim after having just saved the life of Bilal, who had murdered in the name of Allah. She was almost relieved when he broke the strained moment of silence.

"You are here to see Shalman?" asked Mustafa.

"Yes," and before she had time to think about what she was doing she added, "I'm taking him this . . ."

She took the stone out of her pocket and unwrapped it carefully, handing it over to the elderly archaeologist. He looked at it thoughtfully, turning it over in his fingers.

"This is not in my expertise; it's not Arabic. It's Hebrew. But it looks very interesting. Where did you find it?"

"In the hands of a Palestinian terr—" she began, but cut herself off before she completed the word. Mustafa looked at her as if he understood and slowly handed the stone back to her with a frown on his face.

"Shalman will be excited to see this."

Yael didn't know what to say, so she said nothing as she folded the stone away into her pocket once more.

"It is good to see you, Yael."

"Yes." It was all she could say.

Then the old man turned and shuffled off down the corridor.

———

SHE WALKED ON until she came to the outer office of Shalman's suite, and his secretary of thirty-five years beamed a smile and walked around the desk, hugging and kissing her like a beloved daughter.

"*Nu*," said Miriam, looking her up and down, "you've lost weight."

"Don't start," Yael said with a smile. "No, I'm still not married;

no, I don't have a boyfriend; no, I'm not joining an online dating club; no, I'm not interested in your neighbor's son; and no, I'm not ill. I'm just busy."

"Did I say a word?"

"You're a Jewish mother!"

"How've you been? Seriously, you look tired."

"You'd think there was a war on. We're still packing them in, ten operations in a day. Mines, bullets, accidents. It never stops. God help us if Iran or some other basket case decides to get nasty. Peace is busy enough for trauma surgery."

Miriam smiled. "I'd better let you go in. He's been ringing every half hour, asking whether you've arrived yet."

Yael grinned and walked to her grandfather's office door, knocking gently. She heard his chair scraping and waited for him to open the door.

He stood there, diminutive, overweight, balding, white-haired, and pink-faced despite the cold air-conditioning, but just as beautiful as she'd always known him.

"*Bubbeleh*," he said, and hugged her.

"Shalom, Shalman. How are you?"

"Now, good. An hour ago, lousy. But come. Sit. Miriam, tea. And some cookies. The chocolate cookies, not the ones you usually give me."

"But your doctor said—" Miriam began.

"*Phooey!*" he said. "*I'm* the boss. Not him. What does he know about chocolate cookies?" He winked at Miriam, and said softly, "Miriam and my doctor conspire to stop me eating chocolate, but sometimes I'm clever and I fool them."

"But, Zaida," Yael said, "you know you shouldn't . . ."

"Not from you! I have enough trouble with Miriam," he said, grinning and holding his granddaughter's hand as they walked into his huge office. They sat on opposite couches, the coffee table separating them.

"It's been far too long, Yael. Why have you stayed away so long?"

"I had lunch with you three weeks ago," she said defensively.

"In three weeks, I could have died and gone to heaven. I'm an old man, *bubbeleh*. Three weeks is a lifetime."

She smiled. Her beloved grandfather Shalman was laying on a guilt trip. Why did Jews always play the guilt card? she wondered. Her mother had always laid on the guilt when Yael didn't call her regularly. Her excuses that she was busy or out of town never cut any ice. "What?" her mother always used to say. "There aren't any phones where you live? And why don't you phone your mother more often? Sure you're busy. We're all busy. But who's too busy to pick up the phone and say, 'Hello, Mom'? She's all alone in that big apartment with nothing to do except have tea with the girls. What are you, the secretary-general of the United Nations, you're so busy?"

Yael didn't let the guilt trip bother her, but she suddenly felt sad, sitting in Shalman's office, conjuring images of her grandmother, Shalman's wife, all based on photographs taken with an ancient Kodak. But she had died before Yael was born, when Yael's own mother was a baby, so all she really had of her were a couple of indistinct photographs and the narratives from other people. Yael's sadness was because her grandfather had been so devoted that he'd spent the rest of his life in almost perpetual mourning.

Shalman was looking at her, waiting for a response. "I'm just so busy," said Yael apologetically. "The hospital, my work. What can I say?"

Shalman looked at her sternly. "You can say that you'll have lunch with me every two weeks. Is that too much? You're all I have left in the world, darling, and—"

"Bullshit, Zaida!" she said in exasperation. "You think nobody knows about you and Miriam? Or five years ago, you and Beckie? Or before her, that research assistant—"

He put his finger to his lips, and motioned to the roof. "Shush! You want your blessed grandmother *aleha ha-shalom* to hear what I've been up to since she died? God rest her beloved soul."

Yael looked at the old man with a depth of affection, part granddaughterly, part maternal; she loved him so much, but his loneliness was of his own choosing.

"Why didn't you marry again after Judit was killed? You were a young man. You had a young daughter. Yet you never married."

He looked at her mischievously. "I had lots of good times with ladies. Why should I upset so many by choosing just one?"

"C'mon, Zaida. We all know about your affairs. But why didn't you marry? Seriously!"

The old man shrugged. "After your grandmother . . ."

He shook his head sadly. There was no need for him to finish the thought. It was eloquent testimony to Judit's extraordinary qualities. Yael only wished she could have known her as she knew Shalman.

Then the twinkle came back into his eye, and he said, "Yael, darling, love is blind, but marriage is an eye-opener. Why get married again when I was looking after your mother and dozens of women felt sorry for me?"

Yael burst out laughing. She loved his irreverence with all her heart. But there was always something in his eyes when he made such jokes, and Yael had often found herself wondering if it wasn't a façade hiding some deeper, long-forgotten event. From the time she'd first begun inquiring about her family's history, her mother's mother, Judit, had always been spoken of with reverence—too much reverence—and to her young and inquisitive mind it always seemed as though her grandfather and her mother were trying to hide something from her.

Miriam reentered with a tray of tea and chocolate cookies and set it down on the coffee table.

"I think I can make up for your disappointment in me. I have a gift for you. I think it's very old, but I'm not sure it's anything important . . ."

"Oh, yes?" Shalman said with a raised eyebrow.

Yael drew the object from her coat pocket and placed it unceremoniously on the table, wrapped as it was in a bandage taken casually from the hospital. Shalman wrinkled his nose as if fearing the swaddled object might be some macabre hospital souvenir or practical joke—a severed finger, or worse . . .

"What's this?" he asked quizzically.

"Not sure. Probably nothing. Something for your collection of historical tidbits. Maybe just a peace offering," replied Yael with a smile.

Shalman gingerly began to unwrap the object, his curiosity piqued. Yael turned her gaze to the window and unconsciously changed topic.

"So I thought we might go out for lunch. I can make time. Beautiful day outside . . ."

Shalman suddenly cut her off. "Where did you get this?"

Yael turned back to see the small object unwrapped on the table and Shalman's eyes wide and staring at her.

"It was in the hands of a Palestinian kid who tried to blow up the Haredi at the Kotel. The police shot him, arm and leg, and—"

"Where?" Shalman cut her off sharply. "Where did he find it?"

"He tried to explode a bomb underground, near to the entrance to Warren's Shaft—King David's tunnel."

Shalman leapt to his feet, holding the object tenderly in his hands, retreating to his desk to examine the stone more carefully. Yael continued the story, although she doubted that her grandfather was still listening.

"Only the detonator cap went off, thank God. But it must have brought down some masonry. Anyway, he was brought in unconscious for me to operate on, and I found that in his hand."

Shalman studied the object methodically yet held it like a newly delivered granddaughter. He read the inscription, turned it over, turned it back again to reread. Then he viewed the sides, then the reverse, then the obverse; then he reread the inscription, then he turned it over and then over again.

Yael realized that she'd been holding her breath and was surprised at herself. She wanted to ask what he was thinking, but knew to keep silent.

Finally Shalman looked up at her and smiled. "You have . . ." He couldn't continue. She was surprised by the emotion in his voice.

Holding the object, he stood from his desk and walked over to his library, taking one book, then another, flicking over some pages but not really looking. Instead, energized, he walked to the window and continued to look at the object that the Palestinian boy had grasped with a handful of dirt just before he blacked out.

Yael sat there in fascination, wondering whether it was her grandfather's usual sense of exaggeration or something else.

"Well?" she asked after what seemed like minutes of silence.

Instead of answering, Shalman bellowed, "Miriam!"

Suddenly the door flew open. "Fetch Mordecai. And Zvi. And Sheila. And fetch Mustafa . . . he'd be fascinated by this. And . . . oh, hell. Fetch everybody! Now! Immediately! Go! I don't care if they're in a meeting. Go! You're still there. Why? Go!"

"What?" asked Yael.

Shalman shrugged, suddenly coy. "What do you think it is?"

"Don't play games, Shalman."

"No game. I want to know. What do you think it is?"

"If you don't tell me what it is, I'll take it to the Bible Museum."

"Don't even joke! Treasure hunters and publicity hounds. Amateur *mamzers*!" He motioned with a theatrical gesture for Yael to come over to the light of the window. On the sill, there was a magnifying glass. Holding the stone, he turned it slowly, lowered his voice to a reverential whisper, and said softly, "It's a seal, of a mason from Solomon's Temple, when he was building the underground walls. It's perfect. It's intact. It's wonderful . . . I've never . . . didn't even think that in my life . . ."

"That's it? A seal? You've got to get out more often, Shalman, and get some perspective." It might have been a casual joke, but again the words were harsher from her lips than she intended them to be. She turned away from the window.

Yael turned suddenly when she heard a gasp from the doorway. Shalman also turned and saw Miriam still standing there, looking on in rapt attention.

"Go! Now! Bring them all."

He turned back to Yael, and calmed himself down. "It says, '*I, Matanyahu, son of Naboth, son of Gamaliel, have built this tunnel for the glory of my king, Solomon the Wise, in the twenty-second year of his reign.*'"

Yael turned back to face her grandfather; she'd never seen his face so luminous. He'd always been a lovely old man to her, but now he looked zealous, electrified.

"I have to get Zvi to give an exact translation—not just the words, but their meaning, the nuance, but I'm pretty sure . . ."

Yael stared at him lovingly, the significance of what he had just said not lost on her. Shalman's thin voice shifted register into his "lecture voice."

"Let me try to explain . . . The tunnel builder, Matanyahu, son of Naboth, son of Gamaliel, mounted it somehow onto the wall so that everybody who passed by climbing up the tunnel would see it and know who'd built it. And God would know that he built it." Shalman stopped and faced Yael directly with a smile. "Or something like that." He lowered the object. "Over the millennia it must have got covered up by dirt or mud or something. But after three thousand years, to know the name of the man who built the tunnel under David's city . . ."

Suddenly there was the sound of footsteps approaching quickly. The door flew open, and two elderly archaeologists rushed into the room.

"A seal!" shouted one.

"From the First Temple," said the other.

Furious at being upstaged, Shalman yelled in fury, "Miriam, why did the Almighty give you such a big mouth?"

———

IT WAS ALWAYS DANGEROUS, but Yael's life was so pressured that the moment she felt the vibration, she picked up her phone, one eye on the frenetic traffic ahead of her, the other eye on the illuminated screen, and quickly read the words of the text message.

It was a request that she return to the hospital as quickly as possible. That meant one of three things, or maybe all three at the same time: one, an urgent new case, somebody who needed surgery immediately; two, one of her patients was in postoperative trouble; or three, the chief surgeon was being pressured by the hospital administration to achieve some sort of new efficiency and he needed Yael's help to frame a response telling them to go to hell but without upsetting them too much.

She was on her way back from the Israel Museum anyway; she always returned, even for half an hour, to check personally on the recovery of all her patients before quitting for the night. Pulling into the parking lot, she wondered which of the three usual summonses it would be this time—or maybe there'd be a fourth that the bureaucrats had suddenly invented to ensure that the doctors knew who was running the hospital and who was paying the salaries. It was all so infantile, and so typical of Israeli bureaucracy—another reason why Yael had declined the past two promotions she'd been offered from the hospital, preferring instead to do what she loved most and not accepting more money for a new level of administrative responsibility.

Walking quickly toward her boss's office, she nodded to the secretary and went straight in.

"So, what's up?"

Pinkus Harber was only ten years older than Yael but looked as if he could be her grandfather. Like Yael, he had no life outside of the hospital. Twice divorced, with four kids who lived elsewhere, he was the archetypal obsessive personality who'd driven himself into the ground. She adored him, as he adored her, and once, in a reception at the hospital, he'd tried to get too friendly and she'd deflected any hope he may once have harbored about a relationship. But it hadn't affected their professional or personal bond, and they remained both valued colleagues and dear friends.

"Your last patient, the Palestinian kid . . ."

Yael waited for the bad news.

"We have to go in again. He was doing fine in recovery, but then an hour after we took him back into the ward, his BP suddenly dropped massively and we had to pump him full of adrenaline. We nearly lost him. One of his major arteries must have bled."

Yael frowned and recalled every moment of the four hours she'd spent repairing his body. She shook her head in surprise. "No, not possible. There were no major arteries. He was incredibly lucky. The bullets missed all the biggies and only minor ones were lacerated. I fixed them up. I checked his BP after the closure, and it was fine and rising. It's something else—gotta be."

Pinkus shrugged. "What?"

"Dunno, but it couldn't be from surgery. I didn't miss anything. I didn't go into his body cavity or his chest or anything like that. I don't think we should reopen him—not yet. Let's just observe him for the next twenty-four hours and keep him on meds and support and see what happens. I suppose you've ordered close observations," she said. "Have we got a reading on his iron yet?"

"Very low. Probably thalassemia. He's got a huge hemoglobin count and a low red cell count, so I've ordered a profile."

"Do you think it could be something else?" she asked.

"He wouldn't have gone into shock after the operation because of his thalassemia. Half of the Arabs suffer from it. No, it's something else. But I agree that we can afford observations for twenty-four hours rather than schlep him back into surgery. Oh, and there's one more thing . . ."

The look on his face told her that it wasn't good news. She waited for him to speak again.

"His blood group . . . AB negative . . . very rare, of course. We have a supply shortage. Donations are almost impossible. I know that we can use a negative, but . . . what I mean is . . ."

Yael shook her head, knowing exactly where this was going. AB negative blood types accounted for only one percent of the Israeli population. She herself was one of the very, very few in the country, which was why she was always called upon, every four months, to donate some of her blood.

"No way. No damn way. I sweated blood for him for four hours. I'm not giving him any more, especially my actual blood. Anyway, fill him up with universal O neg. He'll be fine."

"Not sure if I want to risk it if he's suffering from thalassemia. He's been through trauma, and I'm concerned about an adverse reaction. Better for him to have AB negative. And that's where we have a problem, because of supply shortages."

"Isn't there . . ."

Pinkus shook his head slowly.

"Anywhere?" she asked.

Again he shook his head. "We've phoned Tel Aviv, Haifa, everywhere. It's in such short supply."

Yael sighed. "My damn *mazel*. That's all I need. An Arab with my blood group."

Pinkus grinned. "Israel is the land of coincidence."

By the time she returned to the intensive care unit, Bilal was stabilized, but she knew just by looking at him that the pallor of his skin and the deflated nature of his body meant that he was on life support. Again she searched her mind for something she'd missed when she was operating inside his body. But after she'd repaired the damage to his blood vessels and his muscles, and pumped him full of a cocktail of intravenous antibiotics, he should already have started to recover. Nor did it seem to be a severe adverse reaction to the medicines she'd prescribed. A young man in full strength shouldn't be behaving like an old man grasping at staying alive.

She checked his charts and was worried by his vital signs. But she had no idea what it could be. Still, now that he was stabilized, even though on virtual life support, she had the time to check other things. He could have had a problem with his liver, his kidneys, his gut; something outside of her operation must have happened to have caused such a massive blood pressure drop. If he was suffering from thalassemia, then he'd be anemic, but after the operation his blood pressure had been normal.

The cause usually had to do with loss of blood, but from where? Could one of his organs have been ruptured? Impossible. Could she have missed something? Possible but hugely unlikely— not because she was infallible, but because she'd checked really carefully. And there were no puncture wounds on any other part of his body that could have damaged internal organs.

Perhaps he'd swallowed something and was being poisoned; but again, they'd done a toxicology screen and his blood seemed to be clean. In confusion and concern, she walked to the nurses' station, smiled at the nurse in charge, and picked up the phone, asking the operator to put her in touch with the head of internal medicine.

She explained in a few terse sentences her patient's condition to Professor Elon Talmidge, who asked her, "Have you done a CT scan? An MRI? X-rayed his chest and stomach? We might need to do some nuclear medicine to find out what's happening inside and see if there's a problem with his organs or some blockage or something. But isn't this guy the terrorist who killed the guard?"

Yael told him who the patient was.

"I'm talking about a lot of investigation. Seriously high-end medicine. This kid will be going to prison for the rest of his life. It seems a bit of an extravagance, if you'll forgive my saying so."

"And how will that sort of statement sound on Arab television, Elon?" she asked.

"I don't give a fuck. But you're right: we should find out why his BP dropped so drastically. Pump him full of blood and I'll order the tests."

"That's another problem," she told Elon. "We've run short of AB negative and I'm probably his only source."

He remained silent. It was the silence of condemnation. She could feel him looking sternly at her, even through the phone, just as he'd done when she was at the university and he was her professor.

"Okay, I'll set it up. You order the X-ray and other tests and I'll order the bloodwork, and then we'll find out what's what," she said.

She put down the phone and began to write instructions to the pathology department. But when she thought about their having the same blood group, out of interest she wondered what a comprehensive DNA profile would show. His DNA spectrum could explain much about his family history, even going back aeons.

It took twenty-four hours before she began to feel stronger after giving her blood. She barely considered the irony that the kid would survive to live for the rest of his life in a prison. She picked up the reports and wondered whether she would have enough energy to go out tonight to a new stand-up comedy club that she'd been told was very edgy. She yawned and decided to go home, order some takeout.

When she read his results and looked at the pictures from the CT scan, it all became as obvious to her as it had been to her colleagues. The young man was both incredibly unlucky and extraordinarily fortunate. Unlucky that there was a massive growth of rogue blood vessels on the outside of his left kidney, an angiomyolipoma, which had burst and bled at least two liters of blood into his stomach. Yet unbelievably lucky that it had happened in one of the world's leading hospitals. Had it happened in his village, and had he been taken to a Palestinian hospital, there would have been no hope of it being diagnosed, let alone treated. He might have lived, or he might have died, but he would have been extremely sick.

Because Yael was weakened from giving him blood, the head of surgery had refused to allow her to observe the rare and complex operation. So one of the hospital's senior renal surgeons had been called upon to insert a catheter in the kid's leg and follow its progress up his arteries until he'd maneuvered it into the blood vessels that were the source of the growth. There he filled the vessels full of a mixture of ethanol and inert particles, nonreactive gloop designed to block the blood vessels and kill them off. In time the growth would wither and die and normality would be restored. In the meantime, he'd had a large infusion of Yael's blood, the operative procedure had been successful, his bodily functions had returned to normal, and he'd soon be sufficiently recovered to return to the police, then the courts, then prison.

Yael put down the scans and picked up the pathologist's report on his blood and DNA. She looked closely at the pictures of the DNA sequences. She studied the vertical lines and read the report. Then she looked again at the sequencing pictures and frowned in concern. She stood and walked over to her filing cabinet, pulling open a drawer and searching for a file. Some years earlier she'd participated in a heritage study among Ashkenazi Jews conducted by the Technion, the university in Haifa. She found the file and withdrew her own DNA sequencing. She looked at it carefully and realized that, despite the air-conditioning, she was sweating profusely.

———

942 BCE

FROM HIS VANTAGE POINT on the flat roof of his palace, Solomon watched the two men walking down the steep hill on which the city of Jerusalem had been built. Most of the original buildings of the Jebusites had been demolished. New houses, shops, markets, and palaces had been constructed. And it was a beautiful city, pleasing to Solomon. He smiled as his mind settled on his lesser wife, Naamah. The previous night she had caused him to shout out in joy, doing things to his body that he was certain the Lord Yahweh would find offensive. Yet the words she had whispered to him as he lay spent on the bed, about how the priests weakened him in the eyes of the people, haunted him.

His first wife, Tashere, would be waiting for him tonight. She always waited. But he would not go to her. Naamah was in his thoughts, residing somewhere between lust and desire. Descending two levels in his palace, he walked along a corridor and through a courtyard covered in vines, and entered Naamah's separate apartments. Though he'd not told anybody he was visiting his third and lesser wife, it was as though her servants were expecting him. Solomon was met at the vestibule of her apartments by two rows of bare-breasted women, some from her nation of Ammon, some from Nubia, and some he thought might be Egyptians. They bowed as he walked past them and held out trays of bread cooked in spices, honey from the comb, and thinly sliced meats. He took a slice of fig covered in honey as he walked toward Naamah's rooms.

He found her naked except for a sheath of the sheerest gossamer covering her body, lying on her bed propped up on one arm, and smiling at him.

"I knew you'd come to me tonight, my king, my lion," she said. "I know what mood you wear after you have spoken to those priests of yours. You desire to have your mind and body eased by your loving wife from Ammon."

Solomon straightened to his full height and looked at her with skepticism in his heart. "And what if I'd have chosen my first wife tonight? What if it had been Tashere the Egyptian I went to?"

"Then you would have enjoyed a long and restful night's sleep."

Solomon snorted and stepped closer to the bed. He felt a stirring in his groin.

"Come to me, my lion of Judah. Let your Naamah soothe your mind and excite your body."

Solomon, lord and master of Israel and many lands and nations beyond, was helpless in her presence. Any resolve he might have had with other wives, no matter how skillfully they pleasured him, disappeared immediately when he was with Naamah. She wasn't the most beautiful, nor was her body as comely as many of his other wives, nor was she as young and nubile, but she knew how to pleasure him, drawing him to her like bees to a ripe and newly opened flower.

He slipped off his cape, undid the fastenings on his tunic, and in the blinking of an eye stood there naked, prone, and rigid. Naamah smiled and beckoned him with her finger to come to her. Solomon mounted her bed and reached for her breast, cupping it in his hand as he kissed her tenderly. What he didn't see was Naamah beckoning with her fingers behind his back to three of her most beautiful naked slaves standing just beyond the doorway. They entered her bedchamber, climbed onto her bed, and pleasured Solomon while he was still kissing Naamah.

It took longer, much longer than the previous night, for her lion to be spent, emptied, and satisfied, but as with all men the end came loudly and definitively. As he lay back on her cushions, she dismissed the three slaves and lay beside him, holding him in her arms.

"Why do you let these priests offend you, my king?" she whispered. "In Ammon, my father would have had them nailed to a cross like the Assyrians and the Akkadians when they wish to punish somebody. It can take a man a day or more to die in agony. If you did that to one of your priests, the others would do your bidding immediately."

His voice hoarse from his cries during lovemaking, he said softly, "I can't go against them. In your land you have many gods, and your father, the king, is the greatest of your gods. But we are not like you. We have just one god, Yahweh. And anyway,

Yahweh tells us that we mustn't be cruel in our punishments."

"My lion, I have just felt the potency of your sword. You have great power. It should be you that wields it, not the priests," she said.

"If I move against the priests, then the people of Israel will spurn me."

"Then appoint a priest who will wield Yahweh's sword for you and not for himself. Then both the priests and the people will be your subjects."

But she didn't know whether he'd heard, because as she stroked his hair she realized that he was asleep.

———

TASHERE, DAUGHTER of Pharaoh Shoshenq and first wife to King Solomon the Wise, had for many years been a devoted wife. But the sands were shifting, and as she made her way to the throne room she eyed with suspicion the people she passed.

Tashere had been the first wife Solomon had taken. When Tashere was Solomon's only wife, she was lavished with gifts and a palace and attention. Now Solomon had hundreds of wives. Each day it seemed she saw a woman whose face she had never seen before. Of course they all knew her and greeted her courteously as first wife, but each diminished her a little and she felt their presence like needles in her skin. Yet, Tashere loved Solomon. And at night when she was alone, she reminded herself that she was his first true love and that, regardless of the numbers of other wives and concubines, none of them could feel this way.

Tashere stopped herself at the great doors to the throne room and waited until the king was walking along the corridor. He saw her, opened his arms and embraced her, but she knew from long experience that his embrace lacked the warmth it once did.

"Was Naamah pleasing to you last night, my king and husband?"

"Yes," he replied flatly.

"It saddens me that you no longer allow me to pleasure you, Solomon."

He stood back and pulled away, looking closely at her. "Shall I come to you tonight?"

She shook her head. "Tonight is not a night for us. The moon god, Khonshu, has traveled again from Egypt to Israel to visit my body and my blood flows. And besides . . ."

"What?" he asked with a thinly disguised note of annoyance.

Tashere hesitated. "Nothing." She looked at him and smiled.

The king seemed to soften as if remembering her as she once had been. "I know that I have a place in your heart. That is all I need," he said.

The compliment stung Tashere like a whip and she drew away from him.

"Not everything is pleasure, my king. You spend so much time looking up to the mountain that you may not see what is at your feet."

"What are you talking about?" he asked.

"I have no power but what you have given me. No wealth but what you allow me. My dowry has already been spent on the timber and the stone of this palace. All I have is your firstborn son, Abia, your heir. And my task is to protect him, to protect your legacy."

Solomon viewed her with dark, intent eyes but said nothing.

"There are those, Solomon, who look upon your son with treacherous thoughts. Sons will kill other sons and it is their mothers who give them the knife."

Solomon leaned back and exhaled slowly. She was unsure of what he might say or do because of what she'd just told him. She waited in the silence, dreading his response, but for the life of her son—and her own life—she had to speak out. Then he bent down and kissed Tashere on the forehead.

"The day is early and my mind is weary already. I don't need such girl-like thoughts from you, my dear first wife. You see shadows where there is only daylight." And with that, he walked away toward the doors of the throne room, which were opened with a waft of air that ruffled Tashere's gown. Silently, her lips barely moving, she said to herself, "But, Solomon, you killed your own brother so that you could sit on your throne . . ."

———

October 18, 2007

EVERYTHING HURT. When he moved, his back hurt. When he twisted his body to look out of the hospital window at the panorama of the Old City of Jerusalem, his neck hurt. His head hurt all the while with a pounding and throbbing ache exacerbated by his dry mouth. And surprisingly his arm and wrist hurt from the handcuffs that secured him to the iron frame of the bed.

Bilal had woken from the operation an hour earlier with the noise of the nurse checking his vital signs and taking his blood pressure. Instinctively he'd tried to move his body, but it was an agony to shift positions in the bed, made worse by being tethered like a dog. He'd fallen back into a narcotized sleep, but the noises from the ward kept bringing him back into the present.

Still suffering the effects of the anesthetic, Bilal struggled to recall who he was, where he was, and why he was there. He remembered lying on the pavement underneath a white wall. There was a mosque nearby. He remembered the pain in his arm and leg, now numbed by the morphine coursing through his body. He remembered falling down into a tunnel and the excruciating agony of an explosion that he had thought had blown his head off. And, most of all, he remembered the crowds that had gathered around him, shouting and gesticulating and shining flashlights into his face in the early-morning light. But that was all he could remember: vague and disconnected images that his addled brain tried to blend together into a coherent narrative, but that he failed to associate with one another as he drifted off.

Vaguely and with his eyes closed, he knew from time to time that nurses or doctors or the police or some other Jewish official would come into his room, walk over to his bed, look at his face or his wounds, check the fluid bottles that fed and drained his body, and then walk out, seemingly satisfied. And Bilal's mind fantasized about remaining asleep forever, not waking up, letting people tend to his comatose body, so that all of his worries and frustrations, his anger and resentment, would be the problems of others, and not him. Even in his dulled mind he knew that being alive was a curse, not a gift. As the veil lifted from his brain, he remembered that he would have to face Jewish punishment for his actions as well as Islamic punishment for his failure to become a martyr and being deprived an eternity of paradise and seventy-two black-eyed and beautiful virgins at his disposal every day of his death. The greatest punishment was that his life would be the same as before, only spent in prison. Death would have been a release.

Death? Where was the sweetness, the peace and beauty, of the death that his imam had promised him if he failed to escape from the Jews? His imam knew everything and had assured him that if he didn't manage to get away, the Jews would surely kill him—stick him in the heart with their knives or shoot him in the head with their pistols. A moment of pain for an eternity of joy. His imam had promised him that they wouldn't allow him to leave the temple alive. His imam never said anything about Jewish doctors fighting to save his life!

But here he was, in a Jew hospital, in discomfort, his body aching, attached to lines and drips and machines that beeped every couple of seconds, with people fussing over him as if he were somebody important. What had happened? How had it come to this?

Bilal searched his leaden mind for linkages. He tried to think back to those days when everything had seemed possible. When he'd first been encouraged by his best friend, Hassan Khouri, to come along to the mosque because the new imam had so many answers to the young men's questions. In the beginning the imam treated him with indifference, and then like an employee, asking him to assist in the mosque after he'd finished working for his father. Then he became the imam's driver, taking the holy man from place to place, and the imam even paid him for his time and trouble. Yet, never did the imam seem to place faith in him or his abilities as a Muslim until the day he pulled him aside and told him that God had identified him as the man to undertake the mission to blow up the Jews in the temple.

His mind was clearing now, and he struggled to keep his eyes open. He had left the comfort and security of sleep and was aware of who he was, where he was, and how he was. A nurse came into his room and saw his eyes open.

"How are you feeling?" she asked. She spoke to him in Arabic, accented but clear. How did she speak his language? he wondered. By custom, he sneered at her. Why should he talk to a Jew?

She picked up a button device and placed it in his hand. "This is self-administered morphine. If you begin to feel pain or discomfort, press the button once, and it'll deliver a small amount of painkiller."

She turned and walked out. He pressed the button and waited. Nothing happened immediately, but within a minute he felt his aches begin to recede and his pains become less sharp. He actually smiled. But the drug made him tired, and he closed his eyes.

Determined not to think dark thoughts, Bilal tried to remember back to those early days in the mosque when all of his anger was muted by the imam's gentle words and his questions were answered by the imam's incredible knowledge. Even when the imam became angry and cursed the Jews and Israel, Bilal felt a sense of wonder and for the first time in his life a sense of excitement for his future, of possibility, of something better when the Jews were gone.

When he'd been the imam's driver they'd talked and talked about the happiness he would experience when he and his parents were living in a luxury apartment in the center of Jerusalem, once the Jews had been driven out. He would have an important job in the government, perhaps even traveling overseas, and his parents would never have to work again, because the Palestinian government would be wealthy and pay them a pension. It was a wonderful future to look forward to, and Bilal remembered how his chest had swelled with pride that he would be playing his part in the security of his people. He had purpose. He would be someone important. Like his beloved brother, imprisoned by the Jews for trying to free his land . . . his people.

Bilal thought of one particular day when he'd driven his imam to a village south of Jerusalem, a long way from his village of Bayt al Gizah, on the road to Bethlehem. On the outskirts of the village, the imam had ordered him to stop the car and to remain in the driver's seat while he met somebody in a private house.

And he would have done exactly what the imam had demanded had it not been for the girl. She was no more than sixteen or seventeen, with huge dark eyes and a seductive look. She'd walked past the car, glanced in, saw Bilal, smiled at him, and then walked on. But her glance was enough to entice him out of the car and defy the imam's instructions. In Bayt al Gizah he was nobody—he would have only dreamed about the possibilities and regretted the lost opportunity—but today he was the imam's driver, he was in another village, and he was behind the wheel of a car, making him a man of position. So he got out of the car and for half an hour Bilal and the girl, whose name was Almira, talked and joked and he arranged to drive down from Bayt al Gizah and meet her again.

It was already evening, and he had hurried back to the car so his absence wouldn't be discovered by the imam. Passing some houses, he glanced into one of the windows. The curtains were partly closed but there was sufficient space between them for Bilal to see inside. There was his imam, talking to a man. Not an Arab or a Palestinian. From the expensive suit and white shirt worn open necked and without a tie, the man was obviously a Jew. He was middle-aged with an amazing stripe of white hair surrounded by graying hair. It looked as if he were wearing an animal on his head. Bilal smiled at the thought but remained crouched so that he couldn't be seen. And out of the shadows in the room a shape emerged. Remaining hidden outside in the umbra of the room's light, Bilal looked inside and felt a sudden shock. As the third man leaned forward to pick up something from the table, his shadowy outline suddenly became distinct. A large round hat with a wide brim, ringlets falling down the sides of his face, a bushy beard, a long black frock coat . . . and then the man sat back and was lost in the shadows.

Now Bilal didn't want to think anymore. He pressed the morphine button again and drifted back to sleep.

———

STANDING AT HIS WINDOW, he looked over the valley and saw the blinding golden cupola of the Dome of the Rock and before it the revered mosque of al-Aqsa. In the distance, he saw the rest of the Old City of Jerusalem, and although he couldn't see them, he knew with absolute certainty that a thousand Jews, and a thousand more, were praying at the Western Wall of the Temple of Herod, the temple that had replaced the Temple of Solomon. He shuddered in disgust that the infidels, those who had rejected the word of Mohammed, were allowed to congregate so close to such holy centers of Muslim belief.

Abu Ahmed bin Hambal bin Abdullah bin Mohammed, the imam of Bayt al Gizah, a Palestinian village on the eastern slopes of the Kidron Valley, which separated it from Jerusalem, tried to restrain his anger. Not with the Jews, for he knew in his heart that they would soon be driven out of Jerusalem westward into the distant Mediterranean. Not with the police or Shin Bet or any of the other repressive organs of Jewish control over the lives of his people. No, his anger and fear were because Bilal was not dead. And his anger was also directed at himself for having trusted such a vital mission to such a bonehead.

Of the twenty young men who sat regularly at his feet and listened to his sermons and shared his hopes and aspirations for the future of the Palestinian land and people, he could have chosen anybody. Any number of young men would have taken the mission in desire of becoming *shahids*. The attempt at desecration of the Jews' most holy place was more important than the deaths of a handful of black-hatted Jews bowing and scraping at a wall.

But Abu Ahmed bin Hambal had chosen Bilal, in part out of pity for the idiot and in part because he knew he wouldn't return. But instead of succeeding in exploding his bombs, or more likely dying before any great destruction, the imbecile had managed to be wounded and was now in a hospital and would be tried, and then it might all come out. For a youth such as Bilal was like a stalk of wheat on a mountaintop: a strong wind and he would bend. And when the Jews' Shin Bet security agency began to torture him, he would bend so quickly that he would tell everything.

Were he an imam in Egypt or Saudi Arabia, such an exposure would have meant little. The Americans would do their best to find him with flying drones and satellites, or they'd send in a killing party from Delta Force, only to see their soldiers left as bones in the desert, killed by the imam's loyal protectors.

But if Israel's secret service, Shin Bet, came after him, then his chances of survival were negligible, for they had spies and turncoats and traitors throughout the Palestinian communities, and nobody knew who was in their pay. He shuddered when he thought of what Shin Bet could do to him, even though he continued to enjoy a layer of protection from their highest placed operative.

———

942 BCE

AS AHIMAAZ WALKED THE STREETS from the temple back toward his home, a servant approached from a dark alleyway and demanded that he follow. When Ahimaaz asked to know who wanted to see him, the servant replied simply, "Queen Naamah," and continued on.

Now Ahimaaz stood in front of Solomon's third wife and felt her radiating presence, which filled the room like light. He had barely time to ask why she wished to see him, when the queen dismissed the servants with a wave of her hand and drew Ahimaaz down to sit on a long, low bench.

"The king is frustrated," she said in a surprisingly gentle tone.

Ahimaaz did not need the context of her statement explained to him.

"I know, Majesty, but even a king as powerful as Solomon can't defy God."

Naamah nodded slowly and said, "A country ruled by priests! Such an interesting place. But who is it who rules over the priests?"

"The high priest," he said bluntly, but found himself strangely confused.

"Ahh . . . your brother . . ." Naamah smiled, then turned her body more fully to face him, well aware of her nipples showing through the translucent gown.

"Ahimaaz, you are cunning yet powerless."

Ahimaaz flinched at her beauty, but her words were an insult to a priest, especially from a pagan queen. "Powerless? How can you say that? I am close to the high priest, and I—"

She cut him off immediately. "And you perform menial tasks; you fetch and you carry, and you teach women and boys."

Ahimaaz looked at her with a mixture of anger and suspicion, but he remained silent and allowed her to continue.

"But you could be so much more . . ."

To his surprise she then turned and began to walk away toward another room. Without realizing what he was doing, Ahimaaz ran after her and held her by the arm. "What do you mean? How can you, a foreign queen, say such a thing to me, a priest of Yahweh?"

Naamah looked him up and down. "You Hebrews are so innocent, so trusting. For all your knowledge, you understand so little." She leaned in closer. "Power is not inherited or given by gods. Real power must be taken and only those fit enough to take it will ever hope to hold on to it. The people are only safe in the hands of such men. Did your god make you such a man?"

"Yahweh made me to serve him," Ahimaaz said, and suddenly realized that he was in the queen's bedchamber. He looked around in sudden fear.

Naamah smiled and said, "Don't worry, little man. The king has another wife to distract him tonight." But Ahimaaz still felt uncomfortable in such intimate surroundings.

Naamah laughed softly. "This god of yours, this Yahweh! Do you serve him adequately? Or are you failing to live up to"—she searched the air for the right word—"expectations?"

Ahimaaz felt a hand on his arm and found himself drawn down to sit on the edge of the queen's bed with her dark face close to his.

"If you were high priest, could you not serve your Yahweh better?"

In his most secret and private moments, Ahimaaz had entertained such thoughts, but the idea had never been voiced. Now this woman was saying things he barely dared to think.

Knowing that it could be a trap, Ahimaaz replied, "Why do you say these things, woman? I could no more be high priest than you could be first queen."

Again Naamah smiled and said softly, "But if you were to be elevated, think what that would mean for you."

He looked at her coldly, full of suspicion. "And what would it mean for you, Queen Naamah?"

Naamah answered the question with another question. "Who should lead your people when wise Solomon is gone? Should his heir be the one who is obvious or the one who is worthy?" She reached over and held his hands in hers.

Ahimaaz answered without thinking. "Abia is Solomon's first-born true heir."

Naamah frowned. "And do you think him worthy? Do you think yourself worthy?"

Ahimaaz pulled away from her hands and stood to his feet. "Treason . . ." he began to say, but the look on her face silenced him.

"Listen to me carefully, priest. My son, Rehoboam, is the king this nation needs if it is to live beyond Solomon. Abia is spirited and without caution. He will go to war at the slightest insult. Clever people are required to lead this country or it will fracture between north and south and then both will disappear, overrun by jealous kings."

"And your son, Rehoboam?"

"My son is neither clever nor wise but he is strong, and with me by his side . . ." She let the thought hang incomplete for a moment before adding, ". . . and you by mine, this kingdom could be truly great."

Ahimaaz was speechless while his mind raced. Naamah continued before he had time to recover.

"Solomon must be made to see the better way, and that's where you have an opportunity."

Ahimaaz finished the thought for her. "My brother speaks for God and will never approve such a succession. And while my brother Azariah is high priest, Solomon will never listen to me."

"The high priest speaks for God," Naamah corrected him. "And who may yet become such a high priest?"

"Solomon will never raise me. This is treason you're uttering," he stammered again.

Naamah looked at him with derision. He would never forget the scorn in her eyes. "You're like a cup of goat's milk, Ahimaaz, bland and plain. And as you age you become bitter. There are many priests and my son will be king. And then you will remember my words."

"And if I tell Solomon what you've said?"

She smiled. It was the smile of a jackal. "Words said in a court have less impact than words whispered to a king in bed."

Despite himself, Ahimaaz nodded. Solomon would never believe him. And now he felt opportunity slipping away. "How will you remove—" He quickly stopped himself and chose his words more carefully, as if someone might be listening. "How will you open the way for your son?"

Naamah smiled again. "The kingdom of the Israelites has many enemies. And a son of a king can be impatient for succession. Such a son might find common cause with a father's enemies. And these are all things that can be whispered in the receptive ear of a lover."

Naamah stretched her long neck in a manner so sensual that Ahimaaz felt his groin stir.

"But it's not true," Ahimaaz said in a whisper.

Again Naamah smiled condescendingly. "But it will be true. Once whispered and said, words can easily become truth. I know my husband. It's me, always me, that he returns to when his shoulders need rubbing with oils and when his mind needs distraction from the weight of being king. And that's when he'll begin to question just why Abia is away from the palace and why

Azariah is sending messengers to strange places, and why nothing is being done to build his temple . . ."

Ahimaaz looked at the queen as if confused, but he understood clearly and plainly.

"Join me and you will understand. And in your learning, you will come to appreciate much about leadership. Stay with me and I will teach you how to destroy your enemies without raising a finger. Support me and you will be the most powerful priest in the whole world."

———

October 18, 2007

SECURELY TETHERED by tempered steel handcuffs, Bilal was a prisoner of the bed, the room, the hospital, and the nation. On the second day after his operation, he'd slept much of the night and woken up groggy and in pain, but as the morning dawned, the pain lessened under the effect of the morphine drip and the painkillers he was given, and his mind was clearer because he no longer needed to press the drip as often.

He remembered everything from the time when he left the imam's home to the time when he made the *shahid* video in the bomb-maker's basement, his explanation to the world of why he was becoming a martyr. He remembered being driven very early in the morning through darkness, with no car headlights, to a point in the floor of the valley where he could access David's tunnel once he'd dealt with the guard. He thought he could remember climbing the tunnel after he'd slit the guard's throat, but after that, nothing was clear until the Jew doctor was checking his wounds on the day of his operation. It was a blank, an absent memory, a hole in his mind; try as he might, he couldn't remember leaving the tunnel—or anything else—until waking up in the hospital. All he had were the dreams, some vivid, some indistinct, which had floated through his mind when he was drifting in and out of consciousness.

Bilal knew that he would soon leave this room, this hospital, and be transferred to a prison. At least there he'd be among his own tribe, among Palestinians; in prison he'd be a hero—a hero like his brother; a man of position because he'd brought freedom and prosperity to his land. People would come to his cell and pay their respects, ask him to tell them how he'd carried out the daring and amazing plot to kill so many Jews. But try as he might, he couldn't remember.

The door to his room suddenly opened, and in walked a tall, lean man in an expensive suit, wearing a white shirt without a tie and open at the neck. On the back of his head he wore the skullcap of the religious Jew. Bilal looked at him in surprise and suspicion. But it was his hair that was unusual. There was a thin streak of white hair. Bilal had seen him before.

As though he owned the place, the man walked over to the bed, pulled up a chair, and sat down. "Hello, Bilal. My name is Eliahu," the man said in flawless Arabic, though with a Jewish accent. "I'm with the Israeli government. I've come to talk to you about what you did. But before we get down to details, are you comfortable? Is there anything you want? Food, water? Would you like your parents to visit you? I can arrange all those things."

The man's smile belied the coldness in his eyes. Bilal had seen that coldness before.

"I won't talk with you. Leave here. You'll get nothing out of me, Jew!" he said, repeating words he'd practiced a thousand times.

Eliahu smiled. "Bilal, you were shot and wounded committing a terrorist act. I don't need anything from you to have you sent to prison for life. But if you cooperate, life could be made a lot easier for you and your family. Help us, and I can help you. All you have to do is tell me what you know."

"Fuck off. You're a thief. You're a criminal. I'm a mujahideen.

I fight for the freedom of my people. I'm a warrior for Allah, and you and your—"

"Cut the crap, Bilal."

Startled by the blunt response, Bilal stopped talking.

"I've heard it a thousand times, and it doesn't impress," Eliahu said. "Now, if you want to wallow in slime for the rest of your life, getting raped by lifers and being the girlfriend of really nasty prisoners, then stay quiet. If you want to make life easier, with visits from your parents, maybe even an early release date from a halfway decent prison, just answer a few simple questions. Okay?"

And then a curtain was raised in his mind. The man's movement, his gestures, were vaguely familiar. Bilal looked at his face, his hair, and suddenly was shocked by the memory, no longer distant. Through a window, a gap in the curtains.

The man removed his skullcap to scratch his head, just as he'd done when he was sitting in the front room of the house in the village. The recollection, once vague, indistinct, suddenly became vivid and present. And terrifying. This was the man sitting with his imam. But how? He was with the Israeli government. Why?

Bilal remembered the phone. A gift from his friend Hassan, a phone he'd pickpocketed that day from a Jew. A new phone, a smartphone. He remembered returning to the car after speaking to the pretty girl. He had taken her number and keyed it into the phone's address book. The device had a video camera and he recorded her smiling at him. She was shy but she didn't stop him. He recorded her a second time, giving him her name and telephone number. She giggled in shyness, but he could see in her eyes that she wanted more.

Walking back to the car, he had played the video of the girl back to himself. It was the first time he'd owned such a camera phone. He pressed RECORD again and enjoyed the way the colors of the streetlights blurred and flared in the darkness. He lifted the camera up and saw the glow in the crack of curtains covering the window in the small house where the imam materialized on the screen. Like the photographer on *Candid Camera*, he'd hidden outside the house, taking a video of what was happening inside.

Later he had shown the video of the girl to his friend Hassan to prove he wasn't making it up. Then they watched the video of the house, laughing at the man inside the window with the white streak of hair. Hassan said it looked like a skunk, ridiculing the old Jew in the hat with the ringlets of hair.

Now the man was beside his bed. Bilal was chained and it was impossible for him to move.

Was this man here to kill him? His mind was in turmoil. Looking at him, Bilal was terrified. Was this Malak al-Maut, the Angel of Death? Was this man here to put an end to his life? Was he suddenly going to take out a blade and slash his throat, just as Bilal himself had killed the Jew guard? Would he die a coward and not a *shahid*, die chained like an animal to the bed?

Confused, terrified, Bilal closed his eyes and began to pray. He held his breath, waiting for the agony before the ecstasy. But not being a martyr, how could he be taken up into heaven? *O, Allah the Compassionate,* he thought, *where is my imam when I need guidance?*

"Bilal? What's wrong with you, boy?" asked Eliahu, a mix of suspicion and annoyance creeping into his voice.

Eliahu Spitzer put his hand on Bilal's arm, but Bilal reacted with a shudder and tried to pull his arm away, only to be restrained by the handcuffs.

"I'm not going to hurt you, Bilal."

But Bilal wouldn't open his eyes. Instead they remained tightly squeezed shut. Only his lips were moving in silent but heartfelt prayer.

"Either you can talk to me here in safety or we can talk in the prison. And let me assure you that if your brothers in jail learn that you're talking to Shin Bet, your life won't be worth a cracker," said Eliahu.

Still Bilal refused to open his eyes. Still his face remained a mask of pain, as though a knife had already been stuck into his guts and was being twisted by the man sitting beside his bed. He wouldn't say a word to this man until he'd spoken with his imam.

Fed up, the Shin Bet agent said softly, "Okay, kid, have it your way."

Bilal remained stubbornly mute. Eliahu stood and walked toward the door. For the first time since remembering who the man was, Bilal opened his eyes and watched him leave. He looked up at the ceiling, his mind a whirl of confusion and doubt. What was going on? What in the name of Allah and Mohammed and all the angels was happening?

———

YAEL TRIED TO MAKE IT a normal postoperative visit, but even as she walked down the corridor of the men's surgical ward, it was obvious that this patient was very different from all the other patients in the hospital. For starters, how many men who had just been through an operation were given an armed police guard stationed outside, checking the identity of everybody who walked into the room? And how many patients were handcuffed to their bed?

Yael smiled at the policeman, who nodded back. She hesitated before entering the patient's room, even though she'd already been in there twice during the day to check on him, just in case the policeman wanted to see her ID card. But he immediately returned to his inspection of the corridor and Yael pushed open the door.

Bilal was looking nervously to see who was coming in. When Yael emerged from the doorway her eyes met his and he lay back down and stared at the ceiling, as if to pretend she wasn't there.

Yael walked to his bed, picked up his chart, and read it. His vital signs were good for postoperative recovery, but his blood pressure had risen considerably since the morning. She wondered why. But he seemed to be recovering well from the two operations, one to stitch up his wounds, the second from the surgery on his kidney.

She put down the chart and walked around to his bedside, sitting on a nearby chair.

"So, how are you feeling?" she asked in Arabic.

Bilal looked at her closely, again confused at hearing his language from the mouth of a Jew. It was unnerving and so different from what he'd experienced when he was in the shops and *shuk*s of Jerusalem, where the Israelis were always so gruff and aggressive and suspicious of him, always refusing to speak with him in his own language.

He shrugged, but his right arm, handcuffed to the bed, made the gesture difficult.

"Do you need anything?" she asked.

Again he tried to shrug.

"Are you in pain?"

He said nothing and stared at the ceiling.

The revelation about their shared DNA rang in Yael's mind like a bell as she looked at the boy, but she couldn't find the words to frame questions that would give her the answers she sought. Instead she fell back to the instinctual questions of a doctor. "Can I examine your wounds? I want to make sure they're healing properly."

Again he made an attempt to shrug. Yael didn't notice and unwrapped the bandages, first on his leg and then his arm. They didn't talk, but she could tell that he was scrutinizing her and she felt his hostility. It wasn't unusual but it was unnerving.

Satisfied that his wounds were healing nicely, she smiled at him. A silent moment passed, an opportunity for Yael to fill it with questions she was anxious to ask. But instead she just remarked, "Your wounds weren't all that bad. But the angiomyolipoma could have been very serious. I spoke to the renal surgeon and he told me that it was so large, he feared they might have to remove your kidney. But fortunately he was successful in the operation. We just have to monitor your urinary output for a few days to ensure that the left kidney is working properly."

Bilal frowned. It was obvious that he had no idea what he'd suffered two days previously.

"Has anybody explained why you needed two operations?" she asked.

"Two?" said Bilal in obvious confusion.

Yael realized that nobody had told him, and he probably hadn't realized he'd been wheeled into surgery a second time while still unconscious from the first. It could have been an oversight on the part of busy nurses, or, more likely, Bilal was simply being ignored because everyone in the hospital knew who he was and what he'd done. Yael told him precisely what had happened in the recovery room and why such an extensive second operation had been necessary.

He looked at her in a mixture of amazement and incredulity but said nothing.

Yael continued on to fill the silence. "You were fantastically lucky you were here when it happened, or you'd have been very seriously ill."

"You operated on me?"

Hearing something that wasn't an insult took Yael by surprise. "Not me. Another surgeon, head of renal. He's very good. He was—"

Bilal cut her off sharply, the details lost on him. "Why? Why did you save me? Why did you stop me from going to paradise?"

"You're going to prison, Bilal. That's a very long way from paradise."

Bilal's jaw stiffened. "I am not afraid," he declared with all the bravado he could muster. "The man who came to me this morning, I showed him that I wasn't afraid."

"You didn't succeed, Bilal." Yael's tone was remarkably soft and calm. "Your bombs didn't go off, people were spared, and you didn't die a martyr."

Bilal's eyes narrowed.

"You failed, Bilal." Yael's words came not as an accusation but with a tinge of sadness that surprised her as she heard her own voice. She turned to leave. But Bilal's anger rose behind her and she heard the rattle of metal as he pulled at his handcuffed wrist.

"When I see my brothers in your prison, they will greet me as a hero. They will cheer my name!"

And it was in that moment that Yael realized how naïve she had been and, worse still, how blind Bilal was. He *had* failed. He had been sent with a task to kill, and in his failure had achieved too little. Yael knew Bilal's brothers in prison would not offer him the hero's welcome he expected.

The revelation brought the reason for her visit to her mind and she turned back to the room with images of DNA strands floating in her brain. But before she could formulate questions about where his family was from and who they were, Bilal launched into a spiel.

"You say I failed. Maybe. But behind me come thousands. And they will drive you into the sea. This is not your land. It is my land. You occupy my home, you made my family into refugees, you build giant walls through the middle of our towns, and you kill my people. We live in tents, in dirt, while you live in palaces. But your time is ending!"

Yael looked at him, torn between wanting to tell him the truth and wanting answers. Before her she saw little more than a kid fed a diet of distortions that gave him an identity, a reason to be. There was no point in trying to convince a fanatic he was wrong. For Bilal, just as for many in the West, Israel was a colonizer, an aggressor, an imperialist. But the narrative he'd been taught was simplistic and naïve. Yael, too, had her own recitations. How

Palestinians tore up the UN partition plan and seven hundred thousand Jews were expelled from Arab nations and made refugees, all of whom had been absorbed into Israel and become valued citizens. She wanted him to see the hypocrisy of Syria and Egypt championing the Palestinian cause while refusing to give them citizenship, using them as tragic pawns in a twisted game for their own political ends.

But she didn't.

In that moment, with the young man in front of her, the image of their matching DNA overshadowed politics and culture and she said nothing. Moreover, she thought of the prison that awaited him and the yawning chasm between his expectations and the hard reality he faced.

Her scowl softened and instead she asked a question. "Bilal, do you know where you come from? I mean, where were you born?"

Bilal was caught off guard by the sudden change of topic and answered before he could stop himself. "I am Palestinian," he declared.

"No, I mean specifically. In what town?"

"I was born outside Nahariya in the north of Israel. We came to Bayt al Gizah when I was two." Again Bilal answered the question as a prisoner of war might declare his name, rank, and serial number: a kind of badge of honor, proof of his identity and purpose.

"Do you know where your father or your father's father came from?" she asked.

"We are Palestinian!" he declared once again in an elevated voice. "My father's family lived for thousands of years in Palestine. Why do you want to know, Doctor? Why is this important? You've stopped me from going to paradise. Now I'm going to prison. Why do you need to know this?"

She'd already said too much. The last thing she wanted to do was to alert him to the information that was troubling her. So she shrugged. "It doesn't matter." She turned and started to walk toward the door.

"I will give you no information. I gave none to the man from the government. You will get nothing out of me, Jew!"

She left his room, but instead of walking away she dallied outside his door for a moment, thinking. The security guard looked at her questioningly. She smiled at him and sneaked a final look inside Bilal's room. She'd left a boy full of bluff and bluster, mouthing hatred taught to him by older and more malicious people. But now he was lying on his hospital bed, his free arm over his eyes. She was sure he wasn't, but from the look of him he could have been sobbing.

———

THE MUSEUM'S THEATER was big enough to be impressive but small enough to deny anonymity to anyone in the audience. Half a dozen print reporters were sitting in the front rows reading the press release. There were four television cameras in the stages of adjustment for height and focus, positioned at the back of the room. Radio reporters entered en masse and put their microphones on the table; the cords and the mics themselves reminded Yael of the head of a Gorgon.

Yael sat several rows back from the front and behind the reporters, unconsciously putting herself out of their gaze in case it turned her into stone. She never liked the spotlight and even resented speaking at the conferences and seminars that were part and parcel of her job as a surgeon. She wasn't shy and retiring, and had even received prizes in school for public speaking, but she much preferred working with a small, intimate group in an operating theater. Yet, even sitting behind them, she felt the focus of the reporters on her, probably wondering who this person was.

But her thoughts were mostly elsewhere. She wasn't thinking of the biblical seal or of the presentation to the media. She was thinking about irregular lines on a DNA profile and then of the fragments of rock slipping from Bilal's fingers. The one-in-one-hundred-thousand coincidence, having compared his DNA with her own . . . How could he and she be so closely related they could have been brother and sister?

And every time she thought about it—whether it was driving home from the hospital or out at a Jerusalem nightclub—it kept coming back to haunt her. As a surgeon, a specialist doctor, she had access to other experts in the field, but she wasn't willing to consult with them. Any questioning of blood relationships in the fraternity of the medical profession posed the danger of her being branded a racist. So the questions kept bouncing around in her mind.

Bilal was a child of a people still living a life, an existence, that had barely changed since medieval times, in an impoverished village where nothing had changed in millennia; she was the daughter of Israeli academics and professionals. Both Yael's sets of grandparents had migrated to Israel from Russia or Germany or Austria just before the closure of the borders and the beginning of the Holocaust. Their prescience and understanding of the reality of Adolf Hitler and their luck in having been able to leave Europe had saved their lives. Before that, her mother's family had come from Latvia and her father's grandparents had been living in Russia, but the family history, because of migration and escape from persecution, was clouded in supposition and mystery. Even long before her grandparents' generation . . . She tried to remember but couldn't recall if her grandparents—all of whom, except for her beloved Shalman, were now dead—had ever told her.

Her rational side knew that DNA had nothing to do with education or status and everything to do with heritage and biology and linkages over millennia, but emotionally she couldn't equate her ancestry with that of Bilal; their worlds were so far apart. And now Bilal was waiting in the hospital for her approval, as his doctor, to be transferred to a prison cell and into custody to await trial for murder. And when that process was complete, Bilal would disappear into the ranks of the civil dead forever. Why had she not signed the release forms? Why was she hesitating?

Her thoughts were interrupted when the door suddenly opened and in filed Shalman, followed by Dr. Zvi HaSofer, who in turn was followed by the head of the museum's ancient coins department, Dr. Sheila Ragiv, and one or two others whom Yael didn't recognize until they sat in their allotted seats and she read the nameplates arrayed in front of them.

Quite used to press conferences and wanting to keep the meeting informal, knowing that less than a minute of the conference would be used by the television stations, Shalman wished everybody good morning. "As you'll have seen from the press release, today we at the Israel Museum are delighted to announce the acquisition of a major find, an artifact dating back three thousand years to the time of Kings David and Solomon. Indeed, this is the world's first direct contemporaneous link with these two great kings. Their existence is no longer mythical or anecdotal. We now have proof positive from archaeology, not just from the Bible, that they lived."

A huge image of the stone Yael had unearthed from the hand of Bilal was flashed up on the screen behind the speakers. For the first time Yael could see the delicacy of the inscription and the perfection of the Hebrew writing. For her, as for any child in an Israeli school, reading the inscription posed no problem, for modern Hebrew was based on the ancient letters and words of the Bible. The founders of modern Israel, faced with the problem of immigrants with different languages from dozens of different countries, used ancient Hebrew as a modernized language to unify its people.

"The inscription and its translation into English, Arabic, French, and Spanish is written for you in the press release, where we have also given a chronology of the known historical events around the period, the meaning of the words in their three-thousand-year-old context, and the significance of this treasure to the Jewish people.

"So let me come to the find itself. This object represents one of the most important discoveries of recent biblical archaeology. This inscription is one of the earliest proofs of the Hebrew presence in Jerusalem in the reign of King Solomon. It must have been written within decades of the capture of the city by King David from the Jebusites, when Solomon the Wise, his son, ruled. This puts the date of the inscription at around the middle of the tenth century BCE, most likely around the year 958 BCE. Its archaeological importance is of the very highest order."

The reporters did not wait for an invitation for questions and one jumped into the pause. "Who made the find?"

"It was found in debris at the top of the shaft, just before the steps that lead up to the walls of Herod's Temple," Shalman said quickly.

"By whom? Who found it?" asked the reporter again.

"One of our people," Shalman answered. But his evasion made the other reporters sit up and take notice.

"And the name of the archaeologist who found the object?" asked another.

Shalman breathed deeply and sighed. Yael sat uncomfortably. He knew she'd resent the attention and would berate him for it later. A silence descended on the room, broken only by the faint electrical murmur of the television cameras.

"The lady who brought it to us is sitting in the back row," he said, nodding toward Yael.

All turned and looked at her. "Who is this lady?" asked a woman reporter from Channel 3.

"Her name is Dr. Yael Cohen," Shalman answered. "Yael, why don't you come forward and sit with us?"

Unwillingly and uncertainly, she stood and walked to the podium. Yael was the type to draw attention, tall and slender, with long black hair, huge eyes the color of a desert night, a sensual blend of experience and innocence in her smile, and her obvious reluctance to be in the spotlight. The questions began immediately, blending into one another.

"How did you find this stone?"

"Are you a professional archaeologist?"

"Did you sell the stone to the museum?"

"How come you found the stone? Were you digging?"

Yael stared blankly at the field of camera lenses, lights, and expectant faces. Her mind focused on the insistent questions from the reporters and she realized how pregnant was the pause she had left in the air. "No, I'm not an archaeologist. I'm a surgeon, and I'm very proud to say that I'm also Professor Shalman Etzion's granddaughter."

"You're a surgeon?" asked a reporter. "How did you come by the stone?"

Yael looked at Shalman, who shrugged. It was too late to avoid the truth. "A young Palestinian carrying bombs was shot and arrested when he used the tunnel to gain access to the Kotel. One of the detonator caps exploded, bringing down some of the masonry. I operated on that boy and in his hand I found . . ."

———

WHAT SHOULD HAVE BEEN a half-hour press conference turned into a one-hour inquisition, with demands for separate interviews, television appearances, staged photos of Yael sitting on a desk with her skirt slightly hitched up, legs showing, pointing to the blown-up writing of the stone on the screen.

When the circus was finished, Yael prepared to leave, but found a tall, muscular reporter to whom she hadn't spoken standing nearby looking at her. She knew instantly that he was American, and from his looks had probably been a college football player. All muscle, but was there a brain?

"Dr. Cohen, could you spare me one more minute of your time?" he asked. His Hebrew was perfect but his accent jarred on her. What was it? New York? Chicago? And she was surprised by his voice. It was deep and melodious and attractive, like a baritone. But she had commitments at the hospital and she told him, "I'm sorry, I'm already late for an appointment and I don't think there's any more I can answer."

Subtly ignoring her protest, he took out his card and handed it to her.

> *Yaniv (Ivan) Grossman*
> *Senior Correspondent, Israel, for ANBN*
> *American National Broadcast Network*

Then she remembered his reports from the Golan as fighting between Syrian and Israeli forces raged in the background. As an Israel-based correspondent for a US network, his reports were sometimes broadcast on Israeli television. Yael felt slightly embarrassed that she hadn't recognized him.

Yaniv Grossman smiled his devastating smile, full of perfect American teeth and apple-pie cheeks, and said to her, "You're a fascinating woman, Dr. Cohen. The find is fantastic but I think you're just as interesting. I'd like to do a background piece on you. For American audiences. You're beautiful and smart. You're the face of modern Israel."

"I don't know about that," Yael said, and hoped desperately that she wasn't blushing.

"Well, US audiences rarely see any Israelis who aren't rabbis, feral settlers, or soldiers, so you'll be like a breath of fresh air." He let out a small chuckle, deliberately self-deprecatory as a counterbalance to his fulsome and, she thought, fawning approach. "What do you say?"

She shrugged. "I'm just a doctor who got lucky. I'm sure there's very little about me that your viewers would be interested in."

"Oh, I don't know about that. You'd be amazed at how interesting I can make you, Miss Cohen. It is *Miss* Cohen, right?" he said.

As Yael walked out of the museum, she wondered whether she'd just been propositioned for a television program or for a date. Certainly he was handsome, but the slickness of his American attitude annoyed her. Where some might have seen confidence she saw only entitlement. But the contemplation of Yaniv Grossman only partially distracted her from the thoughts in her head that seemed to be coming from twisting strands of DNA.

———

942 BCE

AHIMAAZ LAY AWAKE, staring at the low ceiling of his house, thinking about the things that Naamah had said to him, wondering whether he'd ever get to sleep in the palace of the high priest. For years he had accepted his lot of being a minor functionary in the priestly hierarchy of Israel. Azariah, his brother, was the favored one, the gifted one in the family.

But now he held in his grasp the chance of becoming high priest himself. Suddenly he had a patron, a woman who had recognized his talents. And why not? Why shouldn't he be the high priest? As a descendant of the line of Zadok, why shouldn't Ahimaaz rise to the top? He knew as much, was as devoted to Yahweh, and prayed just as fervently as any other priest.

Yet, though he smiled and bowed, willingly did Azariah's bidding, and had married Solomon's daughter Basmath, Ahimaaz was never the one to whom the Israelites looked for rituals or comfort or advice, nor the one upon whom the king called in time of need.

As third in charge of rituals, he was sometimes invited to the home of Azariah when there were matters of importance to discuss. But Ahimaaz knew that Azariah's invitations were delivered at the behest of King Solomon, who asked the high priest to include him. It was both the advantage and the curse of being married to Solomon's daughter.

Try as he might, he had begged Basmath to intervene on his behalf with her father, to get her to use her influence so that Solomon would elevate him to the position of second in command of the priesthood. Yet, she had refused. He knew that she held affection for him but she would not raise a finger to intercede on his behalf with her father.

But now, as if from nowhere, Naamah the Ammonite had delivered power into his hands.

The next day a message came to him from the third queen, delivered by a female servant, evidently one she trusted. The message gave Ahimaaz the task he must do to set the wheels of his ascension in motion, though the message was phrased as a pondering question rather than an instruction.

What if Azariah was the worshipper of pagan gods?

Could he? Could he plant such a seed? Place a pagan idol in his brother's house?

Was it only last night, in the fierce heat of Elul, that Naamah had brought these ideas to him? He knew that for the past few months she had done more than sow doubt in Solomon's mind; she had played him like a harp. By allowing him to find certain documents, by having servants tell him that Abia and that Azariah seemed to disappear without trace for long periods during the day—by telling him that his first wife, Tashere, was writing to foreign kings without Solomon's knowledge—Naamah's lion of Judah had growing concerns about the loyalties of his son and heir, and his high priest.

———

THE IDOL WAS HEAVY in his clothes. Secreted inside an internal pocket of his priestly robes where he normally kept the money Israelites gave to the priesthood on visiting the house of the Ark of the Covenant, Ahimaaz felt its density weighing him down as he shuffled in the dead of night toward the lavish house of his brother. He felt debased by the closeness of the pagan idol to his skin.

When Jerusalem was conquered by Solomon's father, David, the fervor of the citizens to destroy all that had been Jebusite was so great that a tide of burning and smashing was unleashed on all the images of their gods. The idols and statues, shrines and altars, were put to the torch and the axe. Forbidden to set foot on the top of the mountain on which their evil temple stood, the people vented their horror and disgust on the Jebusite houses, the household gods, and the workshops that made the idols.

Ahimaaz was hard-pressed to find even one idol that didn't belong to one of Solomon's foreign queens or concubines. Such artifacts were rare and, worse still, the act of acquiring one would see Ahimaaz face the same fate he had determined for his brother. In the end he had traveled beyond the walls of Jerusalem to a tiny village where nearby caves held ancient graves of the Jebusites. At first he was met with nothing but dirt, sand, and bones. He despaired but kept digging with his hands through the pagan bodies and tearing at their shrouds until he found what he sought. It was small, only slightly larger than a man's hand. Dense and heavy and made of black marble or some such stone. Or Ahimaaz thought it might be made of copper that had been burned in a fire. But when he looked more carefully in the light, he saw chips and cracks over its surface, which told him it was stone. Though time had worn it down, it was still a ghastly image of Moloch, the god with horns and an open maw. Ahimaaz smiled wryly at the idea that Moloch was an Ammonite god, the god of Naamah; it was fitting, then, that this should be the instrument in her plan.

Ahimaaz was met at the door of his brother's house by a servant. The young woman knew Ahimaaz on sight even though he was an infrequent guest. "The high priest is not here," she told him. But he knew that already and had planned his visit to coincide with his brother's absence. He explained that he needed access to the high priest's study and the scrolls and parchments that were kept there. Ahimaaz had prepared a detailed story but it was unnecessary. The young girl was not one to question a priest of the family of Zadok, and spoke no word of challenge.

Azariah's private study was remarkably small and unimpressive, little more than an antechamber to the otherwise lavish house. Ahimaaz chose in that moment to see this as a sign of his brother's misdirected priorities, valuing showy opulence over pious reverence. Yet, the small room was laden with shelves of scrolls and parchments, stone tablets and waxes. There was no shortage of places in which to secrete the idol.

He cast his eyes about the room as he took the pagan statue from his robes. A small shelf stood alone against the smallest wall at the end of the room. Stacked with scrolls like the others, it nonetheless appeared to be special in some way, perhaps holding the most important texts. A mat was laid in front of it, adorned with bright colors and clearly not of Hebrew origin, a style and pattern foreign to Ahimaaz's eyes.

Yes, this would be the place, he thought to himself. But as he took short steps toward the shelf that he intended to be mistaken for a shrine, Ahimaaz suddenly stopped. In one corner of the room, leaning casually against the wall, was an object wholly out of place. In a study replete with scholarly pursuits and the dry solemn air of a library was a child's toy.

A spinning top, wide as a dining bowl, wooden and covered in colored paint panels. It was worn, the hue faded, the edges chipped and bruised from years of play. But the sight of it upset Ahimaaz. It was foreign and yet familiar. Ahimaaz knelt beside the toy and reached out to pick it up. Years had dimmed his memories, yet the feel of the spinning top in his hand brought them back in vivid color.

Ahimaaz and Azariah as children sitting on the cold stone floor of their father's house. He younger and looking in love and admiration at Azariah, who seemed to know so much. Cackling laughter as the boys each spun the top and watched the colors blur and blend into a streaky white. Setting up wooden stick soldiers and watching the army of David defeat the army of the Philistines and bring down the giant Goliath of Gath. Ahimaaz lying, belly pressed flat and chin on the floor, as he watched his brother spin the top with a thin rope with greater speed and dexterity. Watching it spin on a single spot, the colors blending until they became a blur of white before teetering and sprawling over. And the colors magically reappearing.

Ahimaaz shook off the memory and looked down at the objects in his hands—a child's toy in one palm and the image of a child-eating idol in the other. He couldn't be a child anymore; he could no longer be dazzled by his brother's spinning of toys. Ahimaaz dropped the top back into the corner, placed the gruesome statue just out of sight on the shelf, and walked away as quickly as he could, leaving the childhood memories behind him.

———

IN THE END, it was so much easier than Ahimaaz dared to believe. The idol was found by a servant, a girl in Naamah's pay, and, as instructed, she brought it to Solomon's treasurer, who reported the high priest's great act of heresy. But this was only the second blow to Solomon that morning, and not the only arrow to find its mark. When the news of the idol was brought to the king, he already held in his hand a scroll under his own seal, written in his own court by his son Prince Abia. A scroll intercepted by a soldier in Abia's retinue but faithful to Solomon. When he opened it and read the words supposedly written by his son, he wept. His own son had written to Og, king of Bashan, asking him to supply him with an army so that he could deliver Israel into Og's hands and rule in Solomon's place as a vassal of the great king.

So when Ahimaaz walked into the throne room, it was in an uproar. And he watched in breathless awe, silent and brooding, while his brother Azariah was exposed. Despite the protestations the high priest made while he was being rushed out of his palace, Solomon had refused to listen, shouting at him that he had transgressed against Yahweh and that he would be banished from Israel forever.

And on the following day, the lies and gossip that Naamah had been whispering into Solomon's ear grew to fruition. Abia, Solomon's firstborn son, was accused of treason, of plotting with foreign kings to overthrow him. Abia protested his innocence but was banished to the Valley of Hinnom and beyond. Tashere screamed at Solomon that the allegations were lies, but she refused to beg for mercy, instead turning and addressing the court and swearing to bring ruin on the heads of all who had slandered her son.

Solomon's fury at Abia's treason would not be abated, but to command Tashere to follow her son into exile would have meant war with the Egyptian pharaoh. Instead she quietly retreated into the palace, where she wept and rent her garments as though her son had died in battle.

In the large square of Jerusalem's upper public marketplace, a crowd gathered. Rumors had been rampant in the city, and the people came to hear the king's herald announce what was happening. Their shock at the cherished high priest's betrayal of Yahweh was enough to make everybody weep.

And when it was announced by the herald that Ahimaaz was to be the new high priest for the forthcoming Temple of Solomon, people turned to one another and said, "Who did he say? Ahimaaz? Who's Ahimaaz?"

October 18, 2007

ELIAHU SPITZER WATCHED the live television broadcast from the lounge suite in his office on the third floor of a nondescript building in the middle of Jerusalem. As deputy director of the Arab affairs department, he was entitled by the bureaucrats to an LCD TV, which he'd initially enjoyed, but he found that he lost the privacy of his office when crowds of employees would congregate to watch a sports match beamed live.

Shin Bet's headquarters were about as different from those of Britain's MI5 and America's CIA and FBI as it was possible to imagine. He knew all three agencies well and visited them regularly to discuss internal security prior to an official visit by somebody important. But while the Brits were always pompous and looked down their noses at him, and the Americans were his bestest lifelong buddies until he asked for something, these other nations' offices were strictly hierarchical. His organization, Shin Bet, responsible for internal national security, was strangely open and informal. If the janitor wanted to watch the news while Eliahu was sitting at his desk, he'd probably just excuse himself and switch the TV on.

Even the building itself was unusual by international standards. At ground level were shops and a narrow corridor open to the street but guarded in its recesses by two security experts. The corridor led to an elevator where the floors were marked 1, 5, 6, and 7. To all visitors, there were no levels two, three, or four. Only by optical iris identification and fingerprint recognition would a potential visitor get to these floors unless escorted by one of the security men if the visitor was known. Those who'd never been before would be interrogated initially by the security guards, then sent skyward by elevator to a bombproof office on the tenth floor, and then, if they were given permission to enter, they'd be escorted down by a mid-level security person to levels two, three, or four for their meetings.

But even so, the government, understanding the danger of placing such an important target in the middle of a commercial area, was in the process of building a large edifice on the outskirts of Jerusalem to house the top secret unit of national security.

When the broadcast from the Israel Museum was finished, Eliahu switched off his television. He returned to his desk and sat there thinking. The Bilal kid had been shot but was still alive. He was recovering well but his contacts in the hospital had told him that there had been some sort of complication with the operation. His man at the Western Wall hadn't been able to inject the kid with insulin and put an end to him, so there was a danger that he could have talked about the imam. That in itself wasn't such a great problem, but it was another complication, and the last thing Eliahu needed was another complication. And now there was an added thorn. This piece of archaeological treasure that had been found by the surgeon, of all people, had made Bilal and his activities into front-page news worldwide. The story could be the beginning of a forest fire.

And to make matters even more complex, the surgeon was like some poster girl for Israeli womanhood: pretty, elegant, stylish, and no doubt making her Jewish parents proud of her in her work as a doctor. The media would love her and that would keep the Bilal story alive for weeks if not months. He knew the media, and he knew with certainty that the moment some news producer with CBS or CNN or ANBN looked at this doctor, they'd milk the story for all it was worth.

Eliahu sighed. It was all becoming so messy . . .

Taking out a Palestinian who was about to desecrate the holiest monument of Judaism, demands for aggressive retribution, the fury of the Jews worldwide, demonstrations and the beginnings of a sharp move to the right, the pacifist voices silenced.

Then more and more terrorist assaults against religious targets. The rise of ultra-Orthodox Judaism in the government of Israel to deal with the outrages. Ridding the nation of these peacenik appeasers until a religious government, a theocracy, was established in Jerusalem. All so simple. Now all so complicated.

He scratched his head under his skullcap, opened his drawer, took out his prayer book, and found the page that gave him a blessing that would bring him some relief from his complications.

———

YAEL WALKED into the doctors' staff room and found all eyes on her. It looked as though everybody in the room was reading the front page of *Yedioth Ahronoth*, one of Israel's major newspapers, or had seen her the previous night on television. And the paper's picture of her, seated at the table with Israel's most prominent archaeologists, was in the middle of the front page. The story was headlined "Surgeon Uncovers Bible Treasure in Terror Patient's Hand," and having read it over breakfast earlier she knew that the reporter had written about a terrorist, a bomb that didn't explode properly, and an attractive trauma surgeon named Yael. There was hardly any reference to the artifact itself or its place in the ancient history of Israel and the Jewish people's connection to the same land for over three thousand years. With all the undermining of Israel's right to exist by Arab nations, especially in the United Nations, surely this was the important story.

"Welcome O great and famous archaeologist," called one of her colleagues, a vascular surgeon dressed in his surgical greens, from across the room as she hung up her coat.

"I'm more used to digging out shrapnel than digging up artifacts."

The other doctors smiled and laughed and offered congratulations amid the usual teasing remarks.

"Is there a case to be made that the stone belongs to the Palestinian kid? After all, it was he who found it. As a surgeon, shouldn't you have put it into a security bag along with his wedding ring?" The question was only half-facetious and asked by a doctor on the far side of the room with a wry smile.

"He didn't even know he had it. And wouldn't know what to do with it if he did." Yael's offhand comment gave her boss, Pinkus, a small opening to raise issues of unspoken politics to the room.

"The Palestinians could use it as a reason to lob a few rockets our way. Not that they ever really need a reason."

Another surgeon put a hand on his arm, said softly, "Pinkus," and nodded to a man who was sitting in a corner, reading a medical journal. Mahmud was a Palestinian surgeon who had trained at the Bethesda Medical Center in America and was a member of the hospital's staff.

Mahmud had seemed as though he weren't paying attention but no doubt heard the comment. He lifted his gaze from the journal and peered over the tops of his small, round glasses. The doctors rarely discussed Palestinian-Israeli politics when he was present, out of deference to him. He was a good surgeon and was well liked by his colleagues. Yael knew nothing of Mahmud's personal life, but from the hours he kept, she often wondered if he felt the need to work twice as hard to prove he was as good as his colleagues.

Mahmud smiled. "I'm thrilled Yael found it . . ." He let the unfinished sentence hang for just a moment before adding, "And when my Arab brothers drive you bastards into the sea, we'll sell it on eBay and make a fortune."

His joke broke the moment of embarrassment; people laughed and went back to their reading. Yael walked across the room to her pigeonhole and withdrew four letters. She glanced at them and saw that two were from the hospital administration, concerning some new rules that had been imposed. She, like her colleagues, made a habit of ignoring such documents. The other letters were interesting; one was a note from the surgical secretary, telling her that NBC and Fox in the States had phoned and would like to set up an interview. The other was a personal letter, handwritten but bearing no postage stamp, so it had been hand delivered to the hospital. Yael Cohen tore it open, and read it.

Dear Madam Doctor Koen

I am Fuad. I am father to Bilal. Last night on TV I see you at museum. Now I know name of my son doctor. You operate him. You save him. I write thank you. My wife Maryam she say thank you doctor. Yes my son did a very bad thing. Allah forgive him. But work you do save him and I thank you. Excuse my writing. I am not educate man. Wife Maryam no read write.

Fuad. Father to Bilal

Yael smiled awkwardly to herself and returned the letter to her pigeonhole. She went back to her table to read the morning newspaper, but after a minute returned to the letter and put it into the pocket of her gown. She wanted the address.

———

A MAN DRESSED in the robes of a Muslim cleric entered the hospital. He asked the receptionist to direct him to the floor where Bilal was a patient. The moment she entered the patient's name into her computer, a red flag caused her to pick up the phone. Within minutes, two senior hospital security officers escorted the imam to a bombproof room in the basement, where they interrogated him for ten minutes, searched his bags for guns, explosives, and hypodermic needles, then his clothes, and ran a metal detector over his entire body. Satisfied that he carried no weapons, they apologized for the necessary precautions and escorted him upstairs to the men's surgical floor. The imam approached the policeman guarding the room, who further interrogated and asked him his purpose.

"I am Bilal's imam, Abu Ahmed bin Hambal bin Abdullah bin Mohammed. I am his spiritual guide through the darkness of this world into the light of the next. I have come to offer him the consolation of Allah before his tribulation begins. I just wish to pray over him and offer him the comfort and solace of Islam," said the imam in calm tones.

The policeman said only "I'll give you half an hour."

The imam, followed by the Israeli policeman, entered the room. The cleric smiled at Bilal as he walked to the bedside chair and the policeman lingered near the door, looking and feeling decidedly out of place. Bilal tried to sit up in the presence of his imam, but the handcuffs allowed him only limited movement. "Greetings, Master."

"Relax, Bilal. I'm here to pray with you and hope that you find peace and contentment in the hands of Allah when you are on the next phase of your journey."

The two looked at each other. Then the imam began to pray, whispering the prayers into Bilal's ear. Quietly the policeman left the room. Realizing that they were suddenly alone, the imam whispered urgently, "Bilal, my brother, listen closely, for what I am about to say is very important." The imam drew a deep breath. "You are to be taken from here to prison. You understand this?"

Bilal nodded.

"There will be a trial. It will be short. You will deny nothing. Truth of killing the enemy will be your only defense. They will ask you who sent you. You know that you must say nothing of me and your brothers. This is clear! Yes?"

Bilal nodded again. This time more slowly.

"In prison you will be with many of your brothers and they will teach you many things, for your journey is not over."

Bilal seemed about to ask a question but the imam answered it before the young man could frame it.

"They will teach you how to fight. How to survive. How to be strong. And when you are strong, you'll be ready to take Palestine from the Jew."

Bilal shook his head. "But how? How am I to fight from a prison cell? I don't understand."

The imam sat up with the faintest hint of a smile on his face. But he lowered his voice to a near whisper and Bilal had to strain to hear. "We will pray for the kidnap of an Israeli soldier and that he is hidden by our brethren. Remember what happened with the Jew soldier Gilad Shalit when Hamas kidnapped him last year from the border and held him in Gaza? The Jews cannot find him. And"—the most minimal of smiles came again—"whoever kidnapped him will make a trade. A thousand of our brothers for just one of theirs. They show their weakness with Shalit; they will show their weakness when we capture the next of their boys. The Jews will have fathers crying like women for the return of just this one, in exchange for our many." The imam leaned close to Bilal and put a hand on his handcuffed arm. "And you will be one of the many."

Bilal's eyes widened. "I will be freed?"

"This I swear to you, in the name of Allah, provided you don't cooperate with them, provided you remain silent concerning the involvement of me and your brethren."

All the muscles in Bilal's face let go of their long-held grip and he seemed to sink into the bed. But he quickly caught himself and turned suddenly to face his imam. "I wasn't afraid! I knew Allah would look after me. If I couldn't go to paradise, then I knew I would be saved. I wasn't afraid, I swear . . ."

The imam smiled gently. "I know, my son. I trust you are strong, now and always. But first I must know something. And much rests on your answer."

The tension returned to Bilal's face.

"Who have you spoken to since coming to this hospital?"

Bilal's eyes narrowed, as if not understanding the question. "No one."

"No one?" asked the imam. "Surely you were not silent. The police have come, no? Shin Bet has been here to question you. Yes?"

"I told them nothing," Bilal stated as flatly and firmly as he could.

"You told them your name."

"Well . . . yes. I told them my name. I was not afraid." To prove his silence, he continued, "I even said nothing to the man who you know, the man from the government."

"Man? What man?"

"The man . . . I . . . when we . . ." Bilal stuttered a response, strangely wishing he hadn't said anything. His head hurt and with his free hand he rubbed his face as if to wake up.

The imam remained silent, looking at Bilal, his eyes utterly impassive. Softly, gently, he said, "What man, Bilal?"

"The man you know . . . I drove you . . . But I stayed in the car. I just . . . When he came I didn't . . ."

The imam's response came sharp and flat on Bilal's stammering. "I know of no such man."

The silence that fell between the two of them was cold; Bilal, sensing that he should say no more, nodded and closed his eyes, not wanting to look at the imam.

"When you drove me? Where did you drive me?"

Bilal remained silent for a long moment. Then he said, almost inaudibly, "I don't remember . . ."

"And have you spoken to any others?"

"No!"

"Not even a doctor? A nurse?"

"The doctor! Perhaps? Maybe I spoke to her . . . but she was only a doctor. And I spoke of nothing."

The imam cut him off. "She? A woman? You have allowed a woman doctor to touch you?"

"Yes. I was asleep. But she was kind. The Jews came and wanted to take me away to the prison. The soldiers. The police. But she said no. She said they had to wait. She stopped them, told the police that I was not well enough."

The imam breathed quietly. "And why did she stop them from taking you?"

"I don't know."

The imam said softly, "My son, you must continue to say nothing. There are things happening that are greater than you. You will be a part of them, provided you remember to remain silent. Say nothing to the Jews, for this is how they work. They question and promise and lie. They will smile and they steal your land and stick a knife into your back. Mohammed, peace and blessings be upon him, said in Surat Al Ma'idah"—the imam closed his eyes—" 'Shall I inform you of what is worse than that as penalty from Allah? It is that of those whom Allah has cursed and with whom He became angry and made of them apes and pigs and slaves.' " The imam opened his eyes again and looked at the boy coldly. "Bilal, remember those words: apes and pigs and slaves. Mohammed, peace and blessings be upon him, was talking of the Jews."

Bilal nodded to show the lesson was understood.

The imam stood to leave, saying a blessing over Bilal, and then walked out of the room. The guard nodded at him, but before he left he asked the guard, "I wish to speak to this young man's doctor. A woman. What's her name?"

The guard said, "Dr. Cohen. Dr. Yael Cohen."

The imam nodded in gratitude and walked down the corridor.

———

YAEL WALKED THE CORRIDORS of the hospital, making precise turns left and right, without ever looking up from the clipboard in her hand. Her feet seemed to know exactly how many steps each hallway segment required before turning as she made her way through the labyrinthine building. She had pushed all thoughts of Bilal and his family and ancient stone seals from her mind and was intent upon her rounds when she all but walked into the lean but muscular figure of Mahmud, her Palestinian colleague.

"God, I'm sorry. I wasn't looking . . ." stammered Yael.

"I've been called many things, but never 'God.'" Mahmud smiled his wry and somewhat mischievous grin, but it took Yael's mind a moment to catch up to the joke. She returned the smile and was about to continue on her way when Mahmud's hand rested on her shoulder.

"How is the boy?"

Despite the number of children in the large hospital, Yael didn't need to ask which boy Mahmud was referring to.

"He's . . . um . . . recovering well. Slowly . . . Did you know him?"

"Sure. All us Arabs know each other. We're all cousins."

Yael blushed just a little and smiled at his facetiousness. But no matter how long she lived and worked with Palestinian people, she found casual conversation hard.

When the grin left Mahmud's face, he removed his small, round glasses and began to clean them with a handkerchief from his pocket. "Bilal? Is that his name?"

"Yes," replied Yael.

Mahmud nodded. "More than bullet wounds, right? Angio-myolipoma?"

"Yeah." Yael found herself transfixed by Mahmud's hand as he rubbed at the lenses of his glasses, rubbed at dust that was long gone.

"That's a rare condition. I would have liked to see that operation."

"He was lucky he was here for us to find it," said Yael.

"Allah works in mysterious ways."

Yael let out a soft laugh.

"I don't know Bilal, Yael, but I know I could have been him . . ." He returned his glasses to his face and used them to focus on her. "Different choices, different opportunities. My father gave everything to send me to school. He said it was the only answer to what you all call the Palestinian problem. Funny for a man who couldn't read. Bilal and me, a fork in the road, and yet we both end up in a hospital. Me to save people; him to be saved—by you."

Yael found herself unable to reply so Mahmud filled the silence for her.

"Thank you, Yael," he said as he walked away down the corridor toward his patients.

———

935 BCE

GAMALIEL, SON OF TERAH of the tribe of Manasseh, had grown rich from buying the rights to impose a levy on all visitors to Jerusalem and placing his own tax collectors outside the gates. He'd bid for the privilege of collecting taxes when the king's treasurer offered for sale the right to tax people passing through the gates of the city. And the deal he'd made with the treasurer had been rewarding for all concerned. The king was earning good money from traders, merchants, and visitors to Jerusalem, who paid a tenth of Gamaliel's estimate of the value of their goods to the king's estate. He gave the lion's share of the levy to the king and kept a quarter part of the tax to himself, and paid a twentieth part to the treasurer for giving him the rights.

Of course, what Solomon and his treasurer didn't know was that Gamaliel always overestimated the value by a tenth part, much to the anger of the merchants, and underestimated the value to the king's treasurer. The difference went directly into his pocket.

Now he'd been called to the palace to sit in an audience with the king himself and with the high priest, Ahimaaz. Why? he wondered. What spoils of office were on offer now? With the temple almost complete and with Solomon's treasury almost empty from his ridiculous demands for gold leaf to adorn the tops of columns, and for huge statues of angels and cherubim and seraphim and lions made only of gold, no wonder the king was without money.

Perhaps the meeting was to demand he increase the levy at the gates to pay for the temple. Perhaps it was to raise new levies from an already overburdened people. Who knew? He told his wife he'd be back before nightfall and left his home to walk the steep pathways up the hill of the City of David toward Solomon's palace.

Gamaliel was shown into the king's throne room and he bowed low before Solomon the Wise. On the far side of the room stood the man Gamaliel knew to be Ahimaaz the high priest, although they had never met.

Solomon seemed to ignore the priest and looked only at Gamaliel from his throne. The king then abruptly stood and began to talk. He talked about the temple, his reign, the troubles he was having with his wives, his relationship with nearby kings, the difficulties with the twelve tribes, and on and on. Gamaliel was not in the least surprised by this long-winded monologue—nor was Ahimaaz, it seemed to him. Solomon, though renowned for his wisdom, could talk from morning to dusk and not realize that the minds of those listening to him were elsewhere.

But the rewards the king held in his gift were great, as was the potential of his wrath, and so those summoned listened in lengthy silence.

Though Gamaliel's eyes never left the king as he wandered

the room, he could feel the eyes of Ahimaaz on him. Did the priest know what the king might say to him? Or was the priest waiting with painful curiosity just as Gamaliel was? Gamaliel was a shrewd and successful man and so was cognizant enough to know that those in power stayed in power by knowing from where future threats might come. Did the high priest see him as a threat?

Solomon turned from the Western Wall, with its miraculous painted display of ferns and flowers, of lions and deer and rabbits and birds, and faced Gamaliel directly for what seemed like the first time. On either side of him were golden statues of lions, and Solomon sat down on his gold-covered ivory throne with its purple cushion filled with the feathers of ducks. With a voice much softer than his previous monologue he said, "As you can see, my temple is close to being finished. The land is sanctified and cleansed, thanks to you, Ahimaaz"—Solomon gave a curt nod in the direction of the high priest—"and the builders from Lebanon will soon erect the roof of costly but beautiful cedars. Which brings me to why I have commanded you to appear before me."

At last, thought Gamaliel. But with the mentioning of the temple he assumed whatever the king was about to tell him had something to do with its building. Again he felt the eyes of Ahimaaz searching him from the other side of the room. Rumors reverberated around the city about Ahimaaz: how he had spent his life studying the scrolls that were written of the life of Father Moses and of the laws he and others had invoked for the community. It was said of Ahimaaz that he knew every prayer for every occasion. His visits to the poor and the sick were spoken of, and how he gave away large sums of his wealth to those in need. No doubt such rumors were the fabrications of Ahimaaz himself to cement his position. Gamaliel didn't envy him. He had no time for priests and their empty declarations and pointless rituals. Yet, he knew well the machinations of the priestly order and that if Ahimaaz was to survive he would have to be very deft.

Solomon picked up a scroll and read briefly from it to remind himself. "Two separate orders of officials are required to ensure the good running of my temple. The first is the priesthood, which will minister to the people, keep the times and meanings of the services, ensure that all the people worship there at least three times every week, and bring the correct gifts as offerings and animals for sacrifice. Since his betrayal of me and my kingdom, Azariah has been banished and therefore you, Ahimaaz, have been tasked with the role of the high priest, and your charge will be maintaining the priestly blessing, the redemption of the firstborn, prayers for skin diseases and mildew, and instructing those who are learned and of the priestly family in the words of the law, and you will control the order and distribution of the sacrifices and the incense offerings."

Ahimaaz looked at the king in amazement. The revenue he would earn from these tasks was enormous. He would be wealthy. He nodded his thanks to Solomon, unable to speak. And then the king looked at Gamaliel.

"Know this, Gamaliel of the tribe of Manasseh, tax collector. For many years, merchants and travelers, men and women from foreign lands, have been coming to Jerusalem to see its splendors and to marvel at the brilliance of its impenetrable walls. And during that time I have allowed you to collect the revenues that accrue from taxing such peoples at the gate. According to our contract, you have given me over half of the tenth part of what you levied when they entered the city. This is true."

Gamaliel looked closely at King Solomon, sitting there on his raised dais, shrouded in his purple cloak, his golden crown sitting firmly on his head. Gamaliel nodded, and said, "That is true, Majesty."

"But while you pay half of what you are paid, my spies have spoken to these merchants and they tell me that what you levied is not what you've told my treasury. You have demanded a tenth share more from the merchants than you've declared to me."

Gamaliel began to speak but the king put up his hand and said, "Silence! Not only have you underestimated your income from these merchants but you've also lied to me about the numbers of people who visit my city. You pay me tax for a hundred people in a week but my men have counted those whom you tax and they tell me that, since the last full moon until the full moon two days ago, two hundred people have entered the city every week."

Gamaliel smiled and tried to hide his nervousness. He knew that he was sweating and hoped that it didn't show. "Majesty, your spies are correct. There have been twice the number of men and women than those who have paid to cross the threshold of the city and enter its walls. But your spies haven't told you the whole truth, for those extra people who enter are residents of the city. They are exempt from paying the levy. They are farmers in the valleys, or workmen on the Mount of Olives, or builders cutting rock. You have received all that I have levied, less my part. And as to the tax on the goods the merchants bring in, Majesty, I levy no more and no less than the value of the goods. I swear by Yahweh, Majesty, that—"

"Lie to me one more time, Gamaliel, and I will cast you out. My first and foremost wife, Tashere, tells me that one of her servants overheard one of your wives speaking in the marketplace. Your wife was boasting about how she had a lot of money because of you and the way you cheat your king.

"The walls of this city have my ears, tax collector. I know everything that happens, and if you continue to lie to me, then you will follow my son into the darkness of the Valley of Hinnom. My men didn't just count the people who entered but asked them where they were from. And they tell a very different tale to your lie. You have cheated me and my kingdom of wealth, money that has gone into your pocket. That is punishable by stoning until death."

Gamaliel looked upon the king in terror and began to answer, but Solomon put up his hand again to silence the man. "The eighth commandment of the Lord Yahweh was that you will not steal, and if I stone you or cast you into the wilderness, you will surely die."

Gamaliel coughed and tried again to speak but no words came out. Instead the king's tone changed abruptly.

"But your death will not suit my purpose. For once a thief is caught and death is the reward of his crimes, then that thief will do anything to remain alive. Will he not? So I will not punish you despite your thefts, for you, more than any before you, are a good collector of taxes. Liar and a thief though you may be, I will use these failings to my benefit. I need money to complete the building of my temple. You will collect it by raising taxes wherever you can. Do not bend the backs of the people too much, but I must have money. You will keep one-third of all you collect and two-thirds will be given to me to pay for my workmen and those from Lebanon. And from time to time, at times unknown to you, my treasurer will seek your records and will count the number of people, how much each has paid, and the purpose of the payment, and he will count every talent, every mina, and every shekel. Should there be one single shekel's discrepancy between what is and what should be, then without question all your wealth, property, and livelihood will be forfeited and your family will be expelled from Jerusalem forever. And you, tax collector, will be cast into a pit and stoned to death from the walls above."

Gamaliel looked at the king in horror and nodded quickly and emphatically.

———

GAMALIEL LEFT THE PALACE chastened and shaken. His head was a beehive swarming with stinging insects. Normally a man of determination, he felt himself flailing on the edge of a precipice, one part of him about to plunge into the abyss because of his deceit, yet the other part elevated to the safety of increased status.

The logic and wisdom of the king was not lost on Gamaliel. Solomon knew that in a world where all men cheated and lied, the only thief who was honest was the thief who knew that all knew him to be a thief, one too afraid to steal again.

It was a long moment in his bewildered state before he realized that he had been followed. Ahimaaz walked quickly behind him to catch him up and tapped him on the shoulder. Lost in his own world of confusion and relief, Gamaliel turned in surprise.

"Priest? You want to speak with me?" he said.

Ahimaaz nodded, and said, "It's a hot day. In the next lane is a stall selling pomegranate juice. Let us drink together. There is much that we have to discuss."

Years of shrewd business dealings brought back Gamaliel's composure and he eyed the high priest suspiciously. "I know the stall you're talking about. The seller waters down juice and charges too much. Why not walk down two streets to the marketplace? There are better stalls there."

It was a big and crowded bazaar: not as large as that of Hebron or Damascus because Jerusalem had been built on a steep hillside, but it was noisy and bustling with the smells and sounds of any marketplace in any city. Some of the stalls sold the meat of sheep and cattle, some sold freshly baked bread, some the produce of the fields, and others proudly offered goods from as far afield as Acco in the north and Lachish in the south, from Damascus, Sidon, Jaffa, and Ashkelon on the coast, from Assyria, Persia, and even India in the east. Everybody, it seemed, every merchant, caravan, and craftsman, was setting their sights on Jerusalem.

As they rounded the corner, the noise of the marketplace grew louder and Ahimaaz wondered whether this was the best place to talk. Sensing his concerns, Gamaliel turned and said, "There's a stall owned by my cousin. The drink isn't watered down and he won't cheat us."

Gamaliel led the way, weaving around the stalls, holding his breath as he passed the tables of meat sellers, whose carcasses hung in haunches, shoulders, innards, and entrails covered in hysterical flies. The acrid smell was soon replaced by that of newly baked bread. Gamaliel took some shekels out of his pocket, threw them onto the table, and grabbed two warm loaves. He handed one to Ahimaaz.

"I wish you God's good appetite."

"Thank you," said the high priest, slightly startled, but the hours standing in the palace had left him hungry. Gamaliel tore off a chunk and chewed openly. Ahimaaz held the bread in both hands and under his breath whispered a prayer.

They sat down on stools at the stall of Gamaliel's cousin. Ahimaaz looked darkly at Gamaliel as he ordered juice, then said quietly, "Do you always eat without blessing and giving thanks to Yahweh for providing it?"

Gamaliel's reply came bluntly. "The Lord didn't provide it. The baker did. And I thanked him accordingly with shekels on his table."

"Is everything not provided by the Almighty?" asked Ahimaaz.

Gamaliel, shorter than Ahimaaz, graying and slightly stooped, thought for a moment before replying. "Did the Almighty give me the right to levy taxes at the gate, which has made me a rich man? No, I negotiated that myself from Solomon's treasury. There were others, but only I came to a suitable arrangement with the treasurer. So why should I thank God? It was me who paid out of my pocket. You, priest, would tell me that what I did was wrong in the eyes of God. So how do you explain that I'm still here, not struck by lightning, not brought down by a divine arrow, but standing before you with bread in my stomach and juice on my table?"

Gamaliel picked up the cup and drank deeply. He didn't know what this priest wanted, but after the brush with death at the hand of Solomon, and now facing a strange future, Gamaliel felt oddly bold.

"And when I prayed fervently and offered all manner of things to the temple, did the Almighty save my second-born son when he fell into the ravine? No, my son died after three days in agony, his body broken. And where is the Almighty when my second wife, whose skin is constantly aflame with welts and ruptures, cries from morning till night and scratches herself so hard that she bleeds? And my daughter from my third wife, while no beauty, is still unmarried and is already fifteen years old and no man, regardless of what I offer as bride money, will take her because her arm is withered."

Ahimaaz was clearly unused to such speeches and found himself without response as Gamaliel continued in a strangely mocking tone.

"Surely conjuring a loaf of bread is a rather unimpressive display from your god if he means to atone for the sorrow and misery of the city?"

Ahimaaz's dismay turned to shock. "How dare you speak in that way, merchant! How dare you think you can understand God's ways! Wasn't it God Almighty who gave us this city? Wasn't it Yahweh who gave our father, Moses, the strength to resist the Egyptian pharaoh and lead us out of our bondage? Wasn't it—"

"Spare me, please. Your sermons are wasted here. I'm a man of business and I make a living from those who come into this city to trade. I have no need for this god of yours, or any other god. The Jebusites had their gods and look what happened to them."

"Our god is the one true God . . ."

"Show me proof and I'll believe you. Do you know what proof is, Priest? Solomon had proof that I had cheated him. I have proof that the bread I've just eaten was baked today. Other people have stone and iron gods that they can see, but our Yahweh is invisible"—Gamaliel pointed up to the sky, and then to the top of Mount Moriah, where the temple was soon to be completed—"and yet we're building Him a home. So when the roof is on the building and the men of Lebanon have gone back to where they came from, will Yahweh reside there? And if He does, will we be able to see Him? When I'm in my house and sitting on a chair, people can see me and nobody can sit on the chair that I occupy. Yet, if Yahweh is invisible, how will we know which chair He's sitting on?"

Ahimaaz looked at the tax collector in fury. "For such words, as high priest of Israel, I could order that you be stoned to death. You blaspheme against the Lord our God. I will have you killed."

Gamaliel smiled as he took out more shekels to pay his cousin for their pomegranate juice. "And will my death make Yahweh appear? No. But it doesn't matter. Let us make a deal. You tend to your congregation and I'll collect my revenues. We're both now in the service of King Solomon and his temple, Ahimaaz, but we're using different doors to enter."

Gamaliel drained the cup of juice and looked at the priest, whose face was red, not only from the exertion of the walk to the marketplace and the heat of the sun, but also from the seditious and blasphemous words of the tax collector. Gamaliel wiped his lips and smiled. "Now, what did you really want to talk about?"

———

October 18, 2007

YAEL STRODE UP THE CORRIDOR and ignored much of what was going on around her. Patients, nurses, fellow doctors, visitors, the low din of clinking trolleys and the hum of machines. But the swirl of brown robes caught her attention. They billowed as the imam walked briskly down the corridor toward her. She saw the imam reach into a pocket deep within the folds of the material and draw out a mobile phone. For a second she was about to stop him, to point to the sign on the wall that declared mobile phones were not to be used in the hospital, but she thought better of it and the pace and purpose of the bearded man with suspicious eyes implied he was leaving. As she passed him their eyes met, his dark and piercing, black pools deeply set into a tanned face. She quickly looked away, unnerved by his stare. But when she was farther down the corridor and many steps past him, she turned her head to look back and saw the phone pressed to his ear. And it was obvious from the position of his body that he'd just turned back from staring at her.

Yael's thoughts were interrupted by the abrupt presence of the uniformed guard outside Bilal's room. He looked her up and down as though he were about to challenge her entry or search her, even though he had seen her a dozen times. But he simply sat back down on his seat without a word and shifted his rifle's strap on his shoulder. As Yael put her hand on the door and her weight behind it, she pondered how out of place such a weapon was in a hospital.

Inside the room, the air was dry and still and quiet, the TV hanging from the ceiling remaining silent while Bilal lay in his bed. He started with a jump when she entered, and at first she wondered if she had woken him from sleep. But red eyes and the adoption of a fiercely resolute posture in the bed suggested something else. This intrigued Yael and she unintentionally quickened her steps to the bedside, but by the time she was close enough, Bilal's face was a hard mask and he refused to look at her, his eyes fixed dead ahead like those of a soldier lined up for inspection.

"How are you today, Bilal?"

Bilal said nothing. Yael's attention was distracted by thoughts other than bandages. As she checked his blood pressure she could not help but think of the blood that connected them. Who was this young man? Who were his family? How deep did the roots go that linked both of them, two people whose worlds were so diametrically opposed? But her musings were agitated by the image of an imam walking arrogantly down the hospital's corridor, a man she knew must have just been speaking to Bilal. She didn't trust any religion or any cleric, no matter how unctuous or bland they were on the surface. To her scientific mind, God was simply an invention to allay people's fears, but organized orthodox religion had grown into a woman-hating and power-hungry institution of medieval costumes and archaic ideas. Orthodox Jews and Christians were bad enough, but when it came to hate-spewing Islamic clerics, Yael's secular tolerance flew out the window.

In lively dinner-party debates with her educated friends she would attest to her discomfort for the faith of her own people, her frustration with the Jewish religious right, her disgust at the sycophancy of the Christian churches toward the Palestinians when its very own communities in West Bank towns had been decimated by Palestinian Muslims.

In her professional life, she kept such thoughts to herself. Now that she was in the hospital, her duty was to her patients. She gazed at Bilal and was concerned about the stress, anxiety, and fear on his face. Such emotions would adversely affect his recovery.

"Did you just have a visitor?" she asked him. "I saw a priest in the corridor."

But he said nothing. His eyes locked on an imaginary spot on the far side of the room.

"You'll be leaving soon."

This statement turned Bilal's head but he remained silent.

"Can't stay here forever . . ." She stopped her inspection and returned the clipboard to the end of his bed. "So we'll be saying good-bye to each other, Bilal."

"I am not afraid of what happens next," said Bilal flatly but unconvincingly.

"So you've said."

"Understand, woman. I am not afraid."

"Yes, Bilal. You're very brave," replied Yael. She was feeling sardonic and didn't mind sounding patronizing.

"I will stand up straight and say to the world that I am a freedom fighter!" said Bilal, exhaling defiance with every syllable.

"Then your trial will be mercifully short."

Bilal turned his head and looked Yael hard in the eye. "I will be a hero! My brothers will embrace me and they will call me a hero. Of that I promise you."

Yael knew she should remain silent and dispassionate. She shouldn't have cared for his beliefs or assertions. They were nothing to her. But despite the bluster in his voice she could not dismiss him. Whatever he'd done, he'd been controlled by others and he was only a kid. Sure, he was eighteen, but in his attitudes he wasn't much more than a boy.

She stopped examining his wounds and looked at him intently. "Listen, Bilal, you're in trouble. You don't understand. These people you think love you . . . they . . ." Yael snatched at words. "You have no value to them anymore, Bilal. They don't need you. And they will abandon you. They've used you for a couple of weeks, and they'll leave you to suffer for the rest of your life."

"You lie!" Bilal spat. "My imam tells me that—"

"Son, listen to me for a minute . . ." Yael put her hand on Bilal's arm. He tried to snatch it away but the handcuff held it and Yael's grip was firm. She could feel his pulse throbbing under her fingers, feel his blood pumping, blood that they shared. She softened her attitude toward him but her grip on his arm remained. "Bilal, you're not safe. You won't be safe in prison. You need to protect yourself. You need to tell the police that you're not a hero but that you've been led astray—"

"You lie!" Bilal yelled, as if he could drown out her words.

Behind Yael, the door was suddenly pushed open and the security guard entered the room to see what the shouting was about. His eyes narrowed on Bilal and Yael turned to him. "It's okay. We're fine."

Bilal yanked with all his strength at his handcuffed wrist in anger and the bed lurched with a force that surprised Yael and brought the guard over to the bedside.

"It's okay. We're fine. You don't have to . . ." Yael said urgently to the guard, but as she did she was conscious that the chance to garner more information from Bilal about his heritage had slipped through her fingers.

"Calm down, boy!" said the guard with one hand outstretched and the other hovering near his weapon. There was no chance the guard would actually use his rifle, but many years serving on West Bank checkpoints had ingrained a muscular memory and a reaction to Palestinians that was not easy to let go.

"You lie!" yelled Bilal again. "I am a hero. I am a fighter. And you lie!"

The guard pushed Yael away from the bed with a sweep of his arm, a strong signal that she should leave.

"Bilal . . . Please . . . It won't be what you think. You won't be a hero in prison. You'll—"

But her words were smothered by Bilal's yelling. "YOU LIE!"

Yael turned her back and moved toward the door with the image of Bilal's enraged face in her mind. She left the room, and as she walked down the corridor her mind began to doubt the science that had been her mainstay since she'd been a university student.

The match between their DNA must be wrong, the idea absurd; how could this idiotic failed terrorist be related to her? This deluded boy shared nothing with her—not heritage, not culture, not reality. The blood profile was a mistake, the DNA map was wrong. Or it was a one-in-a-billion chance that their DNA was identical but that they had no relationship to each other at all. And the proof was in the room behind her, painted in denial and ignorance.

Putting one hand in her pocket as she walked quickly toward the stairs that would lead her back to modernity and the certainty of her reality, Yael felt for the slip of paper that she'd retrieved from her hospital mailbox: the letter from Bilal's father. They deserved to know the truth of their son's fate and Yael needed to put this stupid absurdity to rest.

———

STANDING BY an empty hospital bed, Mahmud had watched the imam from a distance for some time, but although their eyes never met, he knew that the imam had seen him too. Dark Semitic features were common to Arabs and Jews, but the imam would recognize Mahmud for what he was.

Mahmud had been watching as the imam entered Bilal's room. He'd waited patiently for the imam to leave. Now Mahmud stood outside the front doors of the hospital. The sunlight on his face felt good after hours drenched in the cold fluorescent light of the hospital. Before too long the brown robes of the imam emerged from the automatic sliding doors of the hospital and Mahmud saw him blink in the sun.

"*As-salamu alaykum,*" said Mahmud, and he took three paces toward the man. The imam seemed startled by the Arabic words and blinked again as he tried to focus on Mahmud while his eyes adjusted to the glare.

"*Wa alaykum as-salamu wa rahmatu Allah wa barakatuh,*" came the holy man's reply.

"What brings you to the hospital today?"

"I go where I am needed," the imam replied bluntly as he looked Mahmud up and down. "You are a doctor?"

"Yes."

"Where are you from?"

"Beit Safafa," replied Mahmud.

"Ahh . . ." said the imam, as if the name of the town where Mahmud grew up said it all.

Beit Safafa was an Arab neighborhood in southern Jerusalem. For decades it had been split down the middle, an invisible division of hatred and suspicion separating the Israeli side from the Jordanian side. But after the Six-Day War, when the Israeli army drove back the Jordanians, the township became a symbol of cooperation where both Jews and Arabs lived side by side peacefully. But in truth it wasn't where Mahmud had been born. Desperate for his son to grow up away from the tension and violence of the West Bank, which had characterized Mahmud's father's upbringing, the family had moved to Beit Safafa. Arriving poor and illiterate, they lived four people to a single room while his father drove a taxi eighteen hours a day to send Mahmud to school—an education that had been a gateway to a life his father never knew but had had vision enough to dream of for his son.

While the town of his childhood was a source of pride to Mahmud, the tone of the imam's response was very different.

"You grew up among the Jews, then. And now you work among them too."

"Do you know that boy? Bilal?" Mahmud asked, ice in his voice.

"He is a child of Allah. As are we all."

"And did Allah wish for him to carry a bomb?"

The question was so blunt it surprised the imam, but he didn't flinch, instead replying, "Did Allah wish for his people to be brutalized into poverty?"

Mahmud said nothing. The imam continued. "You are a doctor?"

Mahmud nodded.

"You are a good Muslim?"

"My father taught me to be so," replied Mahmud.

"I see . . . Then why are you here? Why don't you use your doctor skills to help your own people instead of helping these Jews?"

"Jews and Muslims and Christians come to this hospital. We treat the sick. We don't ask what they believe. Anyway, what kind of help are you offering to Bilal?"

The imam's eyes narrowed and his lips tightened. "I am guiding him to Allah. Who is guiding you?"

"When does it end?" asked Mahmud. His voice had lost its edge. It was barely more than a whisper. He turned away from the imam and walked back into the hospital.

———

THE OUTWARD CHANGE in Eliahu Spitzer's appearance was minimal but momentous. It was glacially slow but, now that he came to look back on events, inexorable. Perhaps, in all his secular life, in his work protecting the State of Israel from Palestinian terrorists and other madmen, he'd hungered for a higher calling, for a spiritual side to his innate practicality, but there were times when Eliahu's change surprised even him. Yet, when he had a moment of doubt, he remembered back to the events two years ago that had triggered his transformation, and it all somehow came together.

Before his daughter's murder, before his massive heart attack six months later, he had been—like so much of Israeli society—secular. His father, a Polish immigrant, had been ultra-religious, a former Yeshiva student who would have been a rabbi had not the war intervened. But Eliahu rejected religion and in his social life and education embraced the secular Israeli lifestyle.

For him and later his family, the synagogue was a three-times-a-year obligation at the insistence of his wife. He'd met with rabbis many times for his work and been to the ultra-religious corners of Tel Aviv and Jerusalem, but religion had never been anything other than what he'd done for personal cultural reasons. Yet, like a stone on which water drips and drips, after his daughter's murder and his brush with death, Eliahu's secularism eroded and he made room for a deity in his life. He'd actually seen God and it had changed his life forever.

He had two great regrets: the first was his rejection of his father's faith and that his awakening to the Almighty through the sect of the Neturei Karta had taken him over fifty years to realize; and the second was that, because of his position as a senior security officer for the government, the leaders of the sect had begged him to hide his affiliation to the Neturei Karta and to continue working within Shin Bet as usual and further the sect's cause.

He'd been hiding his faith for three years and in that time he'd worked to change the sect's methods of making the Messiah come early. They believed in prayer; so did he, but assisted prayer. He had laid out an ambitious plan for the leaders of Neturei Karta, and they'd eventually given their approval. In the three years since covertly joining Neturei Karta, he'd paved the way for the coming of the Messiah by honing and refining plans to bring about chaos, the destruction of the government, and its replacement by fervently religious Jews. And then all Jewish voices would be lifted to heaven so that the Messiah heard and would come.

Some members of Neturei Karta refused to go along with what Eliahu suggested to their leadership, believing that the restoration of the nation of Israel should be brought about by the will of the Messiah and not at a time dictated by the sect; and when they heard that people might be killed in the process, they were horrified. But their leader, Reb Shmuel Telushkin, reassured them that fighting governments of foreign lands was unacceptable but fighting Zionists who were traitors against the laws of the Bible was necessary.

Eliahu's identity was kept a strict secret from most of the membership while Reb Telushkin prepared him to be a member of the sect in every respect other than wearing the sect's uniform of the black fur hat and the long black silken frock coat and growing his sideburns.

His transformation from secular to Neturei Karta was carefully handled and subtle. After the shattering events he and his family suffered, he changed his appearance only slightly. Now he wore a small blue and white skullcap, the symbol to Jews that he was a religious man. He wore his Neturei Karta uniform of eighteenth-century garb only when he was in their synagogue, carefully screened from impure eyes; not even his wife knew.

The instrument of his change had begun with the murder of his daughter on a school excursion to the Dead Sea. For days he hovered over her bedside, looking at her torn body swathed in bandages, praying to a remote and invisible God for her recovery, one he'd not spoken with since he was a boy with his father in synagogue, knowing that her life was ebbing away as her vital signs continued to weaken.

Others might have sworn off the deity, becoming confirmed atheists because God hadn't answered their prayers; but as the doctors switched off the machinery that was keeping his daughter's shattered body on the threshold of life, Eliahu prayed fervently for God to look after her in heaven, now that he could no longer protect her on earth.

The month of ritual mourning had done little to mollify his hatred of the Palestinians, and he'd smoked and drunk more than usual before and after the crowds had come to his home to comfort the mourners and say evening prayers. Two of the visitors to his home had been Neturei Karta rabbis. His wife was surprised, as was he. But he welcomed any visitor who could lift the burden of grief he felt, even for a moment. At first he thought that they were just ordinary black-hatted rabbis. They kept their identity disguised until the third visit to his house of mourning, when the older man said that they were guardians of the city. In ancient Aramaic, the language of Jesus Christ, that meant they were Neturei Karta. His wife, knowing they were anti-Zionist, wanted them gone, but he accepted comfort from anywhere and took them into his study, where he asked about their beliefs in God and the afterlife. They spoke soft and concil-iatory words into his ears, and for the first time such words from the lips of Hasidic rabbis began to mean something to him. He knew consciously that he was clutching at straws, but he was a drowning man.

Eliahu's wife continued to view the rabbis with derision bor-dering on hatred, but the Shin Bet leader still listened to their words carefully as they enticed him out of the protective shell of his previously secular life. His wife railed against them and their desire to destroy the State of Israel. Soon they became the focus of her grief, expressed as anger and hatred against those who wanted to demolish her homeland and replace it with a Mes-sianic theocracy.

The rabbis of the sect told Eliahu that the only way for him to meet again with his daughter was with the establishment of the Holy Nation of Israel, not the secular state that had been founded by Zionists and the irreligious. They said that this was holy land and that the Lord God was ready to send his Mes-siah to ease all the pain and suffering of His people, provided certain conditions were met. The rabbis begged Eliahu to come and see their mentor and spiritual leader of the Neturei Karta, Reb Shmuel Telushkin, who would explain more, much more, to him.

But when the thirty-day period of mourning was over, Eliahu stopped thinking of his conversation with the Hasidic rabbis. He returned to work after the religious *s'loshim* ended, and threw himself into his job with renewed energy. He wasn't ready to go back onto the streets, and so they created a research position for him. And he ate hamburgers and french fries and drank liters of Coke and Pepsi at his newly created desk in his new office, rarely moved from his chair, took a taxi home, and sat in front of the television watching American cop dramas. The words of the Ne-turei Karta faded.

That is, until the morning he'd just finished a meeting and

was crushed by a pain in his chest. His heart failed just as it had been broken when his daughter died. In the hospital he was immediately injected with thrombolytics to dissolve the clot and was wheeled up to an operating theater to be given a quintuple bypass, a wonder of modern surgery. And it was in the hospital that he saw the light . . .

Literally!

While he was waiting for the operation to begin, he was given oxygen and injected with drugs to keep him alive before the surgeons could open his chest, and while he was lying in the pre-op ward, he slipped into a coma. The trauma nurses hit the alarm buttons and doctors rushed in. He was given electric shocks and wheeled immediately into the theater. But what the medical staff didn't know was that while he had his eyes closed he could sense that massive things were being done to his body. His eyes were tightly shut but he could actually see a brilliance above his head. The noises of the theater, the urgent instructions of the surgeon and nurses—even the smell of the disinfectants and the anesthetic—all faded, replaced by a warm and gentle atmosphere of peace, serenity, and calm, and the smell of jasmine. Jasmine, Shoshanna's favorite perfume.

He opened his eyes and near the ceiling, floating above him, he saw his beautiful daughter Shoshanna, dressed in the white of purity, smiling at him, waving to him, encouraging him to leave his pain and grief behind and follow her into the whiteness. Behind her, he saw an even more brilliant light, which he could hardly look into, but it shrouded his daughter in a sort of halo. He clearly heard her saying, "*Abba*, come, follow . . ."

And he did. He rose from the bed and could see the faces of the nurses and surgeons desperately trying to keep him alive. He saw his chest open, his heart beating, surgeons quickly trying to hook him up to machines to keep the blood flowing. He looked around the room and could clearly see the surgical table on which he was lying, the doctors and nurses, the instruments, the bottles and syringes and medicines and tubes. As he floated, trying desperately to reach his daughter's outstretched hand, calling out her name, he heard a voice in his ear. He recognized it immediately. It was the rabbi who had visited him months earlier when he was in mourning for Shoshanna, the rabbi who was a Hasid and who told him that the answer to his nightmare was the Neturei Karta. The rabbi's voice whispered, "Reb Shmuel."

Fifteen hours later, he woke in intensive care, but all he could remember was the brilliant white light, his beautiful daughter, and the urgent need to see Reb Shmuel Telushkin so that he could understand why the vision had come to him.

He'd discussed it with his cardiac surgeon, who had told him blithely that it was an unusual but perfectly understandable function of oxygen deprivation and the bright lights of the operating theater, and that he was to put it out of his mind. Which he assured the doctor he would do.

But the image stayed with him, haunted him, and even when he was exercising and trying to get his mind and body back to the way they once were, all he could think about was the way his beautiful daughter had looked, so grown-up and peaceful and serene. When he left the hospital two weeks later to go home, the voice and images remained as strong as ever in his mind. After two months of boredom, walking, watching television, and going to the hospital for checkups, and out of curiosity, he went to see Reb Telushkin in Jerusalem's Mea Shearim district.

Yet, Telushkin knew that he wasn't ready to join the sect, and so he sent him home and a month later they began the first of a series of regular talks, prayer meetings, Bible readings, explanations of the Zohar, the Book of Splendor, the Mishnah, the Gomorrah, and other spiritual books, which, despite being a Jew, he'd never bothered to open or read.

It took two full years before Reb Telushkin thought he was ready to join their sect. For the better part of six months, Eliahu had begged to be allowed to leave all of his ways behind him and become one of them. Every day he was increasingly estranged from his wife and wanted to leave the world of security and Zionism and politics behind him. But the rabbi refused his request and told him firmly to remain in his secular life, and only to come to them when his heart and mind could bear it no longer.

When, two years after his heart attack, Eliahu said that he was ready, he was surprised when Reb Telushkin told him that he would be welcomed into Neturei Karta on the condition that he continue to work with Shin Bet. He must maintain the façade of a secular life. The condition felt like an insult, an instruction that compelled Eliahu to lie and be dishonest to himself and to his newfound faith. But Telushkin calmly explained why this act was good in the sight of God, a small lie to bring about a bigger truth.

Eliahu would be their instrument to end the secular predicament, to end the abomination that was Israel. And he asked Eliahu, as an insider in both camps, how best to do it. Decades of experience with terrorism told Eliahu how to use it to pressure the Jewish community worldwide to rise up against the effete government that ran his nation and replace it with what it should all along have been: a theocracy, a dedicated group of rabbis who knew the message of God Almighty and would bring about the arrival of the Messiah and the Golden Age.

And since his heart attack, since seeing his beauteous daughter, since Reb Telushkin and he had planned their strategy, he had managed to obviate every threat to expose him, even if it meant that some people had to be killed for a greater cause. And now another potential threat was arising, one he had to keep his eye on.

Eliahu Spitzer sat at his desk, ruminating on Bilal's failure to be killed. He thought about this young trauma doctor in the hospital. Why was she visiting Bilal so much? His guard outside the door had reported that she had been in to see him four or five times, each time just talking. Far too much for a surgeon.

What were they talking about? And why had Bilal reacted so badly when Eliahu had tried to talk to him, to see what he knew and what he might tell other authorities?

What the hell was going on?

———

935 BCE

GAMALIEL SAT IN HIS HOME and pondered his sudden change of fortune. Though he and his wives were richly attired and they had every comfort their home needed, still his house was just above the middle of the hill on which Jerusalem sprawled. It suffered the stench of the marketplace and took the full brunt of the burning winds that blew in from the desert.

Unlike princes and priests, and Solomon himself with his vast palace at the very apex of the city's hill, Gamaliel's rank as a tax collector on the gates to the city didn't entitle him to a higher position. But now that he was going to enter the temple, where he'd have an office and servants, he wondered whether Solomon or his court officials would grant him the right to build or buy a house much higher up the hill. If he could, then not only would his status as a lowly tax collector and merchant rise but he would be mixing with the sort of people whose patronage mattered: wives of Solomon, princes of his loins, and important people in the army and the palace itself.

His first and foremost wife entered the room, bowing her head reverentially, and stood in the doorway, waiting for his permission to enter. She still bore the marks on her face from the beating he'd given her the previous week. The truth was Gamaliel didn't know how Solomon had discovered his fraud with the tax collection. Nor did he know which of his wives had spoken of his business in the marketplace. But he did know two things: that he had told his first wife too much of his affairs and that she had a big mouth, always chattering to her friends and neighbors. And one of the servants of Tashere, Solomon's first and foremost wife, was probably listening as she'd boasted of their riches and fortunes.

"Yes?" he said sharply.

"She's here . . ."

"Who?"

"The king's first and foremost wife. I swear in the name of Yahweh, husband, I didn't know she was coming. And I didn't invite her. I've never met her. But she just appeared at the door and asked to see you. I swear." She seemed about to cry.

"The king's wife Tashere? She's in my house?"

His wife nodded.

"Well, don't just stand there. Show her in. Immediately."

His wife ran off and returned in moments with the queen, only to disappear once again just as quickly.

Gamaliel stood when Tashere entered. "Majesty . . ." He bowed and waited for her to release him.

Instead she began to speak, and sat on a chair opposite.

"You have been lucky, Gamaliel the tax collector," said Tashere in a near whisper, and she looked about the room in case people were listening.

Gamaliel didn't respond; Tashere didn't expect a reply.

"The money you will raise will be a fortune. But the fortune will be Solomon's. And it will be swallowed by the temple." Tashere surveyed the room, the furnishings, the matting on the floor. "No doubt you will want to rise higher in the city?"

"It is what all of us wish, to be closer to God's house."

"Save your piety for the priests. You wish to rise higher. And you will. But only so far. You will be blocked by Naamah and by that false high priest Ahimaaz. Is this not true?"

He looked at her and frowned. "Only last week, the king commanded me to raise the taxes. I haven't thought about what that means for me personally."

She laughed. "I know that you have been lying and stealing from Solomon, tax collector. But don't lie to me, for I know you and your kind only too well. My father, the pharaoh Shoshenq, employed a hundred of your kind, and all of his troubles were caused by them and the priests of the god Horus. Their bodies were found floating in Mother Nile until eaten by crocodiles. You want money and elevation from your lowly rank, but Naamah and Ahimaaz will ensure that you fail."

Gamaliel remained silent.

"I can prevent this happening. I can make you more than a rich man. I can make you rich and powerful," she said.

Again he was silent, stunned by her audacity.

"I was once the most powerful woman in Israel. Solomon listened only to me. Naamah took this from me by stealth and by using her body. And she took my son from me. They think I'm finished. But they're wrong, for I was not exiled by their lies. They left me alone because they think me weak; they have badly underestimated me. I need something from you, and you need something from me. And that is all it will take to elevate us both."

Gamaliel leaned in closer to hear what she was about to say.

"Money!" said Tashere.

Gamaliel let out a dry, soft laugh. "What a fool you must take me for, great Queen. Your husband, Solomon, has seen my deceit once and he will not hesitate to stone me to death and exile my family if I am so stupid as to risk his displeasure again."

"You are at risk already. Regardless of what you do, Ahimaaz and Naamah will see to your downfall. They have no control over you. Now that the priest knows you, he knows well that he cannot use you. Naamah will seek to place her own creature in your role. You have nowhere to go but further down the hill—if they allow you to remain alive, of course." She gestured toward the markets and slums that leaned against the outer gates and walls of the city, as far from the temple and prosperity as a Jerusalemite could live.

"Join with me, tax collector, and give me sufficient funds from your revenues to raise a militia of mercenaries to deal with Naamah, and I will expel her from the palace and with her will go Ahimaaz. Then my son, Abia, the rightful heir to Solomon's throne, will return and he will reward you for your loyalty to me."

Gamaliel smiled. "My reward will come swiftly the moment Solomon learns I have diverted revenues to you. I will be cast into the pit at the foot of the Northern Wall. No, thank you, Tashere; I don't fancy ending my days being crushed to death by large stones."

She nodded. She'd expected nothing less. "Naamah is a fading light. Solomon is growing tired of her, and her body no longer pleases him. She has to resort to more and more slaves doing more and more unusual things to his body to entice him. Her days are numbered, but she still commands a bodyguard, which will prevent me from getting near to her. Solomon still visits me in my palace and I have more of his ear than before.

"But she's also failing for another reason. Solomon now listens to me when I tell him things about her and her idiot son, Rehoboam, and he is regretting his decision to expel our son, Prince Abia. Soon, in a few days, I will say other things to him that will convince him of Naamah's treachery. That is why I need to pay for men."

Gamaliel listened carefully before saying, "But how do I account for giving you the revenue from the tax collections? Solomon has told me that he will be counting every shekel."

"Naamah is not the only one with creatures. While she controls the priests and high men, she has neglected the lowly men of the palace, men who see her for what she is. The clerks and the scribes and the money counters, these are my creatures—lowly men, but they are mine and they see everything. Solomon will not see any numbers before they have passed through my hands."

Gamaliel raised a skeptical eyebrow.

"I do not need an army. There will be no war. Just the removal of thorns. Naamah and her fool of a son, Rehoboam. Then my son will return as prince of Israel and you will rise higher than you could possibly imagine."

———

IN THE YEARS SINCE becoming high priest, since the downfall of his brother Azariah and the exile of Prince Abia, Solomon's heir, Ahimaaz had worked hard to teach Prince Rehoboam the intricacies and complexities of the laws of Moses and Yahweh. The young man occasionally asked some questions of merit, but most of the time when he was learning Jewish ways in the new and wondrous Temple of Solomon, his mind was elsewhere.

The prince even admitted he would rather be hunting or visiting other lands than spending his time at the feet of his father, learning the perils of kingship, or in the inner sanctums of the temple having rituals explained to him by the high priest.

In desperation Ahimaaz summoned Naamah, Rehoboam's mother, now the most important of Solomon's wives, to attend a meeting with him at his offices in the temple. He had told her to be present after the noonday sacrifice, and he sat and waited for her. And he sat. And he waited.

As the mid-afternoon prayers and sanctifications were about to begin in the western wing of the temple, Ahimaaz felt he had waited long enough and sent a messenger to ask why the queen had failed to attend. The man returned in less than an hour, red-faced and diffident.

"Her Majesty said that she was unable to attend," he said softly.

Surprised, Ahimaaz asked, "Did she give a reason?"

The man didn't answer but looked at the floor.

"What did the queen say?" Ahimaaz demanded.

The man whispered, "She said, 'Queens do not attend priests. If Ahimaaz wishes to speak with me, he will come to the palace and await my pleasure.'"

Despite the cold that was setting in on top of the mountain, Ahimaaz began to sweat. He had not seen the queen in many weeks. After his elevation to the high priesthood was secure, he'd been a valuable tool to the queen and had systematically removed any potential thorns and opposition in the temple while the queen herself cleared the palace of opponents. But with her power now seemingly secure, she no longer sought his counsel, leaving him to his rituals and the instruction of princes.

But Ahimaaz had to inform Naamah of Rehoboam's recalcitrance, his obduracy, and his waywardness so that she would scold him and force him to concentrate. Perhaps he shouldn't have summoned her, but he knew that was what his brother Azariah would have done. Azariah had even summoned Solomon to his home when the great king had allowed his foreign wives to place their idols close to the Ark of the Covenant so they could continue the worship they had practiced in their homes. Wary of Azariah's fury, Solomon had ordered his wives to keep their idols in their rooms. If Solomon had come at the high priest Azariah's behest, why wouldn't Queen Naamah come when Ahimaaz summoned her? Was he no less the high priest?

He donned his cloak, walked from his office, and descended the steps that led to the heavily guarded gate in the Western Wall of the city of Jerusalem. The guards let him pass without hindrance and he descended the well-trodden path to the king's palace. Weaving his way through the corridors to the women's quarters and then to the upper levels to the queen's chambers, he asked her steward for permission to enter. The arrogant man told him to wait while he went into the inner rooms.

And Ahimaaz waited and waited. There was no chair on which to sit, so he paced the floor wondering, then worrying, why it was taking so long for the steward to return. Eventually, after what seemed an age, the steward threw open the doors to the queen's chambers and told him to enter. The man didn't bow—didn't even lower his head in abasement—much to Ahimaaz's growing anger.

When he entered Queen Naamah's apartments, she was seated on a raised chair, a replica of a throne, surrounded by women in gossamer dresses lying around the plinth at her feet, their breasts and hips and legs clearly visible through the voile. He was shocked at such a display. Under other circumstances, he could have been in the inner recesses of a pagan temple, in the presence of sacred prostitutes.

Affronted, Ahimaaz looked at Naamah and said sharply, "Queen, when a high priest demands your attendance, you must come."

She sneered at him in contempt. "Little man, you are a high priest because I made you one. Yet, you sit in your temple and convince yourself that it was the Lord God Yahweh who put you there."

Ahimaaz was suddenly afraid for such words to be said aloud. "Silence. These women—"

Naamah said quickly, "All Nubians, Ammonites, Egyptians, and Moabites. Not one of them speaks a word of Hebrew. And even if they could, I've had their tongues removed . . ." The queen stretched out the last words as if they were a threat.

"I'm here about your son," said Ahimaaz.

"And what of him?" said Naamah, dismissively raising her eyebrow.

"He is lazy, indolent, and unwilling to learn. King Solomon has commanded me to instruct him in the ways of our faith, but in all of the time that I've been teaching him, he has learned nothing. His mind thinks of little but hunting and sport and women."

"I provide him with enough women. As for hunting and sport," said Naamah, "every young man needs distraction."

"You don't understand, Naamah—"

"Queen Naamah," she said, her voice cold.

"Queen Naamah," Ahimaaz corrected himself. "If he doesn't know and understand our laws and our ways, how can Solomon allow him to take over the kingdom? If he is disappointed, he will seek another son."

"And you will be sent into exile for your failure. But don't worry, Ahimaaz, these things so important to you and your god are of little consequence to me. While my son will rule Israel, it will be me who rules my son, and my plans are much greater than your invisible god can contemplate."

"But . . ." was all Ahimaaz was able to say as the blasphemy echoed in his ears.

"You people can see no further than your diminutive little city. Do you think I've worked so hard, used my body with such skill, just to be the queen of a sandy desert and the mother of houses made from stone? Go, Ahimaaz. Return to your little temple on top of the mountain and leave the running of the nation to those of us who understand what greatness means."

Before he could argue, she banged her foot on the plinth and immediately the door to her chamber opened, and the steward walked hurriedly over to where Ahimaaz was standing. He grasped his arm and tried to hurry him out of the door. But Ahimaaz held his ground and said to the queen, "I am the high priest of Israel. Do not dare treat me in this way. Control your son, Queen Naamah, or I will—"

"What? What will you do, little man?"

He swallowed. "I will curse him and forbid him to be the heir. I will refuse to anoint him when Solomon dies. I will—"

Suddenly, furiously, Naamah stood up and walked swiftly down the steps until she stood so close to Ahimaaz that he feared she would push him over.

"Listen to me, you ridiculous, disgusting little man. Go back to your temple and pray to your god that you never meet me again. For if ever I see you, and if ever I hear that you have used your office to curse me or my son, I will have you stripped naked and will order my soldiers to flay all of the skin from your worthless body. Now go. Get out of my sight. And never dare speak to me again."

Truly terrified, Ahimaaz left her chambers, his legs shaking and his head pounding. As he walked back up the hill toward the temple, he felt as though his head would roll off into the dirt.

In the years since he had replaced Azariah as high priest, Ahimaaz had immersed himself in the richness and complexity of the rituals of temple worship. It seemed all he had wanted was fulfilled. People bowed and deferred to him, sought his counsel and wisdom. He could not have imagined greater fulfillment and even believed he heard the voice of his God in the stone of Solomon's Temple. When he was in the Holy of Holies, alone in the darkness with just a single light to shine upon the Shekinah, he would stand still, barely breathing, and in his ears he could hear the breath of the Lord God. And when he stood even longer, the Lord God Yahweh told him what to do, how to behave, which of his priests to reward and which to punish.

But lately the voice had faded and the stones of the temple seemed cold and silent. The other priests cowered before him, spoke only when spoken to. He was asked no questions and provided no answers. He had convinced himself that God himself had orchestrated his rise.

Then he could think only of the small children's top, a toy from his days of innocence, with its painted colors spinning on the floor. And the laughter of his brother . . .

And now he couldn't even hear that laughter. Now all he could hear was the cackling laughter of the queen as he was hustled out the door by the guards.

Even before he reached the outer gate in the Western Wall of Jerusalem, even before he began his ascent to the Holy Temple, Ahimaaz stopped in his tracks and stood in the road. The guards looked at him, wondering what he was doing. Those worshippers who were going up to the temple carrying sacrifices, or who were descending after offering their prayers and sacrifices, stared at him. And then they rushed over to Ahimaaz when he fell to his knees and sprawled in the roadway in a dead faint.

October 20, 2007

ALTHOUGH SHE'D BEEN strongly advised by both her colleagues and the police superintendent whom she'd consulted not to go into the village, Yael went nonetheless, and immediately regretted it. Israelis didn't go to the Palestinian village of Bayt al Gizah, or to most other places that were predominantly Palestinian towns or cities. Even though Bayt al Gizah was just the other side of the valley from Jerusalem in Israel proper, ten minutes by car and clearly visible from the city's eastern side, she'd never been there before. Cars had been stoned, Jews had been beaten, and there had even been several Israelis killed. Yet, Yael was determined to visit the village both to show that she wasn't afraid and to fulfill a promise she'd made to herself: to find out just how she was linked by bloodline to Bilal.

But now that she was parked on one of the potholed, unpaved streets and knew that those looking at her weren't kindly disposed, she realized how foolish she'd been. Her car, for a start, made her stand out as a person to be detested. It was a late-model dark blue Honda sports car, and a world apart from the ten- and twenty-year-old pickup trucks and dusty Fords and Toyotas parked in the narrow hillside lanes of the village. Then there was the fact that she was a woman, exposing her face and her chest in a blouse that, while modest by Israeli standards, showed the beginnings of cleavage, an outrage in a medieval Islamic setting. She bought her clothes to look sharp and modern, from the expensive boutiques along the Mamilla shopping mall in the center of Jerusalem, in stark contrast to the traditional Arab clothes of men and women who, when they weren't wearing a *thawb* or a hijab or a niqab, wore jeans and tops.

And lastly, there was the fact that her long black locks of hair as well as her face were exposed for all the men to see because she wasn't wearing a hijab or niqab, and her body was clearly visible because she wasn't in a chador. Instead of covering herself, Yael was wearing the normal clothes she wore to work, a blouse and skirt that rode just a fraction above her knees, revealing the shape of her legs. She'd driven straight from the hospital just a short distance beyond the valley where her look was completely unremarkable in modern Israeli society to a traditional society where conservative dress and the restrictions on women were mandated by men.

Indeed, it was only a few years earlier that a group of fundamentalist members of Hamas in Gaza, who called themselves the Swords of Truth, had threatened to behead women television presenters and reporters if they didn't wear a hijab.

As she walked toward the house, she wondered if her car would still be there when she left. It was easy to be angry at thieves, much harder to fix the poverty that afflicted many Arab neighborhoods in Israel. Yael knew this but still felt a mixture of anxiety and anger at the prospect of being a victim of theft.

It was a modest house made of limestone blocks. The front garden was neat and there was a small patch of earth where lettuce, radishes, and carrots were being grown. The steep and terraced garden was intersected by a path that led to four stone steps and the blue front door. Yael smiled at the color; she'd been told as a child that it was painted blue because the devil can't swim, and so he'd mistake the house for the sea and leave the occupants in peace. She just prayed that Bilal's parents didn't look upon her as a Jewish devil as she climbed the steps and knocked.

Within a moment it was opened by an elderly stooped man, unshaven and with the ubiquitous cigarette in his mouth. He looked at Yael as though she were a visiting alien. "Yes?" he said in Arabic.

"My name is Dr. Yael Cohen. Are you Bilal's father, Fuad?"

He frowned but the frown quickly became a strange smile. "You're the doctor who . . . I wrote to you . . . You were on the television . . ."

"Yes. I wonder if I could talk with you. Inside your home, if that's all right?"

"Is Bilal well? Has something happened? The operation? He was taken to prison?"

"He's fine. And no, he won't leave the hospital until Friday." She was nervous about being on the front step and spoke quickly. "I've arranged it so that he can stay a bit longer. He wants you to visit him before he goes to prison. I just need to—" But before she could say anything further, she saw that Fuad was looking beyond her, to the street. She turned to see that a group of about twenty young men had gathered around the front gate of the house, and while some were looking with interest, it was evident that others were looking at Yael with menace. Israeli women, especially those who came without men, didn't enter Palestinian villages. They wanted to know why she was here, visiting Fuad and his family.

"Excuse me," Fuad said, and stepped from the house to stand beside Yael on the front step. He shouted to the group of men, "There is nothing here. This is the doctor who saved Bilal's life. Leave now and go back to your homes. Everything is all right. She is in my protection."

With these words from Fuad they all left to walk back to where they'd come from. Fuad looked at Yael and said, "You will be safe now. Please, good Doctor, come inside. You will have tea and cakes. Yes?" And as if he'd just realized something important, he said, "Your Arabic. It's very good."

Yael knew from her education at school of the legendary hospitality of Arab households, and to refuse an offer of food and drink was a great insult, so she walked into the beautifully neat home and was encouraged to sit on a sofa. As was Arabic custom, the sofa was actually a series of deep cushions, and so she sat on the floor, carefully adjusting her skirt for modesty while Fuad positioned himself to her right. Within moments of sitting there, two women, one elderly and the other presumably her daughter, walked into the central room of the house. Both women were carrying ornamental copper trays on which were arrayed a *dallah*, a traditional coffeepot with a long curved spout, and two small handle-less cups along with cakes. The women, whom Fuad didn't introduce, placed the trays on the small three-legged tables and poured two cups of coffee. The smell of cardamom rose from the cups. Yael smiled when she saw the cakes, small diamond-shaped morsels and triangles of sugary, syrupy confections, full of honey and nuts and flaky pastry. Delicious, and although her diet would never allow her to eat such treats at home, she gladly accepted and relished their sweetness and flavors.

As soon as the coffee had been poured, the two women retired from the room. Yael assumed that the older woman was Fuad's wife and Bilal's mother, and the younger was his sister. But as was traditional with Arab men, Fuad neither introduced them nor would he countenance them sitting in on the conversation.

Alone, Fuad said, "You have come here to visit me. It is a great honor. My house is your house, my possessions your possessions. I wrote to you and I apologize for my writing because I am not a man of education. All my life I have been a construction worker; now I am boss of two construction gangs and I am a respected man in my community." His chest was noticeably full of pride but deflated as he continued. "But I ask you, Dr. Cohen, why are you here?"

"I'm here to ask you about Bilal, and yourself." She sensed a moment of suspicion when his eyes narrowed, so quickly added, "Don't be alarmed. Bilal's health is good, and he's well enough to leave the hospital, but I'm keeping him in for some days so that you can talk with him."

Fuad looked at her in surprise. "Is this usual in your country for you people to speak Arabic as well as you do?"

She forced herself not to smile. *"Your country"?* she thought. *"You people"?* It was always like this, separated even though living beside one another. She wondered when it would all end.

"We learn Arabic at school, and as a doctor I treat many Palestinians, so I have learned the beauty of your language and the wisdom of your thoughts."

Fuad nodded sagely, accepting the praise and compliment without comment. Yael heard a slight noise coming from the kitchen. It was obvious that the two women were close by, listening to every word that was being said.

"If Bilal is well, why are you here? Don't misunderstand. I am honored and grateful, but why have you come?"

"It was through your letter that I discovered your address. Because of what he did, all Bilal's personal records are kept secret, to protect you and your family. But the reason I'm here is because of a blood test that I ordered to be performed on Bilal before we operated on him. He has a rare and unusual blood group." Fuad's eyes widened, anticipating bad news as would any father speaking to a doctor about his son's health. "Don't worry, there's nothing wrong, but the blood group is very strange, and I was hoping you'd be able to tell me where your family came from, your family history."

His concern turned to suspicion. "We are Palestinians. We were born in Peki'in. Near to the border with Lebanon. Why do you ask?"

She knew she'd addressed the issue wrongly. It undermined him to be asked in such a direct way. The Arabic mind-set was full of twists and turns and, like the language, often relied on nuance to make sense. "As a doctor I have to understand blood. It's blood that gives us life. And blood is something we pass from father and mother to son. Bilal's blood is very interesting and rare, and I'd like to know where his bloodline comes from."

Fuad looked at her for a long moment, and she couldn't perceive what he was thinking. Then, unexpectedly, he said with a smile on his face, "Bilal came from my loins."

The joke was strangely comforting, like the dry overt humor of fathers the world over. Yael let out a small laugh and Fuad continued.

"My father was born in Peki'in. His father too. My family came to Palestine many years ago. I don't know when. They say from Egypt, which is why our name is haMitzri. In your Jew words, it means Egyptian. But we are all Palestinians. We're told that we have lived here for many thousands of years. Our president Abbas told us that we Palestinians have lived in Palestine for over seven thousand years. Perhaps my family has always lived here. I don't know."

"And Bilal's mother, your wife? Where is she from? What's her heritage?"

Fuad looked at her strangely and asked quietly, "My wife? Why does she matter?" Fuad's question was genuine, born of a traditional way of thinking about families and bloodlines.

"Because—" Yael was about to explain the need to trace the maternal as well as paternal bloodline but Fuad suddenly cut her off.

"Doctor, I thank you for treating my son. I thank you for saving his life. But you are asking about my family. And these are not things I will discuss with you."

They continued to talk for a little while, but it was obvious that he was immensely sensitive about information concerning his family. She knew that Arab families, as well as the tribe they belonged to, kept personal information very private, rarely revealing details such as this. She decided to leave, finished her coffee, and thanked him, asking him to pass on her regards to his wife, then she said that they should come to the hospital the following day if possible to visit Bilal.

He stood and escorted her to the door. There was nobody left in the street, and her car was intact. But as she walked to her car, she wondered if Fuad was so sensitive about discussing his ancestry because it was a traditional Arab reaction, or because there was something he didn't want others to know.

————

DRIVING BACK TO THE HOSPITAL in Jerusalem would take her not more than ten or fifteen minutes at the most, but driving out of the village of Bayt al Gizah seemed to take forever. Apart from the impossibly narrow streets and the precipitous drops on either side of the roads, which had been carved out of the steep hillside, forcing her to drive at slow speed, Yael felt horribly intimidated. Along the route from Fuad's home to the outskirts of the village, young and old men had positioned themselves on both sides of the road.

Fuad's warning to the village that Yael was under his protection had spread from house to house. But that didn't stop dozens of people from lining the streets on the outskirts of the village as she drove slowly away. They were just looking at her and her car. She tried to focus and concentrate on her driving, but whenever she looked at the people's faces, she thought she saw both anger and envy. They had been warned off from harassing her, but Fuad had said nothing to them about intimidation, and that's precisely what she felt.

The menacing stares grew fewer and fewer as she drove out of the village, but she could still feel them. Having been brought up in Jewish cities and suburbs all her life, and with few Palestinians whom she could call friends, her only contact with them was through her patients. She didn't want to think of herself as a racist or a person who instinctively disliked or distrusted Palestinians, as did a number of her friends, but her experience in Bayt al Gizah deepened her concerns that Jews and Palestinians were destined never to live together, and all the high hopes and naïve optimism might never change the relationships between the two peoples. Abba Eban's words came to her mind:

"History teaches us that men and nations behave wisely once they have exhausted all other alternatives."

Yael was afraid, and she was angry that she should feel afraid. So close to her home, in the place she was born, she was suddenly fearful of those all around her; of the Palestinian eyes she felt boring into her. Realizing that she was driving faster than normal as her anxiety increased, she slowed down as she approached the outskirts of Jerusalem and its familiar lights reflected on ancient stones.

At school she had learned her history and the complexity of the diaspora and exile of the Jewish people. Land and culture were ancient, but nations were built and made and manufactured. Israel had been built upon the bones of an ancient culture with a narrative of determined survival in the unwelcoming places Jews had been forced to live. It was a narrative well suited to a people who had nowhere else to go.

And the Palestinians, whose envious eyes Yael could feel watching her as she drove away, had an identity and a narrative manufactured for them by external political forces. A nation dispossessed and a victim of colonization. Both were simple narratives obscured by infinitely more complex truths. The Jews had been exiled and yet they had never truly left, with family lines remaining in villages, towns, and cities. Palestinians longed for a nation of their own, yet history had never known a people called Palestinians. Their narrative had been written for them, and they had become a people with nowhere else to go. The story was flawed and complex, and too much blood had been spilled trying to simplify it.

But all this was very far from Yael's mind as her eyes glanced nervously in the rearview mirror and the mix of fear and anger welled inside her. Why should she feel afraid? Behind her car, lights flashed and she caught her breath. Was she being followed?

Or was she jumping at shadows? She had gone to a village so close yet so far removed in time and place from her home. She had spoken to a reasonable man, a loving father, yet she was at the mercy of his protection from his neighbors, who saw her as an enemy. She was furious that she should need protection.

Yael flexed her hand and shook out the tension, placing her palms back on the wheel with a deliberately lighter grip. The lights behind turned off into a side street and she was alone on the road again. She thought of the blood she had washed off those hands through countless surgeries. Jewish blood and Arab blood all looked the same as it cascaded off her latex gloves and flowed down the sink. But fear and delusion were much harder to scrub away. The realization of her own bloodline's complexity filled her with anxiety, as her own heritage was shown not to be as simple as she had once thought.

She had to control her anger before arriving at the hospital, but the thoughts kept invading her mind. And she couldn't stop her mind from being angry when she remembered her father telling her that, even before the Six-Day War in 1967, those Arabs living on the West Bank and in the north called themselves Jordanians and Syrians. She knew from further education, talking to friends, and listening to lectures that before the First World War the area now encompassed by Israel and the Palestinian Authority was little more than an outpost of the crumbling Ottoman Empire. And before that, their land was occupied by half a dozen different warring Arab dynasties; even before the rise of Islam, the Romans; before them, the Greeks. No research she'd done, no book she'd ever read, had identified a Palestinian capital or a separate Palestinian culture, language, religion, dress, art, cuisine. The people who now proudly said that they'd been Palestinian for seven thousand years were actually an amalgam of migrants, nomads, Bedouin, and residents of sporadic villages.

Yael pulled into the hospital's parking lot and had to sit for five minutes to get her emotions under control. She was a surgeon, so self-control and the ability to handle any sudden and life-threatening emergency were the hallmarks of her profession. The last thing she wanted was to walk into the hospital in her current angry state.

Eventually, calming herself with deep breathing and listening to a Mozart piano concerto on her iPod, she left her car and walked into the hospital. Up two flights of stairs to the doctors' rooms, she entered and immediately found a note telling her to come to the men's surgical ward. It was signed by her boss, the head of surgery, and he had noted the time: the note had been written only ten minutes earlier.

Rushing up the flights of stairs to find out what was wrong, she was confronted by the sight of three tall and officious-looking men standing outside Bilal's room, arguing in restrained but clearly angry voices. She walked quickly to where they were standing with her boss, Pinkus Harber. "What's happening?"

Pinkus looked at her in relief. "These gentlemen are demanding that Bilal be taken to prison today. Now. Immediately. You told them that he would be able to be released today but, according to the nurse, you've given instructions not to release him until Friday. They're insisting . . ."

Her state of distress from her experiences in Bayt al Gizah suddenly returned and she said defensively, "His wounds aren't recovering as quickly as I wanted. He'll stay here until he's safe to be released into your custody."

The oldest of the three men looked menacingly at her, a technique he used with uppity young women. "We're government officials. We're here to take our prisoner into our custody. We don't need your approval."

"What government department? Where's your identity card?" she demanded.

The man looked at Pinkus.

"Yael," said her boss, "I've seen these men's identification. They're from Shin Bet. They have the right to remove the patient, provided you give permission as his treating doctor."

"Doctor," said a younger man, trying to mollify her, "we have excellent medical facilities at the prison. We're taking him now, and he'll go into the prison hospital."

"He's my patient. You're not taking him now. He's staying here under my care until I'm sure that he's well enough to be released."

The third man, shorter than the others, chimed in: "Are you forgetting that this bastard slit the throat of an Israeli citizen and tried to murder dozens of others? The man he killed was Yemeni; he came to this country with his wife and four children, and he'd become a respected citizen. Yet this little bastard slit his throat like a piece of meat. This hospital isn't a health farm for the likes of him. We have orders to take him, and take him we will!"

Now it was Pinkus's turn to be angry. "Dr. Cohen is one of our finest surgeons, and until she says so, he stays in her care. Now, if you gentlemen would kindly leave and return on Friday, we'll get on with our work of curing the sick."

The most senior Shin Bet operative stared at Pinkus, then Yael. "And if I get a court order to remove him?"

Pinkus said menacingly, "The hospital's lawyers will oppose the granting of any court order. It'll take till Friday to resolve the issue anyway. So it's your choice."

The oldest man slowly nodded to his colleagues. They all knew that the next step simply wasn't worth it. Without a word, they turned on their heels. Yael watched them disappear down the corridor. To her surprise, Pinkus said, "After they arrived, I took a quick look at Bilal's wounds. They're healing fine. You know he's ready to be released. So why the hell are you keeping him here? Fattening up the goose before the slaughter?"

She thought quickly for an excuse, but none came to her. So she told him half of the truth. "He's going to prison forever. I know he's a murderer, but he's also a misguided kid. Pinkus, when he goes to prison, he won't see much of his parents for the rest of their lives, and whatever visits he gets will be through glass walls, talking to them with a telephone, or whatever they do to terrorists. I've arranged for his mother and father to visit him tomorrow. At least in here they'll be able to touch him, kiss him, hold him. I'm sorry that you were involved."

Pinkus nodded. "Okay, fine. But don't compromise this hospital any further. Friday is Friday—it's when he's wheeled out to prison. No ifs or buts or maybes. He goes. Understood?"

She nodded, thanked him, and was about to go into Bilal's room when her phone beeped with a text message.

I'm in a taxi nearby. I could be with you in half an hour for a cup of coffee, if you're free. Text me. I'd like to continue our conversation, especially now you're a media star . . . Yaniv Grossman.

Again Yael found herself annoyed by the American's bravado and slick confidence. And yet, she knew some personal time with him would calm the tension she'd suffered since going to the Palestinian village. She texted him back.

I'm free—so to speak.

———

PUTTING DOWN THE TELEPHONE, Eliahu Spitzer ached to reach for a cigarette to calm his fragile nerves. He hadn't smoked in three years at the insistence of his doctors as well as his wife, who hated the stench of tobacco in his hair and on his clothes, yet the urge to smoke in times of tension had never left him.

Instead, he opened another packet of gum and slowly chewed the little white bullet as he pondered what to do next. This damned, bloody, interfering bitch of a doctor wouldn't give up her patient.

He breathed deeply and realized that his hands were sweating despite the air-conditioning. But why? What did the little Arab shit know, other than the imam had sent him to blow up a wall and, right on schedule, he'd been taken down by the Israeli security forces. Sure, it had made headlines as far away as New York and Moscow, but the reaction, both in Israel and in the rest of the world, had been muted, to say the least. Eliahu had assured his rabbi that it would be the first in a series of planned Palestinian atrocities against Jewish monuments that he would orchestrate to build and build until the momentum of the atrocities against ancient Judaism would anger world Jewry, who'd rise up in outrage, swamping the voices of the appeasing left-wingers.

The rabbi had concurred that violence committed to bring about the downfall of the secular government was justifiable. And as an expert in counterterrorism, it was just a small step across the line for Eliahu to go from protector to destroyer. But, unlike most destroyers, his plan was to rebuild a Messianic Israel after the destruction, the foundations of which would be the Torah, and this would lead to the return of his beloved daughter.

In the eyes of Neturei Karta, Israel was an illicit, amoral collection of Jews who should have stayed in the diaspora created by the Romans until the Messiah arrived. Then He would gather up His people and return them to God's land. A small number of blessed Jews had lived in Roman Judea, in Islamic Palestine, in the Crusader kingdom of Christendom, and under the rule of the Ottomans as caretakers, and this was God's will until the arrival of the Messiah and the return of all the Jews from around the world. But then political Zionism had begun the artificial building of the Jewish nation and secular lawmakers had introduced things that weren't in the Jewish law of the Torah, and so the Messiah would not come.

Eliahu reached for another piece of chewing gum as he

remembered his many conversations with Reb Telushkin in the two years after his heart operation. But the first steps in their plan had gone slightly awry. In the ordinary scheme of things, it wouldn't have mattered. The Palestinian kid had failed to be killed, and he could have been seen to in prison or anywhere. But this doctor was getting involved, and that was adding an unnecessary layer of complication. If there was one thing Eliahu hated, it was external complications to a neat and clever plan.

This damnable woman doctor was frustrating him again. What had Bilal told her? What had he said to others? Had he named the imam? For if he had, Eliahu was concerned that if the pressure on the imam was too great, the bastard would tell the cops about him. It was unlikely, and he'd covered his tracks, but he didn't want any cop or colleague in Shin Bet examining what he was doing. Two had already become suspicious and he'd had to deal with them.

But this doctor—she was a problem that needed to be removed! He continued chewing, realizing that he was chewing faster than normal. To calm himself, he began to sing the Neturei Karta anthem under his breath.

> *God is our King, Him do we serve, the Torah is our Law and in it we believe.*
> *We do not recognize the heretical Zionist regime, its laws do not apply to us.*
> *We will go in the ways of the Torah in fire and water.*
> *We walk in the ways of the Torah, to sanctify the Name of Heaven.*

He sighed and felt calmer as he remembered the brilliant white light and the path he'd followed ever since.

———

933 BCE

AHIMAAZ SAT ALONE in the silence of his office—a silence that was not only in the room but also in his mind. Yahweh's silence was the most profound indication that Ahimaaz was abandoned. The duties of the day were nearly upon him but he could not empty the silence from his mind.

There was a knock on the door and he didn't have time to say "Enter" before it opened and Gamaliel the tax collector walked in. The man was so rude, so arrogant, that Ahimaaz nearly ordered him to leave. Since they'd been working together, administering the temple, they'd barely spoken a civil word to each other.

Gamaliel sat himself down and drew out an assortment of papers and accounts relating to money and expenses in the maintenance and construction of the temple. Small talk of small financial matters filled the room in short, sharp statements, yet Ahimaaz saw that there was something in Gamaliel's face. Today he was a different man, his arrogance dissipated.

Finally the small talk between them was broken when Gamaliel abruptly said, "You and me, priest, we are not so unalike."

Ahimaaz raised an eyebrow. Gamaliel lowered his voice, the first time he'd done so since Ahimaaz had known him. Normally he didn't care who heard him or what he said.

"We find ourselves elevated to high office, with much further to fall," said Gamaliel.

In past times Ahimaaz would have been defiant in his denial, but today he was silent.

"We were both raised up and now those who raised us have no need of us. We are expendable and we teeter at the top of a precipice. You and me . . ."

Ahimaaz remained silent.

"I, too, was offered advancement and protection beyond my station. The first wife herself, Tashere, came to me, just as Naamah came to you."

Ahimaaz flinched. Gamaliel smiled and said, "You can't hide anything from Solomon—or me." He pushed himself back slightly from the table and eyed the priest coldly. "Naamah gave you power when your invisible Yahweh did not. Tashere gave me protection when I could not protect myself. But what price did we pay, my dear priest?" Gamaliel didn't wait for an answer and Ahimaaz had none to offer.

The tax collector continued. "Tashere came to my house and asked me to divert money to her so that she could raise a militia to overthrow Naamah. She wanted to expel the third queen from the city, along with her son, Rehoboam. She wanted her son, Abia, to be brought back from exile and be Solomon's heir."

Ahimaaz finally found words. "And what did you do for her?"

"I gave her money. Money from the temple taxes."

Ahimaaz stood up suddenly, his chair falling backward. "How dare you!"

But Gamaliel stood to match Ahimaaz and cut him off. "Protection from Naamah was the price I charged Queen Tashere. What was your price when Naamah bought you? Which of your fellow priests did you cast out? How many opponents did you have removed?"

"Enough!" yelled Ahimaaz, his mind aching with pain. "Enough!"

But Gamaliel persisted in softer and more resolute tones. "And what of your brother? Is this another story of Cain and Abel? How did you convince Solomon to get rid of him?"

The words sucked the air from Ahimaaz's lungs and he sat back in his chair, his face ashen.

"Do not fear. I am no judge. Your god has the monopoly on that. But now is not the time for giving in . . ." Gamaliel sat back down and leaned across the desk to be close to Ahimaaz's face. "Now is the time to protect ourselves."

"What do you mean?"

"Naamah has no need of you any longer. And as Tashere

circles her with soldiers my money has just bought, Tashere will soon have no need of me. You and I must make ourselves needed, valued, by someone higher than a queen."

"Solomon? How?" asked Ahimaaz, his hands trembling. "When he finds out, he will have us killed."

"The truth. The truth about the plotting of his queens. Such truth will set us free," replied Gamaliel with a smile.

"It will be a half-truth," said Ahimaaz, shaking his head.

"Better than no truth at all."

"Is it?"

"My dear priest. We used different doors to enter, but we are both now, as always, in the service of the temple."

———

HE WAS DRESSED in his pure white vestments, those he usually wore only on the great day of fasting and sacrifice as defined by the Levites on the tenth day of the month of Tishri, the day when he and the people of Israel atoned for the sins of their ancestors in the desert after leaving Egypt. At Mount Sinai they had doubted Moses would return and in their fear and loneliness molded and fashioned a golden god creature. Moses descended from the sacred mountain and in his fury smashed the tablets Yahweh had given him, just as today Ahimaaz descended from his mountainous temple and walked through the Western Gate to the king's palace.

Unlike previous occasions when some palace official had stopped him and forced him to wait for some time before seeing the king, this time Ahimaaz walked straight past the servants into the throne room. The look on his face and the staff of office he carried told them to be wary of him. As he walked through the doors of the room, he was announced by the king's servant.

Ahimaaz walked to where Solomon was sitting on his throne and wondered why the king, who normally ignored him as he entered, was looking at him so fiercely. Usually nervous, this time Ahimaaz was confident, for no matter what Solomon did to him—no matter how much he shouted or ridiculed or compared him with his pious brother—Ahimaaz knew that when he confessed, he would shortly thereafter die. And death was welcome.

Ahimaaz had listened to Gamaliel's reasoning, a plan that would see him detail how Tashere stole funds from the temple unbeknown to the tax collector. Gamaliel would be distanced from his crime, and he, Ahimaaz, would be secured by his act of loyalty to the king, no longer at the mercy of Naamah.

But as he stood before the king, Ahimaaz closed his eyes for a moment, and in the blackness that enveloped him saw the whirling of the colored spinning top and heard his brother's laughter. No. There would be no elevation for him. There could only be the truth to shut out from his head the silence of the Lord God and the ridicule of Queen Naamah.

Taller than normal, standing straight despite the king's withering looks, Ahimaaz bowed before the throne. He spoke immediately, which stunned the amanuenses and officials gathered around the walls of the chamber.

"Majesty, I am here on a matter of God's business, and—"

"God's or yours?" asked Solomon, his voice dry and humorless.

"God's business. I am here to tell you something that will affect your kingdom, which involves your heirs and your wives and I who preside over your temple . . ."

"What is it that people call me, Ahimaaz?"

The question surprised him and broke him from the trance of confession he had put himself in.

"Solomon, Majesty."

The king smiled and shook his head. Ahimaaz remained mute. Suddenly, all the courage he'd been mustering vanished, and he shrank into his clothes.

"Not just Solomon, priest. My people call me Solomon the

Wise. I give fair judgments when people with a dispute come before me; other kings look at the way I rule and envy me. And it's because I am fair, wise, and knowledgeable that my people love me. Do you understand that, priest?"

He mumbled, "Yes, Majesty."

"There is nothing you have to say that I do not already know."

Ahimaaz was blank and unsure of what the king would say next.

"I knew you would come. It has been known to me for a long time."

All moisture was sucked from Ahimaaz's mouth, and his eyes shifted about the throne room. Only now did he see Gamaliel standing by the far wall of the room. The tax collector looked hard at Ahimaaz, and the stare told him he, too, was slipping into a strange panic at the king's words.

"I know my wives very well. I choose many. But I choose them carefully. I know, too, my sons—those who remain close to me and those whom I have cast out." Solomon paused, stood, and stepped down from the plinth on which his throne stood. He took three long strides toward Ahimaaz and the priest felt his body shrink under the king's shadow.

Solomon's voice lowered as he drew nearer. "I know of your schemes with Naamah. I know how it came to be that her son, Rehoboam, became my heir. And I know what part you played, Ahimaaz, high priest of Yahweh."

The horror of realization filled Ahimaaz, but he remembered his purpose, his resolve to meet the end he knew must come. But Solomon, for all his wisdom, knew nothing of what was in Ahimaaz's heart, and he burst out laughing.

"And would it shock you to know that I am aware of Tashere's conspiracy with the tax collector?" Ahimaaz heard a dull thud as Gamaliel dropped to his knees on the other side of the room. But Solomon ignored him. "You see, high priest, there is nothing I don't know about what happens in my kingdom, let alone what is whispered between conspirators in the corridors of my palace."

"But . . . but . . . why? Why did you allow it? If you knew . . ."

Solomon looked down at Ahimaaz quizzically as if pondering the foolish statement of a child. "I am the son of David and Bathsheba; my beloved father wanted me, and not my brother Adonijah, to be his heir. And so my mother Bathsheba, Zadok the priest, and others conspired to bring down Adonijah. Just as Naamah and you conspired to destroy my love for Tashere and my responsibility to make Abia my heir.

"None of this is new to me. It is in my blood, and I have no doubt that my bloodline, son after son, will do what my father, David, did when I was a prince and he wanted me to be his heir.

"And because I am of David's blood, when I came to power, to ensure my reign, I rid myself of rivals. I had my brother and his friends killed. And I now control all the lands from the borders of Egypt to the river Euphrates. Kings submit themselves to me, and my caravans travel far and wide.

"I have written over three thousand proverbs and composed over a thousand songs, and my fleet of ships at Ezion-geber has made me both strong and rich."

Ahimaaz was barely listening. His mind was dulled.

"But though I am wise, I am not God. I am not perfect. I went against the word of the Lord, and I married women who were Moabites and Ammonites, Egyptians and Assyrians. And these women showed me that while Yahweh, the god of the Jews, is invisible, the gods of my wives were able to be seen. I built them temples and allowed them their idols in their rooms, to which they prayed, and soon I, too, prayed to them. And I grew stronger and stronger in wealth and territory.

"But my son Abia, he is a disciple of your brother Azariah, and he will allow no other god than Yahweh in this land. He, above all else, is full of zeal."

Solomon stopped himself, seemingly in the middle of a thought, and pondered for a moment. Ahimaaz breathed deeply and slowly while Gamaliel held his breath.

Solomon sighed. "Abia would have gone to war for Yahweh. He would have attacked Egypt, perhaps even Babylon. And he would have expelled all my wives when I was dead. And what would have come of this?"

Solomon waited as if genuinely expecting someone in the room to answer. But nobody did. Ahimaaz knew his death was close. This is not what he had planned, but it would come nonetheless.

"A war, a war fought for Yahweh. But one that would have led to the destruction and enslavement of all Israel. And not just a war between Israel and Egypt but between us and Moab, and between us and the Hittites and the Assyrians. No matter what I said, no matter how I counseled and demanded, Abia was determined to rid the land of Israel of my wives and concubines and their gods. He would have brought destruction to my kingdom. So he had to be exiled. As did your brother, high priest. And no matter what militia she raises, or how much she fights or begs, Tashere will never return to my bed, and our son Abia will never rule in my place. So tell your tax gatherer that I am pleased that he told you these things, as I knew he would."

Slowly Ahimaaz looked up at the king.

"I know what's in your heart, Ahimaaz, high priest of Yahweh. I know what dark pain keeps you from sleep."

The words were a lash across his back, a lash that sent the spinning colors of the child's toy whirling in his mind once more. The laughter of his brother. The two of them running through their father's house. The brother he had played with and laughed with. The brother he had betrayed.

"Your brother will never be returned from exile."

Tears welled in Ahimaaz's eyes. A rush of blood pounded in his temple.

"Abia fell in league with your beloved brother, Azariah. Together they wanted the death and destruction of all those who would not accept Yahweh. And so you were my instrument. You and the tax collector both. My instruments."

Ahimaaz felt his knees, in danger of collapsing. All this time Solomon the Wise had known everything. Had used him.

Realizing Ahimaaz's distress, Solomon continued. "And do you think that Naamah's whisperings into my ear were what convinced me? Are you so stupid to believe that I'm as foolish as you, high priest? That I would allow a wife to dictate the running of my nation?"

Others in the room began to laugh. Soon the chamber echoed with Ahimaaz's shame and ridicule.

"Return," said Solomon. "Go back to being the high priest. Go back to your rituals. And tomorrow, when you wake up, understand that Solomon can see into your scheming heart." He roared with laughter.

From somewhere deep inside him, a weak but insistent voice said, "No."

The room's mirth slowly fell into silence. All eyes upon him. Not least of all Gamaliel from across the chamber.

"No, I will not return."

Solomon glowered at Ahimaaz, but this time the priest did not shrink from his gaze.

"I won't be your high priest anymore. I will be the instrument of no one."

And Ahimaaz tore off his pure white vestments, beneath which he was wearing sackcloth covered in the ashes of the sacrifice, the dress of a sinner, and left the throne room without having been given permission.

The king watched him leave, and for just a brief moment there was a smile of acknowledgment, perhaps even admiration, on his face.

———

October 20, 2007

YAEL WAITED in the hospital's main reception entrance area and saw him leaving his car. She watched him walking toward her, self-confident, self-possessed. In another life, he could have been a movie star; not pretty but ruggedly and strikingly good-looking, he was tall, lean, attractive in a very masculine way, with dark, Semitic looks and jet-black eyes, dressed in easy and casual clothes matched top and bottom with enormous care. Color and style harmonized as though he had a willing wife or a shrewd butler, and he looked as though he knew that he was at the top of his game. To a passerby he could have been any successful young Israeli man, yet she, of course, knew he was an American. She couldn't help noticing that as he walked toward the hospital's doors, nurses he passed turned for another glance.

When he saw her, he beamed his best television presenter's smile, walked purposefully toward her and shook her hand. She was tall for a woman, but he stood a head taller. As they made their way to the cafeteria, she couldn't help but feel that people were looking at them both. The white medical overalls and stethoscope around doctors' necks normally made them invisible in the hospital, but the two of them walking together were turning heads.

They sat with their coffees and Yaniv came straight to the point. "Yael, I said to you that you're the face of modern Israel: talented, clever, professional, and dedicated. If you're willing, I'd love to do a feature story on you, a profile of who you are. It'll be shown in America, and we have tens of millions of viewers, and it'll almost certainly get picked up here in Israel."

"And what do you think makes me interesting? Or different?" she asked.

He smiled and said, "I'm a good storyteller. I can make anyone interesting."

She suddenly felt miffed. "Then you don't need me. If you're

Pygmalion, I'm nothing more than a dumb marble statue called Galatea."

He blushed. "No, that's not what I meant."

His reaction in the moment made Yael soften. A man with such self-confidence caught off guard, floundering before her. It made her feel assertive and poised and helped her see him as a slightly less clichéd American.

"I didn't mean that at all, Yael. Of course you're interesting and fascinating. But it's the angle of the story I choose to take, and the way it's shaped by the editor that makes or breaks a good story or makes a boring story compelling. That's all I meant."

"I know. I was only teasing. So, if I said yes, what *angle* would you like to take?" Yael asked, skeptical of the word's meaning.

"I need to know more about you and your family. When you came to this country, where you're from, what your parents do, what their backgrounds are, your work as a surgeon—what compels and drives you . . . Then we'll—"

"Whoa . . . wait a minute . . . That's a lot of investigation. I don't want to talk about my family. Anyway, I don't have time for this sort of thing."

"It's all research. I won't take up too much of your time. The work you do here in the hospital, you standing near the Wailing Wall if you're religious, looking over the West Bank if you're political, outside the Knesset if you've been a demonstrator—that sort of thing. We'll pick you up, have makeup and hair in another car ready just before you appear on camera, schlep you quickly from place to place, and deliver you back. Like you tell people before you give them an injection, 'It'll only hurt a bit . . .'"

"And the other stuff . . . my parents' background, where we came from . . ."

"I'll interview your family and anybody else appropriate: friends, schoolmates . . ."

"Why? Why all this fuss just because I found an old piece of stone?" she asked.

"It's a bit more than that. You're A-grade talent for TV. Who knows? If I make you famous, you could put this surgery business behind you and become what every young woman really wants to be."

Yael raised an eyebrow.

"A weather girl on TV." Yaniv's smile was his trademark and he used it to full effect.

She forced herself not to laugh. His American bravado might work on a lot of other young women, but Yael didn't want to seem like putty in his hands. He quickly changed tone.

"Look, good-news stories don't come often for Israel in the U.S. media. You and the archaeological find are a good-news story."

"My role was accidental. It all sounds like such a fuss and I did very little. I'm frantically busy. My surgery list is so full."

"For the good of the nation . . ."

"For the good of Yaniv Grossman, is more like it."

"Oh, absolutely!" And he smiled again.

———

ACROSS THE KIDRON VALLEY from where Yaniv was sitting with Yael, in the village of Bayt al Gizah, another meeting was taking place. The mosque was tiny compared to the palatial mosques of Mecca, Medina, or Istanbul, but the intensity of the prayers and the yearning of the congregants were no less passionate. It was a prosaic building at best, with a blue-domed cupola and a minaret that was almost invisible among the nearby houses. It had been constructed in the 1930s following the demolition of three houses that clung to the edge of the cliff, and for years it had been little more than a house of prayer.

But recently the intensity of the sermons delivered by a new and fervent imam, Abu Ahmed bin Hambal bin Abdullah bin Mohammed, had roused the younger men of the town to new heights of passion, their fervor channeled into hatred for the Jews who lived in their mansions across the valley. The imam had tapped into the frustration of the youth, and in the two years since his arrival he had drawn around him a group of men whom he'd dubbed his Army of God. Bilal was one of them. So was his unemployed friend Hassan, who earned his meager income from being a pickpocket in the Jerusalem marketplaces.

All the young men were assembled for the usual Wednesday-night sermon, a gathering of intimates and initiates behind closed doors, where the imam would explain why the young men were disadvantaged and unemployed, why the Palestinians were poor and dispossessed, and why the Jews across the valley were to blame; these Jews, he told them, drove their Porsches and BMWs, living like ancient kings in their ten-bedroom mansions because they were thieves who had stolen Palestinian land, dispossessed the rightful Palestinian owners, and were prospering while the Palestinians were forced to live in squalor. Fueling their anger, the imam told them that he'd heard there was a secret Jewish law, not on the statute books, that allowed a Jew to abuse his Palestinian servants, even kill them, just for displeasing him.

To the young men, for whom prosperity was an idea far removed from the poverty of their lives, the imam's words rang loud and true. He quoted history and the Koran, ancient and modern Muslim leaders, Islamic heroes and great warriors, telling his listeners of their bravery and selflessness in the name of Allah. His knowledge never failed to astound the young men listening because the imam was able to make the great men of Islam come alive to them.

He painted vivid pictures so that, in their minds' eye, they could see how easy it would be to take back all the land stolen from them by the Jews and Christians, to re-create the glory of the ancient Islamic caliphate, the Great Empire of Mohammed, which after his death had exploded out of Arabia and even stretched from India to Spain. And when they were again a great people, they would cleanse Islam itself of the heretical Shi'ites and Alawites and Druze and return all Muslims to the purity of the Sunni religion, which Mohammed had created in the sands of Arabia.

As Yaniv was kissing Yael on the cheek and saying good-bye, the young men in the mosque were sitting cross-legged on cushions, waiting eagerly for their imam to begin his lessons. But on this night it was delayed for some time while he was in his office speaking in hushed tones. Some were listening carefully but couldn't distinguish what his muffled voice was saying on the telephone.

In his office, the imam sipped apple tea as he listened to the subdued and unrecognizable voice of the other man on the telephone. Most of what he said was audible, but the device the other man was using obscured his voice, making it sound as if he were speaking from inside an underground vault on the other side of the world.

"She is a Jew, no? Then why is she not your concern?" the imam asked.

"She's already been too much in the media. If it is one of yours, any investigation will come through my office. And then I can control it." The imam remained silent while the voice on the other end continued, "I wouldn't have thought you, of all people, would be hesitant to spill Jewish blood to bring about your caliphate."

The imam bridled. He hated the Jew Shin Bet man but he was prepared to dance with the devil if he supplied him with weapons and targets and ensured that his terrorist acts were successful, even if the idiot wanted to bring down his own Israeli government.

He said softly, "If I see this thing done by one of my Arab brothers, then it's your hands that will be red with her blood. Not mine. For me it is war. For you . . ." The imam let his words trail off.

"Will you deal with it?" the other voice asked, ignoring the comment.

"Of course," the imam said, and hung up the phone without saying good-bye. He left his office, and as he walked into the adjoining prayer rooms of the mosque, he pondered how strange it was, being in bed with a Jew.

———

HASSAN STOOD in a small chamber adjacent to the main prayer hall. The small space offered a modicum of privacy in a building otherwise devoted to bringing people together in communal acts, although, as the imam often told him, no secrets could be kept from Allah. The pickpocket felt strangely scrutinized and nervous as he waited.

Hassan thought of his friend Bilal, his best friend, and for so long his only friend. But Bilal was gone now. Hassan knew he wasn't dead, he wasn't a martyr, and the whole village knew that the sniper's bullets had not killed him. But still, Bilal was gone, like so many of his cousins and brothers, into the darkness of an Israeli prison. Bilal had failed.

Hassan hadn't been asked to be on the lookout for the woman doctor whom Fuad claimed had saved Bilal from the bullets. Nobody ever thought she would come to the village so far across the valley from where the Jews lived. But when Hassan saw her enter Fuad's house, he knew he must wait and see. He knew the imam would want to know. The imam had spoken of the Jew doctor, how a woman had dared to touch a soldier of Allah, and how he feared for Bilal and the drugs and poisons the Jew doctors might use on him.

Months ago, the imam had put a hand on his shoulder and looked him in the eye and said that one day he would have a special purpose. Hassan had nearly burst with pride, wanting everybody to know, but then the imam had walked away and none of his brothers had been there to see. He knew the feeling was wrong, that it was vanity. But he so badly wanted everyone to see how highly the imam thought of him. If only they could see . . .

Now, once again, the imam had asked Hassan to wait for him so that he could talk to him privately. Hassan's thoughts and memories were interrupted by the sweeping brown robes of the imam as he entered the antechamber.

"Hassan, my son. *As-salamu alaykum.*"

The greeting caught Hassan off guard, but the formal reply came habitually and reflexively. *"Wa alaykum as-salamu wa rahmatu Allah wa barakatuh,"* he said, nerves prompting him to use the most formal reply he could muster.

"There is no need to be nervous, Hassan." The imam smiled. "What have you to tell me?"

As if he were in trouble, Hassan said urgently, "Nothing, imam."

"Hassan, you have spoken to one of your brothers. He told me you have seen the Jew doctor. Yesterday. That she dared to enter our village. Talk to me about what you saw."

Relieved that this was all, Hassan told the imam, "Yes, I saw the doctor, the Jew woman who saved Bilal . . ." The moment the words left his mouth, he regretted using the term "saved." He knew the imam would not approve. Bilal had not been saved. Bilal had failed. But if the imam noticed or cared, he didn't show it. "She was driving a very expensive car. She parked outside Bilal's house. She was in the protection of Bilal's father, Fuad." Hassan hardened his voice, wanting to be clear to his imam how he felt about the woman. "She was dressed in expensive clothes. Her face and arms were uncovered, like a whore's."

The imam nodded. He took a long moment before he spoke again and did not look at Hassan when he did, as if the chamber were full of listeners.

"Our brother Bilal has suffered greatly for our cause. He faced the enemy bravely. But make no mistake, Hassan, our fight is not easy. Allah is with us but we must prove ourselves worthy. Prove that we are deserving of victory." The imam stopped and stared at Hassan, his eyes boring into him like drill bits. "Are you deserving, Hassan?"

"I pray so," Hassan said, and tried his hardest to sound like he meant it.

"Let us return to your brothers. And when we're there, show me, show them, what kind of a Muslim you are, what kind of a man you are."

The imam put an arm on Hassan's shoulders and guided him out of the small chamber and into the open prayer space of the mosque. A half dozen of Hassan's brothers—the chosen young men who gathered fervently to listen to the imam speak after the rest had left—watched as the imam guided him into the space. The imam held Hassan in his gaze, his arm still on Hassan's shoulder in a fatherly grip.

"If a bucket is full of holes, what happens to the water?"

Hassan was confused but not surprised by the question. The imam often spoke in such ways. "The water runs out," he answered flatly.

The imam continued. "And what use is water if it is spilled on the ground? It cannot be drunk. It cannot fill the mouths of thirsty men. Water is most precious; there is no life without water, and so, too, the bucket that holds the water, that holds life, must be free of holes . . ." The imam turned outward, away from Hassan, to spread his arms to the gathered youths. "We are the bucket that holds the water. In us there must be no holes. We must be complete." He turned back to Hassan, this time placing both hands on the boy, one on each shoulder as if about to embrace him.

Hassan felt all the eyes of his brothers on him.

"Bilal failed, Hassan. Water has spilled. I am informed that he has told the Jew security about us . . . We must stop more water from spilling."

Hassan's heart should have soared with pride at the attention and trust of his master in full sight of everyone. But in that moment he felt fearful as the image of the attractive young Jewish doctor passed into his mind's eye. And he saw his friend Bilal lying on a hospital operating table with her standing over him, saving his life.

But Hassan knew what he must do. There could be no mistake.

———

933 BCE

AHIMAAZ DESCENDED THE ROAD from the king's palace toward the gate that led out of the wall and into the valleys beyond the city. The people of the city all looked at him in surprise and bewilderment. Nobody had ever seen the high priest in sackcloth and ashes before. Occasionally priests who had sinned were forced to wear such as penitents, but the high priest, who was supposed to be without sin, wore it on only one day, the ninth day of the month of Ab. This date commemorated the occasion when only two of the twelve spies sent by Moses as scouts to the land of Canaan, Joshua and Caleb, returned and spoke positively. All the other spies returned and said that the land was unsuitable for the Hebrews. And the people had wailed and panicked, and the Lord God Yahweh was furious and said that from that time forward, because of their lack of faith, all Israelites must fast on that day. And only on the ninth day of Ab did the high priest close himself in the Holy of Holies and spend all day and all night praying for the redemption of his people.

So to see Ahimaaz walking through the city, wearing the garb of a penitent, caused shock and disquiet among his people.

Ahimaaz could see the city gate looming as a dark orifice in the bright pale stone of the city's huge walls. Around him people parted; donkeys and carts were led aside by their owners to make way as Ahimaaz walked slowly forward to the gate.

Gamaliel the tax collector ran after him as the people looked on.

"Brother," he called.

Surprised, Ahimaaz turned. When they were standing to-gether, the full heat of the day made both men sweat as Gamaliel struggled to catch his breath.

"Why?" gasped Gamaliel.

Ahimaaz said nothing.

"Why? I don't understand. The king has swept away all trou-bles. You're free to return to the temple." Gamaliel cast his hand up to where the temple stood at the top of the hill.

Ahimaaz shook his head.

"But I don't understand. How can you walk away? You know as well as I what's out there." Gamaliel pointed beyond the gate to the fields and the valleys and deserts beyond.

Ahimaaz put his hand on the tax collector's shoulder and held his eyes in a fixed gaze.

"Out there is my brother."

And with that, Ahimaaz turned and walked away through the gate into the land beyond.

Gamaliel watched him leave until the sun was almost lost to the shadow of the wall. At long last he turned and faced the hill. Slowly, wearily, he began the long climb back to the temple. Per-haps, for the first time in his life, to pray for the safety of the priest, and to give thanks . . .

———

October 21, 2007

DESPITE HER PUNISHING operating schedule, Yael found time between ripping off her bloodied gloves and gown and scrubbing up for the next operation scheduled for midday to walk up the two flights of stairs to the men's surgical ward and visit Bilal. It was perhaps her last chance before he was hauled off to prison to uncover something of the mystery that so haunted her.

She nodded to the guard as she entered his room and found Bilal with his eyes tightly closed, his lips moving in silent prayer.

"Bilal?"

He opened his eyes and glared at her.

"You know, the men from Shin Bet were here yesterday to collect you and escort you to prison, but I wouldn't let them take you." Yael had hoped such a statement might soften him, but if it did, he didn't show it and he didn't respond.

"I've been to see your parents, Bilal. In Bayt al Gizah. And I've promised them that they can come and visit you before you're taken away."

"When will they be here?" asked Bilal.

Yael saw a faint crack in the armor. "Tomorrow. I've spoken to the guard. He's promised not to interfere and to allow them as much time with you as you need."

Bilal's eyes followed her as she moved to the other side of the bed to check his chart.

"You met my father?"

"He's a lovely man. He's worried about you, you know?"

"And my mother?"

"I only met her for a moment. And your sister."

Yael then tried to extend the topic of Bilal's mother unselfconsciously into the conversation. "Where did your mother come from?"

Bilal seemed to answer despite himself. "Peki'in. She was born there. So was I, but I left there when I was a baby. We've been back to see Peki'in when we were children, me and my sister and my brother, but I don't remember it."

Yael said softly, "I know Peki'in. I was there when I was in the army. Did her family always come from there?"

"My grandmother came from Peki'in. And probably her grandmother before her. I don't know these things."

"And your father? Was his family always from Peki'in, or somewhere else?"

He looked at her curiously. "My father . . . once he told me that he would take me to where my grandfather came from, Egypt. I think my grandfather worked for a Jew business. He came here with them."

"So then your mother and father met in Peki'in?"

"I don't know. It was when you Jews made Israel and you forced my grandfather's family out."

Forced out: a complex narrative made simplistic and disposable, she thought. The lies they were told fed on themselves in the landscape of victimhood.

"I made a promise to your father and mother that they could visit you tomorrow. I don't want their last sight of you to be behind bars. That's what I would want if you were my son, Bilal."

Bilal was taken aback by the sudden change of topic and tone. He'd been taught to see such treatment by the Jews as lies and deception. Who was this woman? Part of him wanted to trust her, but the rest of him knew he shouldn't. The good manners his mother had always tried to teach him compelled him to thank her. But he couldn't bring himself to do that either.

The image of the Shin Bet man and the imam, and the phone and the girl and the tunnel beneath the temple wall, and the bullets tearing open his leg, seemed to scorch his mind. How did it come to this? How could he escape? What was happening to him? Who could he trust?

Bilal ran his hands over his face as if to wash it clean before he knelt in prayer. When he opened his eyes again, his jaw hardened and he clung on to the last of what he knew to be true. "I am a freedom fighter!"

The words made Yael angry. "You think freedom comes by killing innocents and blowing yourself up? What does that achieve, Bilal? Who is more free when you're dead? Your father? Your mother? Your brother and sister? Are any of them more free?"

"It's so easy for you, Doctor. Was your father a doctor? Was his father a banker? Was your father's father a fat and wealthy merchant with servants? You know nothing except an easy life. You know nothing except having whatever you want, whatever you need, and being able to do anything you please! You live in a palace and drive an expensive car and have servants—all on Palestinian blood!"

"So your answer is spilling our blood? And this will make your family wealthy, make your people prosperous and happy? Do you know how stupid that sounds, Bilal?"

"If we do not kill, we rot! If we do not fight, we die."

"Fighting for what, Bilal?"

"Fighting for our own nation."

"Every time, since Israel was created, your people have been offered a nation, you've rejected it. You chose war over peace every time."

"There will be no peace until the Jews have gone!"

With anger and frustration rising in her, Yael was ready to respond. It was the Arab states that had never allowed the Palestinians freedom and never would. The Palestinians were pawns in the Arab game they were playing with the rest of the world.

Yael wanted to tell him that the Palestinian expectation of freedom was a farce. Their land had been annexed and occupied and fought over by other Arabs a thousand years before Israel was formed. And since Israel's creation, Palestinians were forced to remain refugees because no Arab states would offer them citizenship. They were tragic hostages to Arab politics, with nowhere else to go, bullied and exploited by other nations. And as the rockets fell on Israel, launched from Palestinian rooftops, Israel was forced to build bigger walls. Walls to protect the remnants of a people who had survived Hitler's Holocaust, who'd come out of two thousand years of persecution and diaspora to return to their home, where they would no longer be outsiders.

Yael swallowed and exhaled. The endless cycle of it all was made visceral in her mind by the blood and the bullets and the bodies of those who lay on her operating table; by childhood friends who had died in the wars.

All bodies look the same when they are bleeding. Israeli and Palestinian. Arab and Jew. Boys, girls, mothers, fathers. All victims of a cycle that seemed as old as history, and from which nobody could seem to envisage a way out.

These images and memories softened her. She looked Bilal in the eyes as if searching him for something of herself.

"You and us, Palestinians and Jews, we have something in common, Bilal . . . Neither of us has anywhere else to go . . ."

PART TWO

October 22, 2007

A S THE SOLIDLY BUILT POLICEMAN wheeled him down the corridor, nurses and doctors avoided looking at him. Normally when patients were well enough to leave the hospital, those doctors and nurses who had cared for their health acknowledged their leaving as a rite of passage. If they were important people, some of the staff lined up in congratulations, wishing the patient continued good health and fortune.

But everybody knew, without even looking at the handcuffs that tethered his wrist to the armrest of the wheelchair, that Bilal would be getting no such reception. Only Yael came to the door of the men's surgical recovery ward to wish him good-bye.

She stood at the window of the ward and watched him being wheeled into an ambulance to be driven to police headquarters, where he would be processed, arraigned by a judge, remanded in custody to await a trial hearing, and then shipped off to prison. She prayed that, for the sake of his mother and father, he'd plead

guilty so that his trial and the awful evidence that would doubt-
less be presented would be over quickly.

When the ambulance disappeared from the hospital grounds
and into Jerusalem's frenetic traffic, she returned to writing up
patient notes for the three operations she'd performed that day,
showered in the doctors' rooms, and prepared for her dinner
with Yaniv. Part of her wanted to have dinner with him: he was
bright, knowledgeable, and certainly handsome, and the advantage he held over other men she'd recently dated in her small hospital world was that he wasn't medical. But another part of her
had dubbed him Ivan the American, and she wondered if, when
this was all over—when things had settled down—there could
possibly be a future relationship; they were culturally the same
but from different parts of the globe. Or was she being just a tiny
bit xenophobic and naïve?

They were going to dine in a new French restaurant that had
recently opened in the exclusive Mamilla shopping mall near the
Old City. For the occasion, she'd brought to the hospital her favorite red dress with a revealing but still modest neckline and
black patent high heels. She quickly called in to the hospital's
hairdresser for a comb-through and style.

Rather than drive and try to find parking, she took a cab to
the Mamilla and walked down the flight of steps and along its
length, passing Jews and Arabs, Orthodox and secular, young
and old, until she entered the restaurant. She was seated and
then waited ten minutes for Yaniv to arrive.

He apologized for being late. "The reason I was delayed was
because I was interviewing the foreign minister and he insisted
on reframing my questions so he gave the answers he wanted. I
told him I'd dump the interview unless he was willing to answer
the questions. It was a bit of a tussle . . ."

Yael listened and might have taken Yaniv's story as bragging
and name-dropping designed to impress her, but he delivered it

with such nonchalance that he might have been speaking of his conversation with a shopkeeper.

"But I won," he added as he sat down. "You can always get them where you want them, if you know how to be forceful but patient."

He asked about her day, and she told him briefly about the three operations and saying good-bye to Bilal. The questions he asked her seemed to casually and easily move past friendship into the territory of interviewer and interviewee, and she wondered whether he was using her as a source for a story.

"You sound sorry that he's in police custody," said Yaniv.

"He may be a murderer but he's also a kid who's fucked up his life. There's tragedy there as much as anything else. Things should have been different for Bilal . . ."

Yael couldn't help but remember Bilal's words to her: *"It's so easy for you, Doctor . . ."*

"A different time, different circumstances," she continued. "Life might have been very different for him and a generation of Palestinians who've been raised as victims, and to hate."

"How was he when he left the hospital? Full of bravado?"

"Of course. But . . ." She thought back to him as he was being wheeled down the corridor. "It was hollow. There's more going on in that head of his than militant rhetoric."

"Not surprising when you think about where he's going."

"Hmmm . . . not just that . . ." Yael sipped her wine and didn't elaborate.

When he'd finished a mouthful of lamb, Yaniv said, "Did the Shin Bet guys get tough? Or are they saving that for when he's out of sight?"

"They're not stupid; in the hospital it's just questions. He refused to answer. But he was rattled. That's for sure."

"If a group of black-suited Shin Bet officers visited me while I was handcuffed to a bed, I'd probably be rattled too."

Yael shook her head. "No, there was only one Shin Bet man who actually interviewed him."

Yaniv raised an eyebrow. "Only one? I know them. They're usually in pairs."

"I met him as I was going into Bilal's room. He was even wearing a yarmulke, which I found odd for a Shin Bet guy."

"It's also odd that a Shin Bet officer would question someone alone. Those guys are pretty officious and love their procedure."

"He had this odd white streak of hair down the middle, graying at the sides. With the yarmulke, it looked almost funny."

Yaniv suddenly looked up at her.

"What?" she asked.

"Dark gray at the sides, white down the middle. Lean build. Really dark eyes?"

"Maybe. Yes. I think so. Why?"

"I've never spoken to him, but if it's who I think it is, he's a seriously heavy player. Division head."

"So?" said Yael.

"Seems a bit heavy for a kid who fucked up his mission. That level, he'd be doing policy or dealing with the heads of Hamas or Hezbollah. Not some failed wannabe."

Yael shrugged. But Ivan the American wasn't willing to let it go. "Why would a top-level Shin Bet commander come out of the office for a kid like Bilal? And on his own?"

Yael remained silent. She didn't see the cause of his sudden interest.

"What did the kid say about this man, Yael?"

"Nothing," she replied. But she knew from his reaction that there was far more to it than that. "Yaniv, what's going on?"

He frowned, and shook his head slightly. "Probably nothing."

"Come on, don't bullshit me."

"No, honest," he said, and tried to concentrate on his meal. But she remained absolutely still, looking at him intently. Knowing that the spotlight was on him, he said softly, "If it's the guy I think it is, something doesn't seem kosher. That's all."

She looked across the table; he seemed to be a bit distant. This was a new Yaniv, one she hadn't seen before. Up until now, he'd been the reporter on a mission, somebody who she half knew was just using her to get to a story; but now she thought she could perceive a different man, an investigative reporter, maybe even in the Woodward and Bernstein mold, making agreements with sources in back alleys, having whispered conversations with people known only by their code names.

Suddenly, she saw him not as a reporter out for his own glorification but as a professional journalist who'd bust down doors to get at the truth. And she liked what she saw.

―――――

Central Area D Prison Facility, Dead Sea, Israel

"IS THIS THE ONE?" asked the Israeli admissions clerk as Bilal was wheeled into the prison reception area.

The policeman who was pushing him nodded. "Bilal haMitzri. Just brought down from the Jerusalem Hospital via Police HQ."

"Why's he still in a wheelchair? Can't he walk?"

"His doctors have said he has to be in the wheelchair until your prison doctor says he can get out of it."

"Bullshit. You!" barked the clerk. "Can you walk?"

Bilal didn't answer, so the clerk asked again in broken Arabic, "Can you walk?"

Bilal tried to raise his arm, but his left wrist was constrained by the handcuffs. The clerk said to the policeman, "Undo his cuffs and see if the bastard can walk. Just tip him out of the chair."

Within a moment, Bilal was on his feet, clutching the desk for support. "Sign the paperwork and he's all yours," said the policeman.

It took half an hour to strip Bilal, examine his orifices, ask him searching and personal questions about his sexuality and drug dependence, his parentage, relationships, affiliations to organizations, religious inclination, and more. He was given prison clothes to wear, and his personal clothes were put into a cardboard box for storage until he was released. His wallet, phone, bracelet, and watch, which had been taken from him when he was shot, were still in Jerusalem under the watchful eye of the hospital's security until they were released by Shin Bet.

"Which means, you murdering bastard, that for the rest of what remains of your life, you'll be living in prison garb, and you'll never see these clothes again," taunted the clerk.

Bilal lowered his head, a mixture of fear and anger welling inside him, and shuffled slowly beside the prison guard from the outer reception areas through a series of electrified doors and steel security barriers into the prison compound proper.

The astringent reek of antiseptic tried but failed to mask the reek of urine, vomit, and sweat that pervaded every corner of the prison. It took days, sometimes weeks, for newcomers to acclimatize themselves to the stench, something between rotting meat and decaying vegetables. Three times a day, prisoners with mops and buckets would trundle along corridors, sloshing the acrid disinfectant over the floors and halfway up the walls in an attempt to overcome the damage done by the prisoners the previous night. The game, when the lights were out, was to see how far each prisoner who was in a normal cell, not isolated, could piss across the corridor. Immune to further punishment and increased restrictions on their privileges, the inmates used their arcs of urine as both a demonstration of masculinity and a way of showing their contempt to their Israeli captors.

From dawn until well after lights-out, the prison was a clamor of noise and din. A bizarre combination of yells, catcalls, obscenities, and prayers. The noises of men locked in cages traveled down corridors, and Bilal, petrified but trying to look brave, at first attempted to block it out with his fingers in his ears, but when that proved useless, he tried to determine where the noises were coming from. But they were all around him.

As he walked toward the cell where he would be spending much of his time until he was tried and sent back to this prison or assigned to a different prison, Bilal hesitated at the entryway. The guard had to push him forward. It was typical of first-time prisoners, the sudden and wrenching realization that this, not parks or cafés or the houses of his loved ones, was now where he'd spend his days. It had a steel bed, a steel urinal, and a steel sink, but these didn't make it much more than the sort of cage where animals spent their lives as captives of a zoo.

Sitting alone on his bunk, Bilal, terrified of the melee of foreign sounds from the prison compound, tried to prevent his head from exploding in panic. It was all part of the insinuation of new and unwelcome experiences he would suffer every minute of every day of his confinement.

Bilal continued to stare at the same spot on the wall, wondering why he was here and what sin he'd committed against Allah for his god to let him live and be treated in such a cruel and vindictive way. Every hour, guards would slide away the hinged plate from the spyhole of his isolation door, look at the inhabitant, and ensure that he was still alive and breathing.

They'd seen a thousand prisoners like him come and go: shocked, angry, vengeful, and swearing retribution. But the ones they worried about were the quiet ones, those who held everything inside until something, some minuscule incident like a dirty plate or the doors opening later than normal, would drive them over the edge. Then they'd either try to harm themselves or they'd suddenly lash out unexpectedly and could be very dangerous.

After a full day of observation, some of the guards began to think that this one was different. This kid wasn't coming out of his shell at all. He remained almost catatonic and must have felt totally dissociated within his new and unaccustomed surroundings. And so he was put on suicide watch, and the guards reported back to the prison governor that Bilal seemed to be spending every minute of his time inside his cell, mumbling prayers from the Koran.

A week later they were increasingly worried. Initially he'd been examined by the prison doctor, who looked at the wounds he'd suffered and the way that the surgeon in the Jerusalem Hospital had repaired his body. It was an excellent job and he'd recovered well.

But because of who he was—somebody who'd attacked the holiest place of Judaism—his isolation had been ordered by the governor so that he didn't become a local hero and a rallying point for the other prisoners. Not that there was much chance of that, according to his guards. He was utterly featureless, uncharismatic, and everyday—hardly the stuff of heroes.

In his second week of incarceration, he received a visit from his imam. Normally, when a holy man came to visit a prisoner, the mood picked up. But when he was told of his imam's visit, the Israeli guard was surprised at the consternation on Bilal's face.

Still, he appeared to be growing more resilient day by day. Though he was still on suicide watch, there was less concern for Bilal's welfare. He was no longer as morose but was now talking to fellow prisoners in the exercise yards, occasionally being impertinent to the guards, and once or twice managing to smile.

The imam had been to the prison before, several times, leaving his home in Bayt al Gizah and traveling down the steep road that descended into the lowest region on earth, the Dead Sea. The prison, designated as Central Area D, was hidden behind a wall of palm and date trees, in the afternoon shade of the massive white cliffs. Farther south along the road that led down the rift valley toward the Gulf of Eilat were the oasis at Ein Gedi, the ancient Essene settlement of Qumran, and the Herodian fortress at Masada. Not that the imam had visited those archaeological areas.

Since leaving the Al-Azhar University and mosque in Cairo and coming to Bayt al Gizah to be the imam to his beloved Palestinian people, he had made fools of the Israeli security services, had gathered around him a young coterie of eager *shahids*—all prepared for martyrdom—and was about to unleash a furious assault against the Jews and their arrogance. But first he had to take care of a little disappointment called Bilal.

He'd hoped that Bilal, the most anxious of all the young men within the imam's group to prove his love of Allah, would have brought some small measure of destruction to Jerusalem's Jewish quarter. Of course it was absurd to think that he could have done much damage, despite what the imam had told him: the security services were hypervigilant around the Wailing Wall. But the whole purpose of sending Bilal to his death was to breach the Jews' security, even for a few minutes, perhaps to explode a bomb, and thus to show the Jews that they were vulnerable. Yet, he had failed in his mission, no bomb had gone off, there was no *shahid*, and another Palestinian freedom fighter was made to look like a buffoon in the world's media. Instead of bringing down the Jews' Holy Wall, he'd singed his hair and discovered a priceless Jewish treasure!

But it got worse, for now there was even the possibility that instead of dying as he should, he'd told this doctor about the Bayt al Gizah group. And worse, a thousand times worse, Bilal indicated that he'd somehow seen him with the Jew from Shin Bet whom he'd met with the old rabbi from Neturei Karta.

The boy had to die, for he was a captive and the Jews would no doubt torture him and extract the information. Fortunately, because of his injuries, he hadn't yet been questioned, but it would only be a matter of time.

Bilal was led, handcuffed to a guard, into a reception room. It was bare with not a touch of humanity to soften its symmetrical gray lines, its imposing steel furniture bolted to the floor, including a single heavy table.

The imam was seated as Bilal was led to the chair. "My son. How are you? Is Allah the Merciful being good to you in this place of punishment and retribution? Have you made friends with your brothers here?"

Bilal smiled at his imam but the priest knew immediately that it was a forced smile. This wasn't the Bilal who had been his willing acolyte in the mosque. "Imam, I've spoken to nobody."

The imam smiled and nodded, trying to offer the youngster some sympathy in his expression. "My boy, you're afraid, and fear is to be expected. When you're removed from the love and wisdom of your father and those consolations that can be offered by your mother, it's natural for you to feel alone and afraid. But remember this, Bilal: in here, in this very prison with its walls and wire, you have a father . . . In here, Bilal, you have the presence of Allah, of God Himself. In here is the God of Ibrahim and his son Ismail, the very God of Mohammed, peace and blessings be upon him. Put your love and faith in Allah, and nothing may harm you."

Bilal nodded. He'd been trying to find Allah in the prison since he was sent here from the hospital, but the noises, the disruptions, the shouting, the anger, and the threats that reverberated around the walls and filled every space made Allah a distant ghost.

The imam turned around to see how far away the Israeli guard was before he spoke. The last thing he wanted was to be overheard. Fortunately, the guard was at the other end of the room, reading a newspaper.

He whispered, "Tell me, Bilal, to whom have you spoken?"

"I swear, imam, I speak to no one."

"You must think hard. You were drugged, Bilal. Your mind affected and under the Jew doctor's knife."

Bilal looked at the imam and didn't answer. He didn't know. The imam smiled and nodded in reassurance. "Don't worry, my son. Allah will never blame you for falling foul of the Jews' tricks.

But how can I and your brothers in Bayt al Gizah be assured of your silence?"

"I promise you, imam, by all that is holy, in the name of the last and greatest prophet, Mohammed, peace and blessings be upon him, that I will die before I break my oath."

Bilal was going to say that he'd never spoken to anybody about the Jew with the white hair, and the rabbi in the room in the village near Bethlehem, but caution made him hold back.

The imam smiled again. "I know that, Bilal, my son. I know that. Now I have to leave you. There are other brothers I have to speak with."

———

539 BCE
Babylon in Mesopotamia

THE BONES OF AHIMAAZ, the former high priest of Israel, were never found. Nor did anybody ask after him. Only his wife and children wondered whether they'd ever see him again and whether he'd found his long-lost brother Azariah.

Yet, strangely, as Ahimaaz's body decayed and dissolved into the ground after he died of thirst in a distant cave far to the south of Jerusalem, his reputation grew, and the days when Ahimaaz had been high priest of Israel became golden. As Rehoboam ruled after the death of Solomon, the children of Israel looked back on past glories and feared what would happen to their nation and to them as a people.

Through arrogance and stupidity, Rehoboam caused the land of Israel—twelve tribes bonded together into a nation by King David and King Solomon—to split into separate lands in the north and south. Judah and Israel, though not enemies, lived side by side for four hundred years as two separate nations with separate capitals, temples, and kingly families. They even took separate names, the south becoming the Kingdom of Judah, composed of the tribes of Judah and Benjamin, and the northern ten tribes becoming the Kingdom of Samaria.

But other nations grew in size and ferocity, and when the Assyrian king, Tiglath-Pileser III, destroyed the northern kingdom, he sent the inhabitants into exile. Two hundred years later, King Nebuchadnezzar II of Babylon conquered Judah.

It had been four centuries from the time when Solomon the Wise laid the first two stones of his temple in Jerusalem until its devastation in the wreckage of Jerusalem left by the invading Babylonians. Nebuchadnezzar emptied the land and took the Jewish people into exile to live within the boundaries of the fabulous city of Babylon, where they formed their societies along the banks of the Tigris and the Euphrates. And in those fifty years of exile, Jerusalem became overgrown with weeds and decay, and the Jews in Babylon grew lazy and indolent, removed from the harshness of their land and out of the sight of their god.

For fifty years the Jews lived by the waters of the two rivers, the Euphrates and the Tigris, which were the lifeblood of the Empire of Mesopotamia, and which made it one of the most fertile areas of the world. Some of the Hebrews remained faithful to their religion and their god; others eased into the comforts and wealth of Babylon and began to worship stone and wooden idols.

And it was an easy life, even for the Hebrews. Apart from dates, which grew everywhere and provided the people with food, wood, and fodder for their cattle, the Jews luxuriated in plentiful supplies of wheat, barley, lentils, onions, and leeks. Wherever they walked in the land between the two rivers, there were grapes and olives and figs. Spices and fruits grew everywhere, and medicines made from the herbs became readily available to the poor as well as the rich.

It was a land of plenty, unlike the harshness of Jerusalem and much of Israel, which was dry and often barren. And so, because they were exiles far from their land, as one generation succeeded another, the love of Jerusalem and the worship of Yahweh dimmed, generation after generation.

Few who were born in Babylon looked to the south where the land of Israel lay; fewer still had any desire to go there. Only a handful of older ones who did remember Israel yearned for the land, and they wrote psalms and songs to the distant glories of Jerusalem, but their yearnings fell on deaf ears.

Certainly few remembered Ahimaaz, the man who was once high priest. The descendants of those Israelites who sat beside the languid waters of the rivers of Babylon may have known his name, as they knew the names of Moses and Aaron, Joshua and David, but to them these were figures in the history of their people, as remote and invisible as God Himself.

Neither did the exiles in Babylon remember Ahimaaz's colleague, the much lesser figure of Gamaliel, son of Terah of the tribe of Manasseh, who had collected taxes so that King Solomon could build his temple. For unlike the descendants of Ahimaaz, who handed the mantle of priest down the generations, the offspring of Gamaliel failed to make a mark on the people; and as one generation succeeded the next, they changed their occupations from tax gatherers to merchants to landlords to financiers of caravans carrying goods from place to place, and now were counselors to the rulers of Babylon.

All was well with Babylon and the Children of Israel, until the appearance beyond the horizon of Cyrus, king of Persia. In the few years since the people of Babylon first heard his name, Cyrus the Great had conquered the lands of foreign kings and was now marching toward their city. The people were gripped by panic.

And the exiles from Israel, having long experience of fighting would-be conquerors, were more afraid than most. The Israelites held Nebuchadnezzar's successors in low regard, and now that King Nabu-na'id had usurped the throne and was ruling with his son Belshazzar, things had gone from bad to worse. Learning of the rise of Cyrus, Nabu-na'id tried to make an alliance with the pharaoh Amasis II of Egypt and had even approached King Croesus of Lydia, but they'd rebuffed him, and so, like a spoiled child, he'd amused himself with things inside the city and paid no attention to the outside world. King Nabu-na'id spent all his time building temples and improving Nebuchadnezzar's hanging gardens, waterways, and parks, and had no interest in defending the nation against the rise of the Persian Cyrus the Great, for his ministers had assured him that there was food for years within the city, and the walls were impregnable.

But the conquest of the impregnable walls of Babylon proved to be so simple, it came close to engendering respect among those captured. Not a stone from a catapult hit the wall, not a spear was thrown nor an arrow loosed. Indeed, until the Persians were inside the walls of the city, nobody in Babylon was aware of their capture by the Persians.

Arrogantly celebrating a feast day of their god Marduk, and all but a few guards watching what was happening in Cyrus's encampment outside the walls, the people of Babylon were rejoicing while Cyrus's engineers executed one of the most brilliant plans in military history. It was audacious—many thought it impossible—yet it happened, and with a minimum of deaths the city fell without a fight.

THE RIVER EUPHRATES RAN underneath the walls of the city, but massive iron girders had been constructed at the base of the walls and deep into the river. Some youths had died trying, but it was now recognized that nobody could hold his breath long enough to swim under the iron girders. So when he knew that the city was celebrating a religious festival, Cyrus ordered the vast river to be diverted. Huge blocks of stone were built into a wall in the river's path, and the flow diverted away from the city. The water stopped flowing through Babylon and was side-tracked into the desert, where it flooded the ancient sands. The level of the river quickly fell, and a small detachment of men was able to walk chest-high through the water until they were inside the wall, where they fought a troop of guards and opened the massive Ishtar Gate. Cyrus's troops swarmed into the city and took possession while men and women slept soundly, confident they were safe from invasion.

The following day, after his surrender, a shocked King Nabu-na'id assembled with his family on the top of the ziggurat of the Temple of Etemenanki in the middle of Babylon to await the arrival of King Cyrus and the certainty of torture and execution. The entire citizenry also assembled, and all the streets leading to the capital were bursting with terrified men, women, and children wailing and praying, waiting to hear their fate. Would they be enslaved? Raped? Murdered?

Arriving on his golden chariot, King Cyrus walked up to the top of the ziggurat in the unusual silence. Even the birds of the city were quiet. The citizens as well as slaves and prisoners held their breath as he began to speak, and were astounded to hear him begin by blessing their god, Marduk. Then he blessed the people in the name of Marduk. Then he said, "Hear me, people of Babylon. Only a fool would destroy a city of this beauty, one of wealth and one producing such an abundance of food.

"I say to all the slaves gathered before me that you will be free men and women as of this day. I will allow you to remain in Babylon should you wish it, and you will live here as freedmen and -women, or you can return to your homelands. I am told that there are 150,000 Jews in exile in Babylon. You are allowed to return to Israel, where you will rebuild Jerusalem and pay me and my heirs a tribute for my protection. There is no reason to allow Israel to remain barren and unproductive, earning me no tribute, while you Israelites are living in Babylon. Return home, rebuild your nation, and all will benefit."

Hearing these words, words that had never previously been spoken by any conqueror in history, the people rejoiced with cheers and screams and praise.

Less than two weeks later, a column of Jews, stretching from the east to the horizon on the northwest, trudged slowly westward out of Babylon toward Damascus. They could have walked directly south toward Jerusalem, but the roads were full of bandits, and the Damascus road to the west was guarded by soldiers and was well used by merchants. It was safer to travel by the western route and then south down the coast. Once they were level with Jerusalem, it was an easy road from the sea, up the rugged hills, to the City of God.

Once they reached Damascus and replenished their supplies, the Jews had two choices. They might travel farther westward toward the coast of the Great Sea and the cities of Tyre and Sidon before heading south to follow the sweep of the land toward Israel and then up the hills to the ruined city of Jerusalem. Or they could walk the route in the hills of the King's Highway and from Damascus they could reach Hazor and then Shechem before climbing to Jerusalem. Joshua, descendant of Ahimaaz and leader of the Jewish people, told his Council of Elders that they should take the advice of travelers and merchants in the marketplaces of Damascus before deciding. Much depended both on what the weather had done to the roads and whether brigands and bandits were active in the areas.

Some of the community rode out of Babylon on wagons, some on horses, some on donkeys and asses and mules, but most walked. Fathers carried young children on their weary shoulders; mothers hefted heavy sacks full of whatever possessions they could carry. Most of those who had decided to leave Babylon were exultant to be returning to the land that they remembered from stories told to them by their parents and grandparents, or from the sermons they heard in the synagogues; yet others, despite wearing a broad smile on their faces, were wary of the difficulties that lay ahead, both on the road and when they reached the ruined city of Jerusalem.

It was the tenth day since the gates of Babylon had opened and the Jews had walked slowly, majestically, out of the city as a free people, their heads held high, westward as the sun rose behind their backs in the eastern sky. Merchants had trodden this road many times on their way to trade in Damascus, but few of their families—indeed, few of the Jews who had lived in Babylon for two generations—had been this far from the city.

The noise of the cheering for their freedom was still ringing in high priest Joshua's ears, ten days' walk westward from Babylon. Those who were intent on leaving Babylon had packed their few possessions and trudged behind him and the other religious leaders. More than fifty thousand Jews decided to return to Jerusalem, but twice that number determined to remain in Babylon, fearing that the one hundred days of traveling were too much for them to undertake, knowing that there would only be fifteen days on which they could rest for the holy Sabbath. And when they arrived in Israel, there would be no relief from exhaustion, as they would immediately have to rebuild the derelict cities and the devastated land.

The road to Damascus was pitted in places, and wagons found it difficult to negotiate the dips and ruts and surface erosion. Where the people traveled through a valley, the path was often well marked; but when they had to climb over a hill that had been more exposed to rain and wind, and where large boulders had fought their way to the surface, the going was slower and more tortured.

The high priest, Joshua, wasn't surprised but was horribly disappointed that only a third of the Jews of Babylon had opted to return to Israel. But he had great pleasure in welcoming as a fellow traveler one of the richest Hebrews in Babylon, Reuven the merchant. Although neither man was particularly aware of it, the stories that were his family's history told of Reuven's ancestor Gamaliel as a close friend and associate of Joshua's ancestor Ahimaaz.

Reuven's wife, Naomi, was pregnant, and the sudden and unexpected status of fatherhood changed him. He and Naomi had been trying for years to have a son, but the Almighty hadn't favored them. And then, just when Cyrus began his siege of the city of Babylon, Naomi announced that she was with child.

The moment Cyrus freed the Israelites from their Babylonian captivity, Reuven announced that he and Naomi would travel to Israel and establish a branch of his business enterprise in Jerusalem, its capital.

For Joshua, it was a coup to have such an important man making the journey. Most of the wealthy, established Jews hadn't wanted to leave their homes and businesses and the comforts found in Babylon to go to a desolate, overgrown, parched, and infertile landscape. Reuven's decision had influenced only a few of the wealthy members of the Hebrew community to leave Babylon, and so a diminished number of Jews traveled west to Damascus and then south toward Jerusalem.

Riding on a wooden wagon, Joshua said to Reuven, "It's going to be much harder to rebuild the land with so few people, but our journey is supervised by the Almighty One and so we will be safe."

Reuven looked at him in amazement. "Tell me, Rabbi Joshua, do Jews ever die?"

"Of course."

"But why, if Adonai is our God and He protects us, shouldn't we live forever?"

"Reuven, don't be silly. You know that God . . ."

The merchant laughed as the rabbi tried to argue, and said,

"You're as much of a fool as is this god of ours. You have a big task ahead of you, Joshua. Not only clearing a devastated land and rebuilding a city, but establishing farms, growing food, setting up trading links for merchants who have little connection with Israel . . ."

"Life will be hard for us all—even for you, Reuven."

The merchant laughed again. "Some of us only know how to make a bed from straw. But others, like me, know how to make our beds from the down of birds. Trust me, Joshua, my wife and I won't suffer hardships."

"But how?"

"You don't think that I would have turned my back on everything I've built during my lifetime? I have good people working for me in my businesses in Babylon. I will develop trading routes into Israel from Damascus, Tyre, and even as far as India. I intend to establish a series of caravanserai throughout the country, and my caravans will bring precious merchandise from the east and return with what Israel can produce and sell. So where once, hundreds of years ago, the caravans used to visit Jerusalem, I will reestablish that trade. It will take two or three years, but it will happen."

"With God's will," said Joshua.

"No, with my money and brains," Reuven said sharply.

———

October 22, 2007

ONCE BILAL HAD BEEN RETURNED to his cell, the imam was led to the general population area of the prison by a scrawny and impassive guard. The two men walked along stinking corridors and through guarded doorways until they reached the inner exercise yard, surrounded by ten-meter-high walls and guard towers every twenty yards.

In the exercise yard, there were hundreds of prisoners, most of them Palestinians, many of them terrorists, as well as Arabs from other nations who had committed crimes while they were in Israel, such as burglary, crimes of violence, and offenses against the state. The moment the imam entered the large area, people milling around or playing basketball or other games stopped almost immediately and began to gravitate toward him. Few knew him but almost everybody smiled at the preacher as they gathered in a large circle around him, hoping that he'd come there to pray with and for them and to offer them solace.

He smiled at the crowd and said to the Israeli guard, "Out of courtesy to our faith, I ask you to leave me while I pray with my brothers."

The guard turned and walked back through the door into the corridor. The imam looked at the prisoners, and said loudly, "*As-salamu alaykum.*"

Almost as one, they responded, but some, more formally, replied, "*Wa alaykum as-salamu wa rahmatu Allah wa barakatuh.*"

The imam held up his hands and said a blessing over all the prisoners. They responded to him and waited for a lesson from the Koran, but none came. Instead, the imam said softly, knowing that he was being viewed with suspicion by the guards, "Are any of you brothers living in the K wing?"

He noticed that two of the men nodded, although they looked surprised and were immediately suspicious. "Let me speak privately with you. For the sake of the Jews, let it look as though I am giving you a private blessing. Other brothers, I beg you to crowd around so that I can speak to these two brothers privately and not be observed too keenly."

The crowd milled around the imam and the two residents of K wing. He put his arms around their shoulders and spoke quietly to them both as though he were praying silently for their souls.

"Your name, brother?" he asked.

One man said he was Mahfuz. The other told him he was called Ibrahim.

"Have you met a young man whose name is Bilal? He came here from the hospital. He was the boy who—"

"He tried to blow up the Jew temple," said Ibrahim. "Yes, I've seen him. He stays in his cell most of the time. He seems as though the sky has fallen on his head. Why?"

"I'm worried about him," said the imam. "He is a dear boy, and he was once a good Muslim. I pray for him every night, I beg Allah to look after him and protect him, but I think that the underhanded Jews have offered him . . . no, I don't know, it's not fair of me to say . . . it's not his fault . . . but since he's been here, he's changed. He talks to them of things, and he won't tell me of what he speaks. Would you brothers take care of him?"

———

BILAL NOTICED the change of attitude among the other prisoners during the first exercise period the following day. His guard checked on him through the peephole in the door, opened it, and walked inside. Sitting on his bed, Bilal looked up, stood, and walked beside his guard in silence along the corridors until they came to the large dining hall where prisoners were already seated at bare steel tables, gulping down bowls of oats, pita bread, and lentils. Although he was allowed to eat with the other prisoners, he was always carefully scrutinized by the guards.

Bilal stood in line for his food, and when it was his turn to be served by one of the trusty prisoners, the food was slopped onto his plate; then, checking that the guard wasn't watching, the trusty spat into the food. Revolted, Bilal began to object, but the prisoner standing beside him turned and hissed, "Shut your fucking mouth or you're dead. Go eat your shit and I hope you choke."

In surprise and shock, unsure what to do, Bilal walked from the food table to find a seat beside other prisoners who he was beginning to recognize. But the moment he sat down, the others looked at one another and shifted away from him, further isolating him.

The guard noticed and came over to speak to Bilal. "What's wrong here?" he asked.

"Nothing," said Bilal.

The guard carefully scanned the prisoners, who averted their eyes.

"If there's any trouble here, even the slightest, I'll have you all in the punishment cell before you can blink. Got that?"

The others at the table shrugged, but the guard stood close beside Bilal. It was something well noticed by all of the prisoners in the room.

When the guard had departed, Bilal whispered to the nearest inmate across the table, "Why are you treating me like this? What have I done?"

The tension in his voice was palpable, but it didn't impress the others at the table. "You piece of shit. We heard about you singing to the Jews." It was the only reply, and the inmate stood and went to sit elsewhere, soon joined by the others, leaving Bilal alone at the table.

Bilal's mind devolved into a panic. How could he convince people that he wasn't saying anything? Why didn't they believe him? Why didn't his imam believe him? Had his imam said something to these other prisoners? He started to shake but fought to control himself, and found a kernel of courage as his hand gripped the table.

He turned to the next table and said, "You just remember who I am and what I did to the Jews. Anybody who comes near me gets his throat torn out. Understand?"

The Israeli guard turned when he heard the commotion and quickly walked back to the table. "I already spoke to you all. What's going on?"

Another prisoner, eating his oats, said softly, "He doesn't like the food . . ."

————

IT TOOK LESS THAN AN HOUR for the guard's concerns to be transmitted to the governor of the prison. Many years' experience foretold what the next steps might be. The prisoner Bilal had to be protected until Shin Bet had finished with him and drawn from him everything he knew. He'd read the initial report about the boy: they considered him a dumb, talentless kid who'd probably been led astray by some local firebrand. They'd get around to interviewing him within a week or so, certainly long before his trial, but he'd have to wait his turn. Despite the potential of the atrocity he could have committed, he'd done nothing except cause annoyance, and he was way down on the list of terrorists who needed to be interviewed. But it was a delay that made the governor worry.

In a cell within K wing, two floors lower than where Bilal was incarcerated, Ibrahim lay on his bunk, waiting for the guards to turn out the lights in the corridor, which extinguished the light in his cell. The two other men with whom he shared the space were already snoring. But patience was one of the attributes that determined survival or death in the Israeli prison system, and in the seven years he had been there, Ibrahim had learned the art of patience.

Punished to residency in K wing for beating another prisoner into a permanent coma, Ibrahim had learned to live with the restrictions. While the other prisoners were allowed to mingle, watch the communal televisions at night, and enjoy limited interaction, Ibrahim shared his days with terrorists, failed suicide bombers, and those who had fired rockets into southern Israel or been caught by the Israel Defense Forces during incursions from Gaza. His only society was the two other prisoners with whom he shared his cell, and the four hours a day—two in the morning and two in the afternoon—when he was allowed under guard into the exercise yard or the meal hall with the other prisoners.

As the lights went out, he listened to the muted noises of the prison suddenly erupt into a cacophony of catcalls, whistles, shouts, screams, guffaws, and obscenities. He heard men walking about in their cells, rattling their metal plates against iron doors or bars. When the glare of the light ended, the prison erupted into the raucous symphony of the night. It was the ideal time for him to continue fashioning the strip of metal he'd stolen from the prison workshop into a knife. It was a difficult process, but one he'd practiced many times growing up in his hometown of Nablus. People often thought that the dagger they were forming had to have a sharpened edge, but Ibrahim knew that was nonsense. The only thing it needed was a sharp point. Once he'd plunged the point into Bilal's chest, the entire knife would slip neatly between his ribs and into the kid's heart; then he'd twist it around a couple of times to ensure that the boy's organs were ripped apart, and that would be that. Or maybe he'd tear his stomach apart and let him die slowly and painfully as his guts spilled out onto the floor and his body drained of blood.

Whatever path he chose for Bilal's end, it would be good night and sweet dreams, traitor! Collaborator! And the chance that this deserter, this informer, would enjoy his seventy-two virgins in heaven would end as his lifeblood oozed out of his body and down the prison's gutters. Ibrahim smiled to himself as, masked by the commotion of the other prisoners, he unscrewed the top of one of the posts of his bed and took out the makeshift dagger.

———

NOW THAT BILAL WAS GONE from the hospital and the chances of Yael seeing him again were remote, the question of their linked blood grew greater in her mind. As a prisoner on remand, there was no reason medically or professionally for her to visit his family, especially after Fuad had treated her so suspiciously when she'd asked him about his ancestry. And so Yael felt strangely isolated, as though she had a major problem but nobody with whom it could be shared.

So she decided to follow their historical relationship, if indeed one existed; to become a researcher of records, a tracer of families, hopefully unraveling the mystery without reliance upon Bilal or Fuad or others who might or might not have any real knowledge, and who were reluctant to tell her anything. And from what little the family had said, the answers could be in the tiny Druze village of Peki'in, just south of the border with Lebanon, in the north of the Western Galilee. With determination, sipping a cup of coffee in the doctors' recreation rooms, she made a decision.

It took her a week, and some deviousness, to arrange for her two-week temporary residency in the hospital in Nahariya, the most northerly major city in Israel and the closest place of any importance to Peki'in. It was where she hoped to find the linkages that would tell her how Bilal's maternal mitochondrial DNA came to be shared with hers.

Yael had worked in the hospital in Nahariya before, in the weeks leading up to the Lebanon war with Hezbollah the previous year. Rockets rained down on towns in Israel from across the border, and when Israel retaliated, they found the targets they hoped to take out were nested by Hezbollah in civilian areas—in mosques, in schools, and on the tops of private dwelling places. Hezbollah's tactics were cruel, well knowing that Israel's army wouldn't want to bomb the rocket launchers for fear of harming innocent people, and if they did, the world's media would excoriate the Israel Defense Forces for bombing civilians.

Yael sewed up the resultant bullet holes and shrapnel wounds while inevitably the world's leaders decried Israel's attack on civilian targets. And so the cycle continued. As she thought of returning to Peki'in, Yael found the experience had affected her more deeply than she had realized.

How quickly situations could change. When she was there only last year, the hospital was frantic with Israeli wounded. Yet, in the months and years leading up to the Lebanon war, the hospital had treated free of charge many sick Lebanese who had walked or been escorted across the so-called friendly fence. But then, at the instigation of their Iranian puppet master, Hezbollah began to fire rockets into Israeli territory. Salvos of indiscriminate rocket attacks rained down on the northern towns and communities. The Western Galilee Hospital, where she was working, took a direct rocket hit and the treatment of sick Lebanese came to an abrupt halt.

Operating in what was effectively a war zone, she'd befriended many of the medical and nursing staff. And to escape from the pressure of the emergency room and surgical ward, she and some friends would take a road trip into the countryside and to villages like Peki'in.

So after Bilal gave her the information about his mother possibly having been born in Peki'in, once she'd finished her work for the day, Yael had gone to a private office and phoned the hospital's director, a Palestinian thoracic surgeon named Fadi Islam Suk.

"Darling," he said over the phone, delighted to hear her voice, "are you coming to visit?"

"Fadi, I need a favor."

"I've seen you on TV, Yael. I don't know there are any favors a lowly doctor like me can do for a celebrity like you."

She could almost see his broad toothy grin down the phone line.

"I need to get away from Jerusalem for a while. I was wondering if you could request me for some filling-in or other work. I've got some people to see up there, but my boss almost certainly won't give me any time off unless I'm needed, if you know what I mean."

"You have a lover in the Galilee and you want to spend time here with him? Oh, I'm devastated; I thought I was the only man for you," he said.

She laughed at the friendly jibe. But even as she did, Yael was strangely aware of the contradiction in the way she saw a fellow doctor and the way she felt visiting Fuad's village.

"I could certainly do with somebody of your skills. We've got a list that is growing longer and longer by the day. Shall I phone Pinkus and beg?"

"That would be good," she said. "But make sure you tell him that only my skills or my knowledge of the hospital will do, or he's likely to send somebody else."

——

539 BCE

IT WAS AT NIGHT on the road from Damascus that the Israelite exiles understood the reality of their journey. When they lived in Babylon with all its oil lamps and nighttime fires obscuring the firmament, rarely did anybody walk beyond the gates after the sun went down. So it was only on very few occasions, and always within sight of the walls, that anybody other than merchants sleeping in tents or under blankets to ward off the cold saw the full panoply of the night sky.

As they slept under the brilliant and luminescent stars that shone radiantly in the pitch-black desert sky, Joshua felt closer to Adonai than he ever did when he had prayed in his synagogue of Babylon. Even Zerubbabel, whose name meant child born in Babylon and who was the leader of the Jewish community, felt closer to the Almighty.

On the twentieth night since the beginning of the return, when the exhausted community had lit their fires, cooked their bread and lentils, and begun preparing to say their evening prayers,

Joshua's thoughts were interrupted by a visitor. Living communally in the open air, people tended to mix more frequently than when they retired to their houses, and Joshua welcomed Reuven as he sat on a mat beside the blazing fire.

"So, merchant," he said, "how is the travel with you?"

Reuven shrugged. "I'm a merchant. I travel a lot. But all you do is sit on your bottom in the synagogue and tell people what to believe. How are you faring? Do you miss your comfortable bed? Are you getting used to a mattress of stones and a pillow of rock?"

"May I help you, merchant? We haven't spoken in some time. Do you wish to ask a service of me, Reuven, or are you here to seek my advice?"

The merchant threw a stick onto the rabbi's fire. The days in the desert were stiflingly hot, but when the sun sank below the western horizon, the nights turned to freezing in the time it took a man to yawn; and where one moment people had sweated under their protective clothes, the next they were hurriedly lighting fires to protect themselves from the bitter cold.

"Neither," said Reuven. "I'm here to rest my bones and warm my skin beside your fire."

The two men sat in the glow of the flames, staring into the burning straw and wood and dung, which flared and popped and glowed. Joshua remained silent, waiting for Reuven to open up to him.

Out of the desert darkness, Joshua's wife, Shoshanna, walked into the light of the fire carrying two cups of hot anise drink and poppyseed cake that she'd baked the previous night. The men took the refreshments and nodded in gratitude. She retired to her tent.

Sipping the aromatic drink, Reuven said, "When my wife first told me that she was pregnant, I was overjoyed. She said she wanted our baby to be born in Israel. I agreed, and we undertook this journey. I'm doing it to increase my trade, but why is it so important to my wife that our baby is born in Jerusalem?"

Joshua began to answer. "Well, our father Abraham—"

"Our home is in Babylon. We could be just as Jewish there as in Jerusalem. King Cyrus has promised us safety and security. Why are we lesser Jews in Babylon? Why are we better Jews in Jerusalem?"

"Yes, we could be both," said Joshua, "but when God prevented Abraham's knife from sacrificing his son Isaac in Jerusalem, and when we entered into the covenant of circumcision—"

"We could pray in the synagogue, live our lives according to our customs. Yet, Naomi insists that we leave the comforts of our home to live like desert nomads. I love her and so I agreed. And I'm happy to set up my trading business in Israel. But you haven't told me why it's so important."

"At the end of our journey, we will—"

"At the end of our journey, Rabbi, we will still have to live in tents until we build proper houses. Even Naomi and me. There are no houses for us to buy. We have to build them ourselves. Slaves captured by our Babylonian masters built our houses back there," he said, pointing to the east. "Yet, we've left those slaves behind, and who amongst us remembers how to build a house? Who knows how to quarry and cut rock? How to hew stone? Who remembers skills that our ancestors knew?"

"The Lord God will show us the way," said Joshua.

"Then pray that He's listening, priest. Because if He's not, we're in serious trouble."

"Adonai is always listening."

The merchant looked at the rabbi quizzically. "Really? Was He listening when Nebuchadnezzar destroyed Jerusalem and so many Jews died?"

"We were sinners. That was our punishment. But when our sins had been forgiven by the Lord, we prospered in exile. And now that our Babylonian masters have been conquered by Cyrus, instead of us being butchered, the Lord our God opened the Persian king's eyes and softened his heart and so today we're free men and women, able to return to our homeland—a land given to us by God on the provision that we remained pure and always worshipped Him. We lost our way and now we are finding it again. Perhaps, Reuven, it is because of men like you—men who have wandered from the path of righteousness, who, like Solomon, have worshipped false gods—that Adonai punished us. Remember the psalm that our fathers composed when we found ourselves in Babylon, when we were led away from Israel by Nebuchadnezzar?

> *By the rivers of Babylon we sat and wept when we*
> *   remembered Zion.*
> *There on the poplars we hung our harps, for there our captors*
> *   asked us for songs, our tormentors demanded songs of joy;*
> *They said, 'Sing us one of the songs of Zion!'*
> *How can we sing the songs of thee, while in a foreign land?*
> *If I forget thee, O Jerusalem, may my right hand forget its*
> *   cunning.*
> *May my tongue cleave to the roof of my mouth*
> *If I do not remember you, if I do not consider Jerusalem my*
> *   highest joy.*

That, Reuven, is why we are returning. Jerusalem is our city, Israel is our homeland. It was and it always will be. It's what makes us a people. We might live in foreign lands, but our hearts will always belong in the city on the hill."

"Yours might, priest, but my heart quickens when I trade goods, when I smell leather and know I can make a profit, when I buy beautiful painted pottery or carpets or cloth cheaply and sell it for a fortune in a foreign market.

"No, priest, you pray to your heart's content, and don't get in the way of people like me."

Joshua bridled at the insult. As their journey progressed, Reuven was becoming more and more unhappy that he'd left

Babylon, and he was taking out his frustration on his servants, fellow travelers, and now on the chief rabbi.

Restraining himself from answering intemperately, Joshua said, "Perhaps this journey isn't for you, Reuven. Perhaps you and Naomi should return to Babylon and let pioneers like your fellow Jews pave the way."

Reuven laughed. "No, priest, my wife wants our son to be born in Jerusalem, and in Jerusalem he'll be born." As an after-thought Reuven said softly, "And I, too, will be happy that he's to be born there. He'll be the first of a new generation of Jews. Who knows what will come of him and those who are born after him?"

It was too much. Weeks of growing insults and aggression caused Joshua to say angrily, "Don't lie to me, merchant. You're merely coming with us to make yourself a greater fortune. You see it as a new and brighter opportunity for yourself. This has nothing to do with your wife, Naomi, and your future baby. This is all to do with greed. That's why you're here, Reuven. I know the greed in your heart. It has nothing to do with your wife's de-sire for a homeland for your son. It's for money. You're exploiting your own people for your own gain."

Although it was dark, Joshua was certain that Reuven was sneering. "The difference between you and me, priest, is that I'm not a liar. I know I can make a fortune and that fortune will be shared by all who work with me—a fortune made by toil and cleverness. Sure, I'll make a lot of money. I've been given a warrant by King Cyrus to open up the trading routes I told you about. But I'm honest in my greed, whereas you . . . you give your people empty lies about a mystical temple and an invisible god of benefit to no one. When they get to Israel, will they see a glowing city on a hill? No, they'll see desolation. You've sold them lies to get them to come with you. I just hope that this god of yours will forgive you."

———

November 2, 2007

ONLY WHEN SHE LEFT Jerusalem or Tel Aviv, Haifa or Jaffa, did Yael come to appreciate the antiquity of the land. In Jerusalem, even though the streets were named after heroes of Israel, they were part of her everyday life and so she often failed to appreciate their heritage. Only when somebody asked, "Who was Ben Yehuda?" did it occur to her that the street was more than just shops and traffic, but that its name, and the man it immortalized, was part of the blood, muscle, and sinew of Israel.

Not that Yael was any different from a Parisienne or a Londoner. Just as somebody in Paris might say, "Meet you on the Champs-Élysées," or a Londoner would arrange to meet at Oxford Circus, so Yael would arrange to meet friends at Ben Yehuda or Derech HaNevi'im without thinking about why the roads had been so named. Who in Paris wondered about the fields or knew that Elysium was the mythological Greek place of the dead, and which Londoner wondered about the circus and what it had to do with Oxford?

But when she left a major Israeli city and traveled into the hinterland, tiny as the country was, she was transported back to ancient and ancestral roots that, she now realized, somewhere in the distant past, she shared with Bilal.

Here was Bethlehem and Nazareth, Dan in the north, Mount Hermon, Mount Carmel, and Mount Gilboa; here the Jordan River, the Jezreel Valley, and Lake Kinneret; here was Samaria and Megiddo and Tiberias. These were names and places familiar to every schoolboy and schoolgirl whose culture was Jewish, Muslim, or Christian. Here was the starting point of much of the myth and mythology that made up the Western world. Where the Greeks and Romans had once spread their culture of Jupiter and Zeus, Poseidon and Athena, throughout the West, all the ancient gods had been trampled underfoot over time by the one god of the Jews, Christians, and Muslims.

Yael breathed in the hot, dry air of the Upper Galilee and drove east from Nahariya to Peki'in, over steep hills and down into deep valleys. It was a tortured but glorious landscape, rocky and isolated, yet with the comforting feeling of white stone towns perched on hillsides. The Upper Galilee, just south of the restive Lebanese border and prey to Hezbollah rockets, was, for all its history of violence, a beauteous place.

As she entered the village of Peki'in, she wondered where in the town center she'd find the records she wanted to examine, if they existed at all. Most of the buildings were typical Galilee stone constructions, and none seemed of sufficient importance to be the town hall.

Would the Druze, who now ran the town, be cooperative or suspicious? Friends she'd asked in Nahariya's hospital had told her that the mayor was abrupt, defensive, and innately distrustful. There were virtually no Jews left there now, and for a small and seemingly peaceful village, Peki'in had a recent history of riots and violence against Jewish residents. Her friends had begged her to be cautious.

But the amazing blood link between herself and Bilal was something she had to understand. She was haunted by the idea of him in prison, in ways she couldn't explain or reconcile. Moreover, she couldn't help but now question who she was. For most of her life, Yael had asked questions about her grandmother, Shalman's wife, Judit, and the questions had always ended in evasive answers. She was beautiful and clever and brave and died a tragic death just after Yael's mother had been born; but whereas other Israeli children knew their family histories, hers seemed to be mired in mystery and half-truths. And now it seemed as though she were related to a Palestinian family whose ancestry was utterly unknown to her.

Just what the hell was going on?

———

GAINING ENTRY TO THE PRISON was difficult enough, but being allowed to speak with a prisoner on remand, a Palestinian about to go to trial for the murder of a Jewish guard, was exceptional. But Yaniv Grossman was used to doing exceptional things. He'd had himself embedded with a forward platoon in a ground assault against Gaza militants, interviewed an Al-Qassam Brigades rocket maker, managed to get a former Israeli prime minister to confess to defrauding the nation in a land deal, and scored a major scoop when he goaded the French foreign minister into admitting he wouldn't be unhappy if the entire Jewish population of France left and found another country as a way of halting Muslim violence and fanaticism. That interview had made international headlines and caused the hapless man's extinction from the political firmament.

With this kind of history and experience, Yaniv was a particularly well-connected reporter. But he'd needed all that influence to get into the prison. It had taken him six days of hectoring and cajoling, but here he was, waiting in the Central Area D prison facility by the shores of the Dead Sea for Bilal to be brought into the room.

The door opened and Bilal entered, followed by a guard. He was led over to the seat on the opposite side of the desk, and Yaniv smiled at him. The guard handcuffed him to the steel chair and went to sit on the other side of the room.

Yaniv would try to speak to him in Arabic, even though his knowledge of the language was clunky and not nearly as fluid as Yael's. But he thought it might help put Bilal at ease.

"Bilal, my name is Yaniv. I'm a reporter from America."

"Yes," said Bilal. "I've seen you on television." Bilal looked him up and down and added, "You look different in real life."

"Really? Fatter or skinnier?" Yaniv volunteered as a joke. But Bilal only shrugged and looked down at the table.

"This must feel a long way from home," Yaniv said casually, pointing around the room. He needed to create some point of trust, but he got the sense that Bilal was not the manipulated fool the Israelis probably took him for. If he was too obvious, the boy was likely to smell it and clam up.

Yaniv studied the young man, and wondered exactly what he was searching for from Bilal. Investigative journalism was a dying art in the age of instant online gratification and disposability. It required the time and resources to pursue a hunch to an uncertain end. Bilal was a hunch. Why had such a senior Shin Bet man, and especially this man, interviewed Bilal alone in the hospital? What he knew, what he saw, might lead somewhere, or nowhere.

"How are they treating you in here?" asked Yaniv. Bilal looked up as if the question was unexpected and Yaniv quickly added, "The guards can be real assholes."

Bilal's deep dark eyes bored into him.

"You know if . . . if you're not being treated right, I might be able to—"

Bilal cut him off. "I'm fine. The guards do nothing. They check on me. They see that I'm still here and then they leave me alone again." His gaze returned to studying the table, eyes well hidden.

"Good. That's good . . ."

Yaniv had interviewed other Palestinian prisoners and would-be martyrs before. Some were hardened, indoctrinated, full of braggadocio and bullshit, impotently vowing revenge and dire consequences. Others were cold and quiet, and spoke in soft, measured, and controlled voices. While rarer, it was the latter type that was truly unnerving. Yet, Bilal was neither of these. The bluster had gone, seemingly knocked out of him like a gut punch. But neither did he seem resigned to his fate. Something had him rattled, and it wasn't just cell doors and prison walls.

"What about your people in here? Your brothers?"

Bilal glanced quickly up from the table. His eyes locked with Yaniv's.

"What do you want with me? I've already spoken to the police. Why are you here?"

A nerve had been touched and Yaniv knew it. But he needed to circle rather than aim directly at the target. "Do you remember your doctor? In the hospital—Dr. Cohen?"

Bilal nodded, and his eyes were now fixed quizzically on Yaniv.

"Her name is Yael. She's a friend of mine. She saved your life, you know?"

"I know."

"She asked me to come here and make sure you were all right."

"She brought my father and mother to me in the hospital."

"Yes, she did. She said they were good people."

Bilal shrugged. But this time his eyes did not return to their downcast position.

"She's going to try and help them, Bilal. Help them to come and see you after the trial. To get you things you might need to make it easier in here."

It was a lie of course, but Yaniv saw that Bilal believed him, his posture changed and he drew a deep breath. He was exhibiting the naïveté of inexperience, with things so far outside of his comfort zone that he was clutching at straws of hope that things might get better. Yaniv wondered how long that hope would last in prison. He pressed on.

"Do you know anyone in here, Bilal? Do you have friends inside?"

"All Palestinians are brothers."

The words were not a declaration but hollow and empty, and Yaniv knew it. Words Bilal wanted to believe were true.

Looking into the distance, Yaniv said softly, "I've got brothers. Three of them. All older than me. We don't get along. We fight a lot. I love my brothers, but there have been times when I wanted to be as far away from them as I could."

Bilal studied his face for what seemed like a very long time. Yaniv thought he was about to speak, but there was only silence and the strange pleading stare. He tried another direction.

"Is there anything I can do for you, Bilal? Anybody I can talk to, anything you want to tell somebody on the outside?"

Suddenly Bilal's brow creased. "Why? Why are you here? Why do you want to help me? You're a Jew. You should hate me for what I did."

Yaniv feared he'd gone too far, too quickly. "I don't think you were born to kill anyone, Bilal. I don't think that's who you were meant to be. Someone's changed you into someone you're not, and I don't think that it's fair. And whatever you're going through in there"—Yaniv gestured past Bilal to the prison beyond—"might be something I can help fix."

And the mask cracked. There were no tears. No scowl. Just a series of muscles letting go across Bilal's brow and down his jaw, and his face seemed to sag under its own weight.

"Nobody can help me. I am alone. I should have died in the tunnel. But Allah . . . He didn't take me. I'm still here. And now . . . Nothing is like it should be . . . Nothing feels right anymore. What I do, what I did . . ." Bilal didn't, or couldn't, finish the sentence.

"We can help you, Bilal. Dr. Cohen and me. We can help you," Yaniv lied with all the sincerity in the world—a sincerity welling up from the excitement of possibly uncovering a story.

Bilal sat back in his seat and Yaniv could see that he was thinking deeply about something. Now, he realized, was the time to press home the advantage. His instincts as a reporter overrode anything else.

"Bilal, has anybody interviewed you about the bombing?" he asked, but Bilal remained silent, lost for the moment in the turmoil of his own mind. "I would expect that somebody from Shin Bet would have spoken to you. Perhaps in the hospital?"

Bilal shrugged.

"You see, the reason I'm asking is that under Israeli law, if the wrong person asked the wrong questions without you having a lawyer present, then that's illegal. They're not allowed to do that."

Bilal snapped out of his trance and with wide eyes stared at Yaniv. "Illegal?"

"Perhaps. And that means the judge at your trial has to take that into account."

Bilal looked incredulous but said nothing more.

"Who did you speak to?" asked Yaniv.

Bilal waited for a moment before answering. "A man. He came to the hospital."

"Was he alone?"

"Yes. He came alone."

"What did he ask?" Yaniv was probing now.

"I told him nothing," said Bilal, his voice containing a hint of pleading as if Yaniv was threatening him.

"It's okay. Did he offer you anything?"

"He said he could help me," Bilal mumbled.

"And what did he want for this help?"

"I told him nothing. I wouldn't speak to him. And he left. But—" Bilal stopped short.

"But? But what?"

Bilal shook his head.

Yaniv switched tack again, sensing he was very close but aware that Bilal was fragile and at any moment could clam up once more. "I know a lot of people in Shin Bet. Would you remember his name?"

Bilal answered with a feeble shake of his head.

"I know Yitzhak Atzmon, the director general, but he wouldn't have come to see you. He's old and fat," Yaniv said with a laugh, hoping to coax one out of Bilal. But to no avail.

"I know Shimon Gutnik, an analyst. He's got asthma, and he wheezes like an old car."

Bilal shook his head.

Yaniv prepared for the name he suspected might get a reaction.

"I know Eliahu Spitzer . . ."

Bilal's eyes narrowed.

"His hair is gray with a white stripe down the middle of his head. He looks as if—"

"He looks like a skunk."

Yaniv smiled and let out a small laugh. "Yes, yes, he does. Is that the man who spoke to you?"

Bilal nodded.

"And he was alone?"

Bilal nodded again.

For a moment Yaniv was lost in thought as he pondered the implications of a high-ranking Shin Bet commander personally interviewing a low-level prisoner like Bilal.

"The man asked me questions. I didn't tell him anything but I . . . I didn't say anything. I was going to. I was going to tell him I'd seen . . ."

"Seen what, Bilal?"

There was a sharp electronic buzz and a red light suddenly shone above the door to the interview room. The guard stood and walked over to the table.

"Time's up. Got to get him back."

Bilal immediately stood and turned to the guard and shuffled toward the door.

"Seen what, Bilal?" asked Yaniv, almost shouting.

Yaniv wanted to ask more questions, but with the guard present, there would be no answers. Before leaving, Bilal turned and said, "Tell the doctor"—he hesitated as if searching for the right words—"tell the doctor I said thank you."

"I will," Yaniv replied. And then Bilal was gone, leaving Yaniv with a thousand questions.

———

AS BILAL WAS WALKING BACK to his cell, accompanied by his guard, eyes were watching him. The coldest and most merciless belonged to Ibrahim, who had the knife in his pocket and was about to use it. He waited until the guard had left Bilal in his cell with the door open so that prisoners could leave the confines and walk along the corridors, speak with one another, and socialize during the day.

When the guard had left, Ibrahim cautiously walked along the north, then the east, and finally the south corridor to Bilal's cell, which he shared with another remand prisoner now that he was no longer in isolation or on suicide watch.

Ibrahim stood there in the doorway. Bilal looked up in surprise. He'd seen the man a couple of times in the exercise yard and the dining hall, but hadn't paid him much attention. The man was small and wiry, but there was a strength about him and a coldness about his eyes and lips that made people want to avoid him.

"Yes?" said Bilal.

His cell mate looked up from his magazine and then sat up on the bed.

"You," he said, nodding to the man in the upper bunk. "Fuck off."

Suddenly terrified, Bilal's cell mate jumped down from the upper bunk, walked quickly out of the room, and made his way downstairs to where people were playing card games.

"What do you want?" Bilal asked, suddenly frightened, wondering whether to get up from the lower bunk.

"You piece of shit," said Ibrahim. "You've been singing to the Jews, haven't you?"

"No!" said Bilal. He'd learned quickly neither to explain himself nor engage in aggressive conversations. And the look in this man's eyes was the stare of death.

"Get up from the bunk," ordered Ibrahim. "I want to talk to you."

"Go fuck your mother," Bilal said with all the vocal weight he could muster, wondering how to get out of whatever was soon going to happen.

Ibrahim checked the corridors, left and right, and knowing he had about five minutes to do the deed and get away he walked menacingly into the cell.

Adrenaline was pumping through Bilal's body. He was still hurting from the operations, but suddenly his body felt as it had when he was years younger, when he was at school. His mind flashed back to the days when he was bullied by older kids, before he'd learned to fight. He'd learned how to punch and kick in the most painful places on a boy's body—dirty, unscripted fights, full of fury and retribution.

Now he was seeing another bully, somebody he'd seen only a couple of times, walk into his cell to intimidate him. *Well, fuck him,* Bilal thought. He watched Ibrahim saunter arrogantly toward him, and when he reached the bunks, Bilal suddenly lashed out with his right leg in a savage kick aimed exactly at Ibrahim's balls. As his foot connected with the other man's crotch, Ibrahim let out a scream of pain. Bilal instantly jumped off the bunk and stood.

It was so totally unexpected that Ibrahim rocketed backward, and as he fell, Bilal sprang forward and aimed another sharp jab of his foot into Ibrahim's face, knocking him sideways and sending him cascading into a chair as he fell. Pumped up with surprising energy and feeling none of the pain from his operations, Bilal picked up the fallen chair and brought it smashing down on Ibrahim's head, shoulder, and arm.

Lying on the floor, Ibrahim tried to shield himself from the blows. He screamed in agony as the chair broke apart across his body. Strength and energy were coursing through Bilal; he hadn't felt like this since the night he slit the Jew soldier's throat: powerful and in control. He picked up a chair leg that had detached itself from the seat and brought it down mercilessly on Ibrahim's back, then his shoulder, then his leg, then his neck, and then the side of his face. When Ibrahim wasn't moving, Bilal straightened up, breathing heavily, and supported himself against the wall. Suddenly the pain of his wounds flared up as some of the stitches broke. Now in agony, Bilal looked down at the unconscious and bleeding man and saw something metallic in his hand, but before he could bend down and take it from him, he heard the sound of feet running in the direction of his cell.

In seconds, guards were inside, their batons raised, and they immediately saw what was happening. One pulled Bilal roughly away from the wall and another brought his baton down brutally on the back of Bilal's knees. They left him kneeling against the concrete wall as his arms were pulled behind his body and handcuffs were slapped on his wrists. Bilal peered around and saw another guard bend down to determine whether Ibrahim was alive or dead.

"He's breathing. Get a gurney." He looked at Bilal and said, "What the fuck's going on?"

"He attacked me," he replied.

Then the second guard cried, "Look!" He pointed to the homemade knife still in Ibrahim's hand.

The guard turned to Bilal and said softly, "You know who this is, don't you? You're either lucky or stupid, kid."

———

BILAL SPENT A WEEK in solitary confinement over the fight. And the silence of enclosed walls gave him time to think. Images of Ibrahim and the knife blended with the words of Yaniv and the memories of the skunk-haired man, his imam, and the strange rabbi Jew in the shadow. His head pounded with confusion. But as the week wound on, the reality of what had happened and what it meant became clearer to him. One of his own had tried to take his life. A prisoner he had never met wanted him dead. While Bilal wanted to scream: Why? he found himself asking only: Who? Who ordered Ibrahim to kill him? The only certainty Bilal knew was that there was no one he could trust. Neither the Jew guards nor his Palestinian brothers. He was alone.

When the week of solitary confinement was over, Bilal walked the corridors back to his cell, accompanied by a guard. He was surprised that as he passed, men who'd once looked at him in contempt now avoided his eyes. If they were afraid of him now, there was a good chance they'd leave him alone. But in that moment the thought of being forever alone terrified him more than Ibrahim with a knife.

Deep down he knew Ibrahim wouldn't be the last. He had to speak to somebody. On request prisoners could have access to a phone to speak to family or lawyers or spiritual leaders. When Bilal asked to use the phone and was given access to a small booth, he phoned the last friend he believed he had.

———

THREE DAYS LATER Hassan was granted permission to visit the prison. He had lied and said he was Bilal's cousin. Nobody questioned it, although he knew he would be searched and his conversation with Bilal would likely be monitored.

As Hassan approached the prison, all the fears instilled in him of what lay beyond those walls, the fate of so many of his brothers and cousins, gripped him. But as he steadied himself and entered the gate, he wondered if there were other forces at work that tied his stomach in knots. He had been instructed to kill: the imam had told him what he must do. The Jewish doctor must die. And yet, he was about to see his lifelong friend alive and breathing because of that same doctor. Would Bilal know what Hassan had been ordered to do? Would Bilal owe honor to the woman who saved him? More than anything Hassan knew that Bilal would see through any lie that he told, and Hassan was afraid of the truth.

He and Bilal sat opposite each other in the reception room where wives and children came to see their husbands and brothers.

"My brother, you look—" Hassan began, but the urgency on Bilal's face stopped him talking.

Bilal whispered, "They're trying to kill me. Hassan, I need your help."

Hassan was shocked but Bilal didn't wait for a response.

"One man with a knife. I broke his arm and beat the shit out of him, but they'll come again."

Hassan was horrified. "Who? Who would want to kill you? They know who you are. They know you're the one who bombed the temple."

"Hassan. Nothing is right. Nothing in here is right." Bilal clenched his teeth and fought back tears. He would not let Hassan see him like a woman or a child.

Hassan for his part was shocked to see his friend in such a state and saying such things. He'd always looked up to Bilal for his strength of character, his courage. "What did you do?"

Bilal's fear became anger, his words said through gritted teeth. "I did nothing. I said nothing. I told the Jews nothing. I spoke to no one. I did what I was told to do. I did everything the imam wanted . . ." The words caught in his throat. Hassan put a hand on Bilal's arm, not knowing what to say.

"Hassan. I can't trust anyone. Only you. You're the only one."

"What can I do?" Hassan asked as Bilal stared at him.

"There is someone . . ."

"Who?" asked Hassan, leaning in and lowering his voice conspiratorially.

"The doctor . . ."

The words hung in the air and Hassan's eyes opened wide. "The Jew doctor? The one who operated . . ." he said, stunned by what Bilal had just told him. "The Jew?"

"Hassan, you must trust me and do what I ask you. She is a Jew but she helped my family; she helped me. She saved me when I would have died. And now . . ."

Hassan's mind was spinning and he struggled to grasp anything firm. "But why are they trying to kill you? Who's trying to kill you? I don't understand."

"I don't know. But, Hassan, you must trust nobody. I trusted everybody and I'm in here. You must trust nobody. Do you swear to me? Nobody."

"But who?" he asked. The tension in his voice showed he shared Bilal's concern.

Bilal leaned closer. "The imam," he whispered.

Hassan's eyes widened in shock. He was speechless.

Softly, conspiratorially, Bilal said, "I drove the imam to a village near Bethlehem. He ordered me to stay in the car, but there was the girl. Remember? The video I showed you?"

"I remember," replied Hassan.

"On that night the imam was in a meeting with important people."

"So? The imam meets with important people all the time."

"He was talking to a man with white hair on his head. He was talking to a Jew!"

Hassan looked at Bilal, showing no comprehension of where Bilal was going with this.

"That man with the white hair. He came to me. He works for the secret police. He works for Shin Bet."

Hassan slowly shook his head. He failed to see the relevance.

"Why was the imam talking to a Jew from Shin Bet? Why are my Palestinian brothers trying to kill me? Please, Hassan, my brother, go to the doctor. She is the only one who can help me."

"Bilal, my brother, I came to see you because . . . your parents . . . I don't know what to do. I don't know if I can. I'm not good at this."

———

539 BCE

JOSHUA THE PRIEST feared that the number of Jews who camped outside the walls of the city of Damascus after their long twenty-day march would be considerably fewer than those who would leave with him to travel to Jerusalem. Many who had arrived exhausted had been overwhelmed by the seductive charms of the city. Damascus was like a perfumed dancer, a sacred prostitute in a pagan temple, open, willing, full of fragrances and soft fabrics, and always ready to ensnare the unwary.

Damascus was still under the control of the Babylonians even though Babylon had recently been conquered by King Cyrus the Great of Persia. But for those Hebrews who entered the city after their exhausting weeks of walking, it was a reminder of the lifestyle they'd once enjoyed back in Babylon but now had left far behind. The hardship of the road, the constant traveling, the robbers and bandits, the freezing nights spent in tents or under the stars and the fetid heat of the day—all contributed to their misery as they trudged along, and to their joy as the huge walls of the city came into view.

When they wandered through the gates of the city, the coolness of the houses and drinking places, the life and vitality, the colors and smells of the city of Damascus, made many weep. And they wept louder when, to their distress three nights later, Joshua called a meeting of elders to announce that in the next few days they would leave to journey onward to Jerusalem.

They had left Babylon in a spirit of adventure, knowing that they would be the chosen and righteous ones in the eyes of their

Lord, Adonai. But the rigors of the journey had caused many to reconsider their decision and some, Joshua knew, were thinking either of staying in Damascus or returning to Babylon.

He was so concerned that he prayed both to the Lord for guidance and to his ancestor Ahimaaz for strength of purpose. Joshua often prayed to Ahimaaz in those quiet moments when he was alone in the synagogue. To be the descendant of one of the greatest of all high priests, whose reputation as a son of Zadok had grown with each generation, was a gift from the Almighty. Among those who remained faithful to the Lord, Ahimaaz was revered for his wisdom, his knowledge, and his steadfast uprightness. The legends spoke of shouting matches between Solomon and Ahimaaz over the false idols and pagan gods that the king's many wives and concubines had brought into the palace. Being a descendant of Ahimaaz gave Joshua an authority that no other rabbi or priest held.

But Joshua's authority was being undermined just six streets away, in the northern part of the city of Damascus, a hilly area of rich people's houses where cool winds blew and the stench of the marketplace was absent. Ten Hebrews had climbed the hill to reach the house where Reuven, the wealthy merchant, and his pregnant wife, Naomi, were staying.

As the men sat in the shaded alcove in his garden of spices, fruits, and flowers, they looked in expectation at Reuven, who had asked them to come to this meeting.

"Friends," he said, although this was one of the few times that they had been allowed into his presence; none had ever been invited to his palatial home when they all lived in Babylon, "it is time, I think, to ask ourselves who we are and what we are."

They looked at him in surprise. He'd asked them to come to his temporary home in secrecy, and none had any idea what was the purpose, so his statement was intriguing.

"We were an exiled people in Babylon, but for fifty years of our exile we gained respect in the eyes of the city and the king;

now that Babylon has a new king, we are no longer slaves or servants but proper citizens of his empire. Cyrus has asked us to return to Israel, rebuild that devastated land, use our abilities and make it flourish."

Abiel, of the tribe of Benjamin, interrupted, and asked, "Reuven, why are you telling us what we know?"

He looked at him and smiled, asking, "Then if you know this, tell me who we are. Tell me what we are, Abiel."

"We're Hebrews. We're returning to our land and—"

"And who leads a people?" asked Reuven simply. "Do we have a king to lead us? No! Our last king died when we were exiled. So, without a king, who leads us?"

Each of the men looked at the one next to him. Nathan, of the tribe of Judah, said, "Zerubbabel leads us, and his uncle Sheshbazzar with him. They are descendants of the royal family of David through the line of King Solomon. Sheshbazzar carries with him all the things that Nebuchadnezzar stole from our temple. He will return them, and then . . ."

Nathan stopped talking because neither he nor the others gathered nor anybody among the Israelites really knew who would rule in Israel on their return. Reuven nodded and couldn't suppress a knowing smile. "Precisely! We're following Joshua because he is our chief rabbi and Zerubbabel because he is descended from a line of kings who lived five hundred years ago; but are these men leaders? One knows the Lord God Adonai, and the other is an old man who has to be carried from place to place on a litter.

"And when we arrive in Israel, who will direct the building? Who will marshal the farmers to begin clearing the land and planting crops so that we don't starve in the coming months? Who will ensure we're strong enough to defend ourselves from the Egyptians or the Phoenicians, or from being robbed by desert nomads?" asked Reuven.

The group fell into silence, not because these questions hadn't occurred to them since leaving Babylon, but because nobody had raised them aloud.

Daniel, of the tribe of Judah, asked quietly, "Are you proposing yourself as our king, Reuven?"

The others looked at him in surprise. "No," Reuven said immediately. "I am a merchant. I have the ear of King Cyrus, and through my relationships in distant lands, I'm known to many rulers and the rich men in their cities. But I have no wish to become a king. No, what I'm saying is this: that today and tomorrow we have no leadership. We therefore must create a leadership that the people will follow, will respect, and will venerate. Wound a camel and it will limp on; cut the head off a camel and it dies immediately. Without a head, a people will not survive in a hard and challenging world."

"We have leaders," said Abiel. "We have our chief rabbi, Joshua; we have Zerubbabel; we have—"

"And you would be led by men who know how the Lord thinks but who know nothing about administration, the laws of our land, how to create and run an army? Shall I go on?" asked Reuven.

"So you *do* want to be king!"

"No, I want all of us to be kings! I want a ruling council made up of men with different skills. Some of you will be important to the future running of the nation, and we will find others with great skills who will join us. But you are here to listen to my idea and to take it further. Do you all agree?"

"A council? Such as the king of a nation uses to advise him on what to do? But it is still the king who makes the decisions. That is the nature of our lives. If we have a council to run the affairs of the nation, then which of us will make the decisions?" asked Daniel.

"I knew that this would be uppermost in your minds," Reuven answered. "The council will have an uneven number of members at all times. If more than half agree, then that decision will be binding on the rest. We will sign a pledge that we will abide by the rule of the majority. Is it agreed?"

They sat in silence, contemplating a form of government that none had heard of before. They looked at him in both surprise and confusion.

"What I'm proposing is that the rule of the land, now that we no longer have a king, should be determined by those of the people who are able to govern. Just as all kings have ministers and advisers, so we will be ministers and advisers, and—"

"And we won't have a king to make the decisions," said Daniel. "In Babylon we were governed by our chief rabbi Joshua, and by Zerubbabel, of the line of King David, with his uncle Sheshbazzar. It was always to be that when we returned to Israel and reestablished Jerusalem as our capital—that Zerubbabel would be our king. So why are we sitting here, talking about a council of governors, when we already have a king in line for the throne?"

Reuven had anticipated the question and was ready with the answer. But knowing the value of creating tension in a negotiation, he sighed, shook his head slightly, and took a sip of his pomegranate water. Softly, as though explaining something simple to a child, he said, "For five hundred years we've been governed by kings who have progressively weakened the Jewish people by their incompetence and avarice. For the same amount of time we've also been governed by rabbis who tell us that all of our problems are caused by our failings, our lack of faith, and so Adonai is punishing us. So, because of inept kings and because we weren't faithful enough, ten of our twelve tribes have disappeared, our land has been ruined, our capital, Jerusalem, was reduced to rubble, our temple was destroyed, and our people were made slaves of the Babylonians.

"Well, I've had enough of kings and certainly enough of rabbis. It's time that we, the Jewish people, took responsibility for our own government. We will gather the best men of the land, and it is we who will govern—"

Infuriated, Daniel interrupted. "We Jews are a people because our kings are from the line of David; we are one people because we have one God, Who brought us out of the land of Egypt, the land of bondage, where we were slaves. How dare you sit there and denounce our kings and our rabbis and suggest that we are more capable of being rulers? God will strike you dead for this, Reuven the merchant."

Theatrically, Reuven stood, stretched out his arms, and shouted up to the sky, "For my blasphemy, Lord God Almighty, strike me dead. Send a bolt of lightning through my heart . . ."

Everybody looked up at him in shock. Reuven stood there for a long, long moment and slowly turned to Daniel. He shook his head. "I'm not sure that God is listening."

———

THEY MET IN A SHOP selling spices in Damascus's eastern market. They smiled at each other and kissed as sisters. Rabbi Joshua's wife, Shoshanna, was buying leeks and onions for their evening meal. Naomi, Reuven's wife, was searching for a gold clasp to decorate a new robe she'd bought, now that the baby was growing so big that her clothes were starting to be too tight.

"Sister," said Shoshanna, "you look so pale. Is the pregnancy difficult for you?"

Naomi nodded. "Girls half my age seem to have no problem growing a baby in their womb. I'm suffering because of my years and because I am slight of body."

"Come, let's go and find an inn and drink a cup of spiced water to refresh us," said Shoshanna, leading her by the hand to a place she'd found the previous day where the owner used fresh and not dried herbs in his water. They sat and sipped the hot liquid, and it immediately refreshed both of them.

"Soon we'll be in Jerusalem," Shoshanna said. "Joshua says that we'll be leaving here in a matter of days, and then it's only a two-month walk until we return to our homeland. Isn't that marvelous?"

Naomi nodded. "It coincides with the time of the birth of my son. The Lord God has been kind to me. I hope it pleases Him to continue to be kind and to allow me to finish my journey in good health so that Reuven and I can enjoy many years of pleasure with our son."

"Why do you say that?" asked Shoshanna. "Don't you think that you'll finish the journey?"

"Only God Almighty knows whether I'll survive. I've been feeling so exhausted these last few days that I don't know whether I can continue on to Jerusalem. Perhaps I should stay here until the birth."

"No! No, you can't do that. Your son must be born in Israel, and especially in Jerusalem. He will be the first of a new generation of Israelites."

Naomi nodded. "But if my body is too weak, I may be forced to stay here, in Damascus."

"But that means that Reuven will remain with you, should that be your decision. My husband was counting on Reuven to assist him in rebuilding the nation."

"Joshua? Is he on the council of governors?"

"What council?"

Naomi flushed. "Oh, nothing. I must be confused." And she hurriedly looked down at her cup of herb water.

————

THE FOLLOWING DAY Rabbi Joshua climbed the hill in the north of the city of Damascus with grave fears on his mind. When he was sitting in Reuven's home, he began immediately. "I am told by Daniel, of the tribe of Judah, that you convened a meeting of some citizens and proposed a council of governors to rule Israel on our return. It is to replace me as the chief rabbi and Zerubbabel, the grandson of our last king, Jehoiachin, and a descendant of King David. Is that correct?"

Reuven had anticipated that Daniel would go immediately to Joshua and tell him of the nature of the meeting. "Yes!" he said tersely. "And no! You will always be the chief rabbi, but the days of Israel having kings is over, Joshua."

"Then who will lead our country? What will this council do when we get to Israel?"

"Govern."

"It is the role of kings to govern, and above them the Lord God Almighty. It is not for you or any other to decide who shall govern."

"And who is our king? Who determined that he would be king? What say do the people have in who should lead them in the perilous times ahead?"

"The people are under the rule of God, through their king. As it was in the days of David and Solomon; as it will be again when we rebuild Jerusalem."

"And after David and Solomon's rule . . . let me think . . . who did we have as kings? Who did Almighty God decide would reign and protect the Israelite people? Oh, yes, we had Rehoboam, who lost us ten of our twelve tribes; then we had Abijah, who tried to reunite the kingdoms of north and south Israel, but lost; after him, we had Asa, another failure, and then Jehoshaphat . . . Need I go on, Rabbi Joshua? One more useless than the other."

"You lie," said Joshua. "These were good men who tried but failed to reunite our kingdoms. But they were of the line of King David, and so God decreed that—"

"God? Forgive me, Joshua, but I get as much grace and favor from worshipping the wooden and stone idols of Marduk and Ea and Apsu as I do from lifting my face to heaven and asking the clouds to come down and help me. God will not lift stone upon stone and rebuild Jerusalem. Only we can do that, with or without the help of a god or gods.

"And it was for this reason that I called the council together. Men of trade, merchants, builders, metalworkers and woodworkers, farmers and scribes. Each brings a skill to the governance of the land. Each will contribute and make decisions. And in that way—"

"Then you want to be the king of Israel!"

"Fool! I want no kings of Israel. I want no priests to rule over us. I want our land to be ruled by those best able to rule it, not men who climb onto the throne from birth because their fathers had ruled."

"Blasphemy, Reuven. For this I could have you stoned," Joshua said, barely able to contain his fury.

Reuven smiled. "Stoned? But there are no stones in the desert, Rabbi—only sand, and that slips through your fingers."

———

November 2, 2007

THE VILLAGE was as she remembered it. Perhaps it had grown marginally on the outskirts, but she could see that little had changed in the older parts as she drove her car through the precariously narrow, steep streets until she came to the middle of the village.

She parked the car in a lane and walked into the town. She breathed in the midday air of cooking, an aroma of olive oil, hummus, *t'china*, and roasted meats. It was as though nothing had moved forward or developed since she'd been here last. Indeed, in these villages, little had changed in hundreds, perhaps thousands, of years. Yael looked up toward the roofs of the houses. Apart from the occasional television aerial and electrical wires connecting homes to poles, she could have been looking at a biblical or medieval village.

Four streets away, a much older and dustier car pulled into

a side street and parked. Its driver, Hassan from the Palestinian village of Bayt al Gizah, close to Jerusalem, had followed Yael from where she lived and tracked her on the long journey, often finding it hard to keep sight of her sports car as she accelerated up hills and down into valleys on her way north. But luck had been on his side, and she was unaware that anybody was tailing her.

Dressed in jeans and a frayed T-shirt, Hassan walked in the shadows of the buildings toward the center of the village. There he stood beside a wall of a house, peering at the small reservoir of water that came from the spring in the village square, the single café with its primitive awning, and the houses clustered around; and he looked carefully at the raven-haired woman who'd left her car and was walking into the village. She was the reason he was here.

Yael sat at the café and slowly sipped a freshly squeezed orange juice. She was the sole customer. Indeed, there were very few people in the center of Peki'in. Occasionally an elderly man or woman would walk out of one of the narrow lanes that led to the village square, look at her, scowl, and then walk away down one of the other lanes. One of the men wore very baggy trousers, the middle of which reached down to his knees. Hassan had never seen a Druze man wearing his distinctive clothing.

Yael, having been here before, admired the Druze, who now controlled the village. They were a peaceable and loving people despite the recent assaults against the few Jews who lived in the village. She smiled as she watched them passing in the streets. The women usually wore blue or black dresses with their heads covered by a *mandil* and shuffled along in red slippers. But the initiated men, the *uqqal*, wore baggy pants that were tied at the ankles. In their tradition, they believed that a man, not a woman, would give birth to the Messiah, and his body would drop suddenly from the body of the man. So, in order to prevent the Messiah from hitting the ground, all initiated men dressed in baggy trousers. Yael thought that the strange pants seemed perfectly in keeping with the huge mustaches with hand-waxed tips the men sported.

The owner of the café came and stood in front of her. He tilted his head and smiled. "I remember you. Many years ago. Here with the army. In uniform. Yes?"

"You have a very good memory," Yael said somewhat incredulously, and could not escape the fact that being alone in this village with this Druze man made her uncomfortable and wary. She worried about the stories she'd been told about the Druze villagers of Peki'in driving out the few remaining Jews because of some nonsense about mobile-phone aerials. And it really was nonsense; a story had spread that the aerials that had been erected would cause cancer in the Druze population. But peace was now, apparently, restored.

The man looked Yael up and down as if appraising her in advance of what he was about to say next, then smiled. "Your friends were rude. Your army friends. I remember."

"I don't," she said, trying not to sound offended.

The man shrugged. "Yes, you do. You apologized for them. Why, I remember you . . ." He tapped his temple to confirm the memory. "But no matter." He changed the subject. "You want food? Something to eat?"

"No food, thank you. Just another orange juice."

The man retreated from the table but then turned back to Yael, whose attention had drifted to the deserted street.

"Not all the Jews have gone, you know."

Yael turned back to face him, uncertain of what he might mean.

"One old Jewish woman still lives here. A few others."

"It's a shame so many left," said Yael. "This village was Jewish since the time of the Bible." She finished her juice, but if the man appreciated the barb, he hid it behind his mustache.

"But many Jews love to come visit here from all over—from Tel Aviv, Haifa, Jerusalem—to see the synagogue." The smile grew broader and his waxed mustache curled upward in a strange demonstration of pride. "Is that why you're here?"

Yael set down her glass. "I'm looking for someone, for a family that lived here many, many years ago . . ." She told him she was looking for town records, births, deaths, and marriages. The man seemed intrigued but had nothing to offer, and directed her to the town hall and the mayor.

As Yael stood and walked in the direction the café owner had indicated, Hassan followed, keeping to the shadows. When she went into the building, he remained outside, watching.

Moments later she was standing at the counter of the records department of Peki'in, talking to the young man who listened to her request. He nodded, said very little, and disappeared into a back room. Yael looked around for computers so that she could check the records, and then her heart dropped when she realized that a place like this almost certainly wouldn't have computerized their older records. So she'd have to look through year after year of village births, deaths, and marriages in order to find out what she wanted to know. In Jerusalem, a quick registry search by computer would find her what she needed in moments, but Peki'in was a couple of hundred miles north and centuries behind the rest of Israel.

The young man returned and ushered her into a side office, where ten large ledgers were on the table. He told her that these were the records of Peki'in dating back to the beginning of the nineteenth century.

"Don't you have older records?" she asked.

The young man shook his head. "There were no real records kept before that."

"So why did they start keeping records in the 1800s?" asked Yael.

The young man smiled broadly as if he had waited years for someone to show any interest. "Alexander the Great and Napoleon!" he declared with dramatic effect.

"Excuse me?"

The young man took a deep breath. "You see, Napoleon always wanted to follow in the footsteps of Alexander the Great: conquer the world from Egypt to India, just like Alexander did. But Turkey and the Ottomans stood in his way . . ." He gestured with his hands as if tracing a map that Yael couldn't see.

"This feels like a history lesson," she said drily.

The young man was unperturbed and pushed on, unwilling to let the chance to indulge his passion pass by. "Napoleon fought his way from Egypt to Palestine. He got as far as Jaffa, Nazareth, and Tiberias . . ." He again pointed to invisible dots on the map he'd drawn in the air and unconsciously slipped into the present tense as if relaying the events like a sports commentator. "The Ottomans are terrified, right? And they realize that this area is the perfect place to attack the French from the south where they're vulnerable. Not just Napoleon but the Jews and the Arabs who live here . . ."

Yael interrupted the monologue in an effort to get to the point. "What's that got to do with the records?"

The young man seemed taken aback by the question. To him it was obvious. "They kept records so they knew who was here and if they were likely to be attacked. That's when our records began. Napoleon and Alexander!"

The young man's pride in his explanation could not have been more apparent, but it was lost on Yael. Had she been more patient, she might have pondered how little she knew of the turbulent history of her homeland. But instead she looked at the books and turned to the beginning. The earliest records first started for Peki'in in 1802. The ink on the registry was faint but still legible.

Were she a historian, such reading would have been an indulgent pleasure. She read the names, the dates, the locations, and the comments written by the village scribe, who had recorded the ages of residents, inhabitants, visitors who stayed for more than a year, occupations, and ages; the scribe wrote the ages, sexes, defects, and perfections of those who were residents of Peki'in when the area's history was being made. It took Yael an hour to read of the events that occurred in the village during the decades from 1800 to 1850. But there didn't seem to be any mention of a new Arab family who had come to the area.

She was beginning to assume that Bilal's mother's family had been in the area long before that, in which case she might have to go back to Jerusalem and find out what national records there might be that recorded such details. But out of curiosity Yael opened the ledger that detailed the decades 1850 to 1890 and began to flick through the pages. These pages were written by a different scribe from the one who had recorded the earlier decades: the handwriting was different, and the comments about the inhabitants, visitors, and newly arrived residents became more caustic. She smiled when she read such observations as "In Samir's house, a transient from Acre, one Mahmud the stonemason, who claims to have a truthful tongue. But Samir says he eats like a horse."

For the decade 1850 to 1860 Yael read one, sometimes two entries in a section but noticed that the later entries for that decade were suddenly fuller. In earlier decades the population of the village had hardly changed, but as though some event had taken place in history the records showed that, from the end of the 1850s onward, more and more people had flooded into the village. Indeed, in the decade 1860 to 1870, the population of the village swelled by at least a third.

She read the names. They were all Muslim names. But when she read the comments, she was astounded. The scribe had written "Another exile from Circassia. This family, the al-Yazdani, consists of father, mother, and ten children. Where will they be housed?"

Circassia. She'd heard of it. It was somewhere in southern Russia. But why had dozens, perhaps hundreds, of Circassians suddenly left Russia and come to live with Jews and Arabs in

Peki'in and probably other villages? She opened the door and asked the young man, "Can you explain something to me?"

He looked to where Yael was pointing at the register and said, "Ah, the arrival of the Circassians. Few of their relations remain. Most moved on to the south. But Peki'in was one of a number of Galilee villages they first came to when they left Russia. It was part of the Turkish Ottoman Muslim Empire, and so they felt safe here."

"But why did they leave Circassia?"

The young man sat, and sipped his coffee. "In the middle of the nineteenth century, the Russians emptied Circassia of Muslims. They drove them out. The Russians wanted the valuable farming land at the foot of the Caucasus Mountains, between the Caspian and the Black Seas. Very fertile. The Circassians were sent to Anatolia and other parts of Turkey, where they hoped that they would be welcomed by their fellow Muslims, but the Turks hated them and settled them in impoverished mountainous regions and got them to do menial jobs. So many came south to Palestine in the hope of a better life. But the Galilee, and villages like Peki'in, were too small and underdeveloped for them, and so they continued their journey south to Nablus or Bethlehem or Jerusalem for work, and so they could rebuild their lives."

Yael was surprised but didn't want to show it. "So the family I'm searching for could have come from Circassia?"

"Sure. They may have lived in this region for thousands of years, or they could have come a hundred and fifty years ago from Russia. I have no idea."

Thanking him, Yael left the building and returned to her car. Then she drove westward in the direction of Nahariya. What she didn't know was that a much older and slower car, driven by a youth in jeans and a T-shirt, was following her, desperately trying to keep up.

———

ELIAHU SPITZER SIGNED his last piece of paper for the day. He straightened his hair and repositioned the yarmulke on the back of his head. His neck hurt, the small of his back ached, and his bottom was numb. As a man of action, as Shin Bet's most senior field commander before his illness, he used to spend as little time as possible in the office, often less than ten minutes a month at his desk. The rest of his time was put to use in cafés and in safe houses and in Palestinian homes, talking in secret to people he was trying to win over as informants. There were two routes to Shin Bet's success. One was money—the oil in his machine for such tasks as gaining information—but money could never buy loyalty, especially from those who had little. The second was simple blackmail: he would allow a Palestinian certain benefits, such as easy access to a jailed relative, or a well-paid job within Israel, and then, once ensnared, use the threat of exposure of the benefit to persuade the Palestinian to give him information.

Israel's Shin Bet and the nation's external agency, Mossad, were the most successful and feared security forces in the world. Rarely did targets know that one of their own, trusted and respected, had been turned. Yet, never taking credit in public for their successes, always vigilant against the increasing number of Islamist and Salafi breakaway organizations dedicated to the destruction of Israel, Eliahu was at the pinnacle of the nation's security hierarchy.

Until his heart attack. It had come suddenly. He was driving away from a meeting with other security officials early one morning, after breakfasting on his favorite meal, *shakshouka*— brought to Israel by Tunisian Jews, a mixture of poached eggs in a sauce of tomatoes, peppers, onions, and spices—when a crushing pain in his chest and throat nearly stopped him from breathing. Somehow remembering Shin Bet's safety procedures, he drove slowly, forcing himself to cough all the way to the hospital as a way of artificially massaging his heart and forcing it to continue to pump blood. But the moment he reached the doors of the ER, he collapsed. He woke two days later after that fateful six-hour quintuple bypass operation.

Now, three and a half years later, he sat at his desk in Shin Bet's headquarters with time and space to think. This doctor, this Yael Cohen, had left Jerusalem and traveled to Peki'in. Why? Eliahu looked on a map and found the small village in the northern part of Galilee, fairly close to the Lebanese border.

Why would a city doctor go to a backward place like Peki'in? He had checked with his sources in the major hospital in Nahariya and found that her reassignment had been largely unnecessary and completely unorthodox in the way it had been handled. And why had this American reporter for ANBN, this Yaniv Grossman who used to be called Ivan in New York, visited Bilal in the prison by the shores of the Dead Sea?

His instincts told him that they knew something. But what? The imam seemed confident Bilal hadn't talked; yet, when he'd visited in the hospital, the boy suddenly became apoplectic. The imam said that the kid had somehow spotted them when they'd met in secret with Reb Telushkin in a village near Bethlehem, which was why he was going to be killed in the prison. But where did the doctor and this American reporter fit in? What the hell was going on?

His thoughts were interrupted by the sound of gunfire somewhere beyond the walls of the Old City. Or maybe it was just some car backfiring. Either way, it wasn't his concern. Just days ago the Palestinian kid was the only one that Eliahu and his operatives would have had to deal with. But now there were three loose ends to tie up.

———

539 BCE

JOSHUA'S DEEP INNER THOUGHTS were suddenly interrupted by his wife, Shoshanna, who was concerned that he had been sitting outside of the house where they were staying, with his head in his hands. He'd recently returned from the home of the merchant, Reuven, and had said nothing to her.

She approached him cautiously. "So, husband, thinking?"

Joshua nodded.

"You're troubled by what Reuven said? Was it about this council his wife mentioned?"

Again Joshua nodded. Softly and in despair he said, "He and others want to destroy us. They want to cut us off from Adonai, our Lord and God. Some of our people will remain here in Damascus, others will come, but who knows what will happen when we arrive in Jerusalem?"

She said quietly, "If the people have lost their way, if their faith in the Lord is weakening, what is it that will lead them on?"

Joshua searched for an answer but could only say, "Prayer. They must pray to Adonai for strength."

Shoshanna smiled. "You know, husband, when the men leading the camels of a caravan are tired from the journey and want to make camp before the sun sets, the leader of the caravan can demand that they continue until the light fails. That would reward him, but what would it do for the camel drivers other than make them resentful? He could warn them of the punishment they'd suffer by whipping their backsides, but that would make them surly and vengeful. Or he could offer them a reward, and then they would continue, knowing that good things will be available beyond the horizon. So when the journey is long and difficult, good leaders give their men rewards, and they trudge on despite their exhaustion, because they know that it's in their own interests."

Joshua shrugged. "But what can I offer thousands of my people? I'm not a rich man."

"Who is the richest of us all? Who has more wealth than all the kings and all the empires on the face of the earth?"

Joshua stared at her.

"The Lord our God, husband. He is the richest of all."

"But through prayers?"

"Prayers will help, but the people need more; they need another reason to leave the comforts and seductions of Damascus for Jerusalem. They need a reason not to follow Reuven and the others who have set up this council. Give them the reason. Promise them untold rewards in Israel. Swear an oath that in Jerusalem will be riches beyond their imaginations."

"How can I promise that, woman? How can I say what will be there when I don't know?"

"Then how do you know there won't be immense riches in Israel? Stand before the multitudes tomorrow morning and promise them that their lives will be richer and rewarded when they get to the land promised to the Jewish people by God. Tell them that in a dream you've seen gold in the streets, soaring temples, ample food and drink, and everything they will find in Damascus and Babylon, but more so—much more."

"I can't lie, Shoshanna."

"How do you know it's a lie? Have you been to Jerusalem?"

"It's a pile of stones that we have to rebuild with our own hands."

"And beneath the stones? Do you know what lies underneath the rubble? Perhaps it's gold and silver, onyx and alabaster. How do you know that these things aren't to be found?"

Joshua remained silent. "But it would be a lie. I can't lie or bear false witness. The laws of Father Moses . . ."

"Then tell them that in your prayers the Lord has promised that He will provide, and the riches of Damascus and Babylon, of Egypt and Persia, will be theirs provided they finish the journey and use their hearts and heads to rebuild the land. Inspire them, Joshua. Use your voice to raise the people up."

And Joshua suddenly realized that, as the leader of the Jews, he could no longer be a counselor or an adviser, a healer and a comforter, a man of God distant from his congregation.

Shoshanna, his wife, was right. People had followed Joshua and Zerubbabel because of the promise of returning to their ancestral homeland and becoming a free people once again. Nobody had followed Joshua because he had said that returning was the right thing, the Jewish thing, to do.

Yet, now, when doubts and hardships were pressing on his congregation, he had to become more than a rabbi, more than a counselor and healer. He had to become a leader. She was right. It had taken a wife to tell Joshua what to do and how to behave. And tomorrow he would call all of his people into the nearby valley outside the walls and tell them the story of Jerusalem. He would build such a magnificent temple through images in their minds, create such a gleaming white city on a hill, that his people would want to leave Damascus there and then.

He wouldn't lie, as she had suggested, nor would he tell his people that the streets were paved with gold; but he would tell them of the prosperity they could enjoy, the peace and harmony and security they would feel, when the work was done. Some might want to remain behind in Damascus, and if they did, Joshua would bless them and wish them well. And he'd tell them that it was only a walk south to Jerusalem, and they, as Jews, would be welcome there at any time.

Yes! He would write magnificent words to help them envision it, create a landscape on which his people, Israel, could build their houses in the air, see and smell and feel the walls and matting, the cooking hearths and tiled roofs. He would ask them to close their eyes and imagine the streets that led from the Valley of Kidron through the walls of the city, up the hill, past the market stalls laden with food and drink, and up, always up, past the king's palace, to the resting place of Adonai, the very Temple of Solomon itself. He would describe, as his father had described to him, what the temple had once looked like and how it would look again when the Jews rebuilt it. He would do all that tomorrow. He would stand on a plinth and speak across the heads of the multitudes. He would speak loudly so all could hear. His voice would be commanding, strong, and vibrant, and his words would be put into his mouth by the Lord God Himself.

"Husband?"

Joshua opened his eyes and saw Shoshanna looking strangely at him.

"Joshua, are you all right? You were mumbling. You seemed to be in a daze."

Joshua smiled. "Dearest wife. I'm a rabbi, a man of God, and a healer. In His own way, and through your presence, the Lord God, Adonai, has opened my eyes and allowed me to see further than I've ever seen before."

She looked closely at her husband and wondered if he was drunk.

He reached over, placed his hand on Shoshanna's head, and blessed her. *"Baruch Atah Adonai, Eloheinu Melech ha'Olam . . ."*

———

"WHEN WILL WE BE THERE?" asked Shoshanna, Rabbi Joshua's wife. She had run forward to the head of the column of Israelites to where her husband and Zerubbabel were leading their people home on the road south. They were following the tops of the hills from Shiloh to the city of Ai, and then on to Jerusalem.

He looked at her, red-faced from running and concern in her eyes, and asked, "Why?"

"Somebody is sick and needs rest."

"Who?" he asked urgently.

Shoshanna didn't reply. Joshua knew immediately who it was. "Is Naomi worse this morning?"

His wife nodded. "She is much weaker, and now she is show-ing signs of the fever. She drinks water and vomits it up again immediately. I'm worried for her."

Joshua nodded. He said softly, "When we reach the top of this hill, I'm told by our advance guards that the city will be in sight. Then it's just across the valley and up the hill to our new home— our Jerusalem."

Shoshanna sighed. Since Damascus, since Reuven and the others who had tried to convince the Israelites that they should be a ruling council, Joshua hadn't spoken a word to the merchant. And Reuven, who had been soundly rejected by the people of Israel after Joshua's stirring speech about the glories under God that awaited them, had lain low, rarely being seen in the company of others. Since Damascus, his wife had grown frailer and weaker, and now that she was suffering a fever in the last weeks of her pregnancy, Shoshanna was frightened that her body would be spent by the time they reached the broken walls of the ruined city.

Shoshanna walked beside her husband. "Last night we thought that the baby would be born, but the birth women told me that her body is not yet beginning to open and the pains are what must be expected because of the sins of Adam's wife, Eve. But why should Naomi, who is a good and gentle woman, suffer because of Eve? Why should she suffer because of her husband's blasphemy?"

Joshua looked at her but knew that this wasn't the time for a discussion of Jewish law and customs. "God will provide all the comforts that she needs," he said.

"Comforts? The birth women say that she still has two weeks to go before the baby will be full term. Yet, this fever is burning her body and the women fear that it will infect the child unless the baby is delivered immediately."

"Can nothing be done?" asked Joshua.

"The women have given her herbs that should bring the birth to fulfillment. They have bathed her with cold water, which will help to bring down her body's heat. But no matter what they do, Naomi is still burning with fever. One of the women says she won't reach Jerusalem. Reuven told me that he'd rather the infant

ALAN GOLD AND MIKE JONES

died than his wife leave him. Joshua, if the baby dies inside her womb, she will be inconsolable, especially after the rigors of the journey and how close we are now. Every day she prays to God to allow her to see the rocks and stones of Jerusalem. And every day we draw closer, she becomes weaker and sicker. Is God playing a game with her? Is Adonai punishing her because Reuven turned away from Him?"

"Woman, our god is a proud god, but not a vengeful one. He hears our prayers, so if ever you believed in the power of prayer to beg Adonai to help her, now is the time for you to ask Him to intercede. Pray, wife, with all your heart and all your soul and all your might."

"Husband, I've been praying for her from the time we left Damascus, yet God doesn't hear my prayers. What can I do?" she asked, her voice close to tears.

Joshua felt utterly helpless. "It's just two days before we reach God's city. Surely, after all this distance and time, she can travel the last part and see the golden walls of the city. Can't she?"

Shoshanna shook her head. "I don't know. God knows, but I don't. I'm fearful, Joshua. If the baby dies, I think Naomi will go mad. If she dies, then I fear for Reuven's soul."

"Reuven's soul is in God's hands, and I'm afraid that he will be punished for his thoughts. So it's even more important that you pray hard for God's mercy toward them. Pray now, Shoshanna. Pray for God's help for your friend."

When her prayers were ended, Joshua decided to ride back to meet the wagon carrying Naomi and the birth women who were tending to her needs. But when he arrived at the wagon, he could see by their grave faces that things had gotten worse since his wife's visit.

Reuven looked in surprise at Joshua.

"You!" he said.

"Your wife is sick. I've come to offer my prayers, my help."

Joshua anticipated a sharp rebuke, a snarl, and being told to leave, but instead Reuven nodded and said softly, "Thank you, Rabbi."

"You look exhausted, Reuven."

"I haven't slept since we left Damascus, Joshua. My wife said we should remain, but after the people wanted you and Zerubbabel to lead them, and not my group of elders of the community, I knew I had to come to ensure—"

"To ensure that Jerusalem is rebuilt properly?"

Reuven nodded. He reflected for a moment and then said, "Many months ago, in Babylon, you said to me my reason for coming to Jerusalem had nothing to do with Naomi or my baby; it had everything to do with greed. Much of what you accused me of, Rabbi, was correct, but in this regard you're wrong. I want my son to be born in Israel. Since I began this journey, I think more and more that Israel must be rebuilt, must prosper, and must be renewed to become one of the most important nations. Why shouldn't we be as great as Babylon, as Damascus, as Pithom and Carcamesh? Isn't Jerusalem as great as any of these?"

"Jerusalem is great, Reuven, because our temple is the home of the one true God, Adonai Elohim. All the other cities were built because of the desire of ordinary men, of kings and rulers, to show the rest of the world how powerful they were. But Jerusalem is powerful not because of its buildings or treasures but because it is the house of the Lord.

"Allow me to pray over Naomi, so that she recovers and is strong enough to see your son born and circumcised on the mountain where God tested Abraham before telling him to spare the life of Isaac, his beloved son."

Their prayers ended, Joshua returned to his tent at the head of the column, just on the other side of a mountain from whose summit could be seen the destroyed city of Jerusalem.

The cold night passed and Naomi was able to sip some warm vegetable broth that one of the birth women made beside the campfire. Reuven was sitting beside her, watching her drink from the cup. He smiled and she spoke softly, weakly, to him. He had to lean close to her to hear what she was saying. And as his face nearly touched hers, he was shocked by the smell of death.

Naomi never woke up. She died of a raging fever during the night. As soon as the birthing women realized that she was dead, they slit open her body, burst the warm waters, and took the baby from her womb, slapped him hard on his bottom, breathed into his mouth to give air to his lungs, swaddled the boy in cloth, cleaned his mouth and nose, and ran to one of the young birth mothers, paying her to breast-feed the baby.

Bereft, Reuven joined Joshua in mourning prayers in the dawn light. They stood on top of the hill and looked over the valley to the opposite hill, where the sun was lighting up the stones that had once stood one on top of the other as the city of Jerusalem.

And when the prayers had been said, Joshua arranged for Naomi's body to be buried in the caves on the eastern hill opposite the city. And he and Reuven carried the healthy and placid infant up the hill and through the broken archway that led the column of returning Jews into Jerusalem.

———

November 2, 2007

HASSAN KHOURI'S CAR BACKFIRED as it strained to climb out of the lower reaches of the village of Bayt al Gizah. He bent over the steering wheel as if to urge it forward. It was early morning, and dozens of men and women, walking the streets to go to work or to the local shops, looked around in shock at the sudden noise. Explosions, gunfire, and detonations were the terrifying currency of Israeli and Palestinian streets, and every unusual or loud noise caused a shock and people in the vicinity to take notice. Normally a nation that lived at the extremes of life—from despair to unbridled exultation—recent exchanges with the Hamas terrorists of Gaza, culminating in a series of vicious border clashes and rockets, had made all Israelis nervous.

Hassan wasn't aware that people on the sidewalks were looking at him as his car continued to backfire as it climbed the steep hills that led out of Jerusalem. He drove toward the periphery of the city, past hospitals, museums, and television buildings, and soon arrived on the road north from the city to the Sea of Galilee.

Hassan had recently returned from Peki'in, where he'd followed the doctor, Yael, from place to place. Why was the damn woman interfering? Didn't she know her place? Hassan had told the imam of her visits, of the times he'd seen her suspiciously talking to people. And the imam was worried by her activities. Although he didn't discuss it with Hassan, the young man knew that it must have something to do with Bilal, with what he'd told her.

When he'd informed his imam of what the Jew doctor was doing, the decision that she must be killed was made. Prayers were said, thanks were given to Allah, and Hassan was ordered to return and continue what he had begun. The doctor knew too much.

The first time was a scouting expedition. Her image, her hair, her face, were now known so well to him. He had been given a high-velocity rifle, a handgun, and ammunition. He had been told that if the circumstances permitted it—if there was nobody else around and the escape path was clear—he should use the handgun, shooting the young woman in the chest or the head. If he couldn't get close enough because she was surrounded by friends, he should hide behind a tree or a building while she was sitting outdoors at a table or somewhere and use the rifle to kill her. In all the screaming and confusion, Hassan would have time to dismantle the rifle, pack it into a bag, and walk away as though he were a local villager.

The imam had assured him that from the moment the girl fell

dead to the floor to the time he was in his car and far away, the police would only just be arriving at the scene of her death. Hassan would be on the road to Bayt al Gizah and safety well before the police had time to set up roadblocks. The imam had told him that on his way back from the scene of the crime he should pull up in a quiet spot on the northern fringes of the Sea of Galilee and throw the gun and the rifle as far from the shore as he possibly could. Then he was to strip naked, walk into the water, and swim for a few minutes. That, the imam said, would remove all trace of the gunpowder residue so that in the unlikely event that he was stopped at a random Israeli roadblock, the police dogs wouldn't smell anything on his hands. Hassan had packed a change of underwear and clothes so that when he emerged from the water, he could dress himself in trousers and a top that had never been in contact with guns. He would dump the clothes he'd worn to travel to Nahariya in a trash can somewhere along the way.

It was all so clinical, so matter-of-fact. As if the imam were giving him instructions to go to a supermarket and buy food for that night. Hassan gripped the wheel, his knuckles white with tension. Fear? Anger? Doubt? He didn't know; all he knew was that he was about to kill the woman who'd saved the life of his best friend.

Whether she was a Jew or not, his culture, his upbringing— everything he understood about himself as an Arab—told him that he had to revere her for what she'd done for Bilal. As the sun was breasting the Mountains of Moab, his mind was such a maelstrom of emotions that he had to breathe deeply in order to concentrate on the road. He loved the imam, but after what Bilal had told him in prison, what should he do?

He'd never killed anybody before. He'd talked about it many times when he was inside the tightly knit cabal sitting at the feet of the imam, learning about the amorality of the Jews, of their theft of Palestinian land, of their genocide of the Palestinian people, and much more. Everything the imam said explained the misery of Hassan's life and the way his parents and grandparents had suffered all these years. And his fury had been fed and had grown and grown until he was desperate to avenge the degradation with an act of vengeance.

Bombs, rocket attacks, grenades hurled at checkpoints, were all part of the fantasy. That was killing the enemy at a distance; it was impersonal. But a pistol in the hand, a bullet in the head of a young woman, lining her up in the crosshairs of a high-powered rifle, seeing her head blown off—these were no longer what the young Palestinian could aspire to. He'd now been told that he would be going up to a young woman and looking at the terror in her face as he raised the pistol to her head and pulled the trigger. He realized he would no longer be a freedom fighter but a murderer. Hassan felt sick as he thought of Yael's blood and brains splattering and watching her fall to the street. Bombs, rockets, and grenades were all impersonal, but using a gun sat heavily and uneasily with Hassan.

The doctor had saved Bilal's life. And Bilal had begged him to contact her. Yet, now, under orders from the imam, he had to murder this doctor because the imam was certain that Bilal, stupid Bilal, had told her things he shouldn't have. Was the imam right, or was Bilal telling the truth when he assured him that he'd said nothing? Bilal had always told him the truth, even when they'd been lying to others about their little crimes, even when they were kids together. But this wasn't kids' stuff any longer. This was big stuff, adult stuff, matters of life and death, and Hassan felt lost.

And what of Bilal? Had he really seen things that he shouldn't have seen? The imam swore on the Koran that Bilal had broken the most sacred rule by which the group operated. Who should he believe? His mind was so confused, spinning in all directions as he drove north, ever north, toward his moment of decision with the Jew doctor. Damn Bilal! Damn the Jew doctor! And damn the imam. Life had been hard but uncomplicated in the village. But at least there he knew who he was! Now he was confused, frightened, and alone.

The road ahead was crowded, but he knew that by the time he reached Afula the roads would be a lot less busy, and when he reached the Galilee the traffic would almost disappear. That would make driving easier, but it would also make his car more visible to the Israeli police and others who were constantly monitoring the nation. And Palestinians acting as Israeli spies were everywhere, watching every move of their fellow Palestinians and reporting their whereabouts to the authorities.

It took him four hours of cautious driving well within the speed limit to reach Nahariya. He parked his car on the outskirts of the city and caught a bus to the hospital, where he would spy on the doctor. Trying to appear inconspicuous, he studied the building directory and found the surgical wards on the third floor. He took the stairs, not the elevator, and meandered from corridor to corridor, trying to find the room where the surgeons gathered.

"Can I help you?" a nurse asked him.

"No!" he said. "No, I'm looking for . . ."

"A patient?"

"Yes, a patient. My uncle," Hassan lied.

"You really shouldn't be here outside of visiting hours. What's your uncle's name?"

Without thinking, he immediately said, "Ali."

The nurse smiled. At any time there could be twenty Alis in the hospital. "Ali who? What's his surname? Which ward is he in?"

Hassan looked at her blankly.

"Well, what's he in the hospital for?" she asked.

Hassan was suddenly frightened and shrugged. Then he turned and walked away quickly. He ran down the flights of stairs and out of the front entrance of the hospital, praying that the nurse wouldn't call security.

Sleeping in his car in the backstreets of the northern city, Hassan waited for two days before he had the courage to drive up to the hospital's parking lot. He could see the doors where doctors and nurses, patients and relatives, walked in and out, and he sat there, hour after hour for the entire day, hoping that she'd walk out of the hospital so that he could follow her home.

On the third day he was about to phone the imam and give him the coded message that his mission had failed, when Yael Cohen emerged from the doors of the hospital accompanied by two other people. Instead of a white coat, as he expected, she was dressed in jeans and a blue top with a white scarf. He watched her walk toward her car, parked four rows from his. She was young, fresh, confident, and gorgeous. And soon she would be dead.

As she got in, he turned the key and prepared to follow her. They left the hospital grounds and she drove northeast, away from the sea and in the direction of the Lebanese border. But what surprised him was that as she drove out of the center of the city, instead of heading for residential areas, she turned east and headed toward the hills. Her car was far more modern and powerful than his, and as she gunned her machine up the steep hills, she almost left him behind. Only when he came over the crown of a hill by pure luck did he see her far in the distance, on a road to the right and heading south. If he hadn't spotted her, he would have continued along the same road. Hassan turned in the new direction and followed as best he could. Theirs were the only cars on this road. After many miles, up hills and down into valleys, he saw a road sign. And in the distance he realized that she'd suddenly pulled over in the middle of a village. The sign told him that the village was Peki'in. It was his second time here; this time his goal was very different.

He parked in a lane, behind a badly battered and dusty forty-year-old Toyota truck. He took out the sports bag the imam had given him and hurried back to the main street that ran through the village. Hassan looked for her, hoping that she hadn't gone into any of the buildings. But she was nowhere to be seen. So, for the second time in less than a week, Hassan walked in the shadows of buildings on the periphery of the central square where the village's famous and constantly running spring had been dammed and flowed into the wide tiled reservoir. She could have gone in any direction, so he decided to stand in the shadows and wait for her. Though it was late in the afternoon, the heat was oppressive, and as the sun descended into the distant sea, it cast long shadows. Being a tiny village miles from nowhere, there were few cars and even fewer people.

As he waited on the periphery of the village square, he looked around for a tree or a building that would shield him from being observed. He would need such shade if he was going to point the rifle toward her. He would kill her as she emerged from a building into the empty street. He'd drop her when she was walking toward her car. He'd aim the bullet directly at her chest so that it exploded in her heart and she would die painlessly and instantly. He hoped.

It so much depended on whether or not she was alone, or in his sights, or if the setting sun wasn't in his eyes. For any of these reasons he'd quickly pack up the rifle and kill her with his revolver the moment she arrived at the door to her car. Hassan knew this was what he must do, for if he didn't, then the repercussions by the imam against him and possibly his family would be severe. But he silently prayed it would not come to this.

He'd squeeze the trigger carefully as he'd done in the hills above his village of Bayt al Gizah when he shot tin cans: narrow his eyes so that the target was more focused and then fire the gun. He might not even watch her die. He might just avert his eyes, squeeze the trigger, feel its recoil, then put the rifle away and escape.

He planned it in his head but couldn't help but see Yael fall to the ground, screaming in terror, blood spurting from the wound.

Could he do it? Shooting bottles and tin cans for target practice was a lot easier than shooting a woman in the heart.

Bilal's words from the prison rang in his ears. Had his brother really told the doctor about the imam, about the group which was to bring liberty to Palestine? Because if so, then his finger had to squeeze the trigger.

As he took out the rifle, checking that nobody was looking, he realized that his hands were shaking.

YAEL EMERGED from the village's central records repository half an hour later carrying a sheaf of papers. They'd been photocopied for her by the friendly young clerk, and now she had to determine what path of action to follow. In her hands were the records of families like that of Bilal, going back to the late 1800s.

But since she'd been in Nahariya, the urgency of finding out why her blood and Bilal's were linked seemed to have diminished. It had become secondary to her daily routine, and this time away from Jerusalem was a pleasant break. Although she'd conducted a number of surgeries, she found herself trying to justify this time off.

The pressure of her work in the hospital in Jerusalem, the speed and incoherence of the city, all lost their urgency to a calmness that seemed to have descended on her as she traveled north toward Galilee. Perhaps it was the rugged grandeur of the hills and valleys, or the individualism of the inhabitants, or the feeling of being so far from the cosmopolitanism of Jerusalem and Tel Aviv that did it. It was as though she were in a quieter, more laid-back world—a biblical world.

As she walked back to her car, the feeling of always needing to get somewhere, of always having to do something, simply wasn't there. She didn't have to rush back; she could take her time. She could sit in a café and have a cup of coffee. The one she'd been in the other day, the one with the awning, was close by, and so she sat down at a table and ordered a drink.

There were two other people seated beneath the awning at different tables. They were elderly men, and from their dress they were obviously senior members of the Druze community. They looked at her with indifference, quite used to Israeli tourists coming to the village and visiting the ancient synagogue.

———

THROUGH THE SCOPE of the rifle, Hassan could see her clearly, sitting and talking to the café owner about what she'd have to drink. He felt the wheel of the rifle's sights and twisted it to the left in order to make the image of her as sharp as a needle. The crosshairs of the rifle's sights blurred, then sharpened, then blurred again until his sweating fingers fixed them precisely on her head. He looked at the four quadrants through the sights: her forehead was high and she had a fringe of black hair that fell over her cheek before cascading down to caress her neck; her lips and cheeks felt so close, he could have kissed her. She was smiling at the café owner. Her neck was long and slender, and if he looked closely, he could see the delicate lines of her throat above the collar of her blouse. He put the rifle down to wipe the sweat from his eyes.

Hassan reached into the sports bag and took out the bottle of water, which he gulped down. He was thirsty, yet the cold water didn't relieve him. About to pick up the rifle to take the shot, he was disturbed by the sound of a car driving toward him. He immediately hid the rifle with his body and waited for it to go past. He looked at the passengers, who weren't interested in him as they drove toward the center of the village.

Enveloped in silence again, he picked up the rifle and looked through the sights at the doctor. The view was blocked by the broad back of the café owner, who was giving her a glass of something. When he left, she was still smiling at him, engaging him in gentle conversation. Now her whole body was visible again, sitting under the awning, drinking orange juice. He pressed the rifle stock against his cheek, put his finger on the trigger, breathed deeply, said a small prayer, and slowly, cautiously, without jerking the gun, began to squeeze the trigger.

There was firm resistance on the spring of the trigger and then a tiny metallic click. For an instant Hassan found himself wondering how small the sound of a gunshot could be until, through the sight, he saw that the doctor was still sipping her orange juice. Reluctantly Hassan pulled the trigger again. The same resistance and metallic click and silence.

He leaned back from the sight, turned the gun in his hands, and pulled at the bolt to open the breech. The mechanism would not shift. He yanked at it with a strange panic rising in him. What was he afraid of? Missing the shot? That the gun might explode? The wrath of the imam? The fate of Bilal, who had also failed?

Hassan yanked again, vigorously trying to dislodge whatever had jammed the rifle, but to no avail. He looked up into the distance to see the doctor still sitting at the far table. She wasn't leaving—not yet. He stopped pulling on the bolt lever and instead took a deep breath and tried to calm himself. He looked at his hands. They were sweating and shaking. He got to his knees and briskly wiped them on his shirt to dry them. And still the doctor sat at the table.

Hassan reached into the sports bag beside him and his fingers closed around the handle of the pistol concealed inside. It was warm to the touch, the sun heating the bag and the metal of the gun's grip. He drew it out, and stood and stared down at the distant figure of the doctor at the café, the words of Bilal screaming in his ear: *"She is the only one who can help me!"*

AS YAEL SAT GAZING over the empty square, with only the occasional car or pedestrian disturbing the silence, she saw a young man carrying an old sports bag walking toward the café.

He sat down three tables away and stared at the menu. He was dressed in jeans and a T-shirt, common to young people throughout the world. But unlike the Druzim who glanced at her indifferently, this young man immediately looked away the moment her eyes met his. He looked up into the enormous carob tree, then at the pool in the middle of the square, then up at the birds perched on top of the buildings.

Yael didn't give it another thought and slowly sipped the fresh orange juice that the owner had squeezed for her. She read some of the papers, but something drew her to look at the young man again. And the moment she did, she realized that he'd been staring at her. She smiled at him, but he immediately averted his eyes again.

Hassan's muscles felt like coiled steel. She was right in front of him, although he looked everywhere but at her. He willed himself to be invisible. The pistol was lead in his hand as it threatened to slip from his sweaty fingers and clatter on the ground.

They were not alone. There were others at the café. When he did what must be done, he would have to run, run as far and as fast as he could. He might be caught or he might escape, *inshallah*. But as he looked anywhere except at the woman he must kill, he thought of Bilal and the fate of one who had failed.

But still the words of his friend would not be silent in his ears. *"She is the only one who can help me."*

Hassan rose to his feet . . .

———

YAEL WATCHED as the young man suddenly stood and pushed the chair back. He walked quickly out of the café and into the main square. He'd neither eaten nor drunk anything, and he hadn't even spoken to the café owner. Odd. But Yael thought nothing of it except that as she looked at him, he suddenly stopped at the edge of the pool, as though deep in thought, as if his reflection in the water were his alter ego. Then he turned and faced her. In embarrassment, Yael glanced back at her papers until she realized, to her profound disquiet, that he was walking straight toward her table.

She could feel him coming closer and closer and something deep inside her clenched tight like a knotted rope. She didn't look up but her peripheral vision saw his shadow, his shape, as he walked to her table. She felt that she should run, that she should have listened to the warnings of her friends not to come here. People like her weren't welcome here. People like her . . .

The chair opposite scraped backward and the young man sat sharply down on it. Leaning forward across the table, he whispered, "I have a gun. It is in my hand under the table and I will kill you if you speak."

Yael did not make a sound. Her eyes, too afraid to move, were locked on his, fixed like those of a coma patient.

The young man swallowed and whispered, "You are Dr. Cohen. Aren't you?"

"Yes." Yael's voice was dry as dust.

"I . . ." Hassan halted and both of them waited what felt like an eternity for him to speak again. He reached over and drank some of her orange juice. Amazingly, this arrogance annoyed her as much as she was shocked by him saying he had a gun. His hand clenched and unclenched the handle of the pistol beneath the table.

"I was sent to kill you . . ."

She so desperately wanted to scream for help, but Yael was suddenly struck mute. And her fear was replaced by confusion when Hassan continued. "You saved my friend, Bilal, didn't you?"

It wasn't really a question and Yael had no conscious intention to answer. But she felt her lips move nonetheless. "Yes, I did," she gasped. And then reason slowly subsumed fear as a strange courage welled up from nowhere. "Who are you?"

Hassan was sweating profusely despite the breeze. He gulped down more orange juice, but this time it didn't matter to Yael. His next words sounded as though they were forced out of his body. "You must swear to me, swear on the most holy, that you will say nothing to anybody about what I'm going to tell you."

"You have a gun. Just ask and I'll swear to you anything."

The young man looked as though he were sinking into despair. The muscles in his face seemed to twitch as if he might collapse. "You must swear," he insisted through gritted teeth.

"Why? What do you want? What did I do?" The questions tumbled out of Yael's mouth in quiet gasps.

Hassan didn't answer but his eyes didn't leave Yael's.

"How do you know Bilal?" asked Yael, reaching out for something, anything.

The effect of the question on Hassan was profound. His shoulders slumped and his eyes dropped. "He is my friend. My brother. I was ordered to kill you. But . . ."

Yael hung on to the silence, hoping he'd continue.

"It's all gone so wrong . . ." Hassan's eyes suddenly filled with tears, which he didn't blink away. His gaze returned to Yael, but this time it was like looking at a different man: determination had devolved almost at once into exhaustion.

"I was ordered to kill you, but Bilal . . . he told me . . . he said you were the only one I could trust. He said you were the only one who could save him . . ."

EVEN THE PRISON GOVERNOR, who had seen most things in his twelve years superintending one of the most fractious penal colonies in Israel, was surprised by the number of visitors the remand prisoner was getting.

First it was the police taking statements; then a government lawyer appointed by the courts; then his imam; then the kid's cousin; then a journalist, and heaven only knows how he managed to get permission to interview the lad; and now it was a senior officer from Shin Bet.

But provided they had the right clearance papers, there were no grounds for him to object. The governor's sole responsibility was to ensure the kid's welfare and that he showed up for his day in court. After that, he would likely be some other prison commander's problem. Although he'd carried bombs, they hadn't gone off, and his crime was murder, so once he'd been through the courts, he'd probably go to an ordinary prison and not one for Arab terrorists or Palestinian militants, like this prison.

He knew the man from Shin Bet. They'd met in a conference in Hadera on internal security where he'd given a speech and they discussed how to process Palestinian informers in the prison system. That was four years earlier, and he was surprised at how much the Shin Bet man had aged and some of his hair had turned white.

Obviously this kid was something more than your average fanatic and the meeting didn't sit comfortably with the governor—not at all.

———

ELIAHU WAITED in the interview room for Bilal to be brought to him for interrogation. Within a minute the door opened and one of the section guards walked in. He was followed by Bilal. The young man entered with a strangely hopeful air, but that quickly vanished when Bilal saw Eliahu behind the table, and he stopped dead at the door to the room and wouldn't move.

"Inside, you," ordered the guard.

Bilal shook his head. "No. No!"

Eliahu Spitzer stood from behind the desk. In fluent Arabic, he said gently, "Bilal, calm down. I just want to talk to you."

"No!" Bilal shouted. "No, I'm not going in there. Not with him. Put me back in my cell. I won't talk to this man."

"What the hell's got into you, boy?" demanded the guard. "Stop being so fucking stupid." Losing patience, the guard grabbed him by the shoulder and forced him into the room. The guard was a huge Russian who'd emigrated six years before from St. Petersburg, and Bilal was no match for his brute strength. He sat him in the chair and tethered the handcuffs to one of the armrests.

"Why handcuff him?" asked Eliahu.

"Standard procedure," said the guard, who retreated to the wall.

"I want to be alone with the prisoner," demanded Eliahu.

"No," said the Russian.

"I said I want to be alone. Now leave."

The Russian looked at him coldly. "I can't do that."

Eliahu looked at him coldly. "It's not a request."

The guard didn't know who Eliahu was, but he knew, just from his manner, just from the way he presented himself, that he was authority, and as a Russian he knew that he had to do as authority demanded. He knew better than to argue any further. But as the big Russian left the room he decided the governor should know the man was alone with the prisoner. The governor was famous for his micromanagement.

As the guard closed the door, Eliahu turned his attention solemnly to Bilal. "So, my young friend. You seem to have been in the wars," he said so impassively that he could have been having a conversation in a café with a friend.

"What do you want? What are you going to do with me?"

Eliahu picked up his briefcase from the floor and placed it on the desk between them. "Y'know, Bilal, there comes a time when it's better for everybody that a sacrifice is made. Your sacrifice was supposed to be on the Western Wall of the Temple . . ."

Bilal tried to get out of the chair but the handcuffs kept him tethered. He shook them in a vain attempt to free himself, but it was useless, and the chair was bolted to the concrete floor. "What are you doing here? Why are you doing this? I don't understand."

"You've seen things, Bilal. Things you were never meant to see."

Again Bilal tried to break free from his chains.

Eliahu opened his briefcase and took out a hypodermic needle. "Calm down, Bilal. This will make you into a martyr—just what you wanted."

Bilal looked at it in unutterable fear. Here, again, was Malak al-Maut, the Angel of Death. He'd come a second time for Bilal, just as he'd come to the hospital.

Suddenly his body went limp, as though all energy and fight had gone out of him. He was about to die. He could scream but it wouldn't help. He could fight and kick, but the man would just stand behind him. His only hope was to play for time. And pray.

"May I first say a prayer?" he asked softly.

Eliahu smiled. "No, my friend. You'll have plenty of time to pray in heaven . . . or wherever it is you people go."

He pulled out a vial of clear liquid and stuck the hypodermic needle into the rubber end of the bottle. He sucked a syringe full of the liquid and returned the bottle to his case. For some reason Bilal noticed that the Jew didn't push a small amount of liquid out of the needle, as he'd seen on many American television hospital dramas.

Eliahu began to stand, when, above the general noise of the prison, footsteps could be heard in the corridor coming nearer and nearer. Suddenly the door of the room opened and Eliahu hid the needle behind the opened lid of his briefcase.

The prison governor walked into the room with a different air from their first greeting in his office.

"You might be important where you come from, Spitzer, but in this prison I make the rules, and people who come in here obey them. No prisoner can be left alone with a visitor for any reason, ever. My guard stays in this room. Is that quite clear?"

Bilal turned and screamed at the governor, "He was trying to kill me!"

The governor looked quickly at both of them and said, "Shut up, Bilal. Now listen to me, Mr. Shin Bet. You may be a big shit in Jerusalem, but you're not even a fart in my prison."

Eliahu tilted his head quizzically in an image of terse surprise at the interference. He wasn't used to being either commanded or contradicted. "There's no need to be crude, Governor. The matters I'm discussing with the prisoner are of the strictest secrecy. These are issues of national security. There is to be no one present."

The governor's feet were planted and he was not going to budge.

Again Bilal screamed, "He was trying to kill me! In his bag—"

Furious, the governor said, "If you don't shut up, prisoner, I'll have you gagged." Then he looked coldly at Eliahu and said softly and menacingly, "If it's about national security, I'll need to see a court order allowing you to be alone. What do you think we're going to do? Put it on Al Jazeera? Until I'm ordered to by the courts, the prisoner will be accompanied at all times. There's no room to move on this."

Bilal was near to hysteria. "He's trying to kill me!"

"I told you to shut the fuck up!" shouted the governor. "Well?" he said, looking at Eliahu.

Eliahu stood in silence, his eyes never leaving the governor. A contest of wills. Finally he nodded, closed the briefcase, and said, "I'll be back. This prisoner has more to tell me."

He left the room and a shaking Bilal behind.

———

YAEL WAS ALONE in her hotel room. She had closed the blinds, shielding her from the glaring Mediterranean sun, and sat cross-legged on the bed. The phone was in front of her, and when she had reached out to make a call, she saw her hand was still trembling. She was petrified by the confrontation with Hassan, but there was, at the same time, a resolve inside her that refused to allow her to crumble or cry. Her fear, her panic, was replaced by deep and profound anger.

She had tried to persuade Hassan to come with her, persuade him that they could go to the police, but the suggestion had sent Hassan into a panic and he had dashed away, leaving her alone with the memory of a hit man with a loaded gun.

Yael steadied her hand, picked up the phone, and called Yaniv.

She had barely finished telling him about Hassan when he cut her off.

"Yael, be quiet. Stop talking."

"But—"

"Shut up. Not another word. Don't say your location or anything. You need to listen to me. Leave the area you're in immediately . . ."

The area you're in. The phrase was deliberately vague.

"Tell nobody where you're going. Just get into your car; drive on back roads if you can. I'll meet you in the place where we had our first cup of coffee—don't say the name of the place. Take your battery out of your cell phone immediately; take the SIM card out and drive to where we first met. Just say whether or not you understand me."

"Okay. Ok—"

"Not okay!" he shouted. "Yes or no. Do you understand me?"

"Yes!"

"Good," said Yaniv. "Then do it now—immediately!"

He hung up on her. She was offended by his rudeness, but then she realized she was still in shock from Hassan. For nearly a whole minute Yael looked at her cell phone as though it were an unexploded bomb. She followed Yaniv's instructions and removed the battery and the SIM card. She was so frightened that she put them into separate pockets, as though they could talk to each other otherwise.

She threw her things into a suitcase, paid at reception, got into the car, and drove first north toward the Lebanese border, then east toward Jordan and Syria, then south on minor roads until she approached the intersections that divided the country between the hills where Jerusalem was situated and the sea on the edge of which Jaffa and Tel Aviv stood.

In a few hours she parked her car in a side street away from the grounds of the Jerusalem Hospital and walked four blocks toward the back entrance. Two flights of stairs took her to the main reception area, and a minute later she was sitting in the café where she and Yaniv had met and drunk coffee the day after her television appearance at the museum. Yaniv was already seated. He didn't smile at her as she approached the table.

"Are you okay?"

"Nothing about this is okay. What's going on, Yaniv? What could Bilal possibly know that suddenly makes me a target? I'm only his doctor, for God's sake."

"I don't know," he said, and to Yael it felt like the first truly honest thing he had ever said to her. A flat answer without journalistic qualification or bombast.

"I don't know what Bilal knows. He wouldn't tell me. But—" said Yaniv, stopping himself short.

"What?" Yael asked impatiently.

"When Bilal was in the hospital, did he have visitors?" asked Yaniv, but it wasn't really a question.

"Not many," replied Yael. "His imam came. His parents when I arranged it."

"And someone else. A Shin Bet commander named Eliahu Spitzer."

"So? Bilal tried to blow up the Western Wall. Of course security people would want to speak to him."

Yaniv shook his head. "Eliahu Spitzer is one of the most senior men in Shin Bet. Him coming down to talk to Bilal is like the minister of health doing rounds to check on your patients. It doesn't make sense."

"But what's that got to do with these Arabs who want to kill me?" asked Yael.

From her tone, Yaniv knew that she was getting frustrated. "Spitzer was a hugely successful field operative with internal security. But then his daughter was killed in a Hamas bombing of a school bus," he said in almost a whisper.

"I remember that bombing. Four or so years ago. Twelve young boys and girls—terrible."

"A little while later he has a massive heart attack. After a couple of years of recuperation, he goes back to Shin Bet and a desk job. But he comes back a different man. He was always a conservative and hard-liner with the Palestinians, but suddenly, according to my sources, he starts wearing a yarmulke and going to synagogue like clockwork . . ."

"Finding religion when your child dies? Hardly anything unusual about that," said Yael.

"There's more to it. He alienated himself from his colleagues. I know a few of them from my work, and they told me he was a guy who used to be well liked, but when he came back from sick leave he was suddenly introverted and secretive. But that's nothing. According to them, he was saying really bizarre things and acting strangely. Some people in Shin Bet thought he'd gone gaga since the operation and the murder of his daughter. So they began to watch him closely. They were worried about him inadvertently breaching security."

Yael couldn't see anything wrong with the situation. She was used to the consequences of death on people, and it all sounded normal to her. Yaniv knew she was doubting the seriousness of what he was saying, so he leaned forward like a conspirator and said softly, "When they began to examine him closely, they suffered unusual incidents. Two of his operatives died meeting informants in Gaza. These are the undercover agents who look and dress and speak like Arabs, guys who had been working in Gaza for a decade. But suddenly they're uncovered, caught, and killed, and their bodies turn up torn to pieces in a field near Ashkelon. And Spitzer? He doesn't even go to the funerals."

"But that doesn't mean anything . . ."

"Maybe, but both of these guys, according to a contact of mine, had filed confidential internal reports saying they were concerned about the behavior of Eliahu Spitzer."

"Behavior?"

"I couldn't get the details of what they'd written. Those files are buried if they still exist at all, which I doubt. But last year I was tipped off about Spitzer, and I interviewed the two guys' widows. I know that their husbands were worried by the change that had come over him since his massive heart attack. When he came back to work, he threw himself into it despite being told by the head of the agency to take it easy. He was rabid about the Palestinians, demanding more and more from his staff, as though something had been triggered while he was ill. He went from calm and methodical to being an attack dog. Suddenly, he'd throw caution to the wind and send his guys out on reckless missions. So the two guys complained . . ." Yaniv leaned back in his chair and Yael couldn't help but see the journalist's flair for drama come out, despite the circumstances.

"So? That could be put down to the effects of the operation he must have undergone, and his recovery. Not uncommon in people who have suffered trauma and illness. I see it in cancer patients and—"

Yaniv cut her off and continued: "So a week after the funerals Spitzer is seen in the ultra-Orthodox neighborhood of Mea Shearim."

She was shocked. Yael couldn't find a reason to explain Spitzer's behavior. Mea Shearim was a place avoided by all but the most fervent of religious Israelis.

"Black hats and side locks everywhere, and he's greeted like a long-lost brother. People who saw him say he was taken to the home of Rabbi Shmuel Telushkin, one of the leaders of Neturei Karta. He was the bastard who was at the Holocaust denial conference in Tehran."

Yael looked at him in astonishment. "Neturei Karta? You're kidding. Mea Shearim I could understand. That would explain the sudden finding of faith. But Neturei Karta, those bastards . . . ?"

Yaniv sighed. "I need to understand the connection between him and this rabbi. Something's rotten. A top-ranking Shin Bet officer visiting the Neturei Karta, a group opposed to the Jewish state? And a top Shin Bet man visiting Bilal? It doesn't make sense. And now Bilal is terrified someone is trying to kill him . . ."

Yaniv let the phrase hang in the air before continuing: "And then this Hassan kid shows up saying he's meant to kill you but can't bring himself to do it because—"

Yael didn't let him finish. "What does Bilal know?"

"That's the question . . . And the only person he'll talk to is you."

———

As YAEL WAITED in the small room for Bilal to be brought in, the full weight of growing fear began to seep into her. Being fearful of Palestinians who wanted her dead was one thing, but what Yaniv had said about Eliahu Spitzer was like being caught in a vise.

She didn't need Yaniv to explain to her how dangerous someone like him could be. But the shadow of who he was, and the power he wielded within Shin Bet, made her fearful of everyone.

To her mind, anyone could be in league with him; anyone around her could be a Shin Bet agent. Like many Israelis, she had grown up with the perpetual threat of suicide bombings, which had ingrained a hard-to-shake apprehension of Palestinians. But now she was afraid of everyone, Jew and Arab alike, and trusted no one.

Getting in to see Bilal had been surprisingly easy. She didn't need connections or strings pulled as Yaniv had been forced to do. Prisoners were entitled to medical treatment, and as Bilal's doctor with valid hospital credentials she was entitled to check up on her patient after such a complex operation. To sweeten the story, she told the warden she intended to write a medical journal paper on the rare kidney surgery and needed to discuss this with Bilal. She was, of course, searched and had to leave all personal items except her stethoscope behind, but was admitted to the small room and now waited for Bilal to arrive.

Bilal's eyes widened in shocked relief when he saw Yael in the room. But he said nothing until he was seated and the guard had retreated to the corner.

"Hello, Bilal," Yael said in English, her eyes flicking over to the guard to scan for a reaction. He looked from her to Bilal and back and she took this as a sign that he likely spoke English; most Israelis did. She then switched to Arabic.

"Are you well?" Again she looked to the guard, who wrinkled his nose and lost interest, staring at his feet. Reasonably confident the guard didn't speak Arabic and wouldn't understand what they were saying, she pressed on. "Bilal, I've met your friend. Hassan."

Bilal took a deep breath and exhaled slowly.

"Is he okay?"

"I think so," said Yael. "I . . . I don't know for sure. He ran away. He told me you're afraid that someone was trying to hurt you."

"Please, Doctor . . ." Bilal's voice was firm and low but his eyes were desperate. "They are coming for me."

"Who is?" she asked, although she knew the answer. She found herself wanting confirmation rather than an answer.

"Men in here want me dead for being a traitor. But I don't fear them. It's the man with the white hair . . ."

"Has he been to see you?" asked Yael.

"He tried to kill me. Right here in this room." Bilal's voice was flat. Calm. Almost resigned.

"Why do you think this is happening to you?"

With nothing left to hide and no doubt now that his life was close to ending, it was time to speak. In hushed tones he told Yael about the attempt on his life by the prisoner Ibrahim just after the imam had visited; about the visit from the man from Shin Bet—the skunk—and the hypodermic needle. And finally he told Yael about driving the imam to the meeting, about Spitzer and the old religious Jew.

It was this final confirmation that seemed to put the entire thing together for Yael. All the pieces had been inchoate until Bilal spoke of the rabbi. What Yaniv had told her about the Neturei Karta and Spitzer, the confrontation with Hassan, the imam in the hospital. All the pieces refused to align until this one last scrap of information. And over it all were the remarkable strands of shimmering DNA that connected her with this young man.

"I want to help you, Bilal. But I don't know how," said Yael. "I don't know where to begin."

"You don't believe me?"

"I want to, but it doesn't matter what I believe."

"But that bastard Ibrahim, he tried to kill me in here. I broke his arm. The Shin Bet man tried to kill me. A miracle stopped him. They won't just kill me, they will kill my family!" he said.

As emotion caused him to raise his voice, the guard looked up and eyed them suspiciously.

"It's fine," Yael said to the guard with a forced smile. "He thinks I'm trying to steal his organs."

The guard snorted and went back to the magazine he was reading. Yael turned back to Bilal.

"I know you're scared. And I believe you. If what you saw is true, then . . ." Yael didn't really know what would happen if it was true. Instead she said, "But there's no proof. There's no way to prove what you say. He can explain meeting the imam—just part of his job; he could probably even explain away meeting him with the old rabbi—"

"I know what I saw. I was his driver. I was there. I know what I saw."

"But we can't just take your word for it, Bilal."

Suddenly his face went dark, his eyes narrowed as if he were trying to focus on a faint memory. "My phone!"

"Your phone? What phone?" asked Yael.

"That night. The camera on my phone. Hassan stole it from a Jew in the market and gave it to me. I used the camera on my phone. It was new and I was playing around with it. On my phone . . ."

"Where is your phone? What happened to it?" asked Yael, an urgency rising in her throat that she quickly swallowed back in case the guard noticed.

"I don't know. After the bomb, I woke up in the hospital. My stomach hurt. My leg hurt . . . my clothes . . . I don't know."

Yael's mind raced back to that fateful day. She remembered Bilal in triage, remembered surveying his wounds, his closed hand, the fragments of rock that she had taken from his fingers. His clothes were cut from his body, soaked in blood. His cheap plastic bracelet, his shoes, his . . .

"The hospital!" said Yael suddenly. "Your phone. Your possessions and clothes. They're always put into a secure bag in the hospital. It's standard security. After a certain amount of time, they'll be sent to your parents. Your phone might still be in the hospital."

Bilal took a sharp intake of breath and Yael thought for a second he might smile.

She reached across the desk and grabbed his hand, holding it firm.

"No touching!" shouted the guard. She thought he was reading his magazine. She withdrew her hand.

"Bilal, I'm going to do whatever I can to help you."

He nodded. Solemnly. As if he wanted to believe her.

"You stay alive, okay?"

He nodded again.

She'd felt the warmth of his body through his hand. The sweat and texture of his skin. The pulse of blood. Blood they shared.

"My parents . . ." Bilal paused as if unable to say the rest. "Please go to them . . . tell them . . . Tell them I'm sorry . . ."

———

YAEL WAITED UNTIL SHE was safely away from the prison and heading back to the city. Yaniv had warned her not to drive her car but to take public transportation. But she had ignored this suggestion. With one hand on the wheel and the other on a cheap phone she'd bought in a suburban phone store with a pay-as-you-use SIM card, she dialed his number.

"It's me," Yael said.

"Have you left?"

"Yes. I'm heading back to Jerusalem. I think I have something."

"Did you get a new phone?"

"Yes," she replied. So had he. "Bilal said that the night he was there when he saw the three men, he had a smartphone that had been stolen in Jerusalem. Anyway, he said he was fooling around with the phone's camera and that he may have a video of the three men together. He can't remember, but he was pretty excited."

"Where's the phone now?"

"I think it might be at the hospital."

"I doubt it," said Yaniv. "Shin Bet would have taken it for examination."

"Maybe. But I can have a look. It's on my way, regardless."

"On your way to where?" asked Yaniv, concern rising in his voice.

"He's terrified, Yaniv. I don't think he's going to last much longer in there."

"You can't stop that, Yael. He's not your problem. I'll find a way to break the story, but it won't save him. He's history, I'm afraid."

"And that's why I have to—"

"Have to what?" demanded Yaniv.

"I have to see Bilal's parents."

"Are you out of your mind?" he shouted in exasperation.

"I have to."

"Yael, for God's sake, you—"

"I owe them, Yaniv! They don't deserve what's happened to their son. One of their kids is already in prison; now their other son has been locked up. Bilal isn't the source of the problem . . . I have to tell the parents."

"But the phone . . . it's more important than—"

Yael didn't wait for an answer and quickly turned off the phone.

———

ON THE DRIVE FROM THE PRISON, Yael felt a sense of guilt that she wasn't going back to the hospital to look for Bilal's phone. But her mind was set on the image of Bilal's grieving parents and the bloodline she knew they shared.

An hour later she was again sitting in Bilal's family home in the village of Bayt al Gizah. Across from her were Fuad and Maryam. It was the first time Yael had seen the mother and father together for more than a few moments. Maryam's face was streaked with tears but her composure was solemn, quiet, restrained.

"I know this is hard for you to hear. I'm so sorry to be the bearer of such awful news," said Yael.

"You say people want to kill my son? The other prisoners want to kill my son?"

"I think they have been ordered to. I think Bilal knows something that is putting him in great danger."

Fuad shook his head. "My son has gone mad, Doctor. He is talking crazy. He needs some pills for his mind."

"No, Fuad. He's not crazy. He's scared but he's not crazy."

Yael couldn't tell them about Eliahu Spitzer or the Neturei Karta rabbi, but she could ask about somebody they knew. She carefully softened her voice and said, "How well do you know your imam here in the village?"

Fuad shrugged. "He is new. He's not been here more than a year. The young men, they flock to him. But . . ."

"But what?" she asked.

"I say nothing more. To me, I don't like what he has to say. I don't go no more to mosque to pray. Not in a long time. Why do you ask this?"

"A young man was sent to kill me," said Yael, trying to sound matter-of-fact to remove the anger in her voice.

Maryam clapped her hand over her mouth in shock, and Fuad eyed Yael incredulously.

Yael told the couple about Hassan, that he had been ordered by the imam to kill her, the same man of God who also wanted Bilal dead for betraying them.

Fuad and Maryam sat in silence as Yael told her story.

Then Fuad said softly, "You must go to the police. You must have him arrested."

"I can't. Hassan won't testify, and aside from him I have

nothing. The imam will laugh it off, as if I'm the one who's nuts. I didn't want to come here. I didn't want to tell you these things. I was afraid."

"Why did you come here, Doctor? If what you say is true, why did you take such a risk?" asked Fuad.

Yael bit her lip before replying. "Bilal asked me to. He wanted me to tell you that he was sorry." The final word broke Maryam's composure and tears fell unabated from her eyes. Fuad drew in a long, deep breath through his nose and exhaled as if breathing out smoke from a cigarette.

"I don't know what I can do. But we need to make sure that the imam doesn't know that we suspect him."

Suddenly, and completely unexpectedly, Maryam interjected. "Why?"

Fuad looked at his wife in shock. His wife never interrupted when her husband was in the room.

"Because the imam—" began Yael, but Maryam cut her off.

"No. Why are you doing this for Bilal? You are a Jew. He is a Muslim who killed a Jew. Why are you helping Bilal . . . helping us?"

The question was direct and sharp and Yael had no answer. The best she could stammer was "I'm a doctor."

But Maryam shook her head. She became vehement. "No, Doctor. Other doctors would not have lied to keep him in the hospital so my husband and I could see him. And no Jewish doctor would have come here to try to save his life and warn us of these things. Why do you do this?"

"Enough!" said Fuad angrily. "Leave, Maryam." He offered no explanation and Maryam asked for none. She simply stood and left the room.

Part of Yael was angered by Fuad's dismissive rudeness and arrogance, but the rest of her was relieved that she didn't have to answer the question. And as Fuad turned back to face her, she wondered if he, too, wanted an answer. But instead Fuad looked Yael squarely in the eyes and spoke in hushed tones.

"I lost my son. He was lost from me years ago. He wanted more than I could offer. He wanted a reason we live like this. This imam . . . he gave the reason. Now there is nothing for him here. I tried but . . ." Fuad's words trailed off. Yael felt as if she should say something but didn't.

"Guns. Bombs. He thinks there are answers in these things. But there is only blood—first one son, now another." Tears welled in the old man's eyes, and he did nothing to stop them from falling down his face.

———

YAEL DROVE SLOWLY along the road away from Fuad's house. The image of the weeping father scorched her mind. She turned right to ascend the hill that led to the major road skirting the hills of Jerusalem and taking her back into the northern parts of the city. But to her surprise, as she passed a lane that ran close to the rear of Bilal's home, a woman dressed in Arab clothes with a hijab pulled down low and hiding much of her face suddenly jumped out into the path of her car. Yael braked sharply, but before she could recover from the shock, the woman came around to the passenger's side, opened the door, and climbed in. "Drive. Quickly," she said.

Yael didn't have time to answer before the woman took off her hijab. It was Maryam. "Please, good Doctor, drive before I'm seen in here."

"Maryam, what's this about?"

"Drive. I beg you. Away from eyes that look out of windows."

So Yael drove toward the main road, but before she reached it, she turned left into a side street and parked the car.

"Is this all right?" she asked Maryam.

The Arab woman nodded but pulled the hijab over her head and around most of her face so that she would be unrecognizable.

"I don't understand. What are you doing?" asked Yael.

"There are things I can't say in front of my husband. Things that my mother told me and for which I'm sworn to secrecy."

"What's this got to do with me?"

Maryam sighed long and hard. "You're a good woman, Dr. Yael. You saved my Bilal and now, if it pleases Allah, you'll save him again. I don't know why you're saving him, because he killed one of yours, but I open my heart to you and place it in your hands."

Yael said softly, "Things your mother told you? I'm confused."

"She told me what her mother told her, and her mother before her . . . and her mother before that. I don't know when it was. I don't know where it was. I'm not an educated woman. I have little schooling. I have a letter written by a woman who I think is my great-great-great-grandmother. I don't know for sure. I don't understand. I can't read it. It's a letter," said Maryam.

"Can I see this letter? Perhaps I can get it translated for you."

Maryam hesitated. "Dr. Yael, for a hundred years or more, the women of my family have kept this letter from all eyes. When we are given this letter, on the day of our wedding, our mothers tell us a story and swear us to secrecy."

Yael had no idea what this was about, but the gravity in Maryam's voice told her that it was a crucial moment in her life and if Yael were to pressure her, the woman would run from the car like a frightened fawn. So she remained silent and smiled at Maryam reassuringly, reaching over and touching her shoulder.

"My mother told me this story on the day I married Fuad. I break the vow of silence, and I tell you because my Bilal, who has been led astray and done terrible things, I will never ever see again. My Bilal . . ." She began to sob. Yael reached over, pulled Maryam gently toward her, and hugged her while she sobbed. Maryam did not pull away and the two women sat silently for a brief but eternal moment.

"I'm sorry, but when you told my Fuad about why you came to see us, I realized that, for the first time in a hundred years, our great family shame must be made known. It is the only way that I might save him."

Yael wanted to ask a thousand questions, but her understanding of what was motivating Maryam forced her to remain silent.

"He is in that prison because he is a Palestinian, isn't he? If he were a Jew, he would be in a better prison, wouldn't he?"

Yael remained silent.

"If I told you that he wasn't Palestinian, he wasn't Arab, he would be released?"

Of course Bilal would not be released. Jewish or Muslim, he was still a murderer. But such thoughts were a thousand miles away. Maryam's questions were rhetorical, driven by hope and ignorance. Yael continued her silence.

"My Bilal is born a Jew. I am Jew. My mother was Jew. By blood. It is my great shame, Dr. Yael. It is my great secret."

Too stunned to say anything, Yael watched Maryam take a letter out of her pocket, thrust it at her, open the car door, and run down the hill. Watching her disappear, Yael was too stunned to move or even breathe.

When Maryam was no longer in view and had disappeared into the lanes that took her back to her house, Yael sufficiently recovered from the shock to take the ancient letter from its yellowed and creased envelope. It reminded her of taking the precious stone out of Bilal's hand and holding it as though it were divine.

Carefully she opened the folds of the letter. The once-white pages were tinged with brown from age, but the writing in black ink, although faded, was still clearly visible.

Her heart was pounding as she looked at the lettering. It wasn't Arabic; it was written in the Latin alphabet. And German. But it also had overtones of Yiddish. Yael read the first few lines, and tried hard to remember either the German she'd heard from her father's mother or the Yiddish her *bubbeh* had spoken when she didn't want Yael or her brother to know what she was saying. And she especially remembered her grandmother, an elegant and sophisticated Russian lady, who would never use bad language in English yet would swear like a trooper in Yiddish.

Yael read first the Germanic Yiddish:

Um meine liebste Tochter,
  Ich schreibe diesen leter Ihnen in der Hoffnung dass . . .

Quickly, she translated the German into her own language of Ivrit, modern Hebrew. She would read and translate the rest of the letter when she was safely at home:

To my dearest daughter,
  I write this letter to you in the hope that . . .

Yael looked up through the windshield into the distance. There was Jerusalem, shining a blistering white in the afternoon sun, the burnished dome of the al-Aqsa Mosque burning brilliantly like a gold candle on a huge white birthday cake. Then she looked down again at the letter. How was it that over a hundred years ago, probably even a century and a half ago, a mother had written a letter to her daughter in Yiddish and the descendant was today a Palestinian woman, the mother of an imprisoned terrorist?

———

YAEL'S MIND was a sprawling chaos of revelations. Her world had been rocked and the daily grind of surgery and hospital corridors that had been her norm for so long seemed the life of a different person right now.

Yaniv's claims about this Shin Bet operative; the imam being in league with the fanatical Neturei Karta; Bilal possibly being a Jew because of his matriarchal bloodline, a line passed down

from mother to mother since . . . since . . . maybe from the time
when the prophets were wandering the land, warning of doom
and gloom . . . It was all too much.

She had checked in for the night to a tiny hotel in the center of
the city. She feared going back to her apartment. If Hassan could
find her in Peki'in, then they, whoever their agents were, could certainly find where she lived. Going to Bilal's family home had been
reckless but necessary; although she felt like hunted prey, she was
still a doctor, a human being, and her responsibilities had domi-
nated. So she drove straight into the city, stayed where there were
the most people in the most public space, and found a random
hotel—the kind of hotel that took cash and didn't ask for names.

With blinds closed and door locked she sat at a small desk
and struggled to read the letter Maryam had given her in the
desperate hope it might save her son from prison. Its chances of
changing anything about Bilal's fate were virtually nonexistent,
but the letter haunted her nonetheless.

She stared at the strange blend of languages and phrases trying to translate, but she was defeated by the German language.
Sleeping fitfully, she waited until morning, when she switched
on her cell phone. She knew it was early, but she knew that the
person she was dialing was at his office at six in the morning
without fail.

"Yes?" he said.

"Shalman, hi, it's Yael."

"*Bubbeleh,* darling, how are you? So what's new? You're
calling—you hardly ever call. It's so early. Is everything all
right? Why so early? Are you okay? Of course you're okay, because if you weren't okay, you'd have said something. You want
me. Good! What? Anything, *bubbeleh.* Tell Shalman."

She knew that the first few moments of their conversation
would be like this: questions, guilt; he was like a Jewish mother
except that he was her Jewish grandfather. And she loved him so
much for all his quirky ways.

"I have something I want to show you."

"Oh my God! Not another artifact! One is a gift, two is show-ing off!"

"No, nothing like that. Well, not quite. It's a letter. In German. I need you to help me. It's not something that I can translate be-cause I need to understand the nuances."

"Translations, anybody. Nuances, come see me." He put down the phone.

Half an hour later, she was sitting opposite him, drinking cof-fee and eating a doughnut while he read the letter, making care-ful notes. When he'd finished it, he put down his pen, and Yael said, "Well, what do—"

But he held up his hand, turned the letter over, and began from the beginning. "For a translation, I read once. For nuances, twice, sometimes three times."

When he finished this time, he looked up at her and smiled. "From where did this come?"

"From the mother of a patient I'm looking after."

"Some in low Yiddish, some in an attempt at high German. The person who wrote this wasn't very clever or educated, so Goethe or Hegel she's not; this was written by a mother to her daughter. She's obviously trying to impress her with her use of words, yet often she uses confusing phrases and more sophisticated words in the wrong context.

"This letter was written as an explanation for a daughter, al-most an *apologia*, by a lady named Malka; in Hebrew, of course, it means queen, but she didn't call herself by her German name, which would have been Konigin. That would have sounded stu-pid. It was written to her daughter but she didn't call the girl by name."

"Okay, you lost me," Yael said in protest at the incoherent ex-planation.

"*Bubbeleh*, it speaks about a time and a place far in the past, when manners were more particular, behavior more austere, and honor the axis around which families revolved. From what she says, Malka's mother had done something to disgrace her family, leaving Malka and her descendants with a permanent stain on their characters, their bloodline. We're talking here about unmarried sex and pregnancy, the sort of thing that caused girls to be thrown out of the family home. The letter speaks of her mother, who left Circassia and came to live in the port city of Odessa and from there migrated to Germany and settled in Berlin.

"But the main thrust of the letter is to tell her about Malka's own birth, her mother, and her situation. Malka's mother, living in a village in Circassia, had had an affair with a man visiting the area. She'd fallen pregnant out of wedlock and disgraced the family. But she was lucky because the man didn't abandon her. No, he was a gentleman, and when she was forced out of her home by her family, the two fled to Berlin, where they lived in the Jewish community."

Shalman looked up and smiled at Yael. "Very sexy lady, this one, and they chose Berlin because it's cosmopolitan and bohemian, and more likely to accept couples living together."

"Circassia? Tell me about Circassia."

"It's on the shores of the Black Sea, underneath Russia. Back in those days, in the middle of the 1800s, the Muslims were slaughtered by the *mamzer* Russians who wanted the farmland for themselves, and the government in Moscow ordered ethnic cleansing of the nation. All this was about the time that the distant relative of the woman who gave you this letter had the affair with the man and fell pregnant."

He continued. "The letter goes on to say that in Berlin this Malka woman grew up as a German, but anti-Semitism in Europe and wars with France forced the family to move to Palestine and build a home there. They lived in a small town in the Galilee called Peki'in because Malka's father had a business relationship with olive oil producers in Peki'in. It's a very detailed letter . . ."

Yael looked at him in amazement. Peki'in—it was all starting to fit together.

"And the reason that this Malka person wrote the letter to her daughter was because the young woman was about to marry, and the mother wanted her to know the truth about her family history. She begged her daughter to persuade her future husband to leave Berlin and to come to Peki'in and live . . ." He searched the letter for the precise phrase: " 'in peace and harmony and safety among the new immigrants in a land full of potential.'

"Malka tried to convince her daughter that it would be a wonderful new life—and that, my love, is where the letter ends. Is that helpful?"

Yael stood, walked around his massive desk, and kissed him tenderly on the cheek and the forehead. She sat on his desk just as she'd done a thousand times when she was a little girl. He looked up at her knowing that something was on her mind.

"Nu?"

She shrugged.

"You have that look."

"Look?"

He smiled. *"Bubbeleh*, all your life I've read your mind through the expressions on your face. Tell Shalman . . ."

She picked up a photo from his desk. It was one of a very few of her grandmother Judit. She was a tiny figure in the distance, sitting in a circle with a group of other men and women dressed in 1940s flared trousers, a knit top, and a cardigan. Frustratingly, it was in black-and-white, so Yael could only guess at the colors. She hoped that they were a dark blue. She loved dark blue and wondered whether that had been Judit's favorite color too.

"I know more about some Palestinian's grandmother than I do about my own *bubbeh.* She was always a presence in the house when I was growing up, even though she died before I was born. Yet, whenever I asked my mom or you about her, I felt that you were always dodging the issue, as though there were things you didn't want me to know. Why was that? Why won't you tell me about her, what she was like as a young woman, what she liked to eat, her favorite colors, what she did when she first came here from Russia, when you and she—"

"Hoo, ha—so many questions," said Shalman. "Your grandmother, *aleha ha-shalom*, was a wonderful woman. A queen among women. Gentle, loving, kind. She lived a life. In those days, darling, we young people were fighting for our country, our family, ourselves. Judit gave birth to your beloved mother and those few years we had together as a family were the best of my life . . . our lives. When she came from Russia, from St. Petersburg, she was—"

"St. Petersburg? But I thought she was from Moscow," Yael interrupted.

Shalman nodded, wondering if he'd inadvertently gone too far. There was so much which he couldn't tell Yael, so much that, even after sixty years, had to stay hidden. "Yes, Moscow. I don't know why I said St. Petersburg. But when she came to Israel, we lived a life worth living. But all these questions. So long ago. They were hard times. We fought the British and the Arabs and the United Nations. It hurts me to think about it. But now isn't the time. I have a meeting soon, and I have to prepare. One day, *bubbeleh*, I'll tell you more. Today isn't the day."

Shalman waved her away with grandfatherly affection and went back to his work.

Yael kissed him on the cheek and the forehead and walked out. She so badly wanted to tell him of the danger she was in— she so urgently wanted to share her fears with him—but she knew him so well, and predicted that his reaction would be one of panic, hysteria. He'd call the police, Mossad, the prime minister . . . everybody. And she had to keep an atmosphere of calm and confidentiality until she and Yaniv had sorted things through. Love him as she did, Shalman was the very last person in whom she could confide.

As she left his office, he watched her disappear, and spent long moments looking at the closed door. Suddenly overcome by emotions he thought he'd buried forty years ago, he felt himself on the verge of tears. He picked up the picture Yael had been looking at and studied the indistinct face of his wife, Judit. He bit his lip to stop himself from sobbing.

"Why?" he asked himself, suddenly realizing that he had spoken aloud into an empty room. Even after all these years, he was still overwhelmed by the fury.

"Why?"

He replaced the photograph and stared out of the window, consumed with grief and anger and disgust. "Why?" he asked himself again. They could have had such a wonderful life together. They could have been a family like other families; but something had happened to her in Russia, in St. Petersburg, that she'd never told him about. And from the moment he'd met her, when they were both working for the terrorist band Lehi, he knew that there was more to his long-dead wife . . . Something much deeper, and darker.

He sighed and looked again at the photo, shaking his head. It was all so long ago, longer than a lifetime, but it was still raw. And he was still bitter.

From where he was sitting, he couldn't see a man staring at him through a pair of high-powered binoculars from a distant rooftop. He'd been watching Yael's and Shalman's every action on the explicit instructions of Eliahu Spitzer, who had ordered him to follow Yael, see what she did and to whom she spoke, and report back to him in person, keeping no written record.

———

YANIV GROSSMAN WAS CONSUMED by the story. The linkage between Spitzer and the imam and Rabbi Shmuel Telushkin from Neturei Karta was something he could almost taste. And the key to it was Bilal. Yaniv didn't yet have the meat of the story but he knew it was close. Yael would lead him there, perhaps once she'd retrieved Bilal's phone, and whatever evidence it might still contain. All she had to do was to go to the property office in the hospital, tell them that she wanted pills from Bilal's clothing, and put the phone in her pocket.

Even as he thought the words to himself, he felt embarrassment. *Yael would lead him there.* He was a reporter, somebody whose job relied on contacts, often manipulating them to give him detailed and underlying facts. Sometimes—no, often—the people whom he secretly interviewed put themselves and their livelihoods in danger. The only promise he could ever make to them for the risks they took on his behalf was confidentiality and anonymity. He'd go to prison before he'd reveal the name of a source.

And now he was treating Yael as a source. In the beginning, when they'd first met at the museum and he was doing a color piece about the seal that she'd taken from Bilal's hand, he used his charm and looks to coax her into meeting him for a feature. But from the moment he'd seen her on the podium, he'd been captivated by her beauty, her intelligence, her confidence, her poise. And he knew he'd used his position as an American television reporter to inveigle her into meeting him again—and again.

Now he was smitten. Not in love, not like some hormonal schoolboy, but he'd go to bed thinking of her and wake with a smile on his face. He'd count the hours before meeting her. She fascinated him, and he wanted her—badly. But unlike so many women who'd become easy prey for him, Yael had resisted his blandishments, and her resistance had encouraged him to push the boundaries.

And yet, despite his desire to hold her, to feel the softness of her skin and hair, he was preparing to use her to get to the heart and soul of a major story. A wave of embarrassment swept over him as he drove away from the center of Jerusalem. Could he?

Would he allow his professional interests to infiltrate what could be a potentially serious romantic relationship?

Nope. He'd open himself up to her, tell her the reasons he wanted information, and ask her permission to continue. He nodded to himself and smiled.

Love: 1. Journalism: 0.

And how often was a reporter such an integral part of his own story? Woodward and Bernstein had used informants to smash Watergate and bring down an American president, but they weren't involved in guns and car chases. He was a reporter, not a soldier. But what choice did he, or Yael, have? The circumstances were dead against them.

He was thinking through this dilemma while driving toward his apartment in Ramot Alon, his route taking him through the bustling center of the metropolis, within sight of the illuminated walls of the Old City. It was so different from New York, where he'd grown up. He loved Brooklyn—he always would—but no American city could hope to match the insane blends of antiquity and modernity, of popular and classical, of religious and secular, of Jerusalem.

No matter how long he lived in the capital of Israel, nor how familiar he was with its surroundings, he never failed to be moved when he saw the towering fortifications. But this time he barely noticed them, he was so lost in his thoughts. What was Eliahu Spitzer up to? If he was close to, or had even become, a member of the Neturei Karta, then working deep within Israeli security was a scandal of the highest order. One part of Spitzer was dedicated to the salvation of the state, the other part to its downfall.

But how to prove it? And what was the link to the imam who had sent Hassan to murder Yael? With all his digging, Yaniv found virtually no information on the imam from the village of Bayt al Gizah. He seemed to have appeared out of nowhere just a few short years ago. To mastermind a nearly successful bombing attempt on the Western Wall, he must have resources and support. But there was no trace. Yaniv's contacts in the police, Shin Bet, and the antiterrorist agencies told him that the imam wasn't on anybody's radar.

Even if Yaniv did go to the head of Shin Bet and lay the information about Eliahu in front of him, without the evidence of Bilal's phone, it was all hearsay, speculation, and innuendo. And even with the photo of the three men together, Spitzer would probably be able to explain it away. Yaniv knew that he might do some temporary damage to Eliahu's reputation, but any investigation would prove groundless; a man like Spitzer would have covered his tracks meticulously—of that, Yaniv was certain. And worse, if Eliahu realized that he was being investigated, he'd withdraw, resign from Shin Bet, or just disappear.

Yaniv drove slowly in the congested early-evening Jerusalem traffic past the King David Hotel toward the north of the city and casually glanced in the rearview mirror to check the traffic behind him. There were a dozen cars and a helmeted motorcyclist.

Ahead of him, the traffic stopped for lights and the motorcyclist drew up beside his car. Yaniv could see him out of the corner of his left eye. The man suddenly bent down as if to tie his shoelace, but his helmet must have connected with Yaniv's back car door, because he heard a small click. He thought nothing of it, and when the lights changed, he drove on. He switched on the radio and listened to the six o'clock news, but as he left the frenetic traffic and approached the more suburban part of the city, he was able to speed up.

It was there that he saw three young men, all ultra-Orthodox Jews dressed in their eighteenth-century clothes, arguing with a young woman dressed in a miniskirt, high heels, and a top with a plunging neckline. As their numbers grew through a high birth rate and their security became more and more assured due to their ability to wield political pressure on the Israeli government, the people of the Orthodox communities were becoming increasingly militant in their dealings with secular Israelis. And for the past few months they had targeted young Jewish women who wore revealing clothes.

It was obvious that these young men were berating the young woman about her immodesty, probably calling her a whore and immoral. She looked terrified as the three were ridiculing and taunting her. They blocked her path so that she couldn't escape them, even though they weren't touching her.

Yaniv Grossman had spent a career as an observer, a commentator, reporting on but not being a part of world events. But he was also an American, raised in a society of freedom and excess. Seeing archaic misogynistic attitudes like this infuriated him. Yaniv pulled his car over, got out, and ran across the road.

"Hey, you!" he shouted. He knew their preferred language was Yiddish, but he didn't speak it, so he continued in Hebrew. "Leave her alone. Get away from her."

One of the young men, surprised by the sight of the tall, athletic man running at them, called to him, "Mind your own business. You don't understand. God commands women to dress modestly. He said to Eve to cover up her nakedness. But this girl . . ."

It had never left him; it was buried deep in his muscle memory, still strong and potent. Yaniv moved toward them like a soldier on a mission. The boys, all of whom came from *yeshivot*, the religious schools where students studied morning, noon, and night, knew nothing of confrontation short of nonphysical harassment, and they immediately drew back.

"I don't give a fuck what God commands. You live your lives and let everyone else get on with theirs," Yaniv said, moving closer to the girl to shield her.

One of the boys, braver than the others though a head shorter than Yaniv, walked closer to him and said, "People like you call yourselves Jews, yet you have no understanding of what God has comman—"

Suddenly, a shock wave of boiling air, like an oven door opening, enveloped them; then the roar of the explosion, then a massive invisible hand pushed them toward the wall. It was a colossal
blast from the other side of the road. Yaniv turned in horror to
look across the street and saw his car catapulted into the air, high
off the road, as though some giant had hoisted it off the ground.
Then a ball of yellow flame and black smoke erupted from the
panels, blowing off the hood and the front and back doors. The
car flipped over onto its side, landing with a scream of metal, just
clipping a taxi heading northward, the driver swerving to avoid
being crushed by the falling metal. But the taxi hit another car
traveling in the opposite direction head-on.

In all the chaos, when the blast wave hit the group, the boys
screamed and the girl was pushed to the ground, covering her
face. The explosion was too distant to hurt them because the heat
and force of the blast dissipated in all directions, but the effects
shocked and immobilized them. The three boys, shaken but still
alert, recovered quickly and ran away for all they were worth.
Yaniv looked at his car, now on its roof, with a massive hole
where the driver's door had once been, surrounded by snakes of
twisted metal. The taxi and the car with which it had collided
came to a halt amid broken glass and columns of steam from ruptured radiators, hoods raised, horns screeching. The girl on the
pavement burst into tears and moved across to hug Yaniv's legs
for security. But all Yaniv could think about was the motorcyclist
and the click he'd heard at the traffic lights minutes earlier.

———

PROFESSOR SHALMAN ETZION was driving out of the museum's parking lot toward the road that led south and east to the
Dead Sea. Because he was in his car with his iPod playing Wagner's *Götterdämmerung* at full volume, he didn't hear the distant
explosion of Yaniv's car from the other side of Jerusalem.

He drove quickly toward the east for his appointment with the director of antiquities at Masada, the winter palace of King Herod. But before he arrived there, he'd pop in and visit some friends at the ancient archaeological site of Qumran on the shores of the Dead Sea.

Like many Israelis of German origin, he adored Wagner's operas, even though he knew that he was an anti-Semite and a favorite of the Nazis. And like many Germans, when he listened to Wagner in the privacy of his car, he drove too fast, but he was a busy man, and there were places he had to get to.

In his haste, he didn't see that he was being followed by a large black Mercedes four-wheel-drive. He accelerated to beat traffic lights, the Mercedes following; drove too quickly around bends, the Mercedes in his wake.

Negotiating one of the sharp twists in the road, a precipitous drop descending from the heights of Jerusalem to the lowest place on earth, the Dead Sea, Shalman glimpsed the Mercedes close beside him—too close. Why so close? Why was he driving like a *meshuggeneh* on a road notorious for its crashes? What? Was he a maniac?

The car behind flashed its lights; Shalman was momentarily distracted from concentrating on the road, glancing up into his rearview mirror.

Foot on the brake, Shalman tried to slow his descent before taking the long right-hand bend, but the Mercedes suddenly accelerated and overtook him, and just as he was about to correct his wheel, the four-wheel-drive swerved just enough to nudge the front of Shalman's aging Ford. The other driver knew the pressure point of Shalman's car. The old man yelped as the wheel was wrested from his hands from the jolt of the car beside him. He grabbed it back, correcting the steering from his right-hand turn to negotiate the bend, but the front of the car was shoved by the much more agile Mercedes on its right. It was an almost imperceptible move, unnoticed by other drivers coming up the hill, but with the wheel wrenched out of Shalman's hands, the old man was unable to steer, and the car headed toward the barrier.

The Mercedes accelerated past the old Ford, which veered with a life of its own. Shalman tried to wrestle it back, but the steering wheel stubbornly stayed to the left. He lost his grip on the wheel a second time and struggled to retain control. But it was bucking out of his hands as the car's front suddenly veered in a different direction, the front tires fighting against the direction of the curve.

He instinctively slammed his foot on the brake—precisely what he shouldn't have done—and the rear wheels skidded around, turning his car full circle. The elderly man screamed "No!" as his car crashed into the barrier, turned around again, and hit the barrier once more, two wheels leaving the road and tipping it onto its roof. The old car rolled over once and then vaulted the barrier. In horror, Shalman looked into the depths of the valley three hundred feet below as his car careened downward.

He screamed a single name: "Judit!" In that second, he saw her face as his car smashed into the rocks and dirt at the bottom of the cliff.

Drivers behind him saw what was happening, and when they got out of their cars, they looked in horror at the old Ford far below, upside down on its roof, crushed, with steam and smoke rising up the rock face. There was utter silence, broken only by the music that rose up the cliff face. It was Wagner's Brünnhilde swearing eternal vengeance. A shocked American tourist screamed as the car suddenly burst into flames. The music stopped.

Nobody noticed the big black Mercedes continuing to drive sedately toward the Dead Sea. Soon the driver would turn the car around using an exit road and climb the hill toward Jerusalem. The driver didn't even look at the four cars that had stopped, their occupants standing on the edge of the road, looking downward, but he was gratified to see smoke billowing upward in a satisfying column. He had to drive quickly to a private garage and have the dented front fender fixed. Then he'd return to his office in Shin Bet.

———

"I DON'T BELIEVE YOU," she said, sitting down on the tiny bed of the dingy hotel room. Still shaken, Yaniv stood there, shocked by what had happened to him.

"He tried to kill you? You? Why? This is unbelievable. How does he know about you? This is ridiculous. Enough! You . . . we . . . have to go to the police. You have to go to Shin Bet and call this bastard to account. You have to . . ." She was too stupefied to continue for a moment. "You have to . . . do something."

"You don't get it, Yael. We've stumbled right into a shitstorm. They've been tracking us. They know who I am now. They know who *you* are."

"I don't believe the whole Israeli security force is in on some conspiracy!" said Yael.

"No. But we have no idea who Eliahu Spitzer is in contact with or who he controls or who reports to him. We can't tell the police, the Shin Bet, Mossad, the army, or anybody else."

"Bullshit! This isn't Iran. This is Israel. Only religious madmen would be part of this. Nobody else. We have to go to the authorities. The police, surely!"

"And that's half the problem: because if we go to the police, it'll be in a report, and reports are seen by people. We can't take the risk."

"We'll demand that it's kept a secret until he's arrested and put away," she said, but her words were sounding thinner and thinner with each statement.

"And you'd risk your life on something being kept secret? In Israel? I'm a reporter, Yael. I can get to see most everything. I'm not going to take that risk. We have no idea how wide or deep this bastard's contacts go."

"So who can we tell? Who can we go to?" asked Yael in frustration. "Christ, Yaniv, this is Israel, not some Arab country. We're a democracy. We've got separation of powers. Jesus, we've got a fucking ombudsman."

"We can't tell anyone until we have a way out" was Yaniv's flat reply.

"Bullshit. There must be somebody we can get to help us." In her frustration, she repeated quietly to herself: "This isn't Syria or Iran or Egypt. Nobody's that powerful."

Yaniv looked at her in concern. And his silence was eloquent testament that they were indeed on their own.

"Then how can we fight him?" asked Yael.

"You're a doctor. Not a soldier," replied Yaniv.

"In Israel, everyone's a soldier."

It might have seemed a mock retort, but in a country with compulsory national service for men and women alike, and besieged on all sides by hostile armies, it was not an empty boast. Yaniv just shook his head and flopped into a chair.

Yael reached into her handbag and drew out a small black object. She held it up for Yaniv to see. It was a black smartphone with a wide reflective screen.

"I'm not sure I want to see what's on this," she said.

Yaniv stood from the chair and grabbed the phone from Yael's hand. "Where was it?"

"In the secure bag with Bilal's belongings at the hospital," she replied matter-of-factly.

"And you were just able to go and get it?"

"He was my patient, so I told the security guy at the hospital that I was looking for some pills that Bilal had in his pockets. I said I needed them for analysis. And then I just slipped it into my pocket when the security guy wasn't looking. He was too busy with the soccer game on TV to notice."

Yaniv's eyes told her that he wasn't elated.

"Something's not right. Why wouldn't Shin Bet take the phone? Why wouldn't they confiscate all his belongings as evidence?" He let the question hang in the air as he contemplated all possible answers. His gaze returned to the room and he looked at Yael. "The only reason Spitzer wasn't bothered with it is if he didn't need it."

He fiddled with the phone until a tiny drawer opened in its side. "They've removed the SIM card; they must have thought . . ."

Yael looked at him quizzically, not following his train of thought.

"Most people think that all the information is stored on the SIM card, but it's not. Lots of good stuff is stored on the phone, even with the memory card removed. The goons thought that by removing the SIM card, they had all the evidence it contained. They obviously think that they don't need the evidence if they—" His eyes opened wide, and then in a sudden flurry of energy he quickly depressed the switch and brought the phone to life. Swiping fingers briskly across the touch screen, he found his way to the phone's folder of video clips and photos.

Banal photos of feet and a steering wheel, the accidental images of a new user of a new technology. He flicked past them. A video of a pretty, young Arab girl smiling shyly at the camera. He flicked past once more to a grainy image pixelating in the near darkness of a dimly lit street. The shuffling staccato movement and rattling as the phone camera was repositioned in the hand of the user. Finally it came to rest, moving in a gentle arc to survey a street, a wall, a window . . .

As the camera changed its auto exposure, three silhouetted figures came into view. The camera jerked up and then forward before settling again. The silhouettes became more distinct, more in focus. And the light changed again, the dark image brightening as the camera adjusted.

Yaniv's finger tapped the pause button on the screen, freeze-framing the image. Yael wondered why he was smiling.

He turned the camera around so Yael could see. She leaned forward.

"What do you see?" he asked.

"That's him. That's the imam who came to the hospital," said Yael. "And the guy with the white hair next to him is Spitzer." She looked closer at the screen and nodded. "But who's the other man? The Hasid."

"Rabbi Shmuel Telushkin of Neturei Karta," replied Yaniv. "I interviewed him in Tehran at that Holocaust denial conference."

Stunned, she looked at him and said softly, "Dear God."

Yaniv repeated his question from earlier, holding up the phone as if the answer was the phone itself. "Why didn't Shin Bet take this phone? Why haven't they confiscated all Bilal's belongings as evidence? Because they didn't need to. Because they knew everything that he was going to do—the bombs, the Wailing Wall . . ."

Yaniv pointed at the three men on the phone screen. "They set it up."

Yael wanted to protest the absurdity of it all, but the events of the past few days made the words stick in her throat. After what she had been through, anything was now possible.

"I think I know how to stop them coming for us."

Yael didn't respond; she just stared at him.

"But to do it, to draw them out, we have to get Bilal out of prison."

PART THREE

In the 18th year of the Reign of Herod (Known as the Great),
19 BCE

MARCELLUS GRATUS SECUNDUS lay facedown on a towel while a Nubian slave woman carefully scraped the dead skin and aromatic oil from his back, arms, buttocks, legs, and the soles of his feet. Once she had finished, she picked up a sponge from the bucket of warm water, wrung it out so that it was not more than damp, and wiped the noble Roman knight's body from his balding head to his ankles. It was a delicious feeling, and Marcellus Gratus was aroused by the heat of her naked body so close to his and the way in which she paid attention to the small of his back, his bottom, and his thighs.

Marcellus Gratus glanced over to where his wife, Aurelia Juliana, lay facedown on a nearby couch, being scraped by a tall, muscular naked Nubian. He noted with a smile that her slave had been ordered to spend an extra amount of time in massaging her buttocks and all of her that lay within reach of his fingers. He also noted with some disquiet that her slave had the biggest male appendage he'd ever seen. Not even erect, it was twice the size of

that which belonged to his employer. Noticing what he was looking at, his slave girl smiled and whispered in his ear, "I have had
that thing inside me, master, and it hurt me. Very badly."

Marcellus Gratus decided not to tell his wife; she could find
out for herself. He looked around at his slave girl and saw that
she was very beautiful, her shining black skin reflecting the light
of the candle. If he had the time, he would enjoy her body before
the evening meal, because he knew for certain that while he was
engaged on official duties in this backward region of the empire,
Aurelia Juliana would be taking full advantage of her Nubian.

He still didn't understand why Rome needed to control this
regressive part of the world. He'd advised senators that Rome
should be looking toward Gaul and Britannia, which were rich in
ores and minerals, in wood and tin and slaves. But because of the
wealth of Egypt and the grain it produced for bread, the Romans
looked south and east, and so Marcellus Gratus had been asked
to come take charge of the provincial capital of Jerusalem.

He shuddered when he thought of where he was and how different this land was from the epicenter of Rome's life and culture.
Hundreds of years ago, the Jews had been exiled in Babylon but
had returned to rebuild Jerusalem; then they'd been conquered
by Alexander of the Greeks, at the same time as the Gauls again
threatened Rome but were destroyed by the greatness of the
Roman legions. And now he was in Jerusalem, the city that the
Jews called their capital!

Marcellus Gratus Secundus could barely stop himself from
laughing. Compared with Rome or Alexandria, Jerusalem was a
hovel. Since the return of the Jews from their exile in Babylon, it
had had many conquerors and kings. He'd been told the history
since the Persians had released the Jews from their Babylonian
exile, but it was all too complicated. Alexander the Great had
conquered the Persian Empire, and that meant that Jerusalem
and Judea came under his control; but the Greeks wanted to
place one of their gods in the Jewish temple, and that had caused

some war or other and the land fell to the Ptolemies. But they lost it, and it fell to the Seleucids and Antiochus the Great; but the Jews objected for some reason he couldn't understand, and so they revolted and it fell to the Maccabees. But the offspring had quarreled and asked Rome to intervene, and now . . . oh, it was all too confusing, and he couldn't be bothered remembering what had happened in the past. All he was concerned about was ruling for today, handing over tributes to the Senate in Rome, and returning to a higher office in a civilized land.

Shortly after Marcellus Gratus arrived in Judea with Aurelia Juliana, they had come to an easy accommodation with each other. In Rome, it would have been unthinkable for a knight to have indulged his carnal desires with a slave woman in the knowledge of his wife, and unimaginable for a male slave to have access to the body of a Roman matron of rank. These trysts were usually carried out in discreet *lupanaria*, where men and women clients entered the brothels through a series of guarded alleys to avoid a scandal. But in these far provinces, where the eyes of Rome couldn't see and gossiping voices couldn't be heard, things became much easier, and the desires of Marcellus and Aurelia were openly gratified as many times as they wished.

As his slave was rubbing down his body with a warm towel, Marcellus Gratus pondered, as he often did, the differences between this place, Judea, the most extreme region of the eastern Roman Empire, and Rome itself. This hot, fractious, empty, and miserable desert of a land held a few charms, but compared with Rome it was the land of the barbarians. The people were warlike and fanatical in their allegiance to their absurdly invisible god, simple in their needs, their cities little more than hovels, without any great civic buildings or baths or forums or temples; nor was there a single hippodrome of any decent size for the amusement of the soldiers, and the roads between places were nothing more than tracks hewn out of the ground by the feet of countless camels and asses.

Yet, there was a certain attraction to being here. In Rome he was a nobleman, a knight, and respected, but he was fairly low down in the imperial hierarchy and was rarely invited to the residence of Caesar. But things had changed for the better after he fought alongside Julius Caesar and Marcus Antonius in Gaul. After the civil war in Rome, Marc Antony assumed control of the eastern empire and he had asked Marcellus Gratus to join him and assist in the administration of Judea.

In the two years since he'd been here in the hillside village of Jerusalem, he'd barely seen Marc Antony. The noble Roman spent all of his time in Egypt in the company of their queen, Cleopatra VII, who gave him ready access to her body, as she had done to Julius Caesar some years earlier. And knowing the Egyptians, she probably gave her body to her mother, brother, and father as well.

It was all very strange, and had it not been for Marcellus Gratus's sense of duty and responsibility, without a firm ruler the place would have become lawless. But as de facto proconsul, Marcellus Gratus kept a firm hand on the different competing factions, the priesthood, the Israelite hotheads who wanted Rome to quit the province, those who wanted closer ties to Syria or to Egypt, and worst of all, the innumerable people who called themselves Messiahs, who seemed to be springing up all the while. Only last week he'd crucified three of them who had tried to foment a revolt among the Jews outside the temple, yelling and screaming that this god of theirs had spoken to them and told them to rise up against the Sadducees in the temple and to all go and live in the desert or something.

He'd been warned by other knights in Rome that Judea was a land full of madmen, religious zealots, hermits, and a strange people who revered only this single god called Adon or something, a god who was invisible yet was perpetually sitting down in the little temple they'd built to him on the top of one of the hills.

These madmen—and there were dozens of them—called themselves Messiahs, which apparently meant those who had been sent by their god, and all came with visions of some beauteous heaven and salvation and forgiveness of sins. They were of little account, often wandering in the desert, wearing just a loincloth, speaking to bushes and the stars, and rarely bothering anybody; he usually crucified those who gathered a following, which scared the rest of them into staying in the desert.

It was, indeed, a mysterious land, but fortunately they were ruled by a king who had grown up in Roman ways and was fluent in Latin as well as understood the imperial way of ruling. And he'd been told in a letter from Marc Antony that their king, Herod, was going to be conferred by the Roman Senate with the title King of the Jews.

When his black slave had finished toweling his front and back, he held her around her neck while she slipped one of his legs and then the other into his white linen *subligaculum*. On the formal occasions when he wore his toga, he didn't bother with undergarments; but his meeting with King Herod wasn't going to be formal, and so he would wear a simple tunic, which meant that his *subligaculum* was obligatory when he sat down.

His slave pulled the short tunic over his head, placed the gold seal of authority on his finger, combed his hair, and finished dressing him. Then she bowed deferentially and withdrew. He told his wife that he would be in the offices and walked out of the bathhouse, followed by his guards. He climbed the flight of steps, where two soldiers, standing guard, banged their *hastae* on the ground and stood rigidly at attention. The noise of the wooden spears hitting the marble floor told his amanuensis to open the doors and bow as he walked through.

"Excellency," said Septimius Severus, his longtime secretary, "King Herod is expected. His advance guard has informed me that he will be here shortly."

HEROD, KING OF THE north and south of Israel, lover, politician, and omnipotent ruler, son of Herod Antipater the Idumaean and Cyprus the Nabatean, beloved of the Roman conquerors but hated by the Jews of Israel, was overwhelmed with excitement. He had spent much of the morning standing on his golden chariot at the precipitous edge of the mountainside, looking at the city of Jerusalem. His troop of bodyguards, arrayed in lines behind him, was forced to stand in the blistering sun while the black silk parasol gave him shade. Now he was riding quickly toward the city for his interview with the proconsul, Marcellus Gratus, and could barely wait to show him his plans.

It had been so hot on the hill that he was sure the sun had burned the top of his balding head, despite the shade of the parasol. He'd wiped the sweat from his eyes, and although he didn't know it, he and his guards were positioned at precisely the same spot on the Mount of Olives where, nearly a thousand years before him, King David had stood and surveyed the city, which was inhabited by the Jebusites, planning how to conquer it.

But today Herod's eyes saw a very different city, white and gleaming, rich and renowned, proud and holy. His eyes narrowed in wonder as he surveyed the towering walls and the myriad buildings within: the homes of the populace, offices where the business of the nation of Israel was conducted on behalf of the Roman conquerors, shops that sold goods from all over the Roman world, and stalls that sold meat and drink, fruits and delicacies, herbs and spices.

Yet, the beauty of the city was marred when he looked farther up the hill. He shuddered when his eyes were lifted to the top of the mountain called Moriah and saw the temple dedicated to Adonai Elohim built five hundred years earlier by the Jews who had returned from exile in Babylon.

He'd been inside the temple many times and compared its sparseness and insignificance with the towering grandeur of the buildings of Rome, where he'd spent much time. His wife,

Mariamne, had said that the Jews would love and revere him as their one and only true king if he were to knock down the meager structure the Jews called their temple and replace it with the mightiest temple imaginable, dedicated to their god Adonai Elohim, an edifice grander than the pyramids of Egypt or the ziggurats of Roman Mesopotamia.

Herod had spoken to the rabbis about his plans, and while many considered it blasphemy to pull down the sacred temple, others were excited by the idea of a great and grand temple. While he could have compelled them to do precisely as he told them, perhaps executing a few to convince those who opposed him, Mariamne persuaded him to compromise. He would allow them to continue to use their altar and sacrifice whatever animals they wanted, and he would pull down the old temple that had been built by Zerubbabel and Joshua, dismantling it stone by stone. Then he would flatten the top of the mountain and build a massive platform where the huge foundation stones could be laid.

He had the architect's plans and couldn't wait to show them to Marcellus Gratus. His horseman rode his chariot through the great archway that led to the upper reaches of Jerusalem, and people scattered out of the way as the noise of the wheels on the paving stones warned them of his approach. When he reached the gates of the huge home from where Marcellus Gratus administered the nation on behalf of Rome, he jumped down from the chariot, grabbed his plans, and walked quickly toward the atrium.

Marcellus Gratus's secretary, Septimius Severus, saw him approach and ran to inform his master. "Shall I have him wait in the antechamber?" the servant asked.

The proconsul shook his head. "No, admit him. He's a good friend of Rome, so we shouldn't delay."

Septimius Severus bowed politely and nodded to a guard who stood by a door at the far end of the office. In moments Herod walked in and smiled when he saw his friend. He raised his right arm stiffly, his fingers outstretched. It was a salute that also showed that he wore no weapons concealed in the arm sleeve of his tunic. Marcellus Gratus did the same, and they approached each other with a smile. They embraced and clasped each other's wrists.

"So, my friend, what brings you to my quarters?" asked Marcellus Gratus.

"I'm here, friend, to inform you of a significant number of building projects I wish to undertake. I will be taxing my people heavily, so we can expect some trouble. I'll also be importing architects from Greece, Rome, and Egypt, so they'll need guarding and protection from a jealous population."

"Three architects from three countries? That's a big building."

"Architects from three countries, not three architects. I'll have thirty architects working on the different projects throughout the country."

"By the gods, how many projects will you be undertaking?"

Herod smiled. He turned to his secretary and nodded. The man withdrew a dozen scrolls from his bag and began to unroll them on the table. As one, then another, then another were laid on top of one another, Marcellus Gratus shook his head in amazement.

"I intend to make my kingdom into a replica of Rome, but on the other side of the world. I will make my name live forever throughout the ages for the most beautiful and perfect of constructions. From this day until the end of time, people will look at our Roman Empire and see two great pillars on each side supporting the world. One pillar will be Rome with its Senate, its forums, its temples, its hippodromes, its baths, and its theaters. The other pillar, on the opposite side of the world, will be Israel, with the greatest buildings in the East, greater than Egypt's pyramids or the Acropolis of Athens with its Parthenon and its caryatids."

Marcellus Gratus smiled. "You still call this nation Israel; when will you Jews know that its name is Judea?"

"Don't bother yourself with that. Instead, look at my plans, Marcellus Gratus, and tell me that they're not the most exciting and splendid building programs you've ever seen."

They walked to the table and Herod, like an excited school-boy, said, "This is my plan for a new temple, right here in Jeru-salem. I'll have the priests build it of stone and they'll do the woodwork as well, and it will be full of marble and gold."

He pulled the plan for the temple away and revealed a plan for an entire city on the shores of the Mediterranean. "This port city will be called Caesarea Maritima in honor of our emperor and will house a huge theater, an amphitheater, a hippodrome, a vast temple dedicated to whichever god the emperor decides, and a palace for myself by the sea. We'll dredge the harbor so that a hundred ships can dock there in safety."

He pulled that plan aside and cast it on the floor, revealing a plan for a desert palace, which Marcellus Gratus read was called Masada. This looked like an outrageously complicated structure, hewn out of solid rock and built on many different levels; but before he was able to examine it properly, Herod revealed more plans.

"In Jericho, a horrible place on the edge of the desert and overlooking the Salt Sea, I'll build a palace on both sides of the *wadi*, the dry riverbed, but they'll be connected by a bridge, and there'll be gardens and baths and halls for dining and entertain-ment."

Another plan revealed the city of Jerusalem. "And here I'll build a sewage system, which will carry the waste away and dump it into the valley beyond, as well as a water system that will supply the people with all the fresh water they need. And there's the baths and a hippodrome here, and—"

"Stop!" said Marcellus Gratus. "Stop! Enough! By Jove, by all the gods in the heavens, this is madness. Insane. How will you ever be able to afford it? Where will the labor come from? Who will do the building, the construction, the stonecutting? Where will the rock and the wood come from? I've never seen so many plans in all my life. This will ruin Judea, Herod. Ruin the country. You'll be king of a kingdom that is nothing but dirt and rubble."

"No!" said Herod, laughing. "It's time this nation had a strong ruler whose will is absolute. The people, the Jews, are stiff-backed and resentful. But when my buildings are complete and the people look on them in awe—when they see that travelers come from all over the empire just to gaze on these wonders—then they will truly say that Herod is a great king."

Marcellus Gratus looked at the king of the Jews and wondered whether he was truly mad or a man of extraordinary vision. "There will be many who resent what you're doing, who'll fight you. There will be an uprising when your tax collectors whip the backs of people whose backs are already bent under the burden you've imposed on them."

Again Herod burst out laughing. "Then my prisons will be full, my executioners busy, and my torturers exhausted."

"Your people will hate you. Truly hate you. Is that what you want?"

Herod thought deeply, knowing that what Marcellus Gratus said was correct. Wherever he went in Israel, he could sense the hatred toward him of the people of the city and in the country, looking at him and sneering. He was as much a Jew as they were, yet because his family was from Idumaea and even though he was their rightful king, they still considered him a foreigner. He'd threatened, demanded, executed, and tortured enough of them to engender respect for him with the majority, but still he knew that they held him in contempt.

So his beloved Mariamne had persuaded him to build this new temple on the site of the worthless building that the prophets Haggai and Zachariah had overseen in ancient times. He'd been told by the rabbis that the temple, little more than a square building of stone with inconsequential ornaments inside, was erected and completed twenty years after the Jews were released from captivity by Cyrus the Great.

And he knew precisely how he'd do it. He would quarry the white Jerusalem blocks from a shaft he would build and burrow into the higher northern reaches of the mountain, close to the city and the site of the platform on which the new temple would be built. And as it was downhill from the quarry to that part of the city, the oxen wouldn't have to struggle too much. His architects would ensure that the Sadducees did all the heavy building work, for the priests would have little to do once their temple was pulled down and before the new one was erected.

It would cost a fortune, of course, but he would raise taxes to pay for the artisans, the equipment, the architects, the masons, and all the others who would build it quickly and efficiently. He'd been told, according to the records kept in the Second Temple, that the money to build it was raised from the returning Jews of Babylon by a merchant named Reuven, but Herod would use no merchants or others to force the money out of the Jews' pockets. He'd set his tax gatherers and collectors the task of raising the money, and if he had to break a few backs and put holes into a few skulls to ensure the cooperation of the populace, well, so be it.

November 4, 2007

YAEL WAS SWEATING despite the car's air-conditioning. She got out of the driver's seat and the dry, enveloping heat and sulfurous stench of the Dead Sea hit her like a slap in the face. She recalled the numbers of school visits she'd made to the area, especially the trip to King Herod's winter palace at Masada. Living in Jerusalem, she was used to extremes of temperature, but the Dead Sea had an atmosphere all its own. The heat was so intense that it hurt her nostrils to breathe.

Yael hurried into the prison's reception area where it was both shady and cooled by air-conditioning, and told them that she'd made an appointment as his doctor to see the prisoner on remand, Bilal haMitzri. She even carried a folder of papers for him to sign.

"Consent forms and such, so I can use his name in my paper about his medical condition."

The prison officer raised a quizzical eyebrow.

"Just covering my ass so he doesn't sue me later," said Yael as nonchalantly as she could muster. The officer waved her into the security room.

After she walked through an X-ray body scanner, had her bag thoroughly searched, and was examined in intimate places by a female security guard, she was allowed into the prison, leaving her bag and mobile phone in a locker.

Within a few minutes Bilal was led into the reception room by a massive Russian guard. The young man was surprised to see her.

"Dr. Yael. You're here again," Bilal said in Arabic.

Yael looked at the guard to see whether he understood, but it didn't appear as though he did. But she had to test him out, and so she said in Arabic to Bilal, "My friend, I have something very serious to discuss with you and I don't want anybody to understand what I'm going to say. Does the guard speak Arabic? For this is a very private message . . ."

"No, Doctor, I speak to him in bad Hebrew. His Hebrew is as bad as mine."

She winked at Bilal and looked around the room to see whether there were any television cameras or recording equipment. Satisfied that there were none, in a conversational voice, looking at Bilal, she said in Arabic, "Hey, Russian guard. If you can hear me, your mother is a worthless slut and your sister is a cheap whore who sells her body to anyone with a credit card."

Bilal looked at her in astonishment, but Yael saw that the guard didn't even blink, let alone react to the gross insult.

"Bilal, listen to me very, very carefully and say nothing. Don't react in any way. I have to get you out of here."

Bilal's eyes widened but he remained silent.

"You are in very great danger. The authorities will do little and too late. You must do exactly as I tell you. Do you understand?"

Bilal nodded slowly.

"I am going to give you three tablets. Take them, and they will make you sick, very sick, but only for a short while."

Bilal sat back from the table and a flash of fear showed across his face. But Yael reached out across the table and touched his arm. In that moment she feared the guard's attention would be drawn by such an action; she had very little time to make Bilal understand, but the guard was busy reading a paper.

Yael had compounded the tablets Bilal would have to take, doing it herself to avoid implicating any of the hospital pharmacists. She'd obtained the ingredients from the hospital, but asking different pharmacists on different occasions meant that they wouldn't put two and two together. And she'd checked, and double-checked, that Bilal's weight, height, and age meant that he could take the overdose without any long-term effect. Remembering that she'd had an intimate search the last time she came to the prison, Yael had placed the three anticholinergic pills inside the gap where a wire of her underwire bra normally fitted. It was unlikely that a search would find them. And she'd ensured that the hospital pharmacy had a good supply of parasympathomimetic drugs to reverse his illness when he was brought into the hospital.

"The doctor here at the prison will think you have been poisoned, but he won't know how to treat you and he'll call for an ambulance. You'll be taken to my hospital."

Bilal's eyes darted back and forth but he didn't move and Yael prayed that he was comprehending what she was saying and not planning to call for help.

"When you get there, I'll be waiting for you. And I'll give you a . . . um . . ." Yael's Arabic failed her and she struggled for the word. "I'll give you—"

"Antidote," Bilal said softly. A palpable relief welled up inside Yael as he confirmed he'd understood the plan after she'd explained it as quickly as she could.

"So you understand what I'm saying to you?"

Bilal frowned but nodded.

"We can't trust anybody. Not any Palestinian, not any Israeli. Nobody. This is the only way. You have to trust me . . ."

Yael heard herself say this last word and thought to herself how absurd it all seemed. Why should he trust her? Only because he had no other choice.

"So you are getting me out. Yes? But why? What can I do outside? Escape to another country? What do you want me to do?"

"The reason you have to leave here is to save your life. Your imam and the man with white hair are plotting to kill you. When you're out, we will trap them and expose them. We don't know how yet, but we will. But if you stay here, Bilal, you'll die."

"Why not tell the governor? If you tell him, maybe this time he will believe me. Maybe he will save me."

"We don't know who will come after you, Bilal. That's why you have to become very sick immediately, and we'll get you out of this place."

Bilal looked deep into Yael's eyes and said, "When I'm better, can I return to my home and my father and mother?"

She shook her head, feeling sorry for him. "No, Bilal. There's no way I can get you home. You have to pay for your crime." His face was stony and silent. "But we can make things better for you. For your family . . ." Yael felt as if she were lying, but her seemingly honest response, free of false promises, gave him confidence.

"Give me the tablets," he said.

She looked over at the guard, who had turned to glance in their direction. "Not yet, not until he looks away. Just keep talking. I'll keep my eye on him and the moment he's not looking directly at us, I'll slip them to you. Put them in your trouser pocket. Take them tomorrow morning immediately after breakfast. Don't take them when you get to your cell because the guards might not look in for hours. If you take them with lots of people around, you'll suddenly feel horribly ill. They'll get immediate help. Do you understand?"

Bilal nodded.

"You cannot trust anyone, Bilal. Neither of us can . . ."

———

AT HALF PAST TWELVE on the following afternoon, two things happened in nearby parts of Jerusalem. The first was a prison van driven at breakneck speed toward the hospital. The governor had radioed ahead to police headquarters requesting a police escort for a van carrying a dangerously sick prisoner. They were to meet the van as soon as it had climbed out of the valley of the Dead Sea, and lead the way through Jerusalem's frenetic traffic to the city's main hospital's accident and emergency facilities.

And at precisely twelve thirty in the afternoon, just two and a half miles from the emergency department where a nervous Yael worked and waited, a worried Yaniv Grossman walked into the offices of the ultrasecretive Shin Bet and asked to speak to Deputy Director Eliahu Spitzer.

The prison van screeched to a halt, and nurses and paramedics, already alerted, ran out with a gurney, an oxygen cylinder, and a crash cart. Bilal's comatose body, still twitching and as cold and pallid as death, was carried to the gurney and he was wheeled inside.

The Palestinian surgeon, Mahmud, stood waiting. He had known Bilal was coming and knew this was now his part to play.

Yael had been nervous, almost shaking, when she drew him aside and asked him if he'd be willing to assist her in saving Bilal's life. He agreed, although she could sense there was great reluctance. She told him what she wanted him to do. He could tell from the rhythm of her voice that her speech had been prepared, rehearsed. She had no idea how he'd respond and she was desperate.

Mahmud had tried so hard to fit into hospital work life while knowing full well that he might always be an outsider. He ignored the jokes and offhand comments, the passive but invasive prejudices that were normalized around him. And he tolerated the angry looks from his own people who saw him as a traitor. This was the burden he carried. And to shoulder the load, Mahmud had ardently sought to give no quarter, provide no space for the criticism or the glares or the mistrust. He worked longer, he worked harder. He smiled more and laughed more and let nothing be taken as offense. This was his defense mechanism, and it gave him place and purpose and solace within the fraught state of being an Arab-Israeli caught between two worlds.

But when Yael Cohen asked him to help Bilal escape from the hospital, escape from imprisonment for murder, Mahmud knew that if he assisted, then nothing would ever be the same again. There were no normal circumstances that would have made him agree to assist a terrorist—Jew or Muslim—escape from lawful custody; but Yael had explained very dramatically that the boy was a political prisoner, and that her own life was in danger. Reluctantly, he'd agreed to assist. No longer passive or apolitical, this would now be the moment when he crossed a line.

As he stood and watched the gurney carrying the comatose

body of Bilal toward him, he was still not sure why he had agreed to help Yael. A dormant loyalty to his people's cause? The righting of an injustice? No, these were not things that compelled Mahmud. What compelled him was the notion that in another time and another place, it could have been him, not Bilal, on the gurney, a gullible young Palestinian seduced into committing an atrocity and now paying for it with his life.

Bilal's body was drawn up in front of him and he reached for the clipboard notes from the prison doctor, seeing that adrenaline had been administered two hours earlier. Mahmud squeezed only half of the syringe into the boy's arm, running alongside the gurney as it was wheeled into the emergency cubicle that had been made ready.

Mahmud trusted Yael Cohen. He trusted her as a surgeon; he trusted her words. He knew if he was caught as part of this criminal deception against the State of Israel, the authorities would be merciless; but he also knew from Yael how endangered this young man's life was in the prison, and so he'd agreed to join with her in effecting his escape. So for him this would be no political statement or act of irrationality; it would be the act of a doctor saving the life of a patient.

He examined Bilal's pupils, listened to his heart, searched his lips and mouth for the typical discoloration of orally administered poisons, and looked over his entire body with care and precision while he instructed the ward nurse to take samples of blood and have them sent up to the pathology laboratory immediately for fluid, electrolyte, and other tissue analysis. He also wrote and signed forms for an MRI, chest X-ray, EEG, and nuclear medicine to identify what was happening in the patient's internal organs. While these were being prepared in other parts of the hospital, he stuck receptors all over Bilal's body for an ECG to monitor his heart.

Mahmud knew full well what was happening to Bilal and didn't need the battery of tests he had just ordered to bring him back to consciousness. But he played the part he knew he needed to play, to make the ruse plausible and his involvement invisible. It strangely ran against his instincts as a doctor to pretend at being unable to heal when the power to save was right before him.

He said to the nurse, "This is the kid who had the angiomyolipoma." The nurse looked at him blankly. "Dr. Cohen's patient." Still the nurse registered nothing. Finally Mahmud said, "The terrorist who tried to blow up the temple wall." The nurse suddenly nodded in recognition. "We need to prep him for an exploratory op."

"Shouldn't we wait for the test results?" said the nurse.

"I really don't want to wait and have him bleed out internally. Dr. Cohen will want to operate immediately. You know what she's like."

The nurse gave a curt nod and for a second Mahmud doubted whether he had been convincing enough. But he was given no time to ponder as Bilal was set in motion again toward the surgical ward. There, Mahmud knew, Yael would be waiting.

———

YANIV GROSSMAN WAITED for a response from the man who sat opposite him. But instead of reacting, Eliahu Spitzer simply stared back at Yaniv, the slightest trace of a whimsical smile on his face. Yaniv was tense before going in, but Eliahu's cold and calculating manner unnerved him even more as the great gamble played out in front of him.

It was an odd situation for Yaniv. Professionally, he was always calm and in control when he was reporting on television or interviewing a recalcitrant subject. He was known internationally for his incisive yet polite demeanor interviewing politicians or reporting from battle zones. His tall body and intelligent approach gave viewers confidence, and his ruggedly handsome face attracted a bevy of Israeli girls who were regular followers on ANBN's Facebook page.

But sitting opposite the Shin Bet operative in his private office, the reporter's eyes darting nervously from the view of the Old City through his window, to the ornaments on his desk, to Eliahu sitting smugly and comfortably in his chair, Yaniv was a picture of uneasy anxiety.

"And why should I do what you ask, Mr. Grossman?" Eliahu said quietly.

"Because I can help you put an end to this Bilal problem," he said.

"And what problem precisely is that? And why do you think that I have a problem?"

"He's identified you as the man he saw in an intimate conversation with the imam of Bayt al Gizah, and it won't be long before the police work out that he's the brains behind what Bilal tried to do."

The ghost of a smile now broadened to a grin masquerading as a sneer. "I speak to many Palestinians, some imams, some mullahs, some governors, some mayors, and some street sweepers. Why is it unusual for me to have had a meeting with this imam?"

"Why did you try to kill me?"

"Me?"

"A motorbike delivering a car bomb in traffic? We've seen that move before."

"To kill an Iranian nuclear scientist, perhaps, but not a reporter. That would be a waste of resources," said Spitzer, masking a grin. "And not Shin Bet's resources either. That's the sort of thing that Mossad does, quietly and efficiently. It sends a rather strong message."

"But I know that you organized it because you think I'm a

threat. And I've been around long enough to know how deadly Shin Bet is. So I'm not here to play hero and I don't want to die. I want to do a deal."

"I deal with Palestinians and Israeli Arabs. Not respected American broadcasters, Mr. Grossman, even if one has become an Israeli citizen. I think you've come to the wrong department. If you want to do a deal, go to the Tax Office."

"I'll give you Bilal if you promise to leave me alone."

For the first time since Yaniv had entered his office, Spitzer frowned. "Give him up? He's in prison, awaiting trial. In a couple of months he'll be an anonymous nonentity in a prison cell and he'll be there for the rest of his life."

"Is he still in prison?" said Yaniv, hoping for some reaction to play across Spitzer's face. But the Shin Bet officer said nothing and gave nothing away. Yaniv knew—or at least hoped—his words must have had an effect.

"Very soon you'll get a call telling you he's gone. I'm the only one who knows where he is. And I'm offering Bilal in exchange for my life. I know you could have me killed whenever you want to, but I reckon that with Bilal alive, it's the only bargaining chip I have to save my skin."

"I have no idea what you're talking about. I think you should leave or I might have to call the police." The irony of a Shin Bet commander calling regular cops was not lost on Yaniv.

"You know you won't do that. If I'm arrested, the wives of two Shin Bet operatives you had murdered will testify; I'll testify; Bilal will testify; there'll be so much mud thrown at you on every TV station you can name. It likely won't stick, but it'll make one hell of a mess and you'll feel like you're walking through a swamp. All I'm asking is a fair swap. My life for some miserable terrorist . . ."

———

70 CE

ABRAHAM BEN ZAKKAI decided to take the high road to avoid the suffocating reek of sulfur, the noxious fumes of death and decay that suffused the entire area. He dismounted from his donkey as the track started to become steeper, and pulled on the rope to lead the overburdened animal up the narrow path, full of white rocks that were stained with yellow ghosts from the destruction by God of Sodom and Gomorrah. The burning sun forced him to stop at regular intervals, exhausted from pulling the donkey when it refused to continue upward in places where the path was precipitous.

Finding a rock ledge shaded from the scorching intensity of the sun, he took two mouthfuls of water from his flask and fed his donkey from the bag of oats.

Abraham ben Zakkai looked down at the evil sea, indistinct now in the heat of the midday sun, swathed in a heavy gray-white mist that blunted the shore and made the distant Mountains of Moab invisible. Of all the places in Israel where he hated going the most, the Yam haMelach was at the top of his list. He didn't like going to the hills of Galilee, either, because of the madmen, murderers, and robbers who seemed to infest the area, but he would happily be there right now, with its cool glades and abundant waters, rather than in this furnace, which God had abandoned when he destroyed the evil cities that once lived by its shore.

Being a man educated in many languages, he mused on the names used by travelers for the Dead Sea. The Jews, of course, called it Yam haMelach, the Sea of Salt; the Bedouin called it al-Bahr al-Mayyit, or the Dead Sea, a name Abraham thought appropriate; the ancient Greeks who visited the area called it He Thalassa Asphaltites, or the Asphaltite Sea, but later changed it to He Nekra Thalassa, taking up the Arab description of death;

and the recently arrived Roman conquerors knew it as Mare Mortum, also the Dead Sea. He smiled when he thought of the Romans. Militaristic and practical, but not a creative idea in their brains.

Abraham visited the shores of the Dead Sea once a year, for five days at a time. He lived in the open air, lit fires from dead wood and branches to cook his food and frighten away the lions and other large beasts that inhabited the area, and spent his days collecting the leaves and branches of the tamarisk tree, which grew in abundance in the salty soils and crags of the wadis surrounding the Dead Sea. The tamarisk tree's bark was invaluable for curing warts and headaches, and a distillation made by boiling it with a pinch of yellow sulfur was a certain way of curing diseases of the eye.

Abraham had learned his skills as a doctor from his beloved and revered father, Zakkai ben Jonathan, whose knowledge had been gleaned from a long line of healers, herbalists, rabbis, and priests. Though his father was long dead, his reputation would never be forgotten. Indeed, when Abraham ben Zakkai was descending and then living for the five days in the Dead Sea area, he would begin and end each day with a prayer to his father, begging God to allow him to have the same skills and enjoy the same reputation throughout the land as the father, and the father before him.

After sipping his carefully measured drink from the flask of water, Abraham pulled his donkey upward along the path. There was still half a day of climbing before they reached the top and could travel along better roads toward Jericho and then rest for a day before finally returning home to Jerusalem. Always assuming, of course, that he didn't meet a Roman patrol that would haul him into prison to question him about why he was traveling. It had happened twice before, and had cost him his entire supply of gathered herbs and spices as well as the free treatment of the illnesses from which the Roman soldiers seemed to be suffering.

But this time he made it back to Jerusalem without incident, and two days after he'd returned home and enjoyed the company of his family, he was summoned to the house of a rich merchant who lived much higher up the hill, closer to the temple. The merchant, Samuel, was known to be a friend of the Romans, and so, while he would give the same attention to Samuel's servant girl who was suffering from fever as he'd give to any other Jew, he would also be cautious in what he would say to people. In Roman Jerusalem these days, any loose mouth could see its owner end up crucified.

The house was large and imposing. It had acquired the trappings of the Romans, with large marble columns on either side of the wooden front doors, a fountain in the courtyard, and niches for candles in the wall. Having lived and studied in Rome, Abraham was only too aware that such niches normally supported idols of gods such as Jupiter, Janus, Diana, and Minerva. But interestingly, Samuel the merchant had also erected a niche and small shrine for the household gods, or lares, spirits who were supposed to bring comfort and safety to houses that worshipped them. Abraham smiled. He wondered whether there was any trait of Jewishness inside Samuel's body or whether, like King Herod, he was more Roman than the Romans.

Abraham knocked diffidently on the door and, within moments, a large black Nubian slave opened it. He looked with disdain at Abraham and said in a supercilious voice, bordering on insolence, "People of trade do not come to my master's front door. Round the back with you."

He was about to close the door when Abraham said, "That lesion on your neck. An unguent of pine tar, bark from the almond tree, and a tincture of sulfur, the yellow powder I get from the Dead Sea, will help. If you'll let me in, I'll give you some."

The servant frowned and put his hand to his neck where he felt the painful sore caused by a boil that hadn't healed. He opened the door and nodded to Abraham. "You are a doctor?"

"I'm here to cure your servant, Leah. She has a fever." He dug into his sack, took out an ointment, and gave it to the Nubian. "Wash the lesion with water that has been boiled. That's most important. Not water from the well. Wash it with soap and try to clean out all of the pus. Then spread this unguent liberally over the lesion and the surrounding skin. Do the same thing again the following day, and each day that follows until it's healed." The Nubian looked at him skeptically. "If you don't, then the poisons from the lesion may enter your body, and you will die in agony in a month."

Shocked, the servant led him into the house and to where the food was prepared and washing was done. In a side room where four or five of the serving girls slept on the rush mats on the floor, a young woman lay, her face burning, her bare arms wet with sweat; she was panting and gasping and lay with her body in a fetal position.

"Leah? I'm Abraham ben Zakkai. I'm a doctor. Your master, Samuel, sent for me."

But the girl either couldn't hear, or was in such mortal agony that she wasn't listening.

Abraham felt her forehead. It was scorching hot. He realized immediately that her body's humors were out of alignment. He searched his memory for what Hippocrates had written about the humors and the seasons. It was summer, and so this was supposed to match the season of yellow bile, but it was obviously her blood that was in disarray, yet that was supposed to happen in the spring.

He examined her, and from the look of the girl the black and yellow bile were in order but the blood and phlegm were out of their natural orientation. He glanced up at the people gathered to see what he was doing. He had to go beyond Hippocrates and make his own judgment.

"Her blood is too hot and it is causing problems for the phlegm, which is why she has problems breathing. Bring me cold water so that I can cool down her skin, which will cool her blood.

Then take this potion of roots and barks and dilute it in the same amount of water. Get her to sip it slowly—very slowly—for the rest of the day. That will bring down the fever that is racking her body."

They stood there staring at him. "Go!" he ordered.

When he'd ensured that her body was cooled by the water and that the cold, wet towels on her forehead, chest, stomach, and legs were changed regularly for fresh wet towels, he followed the Nubian servant into the master's area of the house. He waited in an antechamber until the master was ready to see him. The noise from the adjoining room was loud: men laughing. Abraham watched as the door was opened and three men, Roman soldiers of elevated rank, walked out into the corridor and toward the front door, followed by a tall, swarthy man in rich merchant's clothes. One of the soldiers peered into the antechamber and saw Abraham sitting there. He didn't smile but merely looked away. It was obvious that Abraham's crude clothes and hat identified him as a Jew not worth knowing.

When the three soldiers had left, Samuel the merchant walked back, and his Nubian servant whispered into his ear. Samuel nodded, looked at Abraham, and said curtly, "Come."

Abraham followed Samuel into his sumptuous office. It was lined with pillars, scrolls, ledgers, tables, and chairs. On the wall were marble busts of Roman gods and dead Roman emperors and figurines of beautiful women in scanty clothing. So different from Abraham's simple yet homely house.

"My servant tells me that you have not just cured Leah but that your salve has already made his lesion feel better. You're a good doctor."

Abraham shrugged. "I use the knowledge I've gained by studying in Greece and Rome. I also use local herbs and remedies, which seem to work well."

Samuel nodded. He picked up a small cloth bag and weighed it roughly in his hand. He threw it to Abraham. "Here: it's more than you expect, but you've saved the lives of two of my servants, so it's what you deserve."

Abraham put the bag into the pocket of his tunic. "You care about your servants? I thought that friends of Rome adopted Rome's attitude toward us."

"I'm a friend of Rome, Doctor, but also a Jew. I treat life as sacred, whether it's a Roman's life or the life of a servant."

"Yet, you sit here with Romans clasping your hands as your friends while Israel's back is crushed under their heel. How can you do this, Samuel the merchant; you, a Jew?"

Samuel looked at him scornfully. "You continue to treat your patients, Doctor, and I assure you I won't interfere. Let me deal with my business with the Romans, and don't you interfere with me. You are no longer required in my house. Go!"

He sat down at his table and started to read a scroll. Abraham knew that the interview was over. He left Samuel's house and walked down the hill to his home. But Abraham didn't notice as he left Samuel's compound that a man was standing in the shadows, observing him leave. The man was dressed in the clothes of an Israelite and could have been a farmer, a craftsman, or one of the growing numbers of men whose lives had been destroyed by the Romans and who now idled away their time betting on the throwing of bones or robbing merchants who came to trade in Jerusalem's marketplaces.

The man waited until Abraham had walked beyond the walls of Samuel's compound before he ran quickly through the shadows and entered the house. He didn't knock, nor did he wait for servants to open the door. Nobody knew he was there. As he walked softly into the vestibule, he felt underneath his robes for the handle of his dagger, the essential uniform of the Sicarii, the group of Zealots, determined at any cost to rid Israel of the Romans. And as one of the Jews who'd been Jerusalem's most important merchants trading with the Romans, Samuel was the man he'd come to see.

Softly, slowly, cautiously, he listened outside Samuel's office for the sound of conversation, but there was silence. All he heard was the noise of vellum scrolls being moved around. He pushed the door open so that he could see into the room, and was relieved that Samuel was sitting at his desk reading, his back to the door.

The man crept from the doorway, as silently as a stalking lioness, until he could hear Samuel's breathing. It was then that the merchant sensed that somebody else was in the room. He turned suddenly and stood in shock when he saw that a man had crept up behind him, an arm's length away. His chair nearly fell onto the floor as he turned to face the man.

They clung together, embracing.

"By the Lord our God, Jonathan, you frightened me. Why creep up on me like a thief in the night?" said Samuel.

"What should I do, friend—announce myself at your door for all to hear?"

"Sit, refresh yourself," said Samuel, pouring him a glass of wine. "How was the assault in the Galilee?"

Jonathan looked downcast. "We lost six good men and several have been wounded. But the Romans have a bloody nose. We must have killed fifty. When I left, they were sending out waves of troops into the hills to try to find where we were hiding, but we know the paths and the caves as well as we know our wives' bodies, and they returned to their barricades empty-handed. The more wounds we inflict on them, the more weapons we steal from them, the angrier they become—and angry men don't fight as well as men who are calm and determined."

Samuel smiled and said, "I'm sorry some of ours died, but I had some generals here before, and they're becoming increasingly worried by what you and the other Zealots are doing. They've even given your men a name. They've called you after your daggers; no longer are you robbers or brigands, but you're now officially Iscariots. How do you like being Jonathan the Iscariot?"

The Zealot smiled, and shrugged. "I'm a Zealot, and proud of it."

They drank their wine, and Samuel said quietly, "I think I've found the man for you. He treated some members of my household and is skilled in the arts of healing. He's been trained in Rome and Greece, and so he probably speaks the Roman tongue better than me. He's what we've been looking for."

Jonathan the Zealot nodded. "Will he come willingly? Is he a patriot?"

"He has no love of Rome. Whether he'll follow you or whether he'll need to be dragged is something you'll have to determine."

———

November 4, 2007

YAEL WAITED for Mahmud to arrive with the unconscious Bilal. She ordered the prison guard to stand outside the doors to the private room. In the corridor, the guard pulled over a chair and sat reading the afternoon newspaper.

Within moments Mahmud arrived and dismissed the emergency porter with thanks. He pushed Bilal into the room, his hand resting on one arm of the youth's prostrate body. For what seemed a long moment, once the door was closed and they were alone in the room, they looked at each other. Silently they acknowledged what they were doing, the roles they were playing, and the consequences that might come for them both.

Then Yael quickly bent over Bilal's body. He was still involuntarily shaking and looked pallid and horribly unhealthy. Now that they were alone, she gave him an intravenous injection of the parasympathomimetic drug physostigmine to reverse the disastrous effects of the anticholinergic drug she'd given him in prison.

Within ten minutes he had stopped shaking, color was beginning to return to his cheeks, his body was beginning to warm, and when he looked at her, he remembered who she was.

His voice was raspingly dry, but he said, "I thought I was going to die."

She put her finger to her lips and whispered into his ear, "Shush, Bilal. I don't want people to think that you're getting better, or they'll take you back to prison. My friend here will take you away to safety." She didn't know why, but for reassurance she whispered into his ear, "My friend is a Palestinian."

Bilal's eyes darted to Mahmud standing on the opposite side of the bed. Mahmud smiled.

"Is the guard on the door?" Bilal whispered.

She nodded.

"Then how?"

She smiled and said, "You'll see."

She gave him a reassuring squeeze on the arm, but she was feeling anything but reassured herself. This would be the end of her career if it was ever found out what she'd done. Career? She smiled strangely to herself. It would be the end of her freedom. She'd be in prison for years. And she'd drag a thoroughly good man, Mahmud, into prison as well.

Suddenly she felt her iPhone tremble in silence in her pocket, delivering a message. It was a simple communication of one word: "Now."

She bent over Bilal and whispered into his ear, "I'm sorry about this, Bilal, but I'm going to give you another injection that will put you to sleep. I swear it won't hurt."

He trusted her and he nodded. She pulled a small case from her pocket, unzipped it, took out a syringe, and rubbed his arm with alcohol. Then she pushed the needle into his arm.

Yael walked smartly out of the room and to the nurses' station. "Can you prepare Theater G? I have to do an exploratory on that Palestinian kid. I think his kidneys are in meltdown. Ask the theater nurse to get a team together."

She walked back to the guard on Bilal's door, who was still

reading the paper. "I think that he's suffering from a secondary rupture to the angiomyolipoma that we treated him for before he went to your prison. If I'm right, he's got a massive bleed into his abdomen. He'll die of septicemia unless I stop the blood and the poisons bleeding into his body from the rupture. Are you okay to stay here? I can't allow you into the theater."

The guard nodded. "Sure. I can't stand the sight of blood. Hospitals make me ill."

She smiled. "This man will wheel him down to the theater." She gestured to Mahmud.

The guard looked at him, then at Bilal's door. "May I?" he asked. "Sure."

He opened the door and saw that Bilal was in bed, asleep, and looking terrible. "I'll go to the canteen and have lunch, if that's okay with you."

"He'll be at least five hours in surgery."

The guard nodded. She smiled as he left the floor to go to the cafeteria.

When the guard was gone, Mahmud seized the trolley and pushed open the door, maneuvering Bilal out of the ward to the elevators. Within another two minutes the elevator descended to the basement of the hospital, where an ambulance was waiting for them. Mahmud pushed the gurney with Bilal lying comatose past a dozen people, who barely glanced at them. He and Yael had a story ready, which they'd rehearsed before Bilal had arrived, and which Mahmud would deliver in a heavy Arabic accent; he'd tell anybody who asked that he was taking the patient for treatment to a specialist decontamination unit in Shaare Zedek Hospital, as the doctors thought he might have been poisoned by radioactive polonium.

But nobody stopped him, and he wheeled the lad out of the rear entrance and straight into the back of a waiting private ambulance. Mahmud secured Bilal's trolley, then dashed to the front seat and started the large gurgling engine.

Mahmud drove out of the hospital grounds at a modest pace, mentally willing the large ambulance to be as inconspicuous as possible. He looked in the rearview mirror to survey the open chamber of the ambulance and could see Bilal's dark features. He lay there with his eyes closed. Nothing would be the same after this and as Mahmud steered the vehicle out of Jerusalem and set course for Peki'in, he wondered what the fate of this young man he was risking so much for would be.

———

WHEN YAEL ARRIVED at the theater, scrubbed and ready for the operation, she pushed open the heavy overlapping polyethylene doors, entered, and looked at the operating table.

"Where is he?" she asked quizzically.

"I was hoping you could answer that," said her anesthetist. "We've been waiting for him."

"Has anybody phoned the ward?" she asked.

"Sure. They said he'd been brought down half an hour ago. We've been to the other theaters and he's not in any of them," said the nurse. "We phoned the porters and they said they'd been given no instructions to collect a patient from Surgical. What the hell's going on, Yael? Who is this patient?"

"It's Bilal, the kid with gunshot wounds; the kid who was brought from prison . . ." She suddenly became silent and looked concerned. "Jesus," she said urgently.

The entire operating room suddenly became very still and quiet. All eyes were on her as she stood in the middle of the room in her operating scrubs, thinking deeply to herself, trying to work out something seemingly impossible. She looked back at everybody; she frowned; they could see that her mind was in a state of disbelief.

"Call Security," she barked. "Jesus, the little bastard's escaped . . ."

And she hoped that her reaction was convincing.

FUAD AND MARYAM knew that Bilal had been taken to the Jerusalem Hospital. The prison authorities had contacted them and informed them that their son was very sick. Maryam, especially, had been hysterical and demanded that they go to Jerusalem, but Fuad insisted that they wait.

So when the letter was delivered anonymously, it came as a hideous shock. And the note about Bilal's death, delivered to his parents the previous day, had been the height of cruelty for its inhuman brevity. In fact, Yael could think of nothing more painful and punishing than to send a note to parents telling them that their son was dead. Worse still for his mother and father were the details Yaniv had typed: that Bilal had been executed by the Islamic Resistance in Palestine for his treachery. But in a supreme irony, right at this moment, Bilal's death would be the only thing that would keep all three of them alive.

Fuad and Maryam were in a state of confusion. One day their son was so sick he was being rushed to the hospital; the next day they received a letter telling them that he'd been executed as a traitor by men of their faith. With Fuad and Maryam bereft and incapable of understanding, the imam took over that moment of their lives and arranged for the funeral.

Yael had never before been to an Islamic house in mourning. As the day began, she'd done her best to ensure that she wasn't followed and went shopping in the Arab *shuk*, where she bought a black hijab and a long dark-blue Arabic gown. She booked a taxi to drive her to the village of Bayt al Gizah, and while waiting she put on the clothes, which instantly changed her from being a modern Israeli to an Arab woman.

Yael lowered the hijab over her brow and draped it across her face, watching in the mirror as her identity slipped away. How much her world had changed. Would anything ever be the same again? She looked at her hands, picturing the blood flowing through veins and capillaries, blood she shared with the young man the letter had pronounced dead; he was a terrorist, and yet he was a man she had broken the law to save.

Everything she thought she was, and where she had come from—everything that once was certain—was now sand shifting under her feet. She stood in front of the mirror and looked at her new self. Those people who had once seemed so foreign and so far away were now a part of her as she would be judged by anybody seeing her as a part of them. And she was afraid.

The taxi driver, not used to leaving the Jewish western part of Jerusalem, found it difficult to reach Bilal's parents' house but eventually got there. One glance told her that it had changed even in the few days since she'd last visited—as had the neighborhood. When she was there the first time, eyes were everywhere, watching her, following her, boring into her in suspicion, focusing their anger on her. This time there were no eyes. People on the street didn't even look at her. As a Jewish doctor, she was an alien in this village; now, dressed as an Arab, she was no longer "the Other."

She walked up the pathway and saw that the door was open. Inside were dozens of people—men, women, and children—sitting cross-legged on the floor, some on mats, some on the bare wood. There was a low moan, almost a hum, coming from the crowd. The men were dressed in dark shirts and black trousers, the women in black robes. Almost all of the women, except for the young girls, were wearing either a hijab or the full niqab. Their eyes looked at her but didn't register anything. She was invisible to them.

She entered the house and made her way down the front hallway to the inner rooms, where Fuad was seated on a low stool surrounded by dozens of men; close to him was the imam, who glanced up momentarily but then looked down again when he saw that Yael was only a woman.

She continued farther into the house to where the women, in

another adjoining room, were sitting on the floor surrounding Maryam. Though it might be culturally insensitive, she wanted to pay her respects to both parents. They thought their Bilal was dead; she knew he wasn't, yet she had to pretend, to try to ease their grief.

Yael knew that she couldn't enter the room of the men, so she entered the room of the women, and some of them looked at her and then back at Maryam. Bilal's mother looked older, thinner, and more haggard than the sprightly woman Yael had first met only days before. Maryam's eyes were red from crying, her cheeks rough, and she had the hollow, withdrawn look of a mother who was bereft and uncomprehending.

Yael bent down to kiss her and pay her respects, but when their eyes met, Maryam looked shocked. Yael put her fingers to her lips and Maryam nodded. But before their embrace ended, Maryam held Yael around the neck and whispered, "Those who ordered Bilal to be taken from the hospital and killed him—they are in this house. It is they who have killed him. You know this. The imam . . . Fuad has to sit with him because we are in mourning, but my husband's anger is so great that I fear for us. Fuad is so hurt that he's threatened to go to the Jews and tell them. But that will mean our deaths. When the mourners leave, we will be alone. I beg you to help me."

Yael so desperately wanted to tell her that her beloved Bilal wasn't dead, but she knew that to do so would be a catastrophe. She kept reminding herself of the absurdity: the only way to keep him alive was to convince people he was dead.

"How can I help you, Maryam? What can I do?" she whispered. She looked into Maryam's bloodshot eyes and felt a pang of distress. How much more suffering could this poor woman take?

"We must leave here," Maryam whispered, her voice even lower so that nobody could overhear. "We must leave Bayt al Gizah. Since this imam, he is poisoning the minds of the boys.

He is dividing our village. If Fuad does what he wants to do, the imam will have him killed. I'm certain. I have now lost two of my sons because of him. Bilal is dead and my other son is in prison. I can't lose any more children, nor Fuad. Please help me."

"Do you want me to help you move to another village?"

"No. The imam is no fool. He will follow us. We must move to Haifa or Tel Aviv and begin our lives again to save our family."

Yael nodded. "I can help you. I can talk to people."

Maryam pulled Yael even closer to her, so that their cheeks were touching, the old lady's lips almost kissing Yael's ear. "No. We must leave this village and nobody must know where we have gone. And to be accepted by the Jews, we must show them my family's Jewish blood. My Fuad, he's a good Muslim, but we can be saved only if we are embraced by you Jews. Your people have to protect us?" It came as a question but Yael had no answer for their fate. Her mind was fixed only in the present.

Maryam fought back tears. "Help us, Dr. Yael. If we are Jews, then my family can live in Israel? Please, I beg you. Please. Help us."

The other women were looking at the two and wondering about their long embrace. Yael straightened up and said softly, "May the blessings of our Lord Allah be upon you and this house, and may your pain and suffering be at an end."

She left the room and looked in at the men, who were gathered around Fuad on the floor, chanting a low invocation. The imam sitting next to Fuad glanced up again and looked at her as she passed the doorway. Stupidly, because of his indifference, this time she didn't avert her eyes but instead stared directly at him. He didn't seem to notice her and glanced down again. Even when she was dressed as an Arab, she was invisible, like so many women in Arabic societies.

As Yael walked to the front door, she passed mourners sitting in the corridor on cushions, just as mourners sat in Jewish houses when somebody had died. Had it not been for the dress of the women and the language they were using, this could just as easily have been a Jewish household sitting *shiva* for a dead loved one.

Outside, little children were playing catch in the garden. One wore an American Aerosmith T-shirt, another wore one sporting Bart Simpson, and a third wore one that proclaimed he was a follower of the Chicago Bulls. She walked around the corner to where her taxi was parked and instructed the driver to take her back to her apartment. As she left the village, she thought about how universal what she'd just seen was. The kids with their American T-shirts, a mother with a young baby, pulling faces and making the kid giggle, and parents grieving for the death of their son.

———

YAEL UNDRESSED, put her Arabic clothes in the closet, and was about to return to the familiarity of jeans and a knit top when there was a knock on her door. Her heart beat faster, as if there were an Angel of Death waiting for her. Yaniv had begged her to leave the country or at least move to a hotel, but she'd determined that she'd stay. She had to see this through to the end or there would never be an end. Yet, now, unprotected and alone in her apartment before she drove to Peki'in, the knock on the door presaged immediate danger.

She did up the buttons of her top and walked to the door. Hers was a security apartment, so it was likely to be a neighbor, but she opened the door with fear in her heart. Standing there were two people in police uniforms, a man and a woman. Their uniforms and badges had enabled them to gain access to the building.

Surprised, she said softly, "Yes?"

"Dr. Cohen," said the young woman, "may we come in?"

"Sure, but let me check your IDs."

The two police showed her their identification. Yael nodded

and let them into the living room of her apartment. Her heart was beating rapidly, and she knew she must show no signs of guilt. This had to be about Bilal and the escape. Dear God, she thought, how had they found out?

"Would you like to sit down?" the woman asked her. "I'm afraid that we have some very bad news for you."

"Tell me what's happened."

"Please, Doctor, sit down."

"I don't want to sit down," she said tersely. "What's happened?"

And the young officer told her that some days ago, a car had crashed through the barrier of the road leading from Jerusalem to the Dead Sea. Before rescue services could get to it, the gas tank, which was rusted and old, had ruptured and burst into flames when it hit the hot exhaust pipe. The car and the single driver had been consumed by fire, and it had taken some time to examine the few remaining recovered documents and trace the owner because he'd forgotten to register the car with the authorities. Unfortunately, the dead body belonged to her grandfather, Professor Shalman Etzion. They were terribly sorry. Could they make her a cup of coffee? Did she have any relatives or friends she could call? Was there anything they could do for her? Would she be able to come to the morgue and identify the documents, as the body was too badly burned to be identifiable?

When they'd gone, she sat in an armchair overlooking the city of Jerusalem. There in the distance was the Knesset and beyond it the museum and her childhood. It was a place of love and sanctuary for her, an anchor in her life where there were marvelous and incredible things and staff who were overjoyed at her inquisitiveness and kept slipping candy into her pocket, all presided over by a loving, kindly, gentle, white-haired, doting grandfather.

Too shocked to cry, she just stared into space, wondering what was happening in her life. She picked up her cell phone and phoned Yaniv. It had been disconnected. Then she remembered that he'd bought new SIM cards for them both. She opened her purse where she'd written his new details and dialed his number. He answered immediately.

Before she could tell him about Shalman, he burst out, "Thank God you've phoned. I'm in the village—have you got the phone? Bilal's phone—"

"My grandfather is dead, Yaniv."

There was silence on the other end of the line.

"He died in a car accident."

The tears that she'd suppressed earlier now came to her eyes as her voice became broken and meandering. "He was a good driver. He's never had an accident in his life. What's happening to me, Yaniv? Is it because of me? I don't know who I am anymore."

She burst into tears.

————

70 CE

TWO WEEKS LATER, Abraham ben Zakkai was returning home from a visit to the distant sea where he had treated a number of people in the village of Jaffa. Exhausted, Abraham pulled his donkey into his home, far below the shadow cast by the massive walls of the temple built by the late and detested King Herod.

Abraham took time to stable his donkey, feed it, and ensure it had enough to drink before he walked toward his house. From the gate he could see long lines of Jews sauntering to the archway that led up a long flight of stairs to the entrance of the temple courtyards. And as was their habit, there were Roman guards standing around, watching the Jews, ensuring that no weapons were carried up to the temple. The only knives the Romans allowed into the temple forecourt were those wielded by the priests when they slaughtered sacrificial animals brought to them by the populace.

Abraham was exhausted from the long and enervating journey, but he knew that his second responsibility, after caring for his donkey, was to visit the temple and give thanks to God the Almighty, Adonai Elohim in heaven, for his safe return and his ability to heal the sick of the land. For years, ever since he was a boy watching his father, Zakkai, tending to all Israelites, from desperately frightened pregnant women to children with hideous diseases to men injured in the fields, he had been gifted by God with the skills to ease people's pains. He had learned his father's and his grandfather's skills with plants and herbs and spices. And because his father had sent him to Greece and to Rome, where the greatest doctors of the day lived, there were many in Judea now saying that Abraham ben Zakkai was the greatest of all the healers, whose family, it was said, could be traced back to the priests in the time of King David and King Solomon of Israel.

Abraham was exhausted and desperate to see his wife and children, whom he missed fiercely, and so he walked from the nearby stables to his house, deciding to beg the Lord God's forgiveness later in the evening for not visiting His temple immediately. The street was already dark, and the lights from the temple cast garish shadows on the walls. He kissed his fingers and blew the kiss into the air, something he'd learned from his late mother, who was always frightened of the dark and of shadows and was worried about devils and demons and especially about Satan, the fallen Angel of God. She and her generation of women thought that if they blew their kiss into the air, God would be touched by their action and protect them.

He smiled at himself. He, a doctor, a man of learning and *scientia*, a man who spoke Hebrew, Latin, Koine, and Greek, and could even converse with the wandering nomads of the desert in their Arab language, blew kisses in the air. He was a man who had trained under some of the greatest doctors in Athens and

Rome, in Alexandria and Ephesus; yet, for all that, for all his travels and learning, he was still his mother's son and followed her ancient ways. For how could he do otherwise?

As he approached his home, some of the shadows in the spaces between the street and his door began to move. He thought it was an odd effect of the fires from the temple forecourt, until one of the shadows suddenly became a man. He stepped out in front of Abraham, followed by two others, then two more. The five men, dressed in the clothes of farmers or citizens of some poor village in the hills, stood between him and his home. They were robbers. Abraham was suddenly frightened.

"I have little money on me, brothers, but you're welcome to what I have," he said, trying not to sound nervous.

"Are you Abraham ben Zakkai, doctor and healer?" asked the first man. His accent wasn't that of a peasant. It was cultured, as though he was a Jerusalemite.

"Yes. What do you want of me?"

"We have some friends who are sick. They need a doctor."

Abraham sighed. "Brothers, I've just returned from the distant Great Sea and Jaffa. I'm exhausted. Aren't there other doctors, healers, you could ask?"

"Not with your reputation."

"Tomorrow, then . . . I'll—"

"Now!" said the leader. The other men moved a step closer.

But Abraham wouldn't be swayed. "No. I haven't seen my wife and children in three weeks of traveling. I have rights. I've had an exhausting journey. I—"

The leader punched him hard in the stomach. Abraham doubled over and was about to fall to his knees, when the others held him under his arms and dragged him backward up the street. To stop him from screaming, one of the men stuffed a cloth into his mouth. He began to struggle but stopped when one of the men hit him hard on the back of the neck. The last thing he remembered was an explosion of light, as though Satan had come down and entered his head.

———

SAMUEL THE MERCHANT kissed his wife and children good-bye and told them that he'd be back in four weeks. His journey, he told them, would take him to Damascus, Baabek, and Tripoli, and then he would return by traveling southward to Sidon and then back again to Acco and Jaffa and then up the hill to Jerusalem and his beloved family.

He hated lying to his wife and children, but as a close friend and associate of the Romans, and as a man who used his position of trust to assist the conquerors, his entire life was composed of lies, evasions, and excuses; but as a patriot, a citizen of Israel, and a man who, like Janus, smiled with one face and frowned with the other, Samuel was of enormous value to the Zealots, a new and fervent group who were planning a final assault to drive the Romans out of Israel. So lying to his wife and children was as much for their protection as for his own. If they were ever questioned, they could in all honesty say that Samuel, their husband and father, was in the north of the country, buying goods with which to trade and bring back to Jerusalem.

He ordered his servants to prepare the wagon, team up the mules, and bring him the baskets of food that had been prepared in his kitchens. Then, despite the darkness of the streets and the moonless night, he whipped the flanks of the beasts and set off north out of Jerusalem. But Samuel hadn't gone more than four streets before he checked that he wasn't being followed, turned his mules, and headed off in a westerly direction toward the Mediterranean Sea, or *Mare Nostrum*—"Our Sea," as the Romans patronizingly called it.

He had been traveling for some time, and was already well

clear of the city of Jerusalem, when in the gloom of the night he saw figures ahead on the road. Only merchants and robbers used the roads at night, and not even the Romans, with all their legions and weapons, their war machines and the strength of their troops, dared to be on these roads at night for fear of attack by fanatics, anti-Romans, and madmen.

As he whipped the mules farther, to the point in the road where he'd agreed to rendezvous with the Zealot party, he vaguely saw five or six men. Nervous in case they were robbers, he drew nearer, his heart thumping, and held his breath. But then he recognized the shape of the leader, Jonathan ben Isaac.

"Samuel?"

"Of course it's Samuel. Who do you think would be riding out on such a night? Julius Caesar? Do you have the doctor?"

Two of the men held a figure between them. He wasn't struggling, but it was clear, even in the dark of the Jerusalem night, that the man was held captive. They hauled him over to the wagon and hoisted him up onto the bed. Samuel turned and saw that the doctor, who he remembered, had a cloth stuffed into his mouth and was unkempt and finding it difficult to breathe.

"For God's sake, take that thing out of his mouth. He's not a Roman. He's one of us," ordered Samuel.

"Not until we're sufficiently distant from Jerusalem," said Jonathan.

"He could scream with all his might and he wouldn't be heard by the Romans. Most of them would be drunk by now, and the guards on the wall would think that it's an animal howling. Now, take that damned thing away before he suffocates."

One of the men looked at Jonathan, who nodded. He pulled the cloth out of Abraham's mouth, ready to ram his hand down hard against his lips if the prisoner began to yell. But Abraham didn't make a noise. Instead, he looked from one face to another. Then he turned to Samuel and said softly, "I know you, merchant. I treated your servants some time ago. Are you behind this?"

"You're required by the army of Zealots," said Samuel.

"The army of Zealots?"

"The Romans have to be removed from the land of Israel by force. We have thousands who'll join us. Already throughout the country, there are hundreds who have left their homes and families, brave Jews, Israelites who would rather die than live in a world where we're nothing but ants trodden into the ground by the Roman heel. Soon the Romans will feel the imprint of our boots on their backsides," said Jonathan.

Abraham struggled to sit up. Jonathan cut the ropes tethering his arms but left his feet tied so he couldn't run away. He sat on the bed of the wagon as Samuel whipped the mules into action.

"Where are you taking me?" he asked.

"Our band of fighters needs a doctor," said Samuel.

"They're wounded?" asked the doctor.

"Until now, those who were wounded were a burden, but now that you're here, they can be saved," Jonathan replied.

"Burden?" asked Abraham.

"We have to move swiftly for the safety of all. If a man is wounded and needs to be carried, it is better to slit his throat. We can't carry him, and if he falls into Roman hands, he'll be tortured. Better to end his life mercifully."

Abraham looked at Jonathan, then at Samuel, in horror.

"Listen carefully to me, Doctor," said Jonathan. "In a few days we're planning a raid against a Roman armory in Jerusalem. Because they think that I'm their servant, they speak more openly in front of me than they should. This is where I learn information that I pass on to my brethren. This is a new armory that isn't yet fully guarded, so we're going to take their weaponry and use it against the Roman army, which will be marching south from Syria into the Galilee. There may be many wounded in the assault, and so you'll be coming with us, to heal those who are able to return without being a burden."

"So you're deliberately provoking a counterattack by the

Romans," said Abraham. "Do you know how many of you will be slaughtered?"

Samuel turned and looked back at Abraham. "We're provoking Cestius Gallus, the legate of Syria, to bring his XII Fulminata legion south into Israel. While they're marching through the valleys of the Galilee toward Jerusalem to put down our rebellion, we'll attack them from the hills. We know the Galilee like the backs of our hands. We'll attack and kill hundreds from our positions high in the hills, and when they start to counterattack, we'll just disappear into caves and out of sight. We know the Roman army: their war machines can only move slowly through our valleys because there are only tracks—no roads—and that will make them vulnerable."

"Are you so stupid, all of you, that you think the Senate in Rome will just meekly accept what you're doing? They'll send tens of thousands of their toughest soldiers against you. They'll decimate our land. You'll kill us all. You'll make this into a land of widows and orphans, with rivers of tears. I beg you to stop this, to reconsider, to talk with the Romans instead of fighting them," he said, his voice breaking with fatigue and emotion. "We've been conquered many times in our history, and God has always driven our enemy from our land—the Assyrians, the Babylonians, and the Greeks. Now it's the Romans, and soon they will realize the folly of conquering a people chosen by God Himself.

"But if we fight, if we show aggression, then they will retaliate a hundredfold. Have you not heard of the punishment of decimation, in which all of the villagers are treated like captives and lined up along the edge of a cliff, and every tenth man is pushed to his death? Will you be that tenth man, Samuel, or you, Jonathan? Or your children?"

"Many of us will die," said Jonathan. "But the remainder will live free, in a free land, and be free to worship our God. But enough of this. We make camp in the clearing down there"—he pointed to a place below the level of the road where their fires wouldn't be seen at night—"and in the middle of the night, we'll return and kill as many Romans for their bows and arrows and spears as we can."

His men cheered, but Abraham's heart sank.

———

THE FOOD WAS BARELY EDIBLE, but it filled his stomach. Exhausted from his traveling, and now from being kidnapped and trussed up like a sheep, Abraham saw the men arm themselves with the evil Sicarii knives that bandits used, as well as bows, arrows, and swords. They'd re-bound him when they left the wagon to rest and make food, but as they left, Samuel the merchant cut his bonds and said, "You're on your honor, Doctor, not to escape. For if you do, we'll find you."

Abraham rubbed his wrists to return them to life. He looked at Samuel and asked quietly, so that the others couldn't hear, "Why are you involved with these Zealots, merchant? You live the life of an emperor, yet you risk everything by what you're doing."

Samuel looked at the Zealots sitting around the fire on the other side of the encampment, talking about tomorrow's raid. Softly, he said to Abraham, "I come from a long line of merchants; my father and his father before him traded with pagans and devil worshippers, with idolaters and all sorts. Like you, Doctor, I treat well all people, regardless of who they are or what they think. And like you, I love my country and I worship my God just as fervently as does any priest in the temple. So because I straddle the world of the Roman conquerors as well as sit comfortably with my brothers in Israel, I'm able to glean information to which others aren't privy.

"I'm no Zealot, Abraham, but I'm useful, and while I live this double life, I feel I'm serving my God and my people. Now, to-morrow, we have a long march to the armory, and neither of us will get any sleep. So I suggest that we rest as best we can."

———

THE FOLLOWING DAY they followed ridges and escarpments, avoiding roads and settlements in order to reach their goal. It took the men a quarter of the night to reach the outskirts of Jeru-salem, until they came up behind the new armory building where the weapons were stored. Jonathan, the leader, put his finger to his mouth, and all of his men stayed in their positions while he crept silently through the woody undergrowth to see how many men were guarding the gates. Worried that a twig might crack and alarm the guards, Jonathan watched every footfall in the moonlight, and silently but surely worked his way to the front of the building.

It was a full moon, and he could clearly see four men guard-ing the gate to the building, plus at least eight more who were sleeping under blankets around the dying embers of fires. Even the guards on the gates were sitting on low stools, holding on to their upright spears to stop themselves from falling asleep. But they were obviously tired, and in the still night air Jona-than could smell the heavy aroma of cheap Roman wine mixed with the stench of the burnt flesh of a pig. He wrinkled his nose in disgust.

Walking more rapidly than before, he used his hands to sig-nal to his men how they should position themselves and what resistance they might meet. Walking around the low mud-and-straw building, they formed the horns of the buffalo, a favorite Roman method of attack. There was no shout of "Attack!" and no order to shoot their weapons. Instead, silently two of the men crept forward and sliced the throats of Roman soldiers who were asleep. In the dark shadows cast by the glow of the dying fires, their movements went unnoticed by the drowsing guards who sat staring at the ground.

With growing confidence, another two men on the opposite side of the building quickly cut the throats of four other soldiers, three of whom died silently in their sleep without a struggle. But the fourth soldier was already half-awake, thinking of going for a piss, when he was held by the mouth as a Zealot tried to cut his throat with his knife. He struggled and managed to yell out. Instantly, the four guards on the gate stood and looked around. As they did so, four arrows hissed through the air, two missing but the other two hitting their targets in the chest and the groin. The two men who had been shot screamed in pain, and the other two guards threw down their spears and reached for their bows and arrows on the ground. One of the two was hit by another arrow in the head, the metal tip slicing through his eye socket and burying itself in his brain. The fourth managed to pick up his weapons, but before he could fire an arrow, one caught him in the arm. Shrieking in pain, he dropped his bow, and two more hit him in quick succession in the throat and the leg.

By this time, those guards who'd not yet been killed and had been asleep on the ground threw off their blankets and stood. But they weren't able to reach for their weapons because the moment they were standing, they were attacked from behind by Jonathan's foot soldiers, and stabbed in their backs, chests, and necks by the Zealots.

It had taken only a short while, yet suddenly where once there were the screams of death, now there was the silence of the grave. With no time to waste, Jonathan made the screech of a night owl, a signal for the man hidden in the trees to bring the donkey and the cart. They broke open the doors of the armory, and before the Romans of Jerusalem realized that they'd been robbed by Zealots, Jonathan and his men had disappeared into the night.

November 6, 2007

YAEL COHEN DIDN'T CRY as she drove north from Jerusalem to Peki'in. There were no more tears left, although she knew they would return. She'd traveled this road a number of times with Shalman, and now she saw his gentle face and heard his beautiful voice all around her. He seemed to fill the valleys and hills. She could remember his face only as a much younger man and, in her mind, she heard his gentle cajoling, his loving support, his tender reproofs. And she smiled at the memory of when he'd taken her around the museum and shown her off proudly to his colleagues, telling them that one day she'd be a great archaeologist.

His funeral would be in two days' time, but no matter how much it hurt her, she couldn't be there. His poor burnt body was being held by the police and the coroner pending its release, just in case evidence was brought to light that his death had been other than accidental.

She had to escape Jerusalem. The police had told her it was a tragic accident, an old man driving too fast and losing control on a bend. But too much had happened; she had seen too much in the past days. She knew the accident for what it was. She knew that somehow, inadvertently, she'd led the killers to him. And that she'd been the instrument of his death was a grief too shocking for her to contemplate. Instead, a hatred of this man began to grow in her breast—this spider in the center of the web he'd spun from his office in Shin Bet to ensnare the people she loved.

And now there was nobody. Not her mother or father, her grandparents, anybody. All dead. All gone. Now she was all alone as she drove slowly on side and minor roads toward the Galilean village of Peki'in. One of the roads north led her through a narrow ravine with steep walls, a two-lane track that meandered beside a little stream. On any other day she'd have pulled over and had a picnic lunch beside the brook, but not today.

She'd never driven north this way on her own, always using

the main mountain or sea roads, and it gave her a chance to appreciate the precipitous hills and rock-strewn valley sides. But the landscape was of less interest to her than her feelings of isolation and distress that everybody around her was in mortal danger. Yaniv had been consoling about her grandfather, but there was nothing he could do, and he begged her to leave Jerusalem, ensure she wasn't followed, and come to him as quickly as possible.

He wouldn't tell her what he'd done, but he tried to convince her that he had a solution. She wasn't in the mood to ask him what. She just wanted not to be alone. All her life, she'd been self-reliant; now she just wanted someone to make things right.

She continued to negotiate the narrow road.

———

SITTING IN HIS OFFICE, Eliahu Spitzer watched the tiny red dot travel along the spidery lines on his computer. The tracking device on the young doctor's car showed that she was traveling north, then east, then west, and then north again. She was obviously trying to avoid being followed.

He smiled to himself. This naïve girl obviously had no knowledge of the craft of espionage. She had no idea about the way agencies such as his relied on satellites and sat-nav and GPS technology to peer down unseen into the darkest corners where their enemies thought that their nefarious activities could be conducted unobserved.

Eliahu opened his desk drawer and took out his prayer book. He thumbed through the pages until he found a suitable blessing for the bounty that the Lord God had provided. There was no blessing over cars, but this one would do. After all, what he was doing was thanking the Lord for delivering his enemy, just as Joshua must have thanked the Almighty for delivering Jericho and Ai.

When he'd finished the prayer, he looked again at the little red dot. She was driving north toward the Galilee. She was going there again; she was going to that tiny little village. He smiled. It would be a date with destiny.

———

70 CE

ABRAHAM BEN ZAKKAI hadn't seen his wife and children in four months. He and the group to which he'd been forcibly enlisted had traveled along the mountainous route north from the outskirts of Jerusalem to Bethel and Mount Gerizim. They hid in the numerous crags and caves in the district of Mount Gilboa and Mount Tabor, raiding Roman encampments, stealing their weaponry, war machines, and animals, and after the raid, when they were being chased by Roman infantry, disappearing into the woods and mountainsides like early-morning mist on a hot day.

Though not a soldier, Abraham tended those who had been struck by spears or arrows and carried to safety by their comrades. He used his herbs and other medicines to cure men who suffered the ailments caused by being constantly outdoors, sleeping and eating in the wild, and living such a harsh life.

Samuel had anonymously sent Abraham's wife a purse full of coins minted by the Roman procurator in Judea, Porcius Festus, as well as another purse containing silver shekels in case the Roman coins weren't acceptable where she shopped for food and drink. She prayed that these amazing gifts came from her husband, even though she didn't know if he was alive or where he was.

Knowing his wife had money and that she and their children wouldn't starve was good news, but Abraham wanted to tell her that he was being held against his will, guarded every night to prevent him escaping, and forced to march with the army when it attacked the Roman foot patrols. But he couldn't because he knew that were he to try to smuggle a letter to her, Jonathan would read it before it was sent.

Abraham woke early the next day knowing that another raid on a Roman patrol would be taking place shortly after morning prayers. He prepared his special fighting brew in a large pot of water gathered the previous evening from the river. Into the boiling pot he put herbs, spices, the stems of mountain flowers, honey, and what he told the men was a special ingredient that he refused to disclose, but which he assured them had been passed down to him from the acolytes of the great Greek doctors Androcydes, Eudoxus of Cnidus, and Hippocrates of Cos. In fact, it was a simple tincture of horseradish—bitter, pungent, and guaranteed to make strong men flinch. But the brew's acrid unpleasantness made the men believe that it really gave them strength, and as long as they believed the medicine was doing them good, then it did them good. Even Jonathan said that since Abraham had joined the group, the men were now fighting with increased vigor and stamina.

As the men gathered up their weapons and prepared to walk from their cave hideouts in the mountains through ravines and escarpments—eventually arriving at the valley where they would wait silently on ledges for the Roman patrol of forty or fifty men to pass below them on the floor of the ravine—Jonathan sauntered over to Abraham, who was clearing away his equipment.

"Doctor, your medicine again has given me and my men the strength to continue our fight."

Abraham shrugged. "That's why you brought me here."

"And to cure those who are sick."

Abraham remained silent.

"Tell me, Doctor, have you taken any of your own medicine?"

"Why would I need to?" he asked.

"Because for months you've been attending to the health of

the Zealot army, but you've not yet seen what the army does or how it does it. So today will be different, and you will need your strength."

Abraham looked at him coldly. They had never liked each other, and although Abraham had kept his mouth shut since his abduction, it was obvious that he still considered himself an unwilling captive and not a participant in what the freedom fighters were hoping to achieve.

"You wish me to accompany you. But if you wish me to fight, you will be disappointed. I am a healer. A doctor. I cure people. I don't kill them."

Jonathan smiled. "I want you to observe. I don't want you to participate. I want you to understand why we're fighting and what it is that we're fighting for."

"Why do you assume that I don't know that, Jonathan? I know what you're doing. I disagree with the way you're doing it."

"And you think that meekly allowing the Roman heel to crush our necks is how our lives should be led?" he said aggressively.

"And how many of our men will die, how many women will be made widows and how many children will become orphans, while you and your army fight? Is there a better way to rid ourselves of the Romans? I don't know, but I do know that violence will lead to more violence, which will lead to more horrors than you can contemplate. You haven't, but I have seen Rome and some of its empire. Its strength is formidable. We aren't even a consideration to Rome when its senate meets. Its emperors are increasingly unbalanced, and if we're noticed by emperors as insane as Caligula and Nero, they'll send armies to crush us as the Romans have crushed the Iceni of the Britons and the Gauls and the tribes of Germania, and then we Jews will be no more; we'll be slaughtered by the thousands and exiled throughout all the countries in the world."

"Nonsense," said Jonathan quietly, hoping that his men couldn't overhear what Abraham was saying. "We've beaten great armies before, and—"

"And look at the nations who sent their armies against us, Jonathan. Without any assistance from us, the Egyptians, the Assyrians, the Babylonians, the Persians, and the Greeks are all gone or are in decline. If we wait, then Rome, too, will stumble and fall. All conquerors seem invincible at the time, Jonathan, but they all make the mistake of growing too quickly; they become arrogant and then their empire begins to fray at the edges like cheap cloth."

Jonathan shook his head. "So instead of just waiting meekly like servants at a banquet for Rome to decay and decline, why don't we give them a hand? Let's prick them in their rear with our sharp needles. Let's annoy them and irritate them with our daggers and spears. Don't you understand, Abraham, that we want them to send an army to try to beat us into submission? This land isn't Britain or Germania or Gaul, where the landscape is flat and smooth. Israel is a rugged land, completely unsuited to vast war machines. Our rocky hills and steep valleys will make their ballistae, catapults, and battering rams useless. They won't be able to transport them, and so they'll have to fight us with hand weapons. And there's no stronger or more resolute army than ours when it comes to bows, arrows, spears, and slingshots, which we'll rain down on them like crushing hail from our sky."

Abraham sighed. He'd been in Rome during the reign of the emperor Claudius, when twenty thousand blue-skinned Britons had been hauled in chains through the streets toward the Senate building after a humiliating victory by the Roman armies. Their leader, sullen and resentful, was pulled by oxen in a cage on a cart. And Britain, Abraham had been told, was just as rugged as Israel.

How little the Jews knew of the rest of the world and what they were facing in fighting against the Romans. The Babylonians, the Egyptians, and the Greeks had produced great armies that they'd marched across the face of the world, but their men had fought as individuals. The Romans, though, had made war into an art as well as a science and were the most deadly force of men ever to have carried weapons into battle. The men were trained over years to fight as one, whether they were a century, a cohort, or a legion; when they went into battle, the soldiers fused together and formed the shape of a turtle with their shields, and when they fought against an enemy army, they used techniques like the buffalo, with the main body attacking the opposition head-on while the horns of the buffalo surrounded the flanks of the enemy and massacred them from the sides and back.

He drank some of the strengthening brew he'd made for the men, praying to Adonai Elohim that it might give him some fortitude. No matter how often he explained the Roman warfare techniques, Jonathan and those commanders around him told him that such weaponry or military tactics were useful in lands where there were open plains, but in the rugged mountains and valleys of the Galilee and Judea, such techniques could not easily be employed.

———

SARAH, WIFE OF ABRAHAM BEN ZAKKAI, walked awkwardly, nervously, to the door of the home of Samuel the merchant, high on the hill of Jerusalem. Her heart beating, she knocked on the door. It was opened by a huge black man, a Nubian, who looked down at Sarah and frowned.

"Yes?"

"I wish to speak with your master," she said.

He smiled condescendingly and told her, "Servants use the entrance in the back of the house. This door is for—"

"I'm not a servant. I'm the wife of Abraham ben Zakkai, the doctor. I wish to—"

The moment Abraham's name was mentioned, the servant beamed a huge smile and opened the door wide. "Please, lady, enter this house. You and your family are welcome here. Your wonderful husband saved my life and that of the woman who is now my wife. He is a marvelous doctor, your husband. I hope he's well and prospering."

She sighed and followed him into the bowels of the house, where he asked her politely to sit in an antechamber while he fetched his master.

Samuel appeared shortly after and looked at her in surprise. "Yes? You're the wife of the doctor? What can I do for you?"

"Sir," she said softly, "my husband, Abraham, is a good man. A loving husband and a father. He has been abducted. I don't know who has him or whether he's alive or dead. I haven't seen him for four months and I'm in despair. Please, please, can you help me? My children are grieving and I have nobody else to turn to. You're a friend of the Romans. Has he been abducted by them and sent to a prison? Has he been taken by this new group all Jerusalem is talking about? I'm desperate. Can you help me find him?"

Samuel looked disconsolate. "Lady, with all my heart, I'd love to help you, but I have no idea where he has gone. I've met him once, briefly, when he came to my home to cure my servants. He has probably been taken as a doctor by these Zealot people, as you suggested. But I will ask and make inquiries. I know where you live and so if I hear anything I'll tell you immediately."

He reached onto his table and picked up a purse of money. He held it out to her. "I'm sure you'll need this . . ."

She smiled and shook her head. "Thank you, sir. You're kind. But I want my husband, not money."

She nodded in deference and made her exit. And he felt ashamed that he'd lied to such a good, loving, and honorable young woman.

———

SAMUEL THE MERCHANT left the camp and returned to Jerusalem to find out more information that could be of assistance to Jonathan and his men. So far, the raids that they'd undertaken had caused serious casualties among the Romans, but far more damaging than dead soldiers to the Roman commanders was the loss of face. Men died all the time in war, but for a legion to lose its eagles, for a cohort to lose its banner, was a loss of face that had to be corrected. And so, under orders from the Senate in Rome, measures were put in place that would see this nasty little rebellion quashed.

Jonathan and his men marched north and west from their secret camp to the ancient Jewish city of Sepphoris, which the Romans had renamed Diocaesarea when they built their fortress. The Zealots weren't going into the city, for they'd be slaughtered by the soldiers, but were planning an attack on a platoon of about eighty men, which constituted a century, returning from a scouting mission and led by a particularly vicious centurion. The Jews would hide in the hills about four leagues from Sepphoris and then rain hail fire, stones, and weapons down onto the valley road. By the time the soldiers' bodies were discovered, Jonathan and his Zealots would have disappeared into the hills, preparing for another strike in another part of the country.

Exhausted at the end of the two-day march over the trackless wastes of the Galilean hills and valleys, Abraham was grateful to be told to watch the massacre of the Romans from a safe place high on a hill. The Jewish Zealots positioned themselves halfway down the hill, concealed by trees, rock ledges, outcrops, and the mouths of the numerous caves. They lay flat on the earth, out of sight of the track that ran through the valley floor beside a thin stream, ready when the first arrow was let loose by Jonathan to send down their spears, rocks, and arrows in a deadly storm that would kill all the Romans in the century. The track led from the north to the south and eventually to the city of Sepphoris, and Jonathan had chosen a place of hiding that was just to the south of a bend in the arm of the valley. It meant that the Romans would march around the bend, blind to their assailants, and walk into the trap.

Abraham lay on the rock ledge high above the theater below him. He could clearly see some of the Zealots hiding and waiting, and from his vantage point he could see the road clearly. There were more than fifty Zealots assembled in the heat of the midday sun, like spiders lying in wait for flies to be snared by their web.

Time passed slowly as Abraham waited. He was both surprised and pleased that the Zealots far below him maintained their discipline, despite the boredom of waiting. On three occasions the men were roused by the noise of travelers walking toward Sepphoris. One was a goatherd urging his animals forward. The next interloper was a man on a donkey singing a song, oblivious to the dozens of deadly soldiers looking at him in amusement from their hideouts. And the third was a group of young girls giggling as they walked back to their homes in the city.

More time passed, and Abraham feared that they would have to spend the night in silence as they waited. Intelligence from a sympathizer in the city of Sepphoris informed Jonathan that the century would be returning this day after patrolling the central parts of the Galilee. They would be led by a burly and aggressive centurion by the name of Marcus Julius Tertius, hated for his brutality and feared by those under his command. Few would mourn his demise.

It was late in the afternoon, when the sun's shadows were casting a darkening gloom over the valley floor, that the men became aware of the noise of animals and cart wheels and leather-clad feet marching beyond the bend in the road. Though not yet in sight, all became alert to the sounds on the compacted earth of the road. The sounds grew louder and louder and Abraham could see all of the Zealots, many now hidden by shadows, silently reaching for their spears, bows, arrows, and rocks. Suddenly the first of the century, led by a tall, heavyset Roman riding a horse, appeared around the bend of the valley. He was followed by rows of soldiers walking three abreast. In the middle of the century were four carts pulled by oxen, laden with food, weaponry, and tents. They were marching straight into Jonathan's trap, and it was so obvious that they would soon be slaughtered. Despite their being Romans, Abraham said a brief prayer to the Almighty for their lives.

As the last of the men marched around the bend, the centurion Marcus Julius Tertius glanced around, held up his hand, and called for his men to halt. Abraham was surprised. They should have continued to march forward into the ambush, because where they had stopped was too distant for the Zealots' weapons to harm the Romans. He, Jonathan, and the Zealot army wondered what they were doing.

Abraham watched in fascination as the centurion dismounted and led his horse to the water. He barked a command, and a dozen soldiers ran to the edge of the track where it rose up the hillside, standing there on guard while the other soldiers sat on the ground and rested, drinking from flasks and eating bread from their satchels.

The Zealots were forced to wait until the Romans had finished their rest period, frustrated that their battle had been delayed. Suddenly, unexpectedly, there was a piercing scream from halfway up the hillside. Horrified, Abraham turned quickly to see one of the Zealots farther up the hill behind him stand, clutching his shoulder. Then he staggered forward and fell over the edge of the cliff, plunging earthward. Another stood, clutching at his neck as though trying to remove a bee's stinger. Frantic, the man twisted and turned and it was then that Abraham saw an arrow that had pierced the back of his neck; its point was sticking out of his throat. His eyes were wide in fear and pain as he struggled to do something, but it was immediately apparent to Abraham that the man was already as good as dead. From the wound, a fountain of blood gushed out of the man's throat and mouth as he pitched forward, headfirst. He fell just beyond the ledge and crashed onto a rock below. There was a sickening thud as the man's head was crushed, and as he fell farther, Abraham saw the streak of blood that colored the rock.

As the dead man cascaded downward, another scream came from behind a tree to his left; then another as the men to Abraham's right and left tumbled down the steep hill toward the valley floor, each man pierced by an arrow or a spear. More men on the opposite side of the valley screamed and seemed to dive from their hiding places on the mountainside down to their deaths. Each was pierced in his leg or arm or back or head by a vile Roman weapon. Abraham held his breath in shock, not knowing what to do. He was well hidden, but any movement would lead to his certain exposure and death.

And then he heard a warlike scream in Latin: *"Aperi portas Inferno!"* He'd heard it once or twice before when he was in Rome. It meant "Open the gates of Hell!" The moment the words echoed off the walls of the valley, breaking the once-peaceful silence, a further swarm of arrows and spears fell from the heights of the hills down onto where the Zealots had positioned themselves. Abraham watched in dismay as the Jews tried to return the assault but instead were rewarded by a hail of arrows. Five, then ten, then thirty Zealots clutched their chests or throats or legs as the arrows and spears found their marks. All around him was the hideous whistle of arrows in flight and the sickening thwack of spears burrowing deep into chests and arms and legs.

The Zealots stood in panic from their hideouts, looking up to the tops of the hills as they tried to defend themselves from the deadly rain of a thousand arrows and spears. But they stood no chance. Hundreds of Roman soldiers had silently gathered on the hilltops in a deadly trap. Some of the Zealots managed to shoot arrows upward toward the Romans, but it was useless, and within the blink of an eye all of the Jews were slaughtered and falling down the hillside into the ravine below. Abraham cowered, terrified, unable to move a muscle. By the good graces of Adonai, he had hidden himself on a rock ledge out of sight of the valley floor, and because of the overhang of the cave's entrance he was out of view of the soldiers on the tops of the mountains.

But he could see some of the Roman soldiers on the crest of the hillside, taking aim at the Jews as though they were killing cattle in a pen. He saw that all of the Roman soldiers in the valley had stood and were running forward. As they reached the Zealots who'd fallen down the hillside, they slit their throats to ensure that they were dead.

It was all over in what seemed like the time it takes to dress for morning prayers, but these poor patriots would never pray again. At the beginning, before the ambush, there was silence, but the moment it started, there were screams from the very depths of Gehenna; then, when the arrows and spears were in full flight, there was a cacophony of shouts and curses and threats and yelps and prayers for help. Then, just as suddenly, there was a mysterious and enveloping silence. And in the silence Abraham knew with certainty that there was death.

It was dark by the time the two centurions met, the burly one in the valley and the commander of the troops who had attacked the Zealots. They came together far below Abraham, beside the river, hugging and congratulating each other, laughing and joking about the success of their operation. And all the Romans formed up and marched out of the valley toward Sepphoris.

Abraham didn't move; couldn't move. He was the only survivor of the massacre. All the Zealots were dead and the Romans didn't even bother to bury their bodies, leaving their corpses as a testament to Rome's dominance and a lesson to any who thought to fight the might of their emperor.

And while Israel and its men were enslaved and killed by their conquerors, Abraham found that he was suddenly free to return to his comfortable life with his wife and children.

———

IT HAD BEEN THREE WEEKS since the Zealot group were slaughtered by the Romans. For them, it was a great victory, but it caused seething hatred and resentment among the Zealots in Jerusalem, who hid their activities by meeting in basements, outside of the walls in the many valleys that surrounded the city, and in eating places where the innkeepers served only those whom they recognized as being travelers or local Israelites—anybody but a Roman.

Samuel, who heard about the raid days after the bodies of Jonathan and his men became food for vultures and crows and lions, was bereft but had to pretend to look delighted when his Roman friends came to call. They gathered in his house, now one of the safest places for the nobility and senior echelons of the army to meet, and ate and drank and laughed uproariously as the Praefectus Alae, the Tribunus Cohortis, and the Praefectus Castrorum and their wives congratulated one another on their recent stunning victories. And Samuel and his wife, Lior, were forced to laugh and drink with them, agreeing that now that the Jews had been taught a severe lesson, perhaps they would behave like all enslaved peoples and respect their masters.

What none of Samuel's guests realized, though, was that the massacre of Jonathan and his men was the turning point in what had, until then, been a minor insurrection. The way in which the bodies of the Zealots were treated—left to become food for wild animals instead of being given a Jewish burial—caused the restrained hatred for the Romans to flare up. Within two days of the news reaching Jerusalem, men, women, and children who had previously observed the curfew were now walking in the shadows of the streets, watching the Romans and how they deported themselves. And they saw how frequently Samuel the wealthy merchant celebrated the Romans' success, how many important governors, senior soldiers, and their wives gathered at his house, and the noises of laughter that erupted out of the windows and over the walls.

The disgust of the people grew with the joyous banter of the Romans along the streets near the temple. And Samuel's friendship was noticed by Zealots who were not privy to Samuel's relationship with Jonathan.

One evening, when Samuel was out dining in the home of the Roman garrison commander, a party of Zealots burst their way into Samuel's home. At first his Nubian slave put up a valiant fight, breaking the necks of two of the attackers; but he was soon forced to retreat from the door where he was trying to block their entrance and was speared to death outside his master's office, where Samuel's wife, Lior, their three daughters, and their two sons were standing in fear, listening to the melee outside.

Lior now realized that she had made a terrible mistake by entering this room for safety, because there was only one door, and if the intruders overcame the servants, she and her children had no way out. She enfolded as many of the younger ones as she could in her arms, and all hid beneath Samuel's table.

"Children," she whispered, trying to keep her voice from sounding as though she were panicking, "your father will be home very soon, and he'll tell those horrible men to go away. But until your father returns, we have to remain here. The nasty men won't dare to enter into your father's office. He doesn't allow you inside, and so they will know to stay away."

But while she was trying to stop her two little girls from crying, the noise of shouting and cursing from the vestibule suddenly stopped. Her heart thumping as though it would burst out of her chest, Lior listened and prayed to God Almighty that the men had been sent away. But when she heard footsteps approaching the office's door, she knew that her worst fears were about to be realized. The door burst open and four men suddenly entered the room.

"There they are," said one of the men, pointing underneath Samuel's table. "Out, Roman whore. You and your bastards."

Her oldest son, Raphael, suddenly lost his temper and sprang to his feet. "You leave me and my family alone. Go away. You're not allowed to be in here and we don't like you." He ran at the first man and started to bang him with his fists, but the Zealot grabbed the ten-year-old by the lapels of his tunic and lifted him off the floor.

"Brave little bastard, aren't you?" he said with a malicious sneer. "Shame your mother's a Roman prostitute and your father licks the Roman backside. But your whole family isn't worth my shit, so you'll die just like the rest of them."

"No!" screamed Lior, and left her hysterical children under the table. She stood and ran to the man in order to save her Raphael. But as she ran across the room, a second man raised his dagger and plunged it into Lior's breast as she opened her arms to rescue her son. Raphael shouted for his mother as the first Zealot dropped him on the ground and kicked him mercilessly in the head. He then stomped on his neck and heard a satisfying crunch, which told him instantly that he'd killed the boy.

The other children under the table were frenzied and kicking their legs in their hysteria. Two men walked over and with a couple of light stabs with their Sicarii knives ended the children's hysteria. The men, satisfied that Samuel's family were all dead, left the room to search the rest of the house and find where the cowardly merchant was hiding.

But the Zealots couldn't find him, and so they rampaged through his whole house, killing all of his servants and scrawling in Hebrew on his pristine white plaster walls "So end the lives of those who lay with the Romans." And just so the Romans would understand that Jewish traitors would be killed for helping the invaders, a man wrote the same message in Latin: *Et ita finis vite iaceret Romanorum.*

When the Zealots were certain that all of the merchant's

family and servants were no longer a threat to Israel, a neighbor, hiding and fearing for his own life, ran to fetch Samuel.

The merchant rushed home, crying and wailing and tearing his clothes while he cradled his dead wife and children. Through his tears and cries, he heard a faint voice calling, "*Abba . . .*"

He looked around and saw his eldest son, Raphael, had crawled behind a tapestry and was lying there, dying. The boy was white from loss of blood and shock, and the wounds in the hair of his head and on his neck showed that he'd been kicked viciously by somebody. Desperate to save the sole remaining member of his family, in a flood of tears Samuel carried the boy to the house of the doctor, who'd recently returned from the captivity of the Zealots to his wife.

Abraham ben Zakkai was in the middle of saying a silent thanksgiving prayer to Adonai Elohim for keeping his family safe while he was abducted by the Zealots when Sarah, his wife of fifteen years, entered the room carrying a bowl of meat stew. It was the third such stew that week, unusual in that the family rarely ate meat more than once a week, despite the fact that he was a doctor and was quite able to afford it more often. But as he said a *b'rucha* over the wine, sipped it, and handed the cup around to his wife and his children to share in the Lord's blessing of the grape, he found his voice breaking. He was so relieved to be home, so relieved to see his beautiful family again, that for the third time that week he was moved to tears.

When all had drunk from the cup of wine, he said a *b'rucha* over the bread, which he tore into portions and handed around to his family standing beside the table. Then they all bowed their heads in their shared heritage of being Jews in Israel, even an Israel under the heel of the Romans, even an Israel being torn apart by the murderous Zealots. Silently, piously, each said his own invocation to Adonai Elohim for his own special needs, and when they'd finished their prayers they sat to eat. Since Sarah's entrance, the small room had filled with the delicious aroma of the stew, the herbs and spices and the freshly baked bread, which the children would use to mop up the divine juices.

Sarah watched the way her husband was pondering his food, gazing down into the wooden bowl and stirring it with his spoon instead of eating it eagerly as their children were. Since Abraham had returned from his abduction by the Zealots, since the massacre of the patriots, she had become increasingly worried about her husband. He'd been distant and withdrawn since he wandered back to their home in the middle of the night, emaciated, exhausted, filthy, and appearing as though all life and spirit had been drained out of him. He kissed her and his children regularly, played with them, read biblical scrolls to them, but she knew him well enough to know that his heart wasn't in it. It was as though he had returned the same man but with part of his soul missing.

When she was certain the children were fast asleep later that night, Sarah sat on the floor at his knee while he rested in his chair. "Abraham, tell me what's wrong. Is it still the thought of those Jews killed by the Romans in the Galilee?"

He smiled and stroked her hair. Shaking his head, he said softly, "No. They're in heaven. But I think of all the other Jewish souls who will soon be killed by the Romans. We're a proud people. Just as we survived the Babylonians and the Greeks, so we will fight to survive the Romans. We've lived in this land since my namesake, Abraham, first agreed to a covenant with Almighty God that we would be a light unto all the nations in this darkest of all worlds; that the sign of our covenant would be to circumcise our sons.

"Yet, our pride will soon lead us into the greatest disaster ever to befall our people. I can feel it in my very bones. I fear for the end of my people."

Sarah looked up at him in surprise and shock. "The end? Of us Jews? No, it can't be."

He sighed and continued to stroke her hair. "Darling wife, I can sense the disaster about to befall us. Maybe not today, maybe not tomorrow, maybe not for years, but one day soon. It depends on whether the emperor in power is insane or just simply evil. Since Augustus, they've all been mad. Tiberius, Caligula, Claudius, and now Nero is emperor and as mad as they come. And from what merchants and travelers tell me, he's so alienated the knights and senators of Rome that there'll be a revolt against him."

"But that's good, husband. If he's replaced . . ."

"He may be replaced by somebody even more insane."

"And that's what is causing you such sadness. I see it in your eyes, your heart, even when you look at me and the children."

"Sarah, my wife. When Father Abraham made his covenant, he couldn't have foretold that a people like the Romans would arise out of nowhere and in the space of a few lifetimes control the entire world. Their power is nothing short of awesome."

Sarah smiled and said softly, "They can't kill a whole nation, Abraham."

"Can't they? That's what the Britons and the Germans and the Gauls thought."

"Is there nothing we can do?" she asked, but before he could answer, there was the slightest tap on the wooden door. It was barely audible, yet the house was quiet and both Sarah and Abraham gazed at each other in concern. Sarah rose to answer the door, but Abraham held her back. "Protect the children. If it's trouble, escape out the back of the house."

He opened the door a fraction and was surprised to see Samuel leaning on the doorpost in a state of exhaustion. Abraham immediately grew furious on seeing this man, the very merchant who'd trapped him, kidnapped him, and sent him for three months to the camp of the Zealots.

"You!" said Abraham. "How dare you come here! After what you did to me, you dare to come here, to my house?"

But the merchant was close to dropping in exhaustion. Instead of listening, he turned and lifted up a huge bundle of clothes off the floor. He was barely able to carry it, and Abraham was stunned when an arm sagged out of the bundle. He rushed forward and helped Samuel inside with the injured boy.

"My son," he gasped. "The Zealots. They thought—"

He sank to the floor in exhaustion from carrying his son such a distance.

Abraham immediately said to Sarah, "Water. Boiling water. Quickly. And my bag with my medicines."

It was fortunate that the lad was unconscious, because when Abraham cleansed the wounds and sewed them together with stitches, had the boy been awake, he'd have been screaming with pain. Abraham covered the stitches with the yellow sulfur powder from the Dead Sea and a salve to protect the wound. As it was, if the boy recovered and didn't gain an infection in the wounds and if the bleeding stopped of its own accord, then the pain he'd experience from the operations would still be almost unbearable for one so young. Abraham would give him medicines to dull the pain, but he didn't envy the young man.

"What happened?" he asked Samuel. The merchant was now sitting on a chair, refreshed by the hot lemon water that Sarah had given him. Samuel told him in simple, direct terms.

"But why would the Zealots . . ."

"My activities as a friend of the Zealots have been known to very few. Jonathan kept me very secret because my information was so valuable. So the others must have looked at me reveling with the enemy and thought I was a traitor to the Jews. The Zealots are going around killing everybody who they see as a friend of the Romans. And the Romans won't tolerate this. They'll bring in a dozen centuries and scour the city. It'll be mass murder tonight and tomorrow and . . . I've been speaking with the head of their army and he told me that they're prepared to kill every Israelite to quell this rebellion."

"You fool of a man. You've brought this on your own head. You've created this," Abraham said, pointing to the bandaged, unconscious body of Samuel's son Raphael. "His blood is on your hands. Not the hands of the Romans. You've brought this pain on our people. And now, because of what you've done, we have to leave. All of us. Once the Romans begin to torture people, they will come to my house and arrest me and my family because for the past three months I've been with the Zealots. They'll never believe I was forced. We have to leave. All of us. Now. Tonight."

"But my son? My Raphael? Can he travel? My wife and my children. I have to bury them." Samuel was ashen-faced.

"We must look after the living and the sick," said Abraham. "We'll pray for the souls of your wife and children. But now we must leave. All of us. Raphael is young and strong. He will survive."

Samuel was disconsolate. "But the Romans are on all the gates. There's a general alarm. All soldiers are out of their barracks and searching the streets for the Zealots who are doing these things."

Abraham nodded. "There is a way. My father knew of it, as did my grandfather. In the days of King David of blessed memory, a tunnel was dug. It leads from the top of the hill on which the temple is built down into the very depths of the valley. Some old rabbis know of it, but few others. We can escape through there."

———

November 6, 2007
The village of Peki'in, Northern Galilee

YAEL PARKED THE CAR in a tiny stone garage beneath a hillside shop, some distance from the house where Yaniv had secreted Bilal away. The house itself seemed almost derelict, with large cracks in the strangely leaning wall that made it seem as if it might topple over at any minute.

With her headscarf on, Yael walked the road from the hill-side shop that meandered beneath the massive carob tree that for thousands of years had spread itself by new roots and growth over almost an entire hillside. Hidden within the hillside was the cave where Orthodox and spiritual Jews believed that Rabbi Shi-mon bar Yochai and his son, Rabbi Eleazar ben Shimon, had spent thirteen years hiding from the Romans, living only off the fruit of the carob tree and water from the spring that still flowed into the center of the village. During their isolation from the rav-ages of the Roman destruction of Israel, the two rabbis suppos-edly wrote one of the great books of Jewish mysticism, the Zohar, the Book of Splendor, a central work in the Kabbalah, the body of Jewish spirituality.

Below where she walked on the steep hillside was the ancient synagogue of Peki'in, the oldest continuously used synagogue in the world. Yet, despite the important Jewish history that infused Peki'in, only a few elderly Jews still lived there, some of them claiming to trace their ancestry back to the priests of the temple of King Solomon.

But Jewish history and traditions were the last things on her mind as she walked as inconspicuously as possible toward the house. Yaniv was looking out of the window, and when he saw her, he immediately came out to meet her. Neither said anything as she stood in front of him. But then, much to her surprise, he opened his arms and embraced her. She'd never been so close to him before, but she felt the comfort of his muscular body.

"I'm sorry, I'm so very sorry" was all he said. "I know how much you loved your *zaida*. It was a terrible thing that hap-pened."

"It was them, wasn't it?" she said. It wasn't a question. "They killed him because of me."

Yaniv didn't answer but led her gently away from the street and up the hill to the shop and the small, disheveled house.

"Keep to the shadows when you walk down these narrow

alleys," Yaniv said. "Try not to expose yourself by walking in the middle of the street."

She turned back to him. It was good not to think about her grandfather for a while. "Why? Snipers?"

"No, satellites."

"Israeli satellites look at the borders, not tiny villages."

"Spitzer has the power to point them anywhere he wants."

She didn't ask any other questions until they came to their house, but made sure she walked in the shadows.

When they entered the house, Yaniv bowed his head under the low lintel and walked into the room where Bilal was lying on the bed, staring at the ceiling. The moment he saw them— saw Yael in Arabic dress and headscarf—he sat bolt upright. He looked as if he wanted to ask a thousand questions. Instead he stayed silent, just staring at Yael and Yaniv.

"Your parents have been told you're dead, Bilal," said Yael calmly.

Bilal gasped and for a moment Yael feared the young man's reaction. "It was the only way to be sure they remain safe, and that we can protect you."

"My mother . . ." Bilal began to ask, but couldn't finish the question.

"You're her son. She weeps like any mother would."

Bilal took the news with a resigned nod as if it were strangely comforting.

Yaniv cut in, "And as expected, your imam was there. He must know you're not dead, so there's no doubt he'll question Hassan about where you are."

"But Hassan knows where I am," said Bilal, close to a whisper. "I told him. So if he tells the imam . . ."

"And that's what we want. That will bring them here."

Beneath the head covering, Yael suddenly shuddered. What was she doing here? She was a doctor, not a secret agent. But if Bilal or Yaniv noticed, they said nothing.

"And the Jew? The Shin Bet man? With the white hair? What of him?" asked Bilal.

Yaniv hesitated to respond.

"He will come after me," said the young Palestinian, fear suddenly inflecting his voice. "He will find me and kill me."

"No, Bilal," Yael said, trying to reassure him. "We won't let that happen. The one thing he fears is exposure, and he knows that if he comes here, he'll be exposed. Once we've dealt with the imam, we'll deal with him." But not even Yael thought that her answer was convincing. They were amateurs in this deadly game. Spitzer could hire any assassin he wanted, without even filling in any paperwork; the imam, too, could get anybody to come in his place. Both of these men could be sitting behind their desks in comfort while their minions did the deed. The risks she, Yaniv, and Bilal were taking were huge. But what choice did she and Yaniv have?

Bilal lay back down heavily on the bed. He was thinking about his future, if there was a future for him. "And when I am put back into prison, I will be killed by other prisoners. I am a dead man." He closed his eyes.

Yael turned to Yaniv. "Can you give us a minute alone?"

Yaniv nodded and left the room, closing the door behind him.

Yael turned to Bilal, and said, "There's something else we have to talk about, Bilal. If we come out of this alive, you'll still go to prison. You have to, and I can't change that; nobody can change what you did." Bilal gave the smallest of nods. "But there is something . . ." She hesitated, trying to find the right words. "There's something I have to tell you. It's going to come as a shock, but it's something you have to know. And once you know it, Bilal, it'll make your life much easier."

She hesitated, and saw the questioning look in his eyes. "Bilal, do you remember when I'd just operated on you in the Jerusalem hospital, and I was asking you all those questions about where you were born, about your mother and father and your relatives?"

He nodded again.

"Well, the reason was that your blood is very similar to mine. So close that we could be relatives, brother and sister, from way back in history. I went to see your mother, and she told me something . . . something about you and where you're from. She told me about her religion today and about the religion her ancestors followed. Bilal, what I'm trying to tell you is that . . ."

———

70 CE

ABRAHAM LED THE WAY on his donkey and was followed by his wife, Sarah, and his children riding their mounts. Samuel rode on his donkey behind the youngest member of Abraham's family, pleased to be in their company, glad that they'd reached an understanding. Raphael, though in great pain, was healing well, and Abraham was pleased that his wounds didn't seem to have become hot through infection.

Though Abraham still harbored anger at the way he'd been abducted from his home and forced to join the Zealots, in the intervening traumatic period the disaster that was being wrought in Jerusalem was so overwhelming that any personal animosity was subsumed by the ordeals all Jews were suffering.

Because of Raphael, their progress was slow, and so they were often overtaken by people on horseback fleeing the havoc the Romans were wreaking. Some would spend the evening around the campfire that Abraham and Samuel made and tell their tales of the misadventure befalling Jerusalem.

For two months, they said, General Titus and his second in command, Tiberius Julius Alexander, had laid siege to the city, starving the inhabitants. First to die were the children, then the elderly, then the women. Those who managed to escape through holes in the walls or in the underground tunnel told of men eating the dead bodies of their neighbors.

And the Romans were employing ballistae to hurl rocks the size of a large dog over the walls of the city. Not only were countless men and women killed in the carnage, but most buildings were badly damaged or destroyed. There were almost no streets that weren't strewn with blood and bile and limbs and torsos.

One morning, after one of the Jerusalemites fleeing had ridden off to escape to a distant land, Samuel was approached by his son, Raphael.

"Father, I was awake when that man was telling you about the Romans. I heard what he said. When my wounds are healed, when I'm better, I'm going to become a Zealot and fight the Romans. I'm going to become one of the Sicarii."

Samuel looked at his beloved son, not yet old enough to be a bar mitzvah, and smiled. He was young enough for Samuel to indulge him in his fantasy. "Good, Raphael. Then you will have to be called Raphael Iscariot, so the Romans won't know whether you're one of us or one of them."

They both laughed, and Abraham turned and observed them, wondering what the father and son had to be amused about.

Their progress toward the Galilee had been long and slow. At each village and town, Abraham had earned money as a doctor, and the others had lived quietly so as not to cause people to talk, until it was time for them to move on. After many weeks on the road, they were in sight of the safety of the hills and valleys of the Galilee.

They rode in silence, thinking about the Jerusalem they'd left behind. Abraham's children, initially in a state of shock, had grown accustomed to spending just a few weeks in a new place and then moving on. The children normally laughed, but they felt the seriousness of the adults, and their voices were stilled.

No matter how Abraham and his wife tried to normalize

the children's lives, they often talked about those days in Jerusalem as they'd gathered themselves to leave. They'd left before the mayhem, but they imagined the stench of death; the screaming and terror of people being hacked to death in the streets of the city morning, noon, and night; and the heart-wrenching sound of the massive stones of the temple and other buildings being torn apart and crashing to the ground. Though far away, in their despair, they imagined that they could smell the burning—burning flesh, burning wood, even burning stone. When he closed his eyes in an attempt to sleep, Abraham saw Jerusalem aflame, its once pristine blue sky now a jaundiced yellow from smoke and fire.

To cheer them as they trudged out of Jerusalem, Abraham had told the children that they were going to a new life, a better life, and so they had to give new names to their donkeys. His son Joshua called his Nero, and his daughter Maryam called hers Caligula, but Abraham, though laughing, told them never ever to use those names in public or disclose their names if they were stopped by a Roman patrol. And when they saw how serious their father was, the children's laughter stopped.

Travelers who met them on the road continued to speak of patrols of Roman soldiers who slaughtered almost anybody they came across. It was no longer the Jerusalem of David or Solomon, of Ezra and Nehemiah, of the Hasmoneans or of Herod the Great. It was the Jerusalem of the Romans, a destructive plague on the world who had turned a wondrous city into a pile of stones, broken bodies, and streets knee-deep in the blood of countless tens of thousands of men, women, and children. The cadavers of Jews were strewn everywhere, torn apart by sword and axe. Heads, arms, legs, and torsos were left lying about like food thrown to dogs. Where a road had to be cleared so that General Titus's troops could move from one part of the city to the next, they'd piled the trunks and limbs and heads one on top of the other beside the walls of houses, in gullies, at the bottoms of wells, in drains, beside the blackened walls of the ruins of the temple—everywhere.

Now in the Galilee, even Sarah began to feel some sense of safety. As night fell, Abraham, who was more accustomed to the country and its terrain than the urbane and sophisticated Samuel, found a path leading up the hillside toward a series of caves that appeared as they climbed higher and higher. Samuel was astounded by Abraham's connection with the land, seeming to know what was around bends in the road or what landscape was available to them, though invisible from where they rode beside the river. Yet, to Abraham, who'd traveled these paths for many years since returning from his training as a doctor in Rome, the sudden appearance of invisible caves was not surprising; the entire area of the Galilee was rich with such features.

That evening they made a fire deep in one of the larger caves. They'd first checked carefully that the cave wasn't home to some large beast that wouldn't welcome their sudden arrival. Then Abraham sent his children out to find a quantity of large sticks and, if they could manage, even larger branches. Well inside the cave, Abraham said a blessing and struck a flint four times. Each time, sparks fell onto the tinder-dry leaves. Once these were alight, despite the irritation that he knew the smoke would cause until the cold night air sucked it out, he blew gently on the nascent flame until the entire interior of the cave was warm and cheerful. The children made fun of the shadows of the rocks and outcrops on the walls of the cave while Sarah prepared the food for the night. Abraham walked out of the cave's mouth and checked that the fire couldn't be seen from down below. The smoke against the night sky would look like a fast-moving cloud to a platoon of soldiers beside the river, looking up.

The little party of escapees from Jerusalem traveled northward from cave to cave, riding their donkeys toward the part of the Galilee where they were certain the Romans were few in number. In this part of Israel, there were not many large towns, especially inland, and so it was less and less likely that General Titus would waste valuable troops or war equipment on villages without a significant population. The only cities of any size north of Jerusalem were Jericho, Emmaus, Shechem, Scythopolis, and Sepphoris, so it wasn't difficult to blend into life in a village.

"Where are we now?" asked Samuel as they entered a valley that seemed to stretch ahead as far as the eye could see.

Abraham sighed. "Samuel, every time we round a bend or see a mountain, you ask the same question. 'Where are we now?' I don't know. I once traveled in an area close to here because of an old lady who makes wonderful potions from the olive that grows in abundance in this area, but it was many years ago and I only remember the name of her village. It's called Peki'in. I'm hoping that if we climb over that hill over there," he said, pointing to an imposing ridge to their right, "we'll find the village. The lady was kind to me and gave me a lot of her medicines without asking for payment. I used them for curing skin diseases, ailments of the head, and even scrofula, though I also added sulfur from the Dead Sea. It seemed to work. I would like to see this woman again if she's still alive, for she might give me more of her potions and then I can treat the sick in this area if we settle here. She's a good woman, but she wouldn't tell me how she prepared the olive oils. She said that if they were for the benefit of Israelites, then she was obeying the will of God, but that God had shown her the way, and she wouldn't show anybody else."

"And this village, Peki'in," said Samuel, "is it a nice village?"

Sarah smiled and turned around to face Samuel as her donkey trod the uneven path. "What do you hope to find there, Samuel? A Roman theater? A Roman bath? Shops that sell the latest style of toga?"

The children burst out laughing. Even Samuel, normally dour, chuckled. But Abraham unexpectedly held up his hand for silence. The others instantly obeyed.

"Off the track. Immediately. I heard the neigh of a horse.

Romans. Hide! Quick, ride toward that copse of trees," he ordered.

Suddenly terrified, the children pulled the reins and turned their donkeys' heads toward the distant mountains. The copse of trees that their father had spoken of was near the foot of the hill, a long distance away. Between them and the trees was a stretch of open field. Riding across such a field would make them immediately visible, and the slow-moving mounts felt no urgency to trot faster, nor did they have a horse's ability to gallop.

Abraham turned to ensure that his family and Samuel were riding as quickly as they could toward the foothills. But when he looked backward, he saw a century of Romans running across the valley floor. Had they not turned off the path, they would have met the troops head-on. But regardless, Abraham knew that the centurion and his second-in-command, the only troops who were mounted, might see them. Abraham had to distract them, to make the soldiers on horseback look elsewhere and give his family a chance to reach the trees and hide in the undergrowth. So he made an immediate decision. He called to his beloved Sarah, "Head toward the trees. I will return and distract them."

"No," said Sarah. "We will hide in the trees—all of us."

"Sarah, go now. There is no time. I have to return. I have to distract them. They're too close. Save the children. I beg of you."

Without another word, Abraham turned his donkey; but before he rode off, he quickly took two stone tablets out of the baskets strapped to the sides of the animal. He handed them to Samuel, saying, "I took these from the temple before we descended into the tunnel. Do not sell these, merchant. They are our devotion to Adonai. Treat them well and give them a good place to rest, now that their home in Jerusalem has been destroyed."

Samuel took them and nodded to Abraham, who rode back to the path they had taken. Sarah, too, began to turn her mount, but Samuel put his hands on the reins and said firmly, "No! Your husband is right. He will be fine. He is a clever man and will know how to deal with them, for like me he speaks their language. But we must protect the children."

He pulled at her donkey's reins and forced Sarah and the children to follow him quickly, Sarah constantly turning to try to see what was happening, far away now, in the path across the valley.

It took Abraham moments to return to the path and continue northward as though nothing had happened. Abraham's heart was beating wildly. He'd met many Romans in the years since he'd returned from studying the arts of healing and medicine, and rarely had spoken more than a few curt sentences. Now he would have to use their accursed language to save his family—and himself. When the centurion on horseback was just coming into view, Abraham began to sing a song he'd learned years earlier in Rome. At the top of his voice, he sang in Latin,

"Julius was the first of his gens, a noble gentleman
Augustus followed after him, with Livia in command
Then came Tiberius, slayer of many
Though Livia ruled the land,
Not even Sejenus could save Tiberius,
Killed by Caligula, mad as a snake,
Dressed in his little boots
But who will mourn for Claudius,
Yes, who will mourn for Claudius
And who will mourn for Rome . . . ?"

He sang it so loudly that it almost filled the entire valley. He was halfway through the second verse, outlining Caligula's evil deeds, when he stopped singing and brought his donkey to a halt on the path, waiting for the centurion to ride up to him.

"Greetings, noble centurion," he said in a voice that was loud and firm and, he hoped, confident. "I am Abraham, a friend of Rome and personal physician to the General Titus in Jerusalem. And who might you be?"

The moment the centurion heard the name of the commander of all the forces in Israel, he became cautious. "Antonius Marcus Spurio, centurion of X Fretensis. We're on our way to Sepphoris."

By the time he'd told Abraham who he was, his troops had run up to where the centurion had stopped and stood there, panting and puffing, desperate for a drink after their exertion but knowing that regulations didn't permit food or water between rest periods. The men bent over double, trying to catch their breath, supporting themselves on their spears.

"Where are you going, Abraham the doctor?" asked the centurion.

"I'm going to Caesarea Phillippi on the coast, to gather those herbs and spices that grow in abundance there, in order to cure those ailments that plague our beloved commander."

The centurion took a flask from a pocket in his cape and looked suspiciously at Abraham. "And what ailments are those, Doctor?" he asked, a note of distrust creeping into his voice.

Abraham smiled and said in a lower voice, "A doctor doesn't discuss with others what ails his patient."

"Some years ago, Doctor, I attended the General Titus Flavius Caesar Vespasianus Augustus in Jerusalem. This was at the time when he was still pleasuring the Jewish queen, Berenice, and I was his cupbearer in services to the god Jupiter. I spoke to him once or twice, and I learned of his ailments. What particular ailments that he suffers are you treating our commander for?"

Abraham began to sweat, but it was nothing to do with the heat of the day. "Centurion," he said, trying not to show panic in his voice but rather composure, "I have sworn by the Hippocratic oath when I learned my trade of medicine in Rome. It says in part: 'What I may see or hear in the course of the treatment or even outside of the treatment in regard to the life of men, which on no account one must spread abroad, I will keep to myself, holding such things shameful to be spoken about.' So I will not discuss the ailments that our commander suffers with you or anybody else."

Abraham looked sternly up at the centurion from his lowly vantage point on his donkey. The Roman officer nodded but continued to look closely at Abraham.

"You speak Latin with a Jewish accent. You're not dressed like a noble Roman. You're dressed like a farmer and you're riding a donkey. So I'm thinking to myself that you're a Jew."

Abraham shrugged. "Yes, I'm a Jew. But a Jew who knows how to sniff the winds of fortune, and my nose tells me that fortune lies with the Romans and not with the Jews."

But the centurion wasn't persuaded. As they rode south, he and his men had killed many a Jew fleeing from Jerusalem. So he asked, "Why is a Jew allowed to treat our commander? We have Roman doctors with us."

"Because, centurion, your Roman doctors, no matter how skilled, do not know the plants that grow in this land, nor the herbs that I brew to relieve General Titus's suffering."

"And what herbs are these?"

"Herbs that grow on the coastal fringes of our land. We have in our land many things that are unique to this area. Your emperors wear togas fringed with the color purple. This is obtained from the crushed shells of the murex sea snail, found only on our northern shores. And there are herbs that grow nowhere else, which cure aches in the head, inflammations of the guts, and eruptions on the skin," he said. But he could hear that his voice was becoming more and more infused with the panic that was rising inside him.

The centurion sneered. "Jew," he said menacingly, "I have your life in my hands. I could have you killed like I'd swat a fly, throw your body into those trees over there, and nobody would miss you. Why should I believe that you're my commander's physician when you'll tell me nothing except that you're a doctor? I've spent the past four months killing any Jew I came across. You claim to be my commander's friend, yet where are your fine clothes and where are your horse and servants? So I'm wondering, Jew, what kind of a healer are you who touches the sacred body of General Titus Flavius Vespasianus? You could be one of these Zealots or a common thief or murderer. Which is why I command you to tell me what ailments my commander suffers, or I'll skewer your body like I skewer a pig before I roast it. If you value your life, Jew, you'll forget this oath and tell me. And remember that I know my commander and what ails him."

Abraham knew he couldn't ride away, as he'd be run down by the centurion. Nor could he talk his way out of this hideous situation. He needed to play for time to allow his wife and children to hide in the copse of trees.

"I will tell you this, centurion, to save my worthless life, but understand that in doing so I am betraying a sacred oath, and for this sin I will have to suffer the punishment of fasting for three days. Your general," Abraham said imperiously, trying to sound as arrogant as possible, praying that his imagination had some basis in reality, "is suffering from marsh effluvia, which he contracted when he was tribune with the army in Germania. The effects are still with him, and at night he suffers pains in the gut, foul wind, and ulcerations on his foot, possibly by inadvertently stepping into some foul miasma in Britannia when he went to reinforce your legions fighting Queen Boudicca of the Iceni."

Abraham held his breath while still staring in anger at the centurion, high up on his horse. If he'd chosen the wrong diseases, his next breath would be his last. If he'd chosen correctly, the centurion could just as easily force him back to Jerusalem and certain death. He looked steadily into the centurion's eyes but couldn't read the man's mind. All the centurion did was stare down at him as though Abraham were a dog obstructing his path.

From far away, in the copse of trees, Sarah sat on her donkey, watching Abraham speaking to the Roman commander. She couldn't hear what was said but held her breath in terror for her husband's safety. For without him, how would they survive in this village of Peki'in? And for his part, Samuel lay on the grasses between the trees, peering at the distant scene of Abraham speaking to the Romans. Why had he done it? Why risk his life? Why hadn't he tried to escape with his family? Was it an act of martyrdom?

———

November 7, 2007

ABU AHMED BIN HAMBAL bin Abdullah bin Mohammed, the imam of the village of Bayt al Gizah, sat quietly listening to the voice on the other end of the telephone. Had he not secretly met this man more than a dozen times, he would never have recognized the voice as belonging to Eliahu Spitzer, one of the most senior spies for the State of Israel. This voice sounded more like a geriatric Mickey Mouse as it was disguised through a series of filters and was beamed by covert microwave transmission signals to a satellite in geosynchronous orbit twenty-seven thousand miles above the island of Cyprus in the Mediterranean Sea; a satellite that had been decommissioned by the Israeli government a decade earlier and was no longer monitored. The voice was calm and controlled.

"And you want me to do what, precisely?" asked Abu Ahmed.

"We've tracked the woman's car to the Galilee, to the village of Peki'in. It shouldn't be difficult to find, even for you. Your people will be invisible in that part of Israel. Apparently he's already dead, so killing a dead man shouldn't be beyond your capabilities."

The imam ignored the sarcasm. "And the girl doctor? And her reporter boyfriend?"

"The reporter came to see me a few days ago. He told me some ridiculous story, pretending to be trying to save his own life. It was so transparent, I felt insulted. Obviously he was trying to flush me out. So he has to go. And the woman, yes: she has to go as well. But tell your operative to leave the man to me. Solving three problems on the same day, and at the same time, will raise too many questions. Anyway, the man isn't as much of a danger. He's a coward and will do anything to save his skin. I'll find him and make his death look like an accident, and such accidents must be made plausible."

"And does your friend Rabbi Telushkin know about this? Does he know that you're killing your own people?" asked the imam.

"I really don't think that you have the right to talk to me about internecine murders. How many Sunni have been killed by Shi'ites, and vice versa? Our objective is the same: to destroy this false government in Jerusalem. But the outcome, I promise you, will be very different. In order to bring about the return of the Messiah—our Messiah—we have to rid ourselves of those who stand in our way. It's for the greater good."

The imam knew all about the useful idiots of Neturei Karta, of course: how they wanted the same result as he did—the destruction of the Jewish state. The imam wanted it replaced by an Islamic theocracy and governed by Allah's law, sharia; the Neturei Karta wanted the state to be destroyed so that it could be born again by the arrival of the Messiah and then Judaism would spread through the world. An absurdly shared goal.

"When will you do your deed?" he asked the Shin Bet officer.

"My actions won't interfere with whatever plans you might have. I have no doubt that you'll go to the village to ensure that all is done correctly. So, then, go to Peki'in and do what must be done. Tomorrow, if you can arrange your side of the events, I'll start to organize mine. Do we have a deal?"

"We have a deal. And once this mess is behind us, what then?"

"Our plans remain the same. War and God make for strange bedfellows."

The imam laughed somewhat caustically. "And what if my god wins over your god?"

"You may have forgotten," said Eliahu, "but our gods are the same."

The imam laughed. "You Jews are a peculiar people. Anyway, I will succeed in my mission. In a small village like Peki'in, these people will not be hard to find."

Eliahu disconnected the phone and listened carefully for almost a minute. If anybody, somehow, was eavesdropping, he'd know it soon enough. A click, a heavy breath, or something. No matter how sophisticated the equipment, experienced men like him could always tell when there was a third party on the line. But when he was satisfied that his was the only ear still listening, he put the cell phone back on his desk and took out his prayer book from his drawer.

He flipped through the pages, looking for a suitable *b'rucha* said by an Orthodox Jew. He said a *b'rucha* for when an Orthodox Jew sees something hideous and evil in the sight of God. That, he thought, should do. Now it was time to tie up all the loose ends. And there was only one man who could ensure Neturei Karta's separation from the incident so that it didn't come home to bite, to ensure that the job was done right, and that man was himself.

———

IN ANOTHER TIME, another place, a different life, Yael might well have fantasized about sharing a bed with Yaniv Grossman. But this was neither the time nor the place and it certainly wasn't a fantasy. The twisted knots of fear still cramped her belly, especially now as she lay on a creaking bed in an airless room. The window overlooked the backyard but the curtains were drawn tight, closed to the world.

The whole house was tiny and cramped. Bilal lay next door, alone in a bedroom that must have felt little different than the prison cell from which he'd escaped. The only other bedroom of the house was slightly larger but nonetheless confined. There was no choice but for her and Yaniv to share the rusted metal bed with its wafer-thin mattress.

He'd stood in the doorway with a strange boyish nervousness she had never seen before. In all her tension, she found it endearing.

"I can sleep on the—"

"Floor?" Yael said. "There isn't any floor."

And indeed there wasn't. The extent of the bed filled the tiny room, leaving only the slimmest space for the door to open.

Yael rolled over onto her side and closed her eyes. Moments later the bed screeched its disapproval as the weight of Yaniv's tall, muscular body unfurled beside her.

She lay there for half an hour, feeling the heat from his body under the sheets, yet no hormones raced, her heart rate stayed the same, and she closed her eyes, willing herself to sleep. There was silence and stillness until Yael heard herself speak.

"You're using him as bait," she said softly. She and Yaniv lay facing away from each other, back to back.

"It's the only way," Yaniv replied without moving to face her, his voice low and matching hers.

"Only way to what?" It was a genuine question.

"To save us. To save him," Yaniv replied.

"Is that what you want? To save us? Or is it just the story you want? The headline?"

Yaniv shuffled on the bed and Yael knew her barb had stung.

"Is that all you think of me?" Yaniv asked after a moment's pause. "After they tried to kill me? After they killed your grandfather? After they tried to kill Bilal? Is that who you think I am?"

"I don't know who you are," Yael said, pulling any air of accusation from her voice. "You're not Israeli. You're not from here. I see you watching this country like a tourist and I wonder what you care about. Do you really care about me, or Bilal?"

Yaniv answered her question without answering her question. "I became an Israeli citizen because I love this country. I care about the story because the story matters. And Bilal's story is the only reason we're still alive. We tripped over an ant's nest, Yael, and there's no going back. We'll never be safe until Spitzer is gone, this imam is gone . . . We either expose them or we kill them . . . and neither of us is a killer."

"And if they come armed? If they're wielding guns? We're not police. Shouldn't we call somebody?"

"It will be okay" was all Yaniv said, but he knew that Yael didn't believe him.

"And what about Bilal?" asked Yael softly.

Yaniv didn't answer. She knew he wouldn't. The reality was that both of them were tyros, two people totally out of their depth. She was a doctor, he was a reporter, and they were playing at being secret agents, in competition with one of the deadliest men in Israel. She had no idea what was going to happen if or when the imam or the Shin Bet guy came to Peki'in. They'd set a trap, but what was the bait? Was it her, or Bilal, or Yaniv? And if they were tethered goats waiting for these predators to come and get them, who was going to stop the hunters?

Yael realized with a shock that she was nervous. She was rarely nervous, hadn't been really nervous since she was a child, and that was when her busy parents had left her and her brother alone in the house or when she was somewhere strange and she was alone.

But she was in bed with Yaniv and wanted to reach out so that he could hold her, reassure her.

She moved toward the center of the bed, closer to him, wanting to hold him, touch him, gain strength from the strength of his body. She was enveloped by his warmth. It was so different from all the other times she'd been physically close to him. She never wanted to be another Yaniv conquest, so she'd kept him at bay. Now she desired him; now she wanted him to hug her, hold her tightly, enfold her. She reached out and touched his shoulder, stroked his arm, and pulled him closer to her.

Yaniv turned and suddenly they were facing each other, their faces visible in the moonlight that had insinuated itself into the bedroom through the thin drapes. Yael pulled him closer to her and kissed him tenderly on the lips. He barely responded, as though it were an inappropriate move on her part. She knew that she was an Israeli beauty and had never had trouble attracting men before. Yet, she felt as though he was deliberately distancing himself from her.

"What's wrong?" she asked softly.

"Not here. Not now," he answered, his voice quiet and sleepy.

"I thought you liked me . . ."

"I do. I adore you. I can't stop thinking about you. But if we're going to make love, I want the first time to be tender and special—not somewhere like this where we're both frightened and anxious. I don't want this to be our first memory."

She kissed him again, realizing that he was right. Wrong time, wrong place, but at least now she was certain he was the right man. What an irony! For the first time in her life, she'd found the right man, and tomorrow they could both be murdered. Well, she thought, that's Israel.

She smiled. They drifted into sleep holding each other.

———

72 CE

AS HE ENTERED THE HOUSE, bending to avoid the low lintel, he smiled. It would soon be the Sabbath, and even though the sun was still hot and he was sweating from walking up the hill, the aromas of Sarah's cooking thrilled his senses. All day he'd been overseeing the work of his servants in the oil presses that he'd built in the olive groves near the village of Peki'in. Since arriving nearly two years earlier, he'd first become a buyer and seller of the olive oils that some of the village farmers produced, then he'd arranged to press them under large round stones in a small workshop he'd created, and now he was selling his oils to villages and towns as far as seven days' traveling distance from where he lived. The money he'd so far earned from the ripe crops had enabled him to pay for the construction of a house at the top of the hill where the breeze cooled the summer, close to the widow Sarah and her children.

Though Peki'in wasn't Jerusalem, a blackened ruin of a city where the streets were still stained red by the blood of the martyred Jews, he had established a comfortable life in the village, and each day, after his work was done, he'd visit the widow Sarah and her children, to whom he'd become attached.

By Jewish levirate law, according to the book of Deuteronomy, Sarah should have married one of Abraham's brothers; but all of them had been murdered, victims of the Roman massacre of Jerusalem, and the law of levirate couldn't apply. So while not a blood relative of Abraham's, Samuel had stepped up to the mark as the closest man to her and was providing her with food and shelter, aid and assistance. There was even talk in the village that one day they would marry. She was still young enough to bear his children, something that he craved so that sons other than Raphael would carry on his family name, but she was still grieving for her beloved Abraham.

There were those in the village who said that she'd mourned enough. King Solomon the Wise had once said that mourners should not be encompassed by grief and should enjoy the fruits of life. In Jewish law, the prescribed time for grieving for a husband was just the length of time for the moon to wax and wane until the next time it waxed. Yet, she had been grieving for Abraham for two years, wearing the clothes of a widow, torn at the breast, as Jacob had rent his clothes for Joseph, and King David had torn his when Saul died. It was Sarah's outward expression that showed the villagers that she was incomplete without her Abraham. It was also a warning to the younger men of the village—or the widowers from other villages looking for the comfort of a wife and housekeeper—that she was not to be theirs.

Samuel the merchant and his son, Raphael, were the only ones who seemed to be close to her, and though her neighbors had been watching closely, he arrived at her house as the sun was low on the horizon, and without fail he left her house when the moon was high in the sky. He'd never been known to stay for the length of the night, so Sarah's purity had never been questioned.

Not that she was the subject of gossip. She was a good woman, loving to her children and helpful to the elderly and the lame, always carrying their bags and foodstuffs to their doors as they wended their way home. But there was something morose about Sarah. She laughed with the women as they gathered in the center of the village where the water bubbled out of the ground in order to do their washing. But while others' laughter was full-bodied, hers was restrained, almost apologetic.

Samuel loved her for her modesty, her delicacy, and her insights. And he loved her children for their liveliness and good humor. The children had adapted to their new surroundings with ease. Though they said they missed the size and busyness and excitement of Jerusalem, they had acclimatized to life in the little village quite well and were often heard in the upper parts of the village shouting and yelling at each other, or playing in the caves near a young and healthy carob tree that was often bursting with fruit.

Samuel entered the home of Sarah and her children, and she turned as he crossed the threshold and smiled at him. She was at the fire, stirring the evening meal. The smell of freshly cooked barley bread and the aromas of mutton, grapes, garlic, and pomegranate in the stew smelled delicious.

"Welcome, Samuel. May the good grace of our Adonai Elohim be with you and make your night safe."

"And may you remain as lovely and comforting and safe as always, dear Sarah."

"How is Raphael today?" she asked.

Samuel smiled. "He's well. He's keeping the company of a young girl, Zipporah, who lives in the lower part of the village. Her mother works for me, and I know her. She's a lovely girl; her hips will bear him many children and already her breasts are large and they will fill with milk."

Sarah smiled, but deep down she'd hoped that Raphael, who'd grown into a delightful young lad of fourteen, would be interested in her daughter, Leah, even though she was only eleven. Apparently it wasn't to be.

As he sat at the table, she brought over a bowl of fresh water from the nearby well, a cup to enable him to pour the water over his hands so that he could say the proper blessing, and a clean towel. As he was saying his *b'rucha* she poured a cup of wine and gave it to him with a platter of olives, figs, and pistachio nuts.

But instead of returning to the fire to continue stirring the evening's stew, she sat and looked at him, picking up a fig and eating it. It was unusual, because she generally allowed him to sit alone while she continued with the cooking and the housework. Samuel looked at her questioningly.

"My friend," she said, "you are aware, as am I and my children, that when Abraham of blessed memory was taken by the Romans two years ago as we were riding to this village, his body was never recovered. We have assumed his death, but he has no grave."

"Of course," said Samuel.

She swallowed nervously, as though she were unburdening herself. "Well, since we've arrived here in Peki'in, you have begun to rebuild your life as a merchant, and from what you've told me, you are doing well. Not as well as your life in Jerusalem, but the Roman invaders have taken all of that away from us."

He nodded, wondering what was to come next. He began to wonder whether she would suggest that they marry. It was unheard-of for a woman to ask a man, but who knew what would happen in these terrible times for the Israelite people? Samuel realized that he wasn't breathing, rapt in the moment.

"And so I was wondering, dear friend, whether you would join with me in building a memorial to my dead husband."

He had been so wrong in his assumptions, and felt shame at thinking in that way. "But without his body . . ."

She shook her head. "No, not a grave. A memorial. Not one like the Romans with their arches or columns, but a building. A synagogue. The synagogue we have here in Peki'in is so small and unfriendly. But a town like this needs a beautiful synagogue, a *bet ha-knesset,* a meetinghouse, now that the temple in Jerusalem has been torn down. For without a beautiful synagogue, where is our Lord Adonai Elohim to reside? And the synagogue could be built on the site of the current small building, but be a beautiful building, full of light and color and drawings, with niches for our sacred vessels and our menorah to celebrate the victory of the Maccabees. And on the wall we will hang the two plaques that we've carried from the temple in Jerusalem, as a permanent memorial to what the Jewish people once were.

"What do you say, Samuel? I don't know what the cost would be, but would you do it for my Abraham? If so, if you did this wondrous thing for him, and for me and my children, then I could put him to rest and move ahead with my life."

He sipped the wine, and looked at her deep-brown eyes. Her face was lovely, framed in a red scarf with wisps of her black hair caressing her cheeks. He had admired her when they first came to Peki'in; then he had revered her for her goodness and patience; and now he realized that he loved her, loved her with all his heart—that he wanted nothing more than to marry her and for them to have their own children, as companions for him in his old age, and for her children and his son, Raphael, when he and Sarah joined Abraham in the heavens.

Since the Zealots had murdered his wife and children before the destruction of Jerusalem, he had often thought of asking

Sarah to marry him, but two things prevented it. The first was his betrayal of his dead wife and the second was because he didn't think that Sarah had accepted Abraham's death.

So he'd eschewed his personal comforts in Peki'in for the joy of remaking his fortune as a merchant. In Jerusalem, he'd risked his wife and family living such a fraught life as a spy for the Zealots. But now he realized that he wanted nothing more than a quiet and peaceful life with Sarah, to share her bed, know her body, love and revere and worship her as he worshipped Adonai Elohim.

And if the price he'd have to pay was to build a synagogue in Peki'in to the memory of her first husband, well, so be it.

————

November 8, 2007

IN THE MORNING Yael put on a warm winter jacket when she got out of bed. The house seemed cold. Even though it often snowed in Jerusalem in the winter, her apartment was heated and air-conditioned and the ambient temperature rarely varied. To go to work, she would get into a climate-controlled car and drive to a climate-controlled hospital.

So being in a simple stone house on a hill in the Galilee, she was closer to nature than she'd been in years, and for a moment enjoyed the sensation of leaving the warm bed and feeling the chilly bite of the air.

She walked out of their tiny bedroom and down the short hall to where Bilal slept. In her mind she played out what else she could possibly say to him about who he was—who *she* was—now that he'd been told the truth.

The revelation she had laid before him the previous night had caused a mix of emotions. At first his reaction had been one of shock, then denial; then, when she explained about the letter and

374

his mother's need for absolute secrecy, Bilal began to understand the implications. He said very little but his silence belied a mind in turmoil that struggled to reconcile the life he had led, the identity that had been built up based on hate, and the reality of the world he was in right now. A life that had Yael the Jew, who had saved his life, sitting in front of him and connected to him by blood.

When he finally spoke, his question was strikingly practical. "If I'm now a Jew, will I be treated differently?"

At first Yael had not known how to respond. In her mind's eye she saw Jerusalem, a city divided. She saw his village and she thought of her own upbringing, her own home. Their worlds could not be further apart.

"Yes," she had said. There could be no other answer.

Bilal had looked down at his very own body as though it were now foreign to him as Yael had pressed forward with the raw truth.

"Your mother believes that if you are known as a Jew, you will be freed or sent to a better prison. That you will be safe."

"Will I?" he asked.

"Who you are, what your bloodline is . . . this doesn't change what you did, Bilal. You killed a man."

"So my mother gave up this terrible secret for nothing."

"She believes it will save you. And she needs to believe that. She has nothing else to hope for."

Bilal stared hard into her eyes, boring down into her soul. "And you, Dr. Yael? Who are you?" Bilal spread open his hands. "If I have your blood, then you have mine . . ."

In that moment the night before, the labels, the divisions, between Arab and Israeli, Muslim and Jew, seemed so utterly incomprehensible to her. Artificial barricades that had wrought such destruction seemed washed away. Now, in the cold of a Galilee morning, their harsh reality lay just beyond the door. In the gunsights of two men who fanatically followed the extremism of their faiths.

———

WHEN YAEL KNOCKED at Bilal's bedroom, there was no answer.

She turned the handle and found that she couldn't open the door, as if something were jamming it. She pushed and called out his name. She pushed again, harder, and it still resisted. But the timber was old, rot had taken its toll, and with a further shove the door swung inward with a creak.

The window was wide-open; two of the horizontal iron bars that had sealed the portal had been removed by deep cuts made into the wooden frame. Bilal was gone.

"Yaniv!" Yael shouted, and he came running, looking into the empty room.

"Shit!"

He dashed back to quickly put on his shirt and trousers. Yael followed. In the hallway Yaniv reached into the small table for his watch and phone. In shock, he realized the phone was missing.

"Jesus!" he said. "The little bastard's stolen my phone."

"The one with the video on it?" asked Yael.

"No. No SIM card. His can't make calls. He's taken mine. He's phoning somebody . . . the little backstabbing bastard. He's phoned the fucking imam . . ."

———

BILAL COULD ALMOST HAVE HEARD Yael and Yaniv starting to search for him from where he was. He was just two streets away, hiding in a corner of the courtyard outside the ancient synagogue, where he and Hassan had planned to meet. He looked at the time on Yaniv's phone and realized that the imam was probably on his way, as he'd arranged. With trembling hands he phoned Hassan's number.

"Where are you, brother?" he asked.

"Close to the village. Where are you?"

"In the synagogue."

"Ten minutes," said Hassan.

Bilal waited in the shade of a corner of the wall. He hadn't slept all night. If what Dr. Yael said about him being a Jew was true, then who was he? All his life he'd grown up to believe in Allah and that Mohammed was his prophet. But now, if his blood was different from that of his friends, if he wasn't the same inside as he'd always been, what did it mean? Was he still Bilal ha-Mitzri, Bilal the Egyptian? Why was he the Egyptian? What did that make him? Was Allah still his god? Had his life been a lie?

Bilal examined his hands, his arms. They were the same as yesterday morning, but last night they became the hands and arms of a Jew. But they couldn't be. It was impossible.

It was all too much. He needed to talk to somebody. But who? Who could he speak with that wasn't trying to kill him? Not the imam, who wanted him dead; not the Jews, who wanted him imprisoned. Dr. Cohen? Could he trust her? Hassan, his brother? Only Hassan could help him . . .

———

ELIAHU SPITZER WATCHED as the kid, Bilal, who had become such a problem, slunk down the narrow streets of the village. The boy wasn't entirely stupid, staying out of the open, but he was easy to track from the clear vantage point on the hill where Spitzer had positioned himself. His high-powered field glasses gave him a clear view of almost the entire village.

Eliahu hadn't known where the boy was in the village. Going from door to door wasn't an option, and there were no informers in the Druze village that could be relied upon. But the Shin Bet officer didn't need such ham-fisted searching. He only had to sit in his hiding place and wait.

He removed the tiny electronic speaker from his ear and slipped it into a pocket. He had earlier been listening to the voice of a young Arab man, apparently named Hassan, and the more familiar mutterings of the imam, Abu Ahmed bin Hambal, as they drove toward the village. The car the imam and Hassan had taken had been easy to bug and from his position he had only needed to wait for their arrival, which he knew would draw Bilal out.

―――

73 CE

SAMUEL THE MERCHANT stood in awe and looked at the doors of his synagogue.

His synagogue.

It wasn't the Peki'in synagogue, or Abraham's synagogue, but *his* synagogue.

Not, of course, that he would ever use this name to his wife, Sarah, or to their newly born baby boy whom they had named Abraham in memory of his mother's first husband, a man the child would never know. But as he'd paid for the stone and the timber, the stonemasons and the carpenters, the artisans and the other craftsmen, he felt entitled, when he was alone and provided he said it silently to himself, to call it "Samuel's synagogue."

It was finished, complete. The final stones had been laid, the women of the village had put in a special effort to sweep the floor and polish the new pure silver seven-branched menorah he'd bought from a craftsman's shop in distant Acre, and now he was making a final inspection before its consecration in the morning by the learned and blessed Rabbi Gamliel of Yavne, leader of those Jews who had not fled from Israel to other lands after the destruction of the temple. Rabbi Gamliel was also the head of the Great Sanhedrin of Israel, the body of lawmakers and adjudicators that had re-formed since the obliteration of the city of Jerusalem.

Such great rabbis rarely left their schools, but Samuel had known Gamliel from his days in Jerusalem when he was a friend to the Romans and a spy for the Zealots. Gamliel was one of the few who stood up for Samuel when he was accused of being a traitor to the Jews by those citizens who were ignorant of his role as a spy. And so, when Samuel had sent word to Gamliel that the synagogue he'd financed was about to be opened, Gamliel asked whether he could consecrate it.

The moment Samuel told his wife, Sarah, who would be visiting the village the following day and officiating at the very first community ceremony and prayers in the synagogue, she looked at him in amazement and then threw her arms around him.

"Truly, Samuel, when I was married to Abraham, I didn't think there could be a better husband in the world than him. But in this past year as my husband, and in the two years before that as the friend who supported me and my children when we were at our lowest ebb, you have risen in my eyes to be a dear friend and a true love. While nobody can replace Abraham, you have become my husband and father to my children, and now that we have our own son, Abraham, we are a family."

In the first several months of building, Sarah had visited the synagogue many times a week, both as a woman standing on the periphery, watching the men working on the stones and the woodwork, and as a worker, assisting the men in carrying panniers of dirt and stones to be thrown into the bottom of the valley. But as the frame of the building was completed and the men cut and shaved wood and began to carve sacred images into the stones, Sarah visited less and less. Samuel thought it was because she was bored, but her reality was very different from his. As the building became more and more complete, it became less Abraham's memorial, and more and more Samuel's donation to the village. She felt guilty for thinking these thoughts, as though the sacred memory of her blessed doctor husband had somehow become lost in the act of building his memorial: the flesh and blood of her first husband was replaced by the physical beauty of the building, the carvings and the ornaments. In ten years or a thousand years, who would remember Abraham the Healer when they were praying to Adonai Elohim? All they would see was a beauteous building, its purpose forgotten, its value vested in its silver and gold, not in the man whose memory it served.

She had said this to Samuel over breakfast on the day he inspected the synagogue to ensure that all was right for the visit of Rabbi Gamliel. Samuel listened attentively and said gently to his wife, "Dearest love, Abraham will live on in your heart and in the hearts of those children who you and he shared. And our love will live on through our own child, our own Abraham, whose blood is yours and mine, and who I'm sure will grow up to be a healer like your first husband."

She smiled and said, "But from the way he grasps my breast when I feed him, I think he will be more merchant than doctor, for no matter how much he drinks, he never seems to be satisfied."

Samuel smiled as he thought back to their conversation. He sat on a bench in the middle of the synagogue feeling the coolness that the stone building afforded. He looked around and saw in delight the niches where ancient columns from the Jerusalem temple had been saved and now stood. He saw the two stone plaques that Abraham had retrieved from the temple after the Romans had thrown the huge building blocks into the nearby streets, pulling it down and leaving one of the world's greatest buildings in rubble.

He knew that his modest building could never begin to equate to the palatial temple that King Herod had constructed or the magnificent edifice that King Solomon had created a thousand years before; but his building was a temple nonetheless, and he loved every stone, every ornament, every niche.

Sitting alone in the middle of his synagogue made Samuel think about who he was and how he had come here. One year he was a wealthy merchant, friend of the imperial commanders, confidant of the Zealots, treading a dangerous path between the two. A year later he was doing everything in his power to earn a living from trading olive oil in a tiny village nobody in Jerusalem, even ruined Jerusalem, had heard of; and now he was making the village prosperous, he had a wife and a son, and he was sitting in the middle of the synagogue that he had founded.

How had he come to this? He knew that he was surrounded by all of the people, now dead, whose lives had gone to create him and his life. He thought of his father and his grandfather and all the unknown and unknowable generations back to the time of Solomon and David and Saul and Abraham. Had Father Abraham passed this way as he walked from his home of Ur in Mesopotamia toward Jerusalem with his son Isaac, instructed by Adonai Elohim to sacrifice the boy, only to be held back when the Angel of God told him not to slaughter the boy but instead to slaughter a ram? Had Abraham, or Isaac, or Jacob or Moses or Aaron, known of Peki'in? Did they know of the wondrous olives that grew in the valleys and on the sides of the hills? Did they know how sweet the water was that bubbled up in the center of the village? Did they know how pure the air was, or how sweet the view was to the north of the mountains, sometimes capped in snow in a harsh winter?

He sat there thinking how wonderful the next day would be, how glorious for himself and Sarah, when Rabbi Gamliel arrived with his students and assistants, and the whole town gathered in the center to see him, to be blessed by him, and to listen to him say his blessings when he officiated at the first ceremony in the Peki'in synagogue.

And as he remained seated, Samuel smiled to himself. Only through the joining of himself, a merchant, with Sarah, the wife of the healer, had all this glory come about. Indeed, the Lord God did work in mysterious ways.

His thoughts were interrupted when the doors of the synagogue slowly creaked open . . .

———

November 8, 2007

BILAL LOOKED AT THE DOORS of the synagogue and wondered whether he should wait in the courtyard or open the doors and wait inside.

While he was thinking, a dusty old Toyota pickup rolled down the central narrow street of the village. Inside were two men, one young and fresh-faced, the other much older, wearing the clothes of a Muslim priest; Hassan and the imam rode in silence amid the noise of the engine.

Bilal heard the car draw near and stop. In the early morning the village was eerily quiet. The only noises were from farm animals in nearby fields and the barking of a distant dog.

The moment Bilal heard the car, he decided that he should meet them inside the synagogue. It would make his imam uncomfortable, but that was good. The young man stood from where he'd been crouching in the corner of the courtyard since escaping from the house and walked quickly toward the synagogue's closed doors. He pushed them open and walked inside. He'd never been inside a Jewish religious building before, and it wasn't what he expected. It was drab, old, with white plaster on the walls, and columns that looked as if they had come from ancient Rome, and above the door was an old, brown, faded handwritten part of some ancient scroll.

Heart pounding, he found a seat and waited for the arrival of Hassan and the imam. He closed his eyes and tried not to think about the conversation last night with Dr. Yael. She'd told him so much and had undermined everything that he had ever known about himself. Yet, she'd also opened a door to hope, to a golden future. He felt like a pauper who'd suddenly seen the inside of a treasure house and been told that he could go in and take as much as he wanted.

He opened his eyes again and looked at the Jewish markings on the walls, at the ark at the front of the synagogue with its Hebrew writing on top, and at the prayer books. Was he really part of this? He'd grown up to believe that this was all evil, but . . .

Bilal's thoughts were interrupted by a blinding light in the synagogue doorway. He looked over and saw the dark outlines of two men. One of them entered. The other stayed.

He heard his imam's voice. "Bilal, my son, come outside. Come here into the light."

"No, Imam, it's better to meet here. Inside. Where we can't be seen."

He saw Hassan turn and hold out his hand for the imam, as though helping a crippled man to walk. Slowly, reluctantly, he saw the imam walk inside the doorway. They lingered at the entrance for a moment, looking into the small building, to adjust their eyes from the brilliance outside.

Bilal stood and bowed slightly as the imam walked over to him. As he neared, the imam looked around at the Jewish symbols adorning the walls, the star of the shield of David, the menorah, and the Ark of the Covenant at the front facing in the direction of Jerusalem.

The imam then turned his attention to Bilal. "My son," he said as he walked toward the young man. He put his arms on the boy's shoulders and kissed him on both cheeks. "It is so good you are alive. Allah the merciful has given you a great blessing."

Bilal said nothing as the imam stood face-to-face with him, still holding his shoulders. Not so long ago such an embrace would have overwhelmed him; it was all he'd ever hoped for. But now there was no similar feeling, no sense of confidence or pride.

The imam continued: "We should not be meeting here, my son, not in this unholy place. But because Allah has willed these Jews to free you, I will stand shoulder to shoulder with you in these times of your adversity. You were right to contact us. And now you can be safe. Now you can come home."

Home . . . Bilal pondered the word and what it might mean now.

"We should leave here. We might be seen," Hassan said, breaking the moment, his eyes darting nervously and refusing to look at Bilal.

Quietly, and looking at the floor, Bilal asked, "How do you know I'll be safe, Imam? Where will you take me that's safe? I can't go back to my parents' home, so where will I go? Egypt? Jordan? How will you get me out of the country?"

The questions took the imam by surprise and Hassan took a small step backward.

"You doubt and question me? You've sworn an oath in the name of Mohammed, peace and blessings be upon him, that you would obey, not question. Why would you doubt me?"

Bilal didn't answer but found himself staring at Hassan, and for the first time since he had arrived Hassan didn't avert his gaze.

"What has happened to change you, my son? You forget yourself. Too long in the company of the infidel," the imam said. His voice was quiet and confident.

Bilal's eyes slowly left Hassan's and he faced the imam.

"The doctor saved my life when the Jew soldiers shot me. She may be an infidel, but by custom, and all that you have taught me, is my life not now hers?"

"Bah!" The imam waved a dismissive hand at the suggestion. "You were not saved, Bilal. A martyr is not *saved* when his martyrdom fails because of the enemy."

But Bilal was not deterred and a stoic tone rose in his throat. Hassan took a step back, frightened and confused by the Bilal in front of him, so unrecognizable from the childhood friend he knew.

"And she saved my life again when she helped me escape from the prison. There were people who would have killed me in the prison. Muslims! Muslims would have murdered me. Yet, she saved me."

"What nonsense is this, Bilal?" The imam's voice changed to anger. "What is making you say these things?"

"I have been told—"

"Who has told you? What have they said?" the imam snapped.

Imam Abu Ahmed bin Hambal stared deeply into the eyes of the boy who'd once been his acolyte, his willing puppet. In that moment he knew that the boy had changed irrevocably and had to be dealt with immediately. He had converted from being a *shahid* to being a traitor.

"Hassan, end this now," demanded the imam in gruff and commanding tones, the voice of a man used to being obeyed.

Bilal turned his gaze to his friend and saw that Hassan showed no sign of surprise at the order from his imam. Yet, Hassan did not move.

"End it now!" bellowed the imam.

---

73 CE

SAMUEL THE MERCHANT looked at the doors to the synagogue and was surprised to see his wife, Sarah, standing there, framed in the brilliant light. He couldn't see her face, dark against the light, but he knew from her shape that it was her.

"Wife?"

"Samuel. I've come to spend some moments together with you, in the peace of the synagogue, and in the presence of Adonai Elohim, our God Almighty."

He stood and reached out his hands toward her, but instead of taking them, she hugged him in a close and loving embrace. But when she looked closely at his face, she could see that he'd been crying.

"Husband. What's wrong?" she said softly.

"Dearest wife. My lovely Sarah. There are things I must tell you. Things I have done in the past of which you don't know. Things that touch upon my acts toward Abraham, your beloved husband, and you and your children.

"Sarah, years ago, when I was a friend of the Romans, I—"

But she put her fingers to his lips and stopped him from talking. "Samuel. Husband. There are things that happened in the past that we can't alter. These are things that we have to live with. But we are today, and we will be tomorrow and next year. We have children who came to us from others, and now we have our own child. The past is the past, husband. We have started our lives again. Ours is the future. Don't let the past damage what we have, what we've built."

He looked at her with such love and tenderness, and tears rolled down his face.

She continued. "Samuel. Husband. When we first married, I was not in love with you. I was still in love with my beloved Abraham. You were a friend, and as a widow with two children, I needed the protection of a friend. You were good to me, and I know that for two or three weeks after we were married I didn't share my body with you, and you never once demanded your rights. For that I was more than grateful. I knew from that simple gesture that you were a kind man and that your heart was fond and loving.

"And it was then that I opened my own heart to you and began to love you. Slowly at first, but more and more, and now, Samuel, now that you've paid for this beautiful synagogue in memory of Abraham, now that we ourselves have a glorious son called Abraham, I've come to tell you how much I love you and to thank you for being such a good and kind husband to me and a father to my children."

He hugged her and realized there and then that all would be well for them. "Sarah, my dear wife. You know how much I love and admire you, and for you I have built this synagogue in memory of your first husband. May this building, dedicated to the

One True God, be a sanctuary for all time, a place of peace and harmony and loving-kindness."

Sarah nodded and said softly, "Amen."

November 8, 2007

SPITZER LOOKED THROUGH the viewfinder on the rifle's sight into the synagogue. He had a clear view and could easily kill the target now. He was settled in position, lying in a block of waste-land cordoned off from the road by rusted corrugated iron and elevated some three hundred yards from the Peki'in synagogue. Lying down on a blanket, staring through the high-intensity scope of his Israeli-made TEI M89SR sniper rifle, his view of the front half of the interior of the synagogue was more than ad-equate. Despite its use as a long-range killing weapon, the rifle was very short in length and easily slipped away into a sports bag. And this is exactly what Eliahu Spitzer would do when his task here was done.

Eliahu lifted the rifle's silencer out of the case and screwed it to the end of the barrel so that neither sound nor muzzle flash would be emitted. Then he brought the rifle back to his shoulder. The crisp black crosshairs of his telescopic sight drifted slowly and incrementally across the space of the synagogue so far away before him. Through the tunnel-vision image ringed in black, Spitzer heard and felt his own breath. Just before he squeezed the trigger, he'd hold his breath. Years of training compelled him to slow his pulse and let his muscles press into the ground beneath him.

Opening his other eye briefly, he adjusted the dials on the

scope and then returned to the tunnel vision of the crosshairs now drifting over the figures standing in conversation.

He saw the imam, his head uncovered, wearing his long robes in stark contrast to the ragged jeans and jackets of the younger men. He saw the one who must be Hassan standing close by and facing the third figure: Bilal.

Spitzer settled the gun sight, stopped its slow drift over the scene to come to a standstill over the head of Bilal. The crosshairs formed a perfect crucifix on the bridge of his nose.

Spitzer's lungs filled very slowly with air.

———

WITH A SLOW, DELIBERATE HAND and eyes never leaving Bilal, Hassan took out a small pistol from inside his loose jacket. Bilal physically shrank in retreat, and yet, as he looked at his friend, there was no shock or surprise in his expression.

Hassan leveled the gun, and his hand shook but he quickly grasped the butt of the pistol with his other hand to steady it.

"Hassan. You're my brother," said Bilal, with pleading in his eyes.

"You betrayed us," Hassan replied.

"No. We've all been betrayed," said Bilal, his voice more resigned than afraid.

"I have to do what the imam tells me, Bilal. I swore an oath in the name of Allah."

"Why?" asked Bilal. "Why?"

Hassan's voice dried up and he couldn't speak. The imam said menacingly, "Because you failed. We can have no patience with failures. You deserve to die because you put us at risk by your failure."

The imam turned to Hassan with cold, piercing eyes. "Hassan, kill him!"

Suddenly they heard footsteps on the stones leading up to

the door. The imam turned at the intrusion and Hassan's eyes flashed in surprise, but he didn't lower the pistol and Bilal was rooted to the spot.

Yael walked into the synagogue. She stared in shock at the three men standing there, but when she saw the gun, instinct made her try to stop what was happening.

"Bilal!" cried Yael.

For a long moment nobody said anything.

———

THE OPEN DOORS of the synagogue afforded Spitzer a perfect view of all of the players in the drama taking place. But then there was a flicker. Though the dark field of vision through the telescopic sight was constrained, showing little more than the head and shoulders of Bilal, the light in the room altered, causing the shadows over the young Palestinian's face to shift.

With a tiny movement of his forearm, Spitzer lifted the sight away from Bilal to drift over the space of the synagogue. It was amazing how much of the interior of the room he could see. The imam and Hassan remained fixed to the spot, but their gaze was diverted elsewhere in the room. Eliahu continued to guide the scope upward toward the subject of their gaze until the face of Yael, like a deer in headlights, filled the sight and behind her, soon after, emerged the figure of Yaniv.

Eliahu lifted his left hand from the rifle and adjusted the telescopic sight to draw it back to a wider field of view so he could see everybody at once. The imam, Bilal, Hassan, Yael, and Yaniv Grossman, the journalist.

"My God, what an odd congregation in a synagogue," said Spitzer out loud, a wry smile on his face as he reflected on the hopes that he and the imam shared for the dismantlement of Israel.

Eliahu Spitzer said a quick *b'rucha* under his breath as he rested the stock of the rifle against the side of his face. The task ahead seemed all too easy.

———

THE MOMENT YANIV followed Yael into the synagogue, he recognized the danger of their situation. He grasped her forearm and tried to drag her back through the door but she jerked free with a strength that surprised him.

She was pleading with Hassan and the imam. "What do you want with him? Let him go?!" To her own ears the words sounded petty and worthless.

"Hassan!" insisted the imam. But Hassan's eyes flashed back and forth between Yael and Bilal, his hand trembling around the pistol in his grip.

"Don't! Don't do this!" Yael's voice was desperate as she walked closer to the three men. "Hassan. Remember in the café? You told me you couldn't kill me. Remember? Don't do this to Bilal. He's your best friend. Please."

"Yael!" Yaniv was behind her, trying to pull her to safety.

"Hassan! Kill them. Shoot!" the imam demanded. But Hassan didn't . . . couldn't. Nor could he move as he and Bilal stared at each other, wide-eyed.

The imam let out a guttural grunt. He snatched the pistol from Hassan's hand and pointed it at Yael.

Yael froze in sudden horror as she stared into the hollow barrel of the gun.

"You're a priest. A man of God!" she gasped, her body rigid as stone.

"Jew! What do you know of God?"

In that instant a part of the imam's head suddenly detached from his body and flew sideways toward the Ark of the Covenant. One second Yael was looking at the imam's face, seeing him sneer with the pistol in his hand; the next she stared into part of his skull, his bloodied brain exploding and splattering against the synagogue's walls. His brain liquefied like jelly and sprayed over the ceiling, the walls, and the floor. Dollops of the imam's brain hit Yaniv and Yael. Both of them looked on in astonishment.

There was no noise of a gunshot, just the clattering of the pistol to the floor and the strangely wet smack of the imam's body crumpling to the floor. For a fraction of a moment nobody moved.

Then Hassan broke the stupefied silence as he fell to his knees in front of the near-headless body of his imam. He put his hand on the chest of the cleric as if feeling for a heartbeat. Yael looked on, her doctor's mind unconsciously considering the absurdity of such a gesture. Then, still stunned and her head spinning, she saw Bilal crouch in front of his friend and grab Hassan's wrist, trying to yank him back to his feet.

"Run, Hassan. Run!" Bilal cried as he hauled Hassan back to his feet. The two childhood friends stood staring at each other for a moment. Hassan then opened his mouth to speak but there was a small percussive thud. Instead of words, blood poured out of Hassan's mouth as he slumped into Bilal's arms.

Another bullet suddenly splintered the wood of a pew close to Yael and she flung herself sideways onto the floor. Her sudden drop in height meant the next bullet flew through the space where she had once been and exploded the plaster on the wall behind, mere inches from Yaniv, who in turn threw himself onto the floor.

Yael looked up and out through the open doors of the synagogue into the bright, glaring Israeli sun. For a moment she was dazed by the light, her eyes squinting. She heard the sound of running feet but whether it came from behind or in front of her she couldn't say. Blinded and blinking, she pushed herself onto her knees as a shadow fell over her and the glaring light dimmed for a moment. Widespread arms wrapped around her and pushed her to the ground, knocking the air from her lungs in a squelching gasp as she heard again the same strange damp percussive thud as her head hit the floor. Feeling the weight on her, she opened her eyes to see Bilal's face inches from her own.

His mouth was straight, not contorted. His eyes were open but not focused. The muscles around his brow and his jaw were slack, his lips close enough to kiss.

"No!" came a cry from somewhere that seemed far away. "Bilal?" Yael screamed.

The young man's body slid sideways off her and his eyes dimmed in death as the bullet exploded in his back and shattered his heart.

When he had slid from her, she suddenly felt a searing pain in her body. Her head hurt from when it had hit the floor, but it was the radiating pain that coursed through her, from her shoulder and across her chest, that worried her. As a doctor, she tried to analyze why she was in pain. She put her hand to her chest and it came away bright red with blood. Her blood and Bilal's blood, mixed together. The bullet that killed Bilal was now lodged in her.

Yael screamed. The high ceiling of the synagogue swirled above her. Two muscular arms slid under her shoulders and she felt herself drifting backward.

And then silence.

———

SPITZER LOOKED THROUGH the scope and realized that the scene was hopelessly compromised. He cursed under his breath. He hadn't seen the doctor and the reporter coming, and five targets made for a much-too-complex kill zone. But he was a patient man; he knew for certain that three had been taken and the rest would have to wait for another day.

He picked up the spent shells from the rifle, carefully unscrewed the scope and silencer, and packed everything away into the small case. He stood, shook his blanket, which he'd dump into a trash can on the way back to Jerusalem, and paused for a moment, wondering. Unlike amateurs, who would run like scared rabbits from such a scene and be noticed by passersby, Eliahu was a professional. It would be hours before anybody came to where he was to examine a possible sniper's location, and so he waited there for a few minutes, pondering his next move.

He then walked toward his car, threw everything into the trunk, and drove cautiously along the narrow, twisting streets out of the village. The image of the despoiled synagogue bothered him, but there was nothing he could do about that. He said another *b'rucha* as he drove along the road to Nahariya, then south to Jerusalem.

As he drove, in his mind's eye he could see the face of Rabbi Telushkin, could feel the aging man's comforting hand on his shoulder and hear his voice, which always seemed so lyrical that every sentence was a chanting prayer. The rabbi would be proud of the work he had done this day.

FEW PATIENTS WERE MORE used to hospitals and their routines than Yael Cohen. She knew most of the nurses in Nahariya's main hospital and all of the doctors, and had walked this very ward a hundred times when she was a surgeon operating here.

After the massacre in the synagogue, she'd been brought by ambulance, unconscious, with a rising temperature from the infection that the lodged bullet was causing her. As a shooting casualty, she was immediately wheeled into the triage section and examined by an intern. But when a terrified and profoundly distressed Yaniv Grossman had explained who the patient was and her relationship to the hospital, a call had immediately been made to the hospital's director, the thoracic surgeon Fadi Islam Suk.

Though he was in a meeting with a man from the Health Ministry, Fadi leapt from his seat and ran at full speed down the four flights of stairs to the emergency room. He strode into the cubicle where Yael was being examined and looked at her pale, almost lifeless face.

"Dear God," he said, turning and barking instructions at the ward nurse. "Get Raoul the anesthetist to prep for surgery; get the operating theater ready—find one that's sterilized. Now. Immediately."

He turned to the intern and barked, "What's happened to her? How did this happen?"

Standing just outside the drawn curtains, Yaniv entered and spoke to Fadi. He explained who he was and that Yael had been the victim of a sniper shooting in nearby Peki'in.

Fadi nodded. "Are you her brother? Who are you?"

"No . . . I'm just a . . ." But the Palestinian doctor didn't let Yaniv finish.

"Okay, look, she's been shot in the upper thorax but her blood pressure isn't weak, which is a good thing; it means that no major blood vessels were hit. But I won't know until we get her into surgery."

Then Fadi took charge. Within half an hour of her arriving at the emergency room, the Palestinian surgeon was operating on Yael, tracing the path of the gunshot and opening only as much of her chest as he needed to to expose the bullet so that he could remove it. It had torn much of the surrounding muscle but hadn't fractured any bones or severed any important blood vessels. Yael was young and strong and healthy; she could fight the infection. Fadi rarely prayed, but as his hands worked and the sweat beaded on his brow, he said a silent prayer to Allah beneath his surgical mask. And one to Yahweh just in case.

———

FOUR DAYS LATER, Yael was sitting up in bed, eating grapes and sipping pomegranate juice and, strangely, beginning to enjoy being a patient. Her private room was full of sunlight, a spectacular view over the Mediterranean, flowers, fruit, dozens of get-well cards, stuffed animals, and a pair of felt lungs inside a plastic rib cage, a joke from surgical coworkers in Jerusalem.

She'd been visited by colleagues and concerned friends. She'd been interviewed by the police, by Shin Bet, and by others who simply explained that they were from "the government."

Her problem was that she had absolutely no memory of what had happened in Peki'in. The anesthetic, the shock, and hitting her head on the floor when she fell with Bilal on top of her had robbed her of the memory of two days of her life. She remembered going to Peki'in desperate to save poor, dead Bilal. She clearly remembered the drive and Yaniv. But from there her mind was a complete blank. She had no memory at all of the synagogue, the shooting, the imam, or the massacre. To her it was a complete blank, and no amount of thinking about it made any of the details reappear. As soon as she was feeling more like a human being, she'd ask Yaniv to remind her of the details.

————

THE TIME AND PLACE of the meeting were sent to Eliahu Spitzer's phone by text message. He had wanted to go to the rabbi's home, a place that felt like a sanctuary, in some ways more sacred than a synagogue to him. But the message was clear about the time and place, and Eliahu made his way slowly to Sacher Park by public transport and then walked the rest of the way.

Eliahu arrived as the sun was setting, bathing the Old City in warm light like rich honey. Christian domes and Islamic minarets were interspersed in amber shades amid clusters of mobile phone antennas and modern glass-and-chrome structures. In this light, at this quiet time of day, everything was beautiful. The bullets and the bombs and the blood that had been spilled here were purified by the sunset and, for fleeting moments, forgotten.

He gazed out across the open expanse to the clusters and strings of people moving through the park. The modern intersected with the ancient, both in the buildings of Jerusalem and its people: women in power suits, police officers in uniforms, youngsters drafted into the army using mobile phones in one hand and clutching high-powered rifles in the other, children in American T-shirts, Arabs in veils, and Orthodox Jews in black hats and frock coats.

Reb Shmuel Telushkin ambled up the path toward Eliahu, his gaze on no one and nothing in particular. Eliahu stood as his mentor and teacher approached, but the rabbi paid no mind and sat down on the end of the park bench without a word.

"How are you, Rabbi? I hope you're well," said Eliahu.

The rabbi drew a deep breath as he looked out across the park, but didn't answer. Nor did he look at Eliahu.

"Your family?"

The rabbi gave a nod as his only response.

"Good," answered Eliahu as a strange uneasiness spread over him.

The two men sat in silence for a long moment until the rabbi spoke with a voice so soft that Eliahu had to lean closer to hear.

"How many are dead?"

"Three," replied Eliahu soberly.

"All of them Arabs?"

"Yes."

"But there were others?" said the rabbi. "The girl . . . the doctor. And the American?"

Spitzer hesitated before answering. "Yes."

"And what of them?" the rabbi asked in a tone that said he knew the answer already but that this, in true Jewish fashion, was to become a teaching moment.

Eliahu didn't answer. He was not expecting to be questioned, and the interrogation took him by surprise. In his head he went through the responses he might give: that the two Jews who survived didn't know anything; that they would be taken care of. But in the silence the rabbi turned to face him for the first time.

"What of them? Such a mess. This is not what should have been. When you came to us, I had such hopes. I thought that out of your tragedy . . . but it wasn't to be." The rabbi sighed.

Eliahu was starting to get annoyed. Where was the praise for what he had done for their cause? Where was the warm hand on his shoulder and the encouragement for what he must do next to prepare Israel for the Messiah?

"Nobody could have foreseen what—"

"God foresees! The Almighty knows everything! You may have been blind to the consequences, but because of your failure we are weaker today than before. Because of you!" The rabbi shook his head in dismay.

Eliahu was too stunned to speak. A grown and experienced soldier, a man who had seen more war than most, and suddenly he felt like a schoolboy being reprimanded.

The scolding continued. "Who is our puppet now, huh? Which Arabs can we call upon to place their bombs? Huh? When this false government"—he waved a hand in the direction of the Knesset—"starts to talk of a peace process once again, who will throw the stones? If there is peace, this false Israel becomes strong. But while there is violence it is weak; it can be torn down and God's will be done."

"There will be others. I can find another imam," Eliahu said desperately.

"Bah!" spat the rabbi. "This failure cannot be endured."

"What are you saying, Rabbi? What can I do?" begged Eliahu.

"Nothing. You can do nothing." The rabbi stood.

"The doctor and her boyfriend, they know nothing. They have nothing to hurt us."

"There is too much attention around them. Too much attention on you. You have failed, and exposed yourself by your failure. It is a matter of time before your Shin Bet brothers come for you."

"Rabbi. Please."

"There is nothing you can do. We have no place for you."

And with that, the rabbi walked away into the sinking sun and fading light.

———

UNUSUALLY FOR A MAN whose life had been dedicated to action, Eliahu Spitzer sat in his office for much of the evening, incapable of moving. He had intended to return home but he was fixed to his chair, his mind in turmoil, ever since returning from his meeting with Reb Telushkin in the park.

He looked around his familiar office: the television, the bookshelf, the photographs on the wall of him smiling and shaking hands with prime ministers, presidents, and heads of foreign delegations. He looked at his desk; there were no papers or files, just a photograph, a computer screen, and a keyboard. Typical of his orderly life, no mess, no fuss, everything in its precise place. It was his Germanic background: everything had to be precisely so.

He couldn't stand the offices of his colleagues, where coffee cups and books and documents obscured the tops of their desks. All that was allowed on top of his desk, aside from the screen and the keyboard, was a photograph of his beloved dead daughter, Shoshanna, when she was just nine years old, smiling at him from the distant past, dressed in a swimsuit, standing on a sandy beach against a blue sea and sky. It was a vacation they'd taken when he'd been posted to America. Where was it? Oh, yes, Florida. She was smiling back at him. Those were halcyon days of innocence and happiness. He would give anything just to hold her again, just to have her young, innocent arms draped around his neck, telling him she loved him and that he was the best daddy in the entire world.

He found himself immensely tired—so exhausted that he could easily drop off to sleep in his chair. All this duplicity, lying, cunning, and subterfuge had drained him of everything, including his own self. But his energy had come from his cause: to create a land of chaos so that the Messiah, the Jewish Messiah, would know that he had to come again and save his people and Israel. None of his former friends or his family understood or even knew of his mission; he'd only seen his Shoshanna, so young and happy in that brilliant light, beckoning him to come to her. He thought he could bring her back when the Messiah returned.

But Reb Telushkin had cut him dead. All the struggles, all the cunning. Why should he continue with it? Why struggle when it was so easy to close his eyes and sleep? And in sleep, in sleeping forever, he'd see his Shoshanna again. Hold her, hug her, protect her.

And he closed his eyes, and in the blackness he saw again the brilliant white light. Framed in the center of the light was the distant face of his Shoshanna. He would do anything to hold her again, his precious, beautiful daughter. Eliahu said a *b'rucha* over his girl, as though this were the anniversary of the day she was murdered.

"Blessed and praised, glorified and exalted, extolled and honored, adored and lauded be the name of the Holy One, blessed be He, beyond all the blessings and hymns, praises and consolations that are ever spoken in the world; and say Amen."

He opened his eyes, suddenly feeling calm and rested. Knotted muscles uncoiled. Now he knew what he would do. He should have done it years ago, but it wasn't too late. In fact, this was the best time to do it. He opened his desk drawer, took out his prayer book, and opened it to Hallel, the Praise of God. When he'd finished saying the prayer, he took out a revolver from the back of his drawer, said another quick *b'rucha*, this one for the rest of his family, and put the barrel in his mouth.

The last word he said before he pulled the trigger was his daughter's name.

Shoshanna.

————

126 CE
The village of Peki'in

IT WAS A BLISTERINGLY HOT Sabbath day. Others hoped that their one day free of work would reward them with prayer and that after the worship they could return to their homes from the synagogue in Peki'in to benefit from the occasional breeze that might blow up from the olive groves below. Then they could rest.

But Abram ben Yitzhak, grandson of the beloved builder of the synagogue—Samuel the olive merchant—and his good wife, Sarah, had a duty to perform and until it was done, he would earn neither respite nor a cool breeze.

Today was the anniversary of his grandfather Samuel's death all those years ago, and so it was Abram's duty to visit the cemetery and say prayers. The young lad remembered his grandfather with enormous fondness; remembered how he would sit beside him in the synagogue and Grandfather Samuel would explain the meaning of every stone, every column, every artifact, and why he had the builders place them there. His favorite moments were when Grandfather Samuel told him of the way he'd escaped the Romans when they'd destroyed Jerusalem, of Samuel's bravery on the journey, of the way he'd saved the life of Grandmother Sarah and her family, of how he'd tricked the Roman centurion when he'd boldly faced him on the road north by sending Grandmother Sarah to hide in the woods, and of how he'd entered the village of Peki'in to crowds lining the streets and thinking that he was the king of Israel.

But those days were long gone. The Romans now owned all of Israel and the surrounding nations, their legions were everywhere, Jews were servants in their own land, and anybody who opposed their Roman rulers was crucified along the roadside. Many of the Jews of Israel, especially those who had somehow survived the siege of Jerusalem, had been expelled, sent to other countries as slaves. But those who remained had learned to live their lives in isolation, and the village of Peki'in was rarely bothered by centurions or their troops, who generally marched north and south along the coast road and the Highway of the Kings.

And so life in Peki'in continued as it had always continued: growing olives in the valley, making pottery, and supplying other villages with herbs and spices, which grew in abundance on the rugged hills.

Abram had lived in Peki'in all his life, and in the past years had tended to his family's graves now that his father Yitzhak was bedridden. Unusually, Grandfather Samuel had written before his death that he wanted his bones to be dug up after two years, when his flesh had been eaten by worms, and placed in a limestone ossuary, a practice that had not been undertaken for at least two lifetimes. He had learned of the technique because he'd lived for many years in Jerusalem, where the cemeteries were full of such bone boxes, as the villagers crudely called them. When his testament had become known two years earlier, there was disquiet in the village, but the rabbi of the synagogue had decreed that there was no part of Jewish law that forbade it, nor did Roman law in Judea deny the right of a Jew to an ossuary, and so it had been done.

Now, as Abram left the small but beautiful synagogue, he kissed the two stones that his grandfather had taken from the destroyed temple in Jerusalem built by King Herod, a curse on his name and may his evil children piss on his grave, and walked the half a league to the village cemetery up on the hill. He found his grandfather's grave and said the memorial prayer, said a prayer for his Grandmother Sarah, placed fruit and bread on both graves, and left the cemetery by a different road. Instead of returning to the village, Abram sat on a rock and scrutinized the surrounding countryside. Satisfied that there were no Romans, no spies looking at his activities, and no villagers to notice what he was doing, Abram walked along a shepherd's track to the upper hills above Peki'in.

He continued to stop and sit on rocks with a commanding view of the village and its roadways, checking, always checking, that nobody was watching him. Only four people in the village knew who was living in the cave he was about to enter. If word spread and the information came to the ears of the Romans, then not only would the two blessed men be crucified but the entire village would suffer decimation, in which one in ten of the residents would be hauled out of the square and whipped, have his eyes gouged out, and then be nailed upside down on a cross of wood as a Roman lesson to all who dared to disobey.

After Abraham climbed a narrow rocky track that led to the top of the mighty hill, the mouth of the cave came into sight. Panting from exertion, Abram stood beside the low-lying limbs of a carob tree and rested. Above the screams of two ospreys circling high in the sky searching for prey, he heard the voices of two men, one older than the other, in heated argument. He smiled and continued to listen to the frenzied words, the fury of one, the denial of the other. Abram could have spent the day just listening to them arguing. The anger, the indignation, the vehemence, the wounded pride, the treachery, the forgiveness, the love, the concern—it was a school for adults, an energetic and animated search for the truth, which he loved listening to.

"Fool of a son," said the father. "How could your mother have given birth to such a blockhead? Don't you understand the beauty of what I'm describing? How could you argue for such a simplistic form of the Divine when you just have to look around you and—"

"Father," interrupted the son, shouting over the other's voice, "my love for you knows no bounds, but your portrayal of the Shekinah shows me that your eyes are dim and your mind needs rest. Moses could not enter the Tent of Meetings because the cloud had settled upon it. And the cloud was the Glory of the Lord. It is the very nature of—"

"Idiot! Imbecile! This shows you have no understanding of the word 'cloud.' What it means is . . ."

And so they continued, and Abram would have listened for much longer had it not been the Sabbath and his mother expecting him home from synagogue and the cemetery. He coughed and called out the code. The interruption immediately made the men stop speaking. From the mouth of the cave, a tentative voice said softly, "Abram?"

In a low, gravelly voice, the boy said mischievously, "It is Yahweh, the Shekinah, Adonai, the Cloud and Spirit of our people Israel."

A man walked out of the cave, beaming with joy. "Abram," said the older of the two men, Rabbi Shimon bar Yochai, who had lived there for the past twelve years. He opened his arms, and Abram walked gleefully forward and hugged the scholar. "How are you, my lovely child?" he asked.

Abram was about to answer, when Rabbi Shimon's son, Rabbi Eleazar, walked out, smiled when he saw his father and the young boy, and joined in the hug.

Eagerly, Abram said, "I've brought you food and—"

"Wait," said Rabbi Eleazar, "let us thank the Lord God Almighty that you are safe and that you have been spared to visit us again."

And the three of them prayed. When they'd finished thanking the Almighty for His many blessings, the two rabbis eagerly waited for Abram to open the sack he was carrying, and gazed ravenously at the food. His mother, one of the few who knew of the rabbis in the cave, had packed cheese and bread, fish caught from the sea the previous day, and pastes of olive and herbs.

Eleazar thanked the Almighty that for at least a few days they wouldn't have to eat the fruit of the nearby carob tree, which, though delicious, was boring after days of eating nothing else. They went into the cave and sat on wooden stools, which Abram had brought to them when his father had become bedridden from a farming accident and handed over the care of the rabbis to his trust.

Yitzhak had first hidden the rabbis when they escaped the vengeance of the Roman commanders in Jerusalem. It was an incident that had become Jewish folklore: Rabbi Shimon was debating the effect of the conquerors on the land when he openly criticized the Romans for constructing marketplaces, baths, forums, roads, and bridges not for the benefit of those who had been conquered but for their own benefit. He mused about the reasons why conquerors rape and pillage a land instead of bringing the benefits of their civilization to those people now under their control. Overheard by a Jewish spy who reported his words to a centurion, Rabbi Shimon was condemned to death, but he escaped to the uncharted wastes of the Galilee with his son. They were taken in by Abram's father and given safety in a distant cave far above the village in the mountains, where they'd lived for year after year.

Abram sat with his friends, the rabbis, and refused their offer of food. "My mother prepared this for you, and I can eat freely when I go home this afternoon," he said.

The rabbis nodded and continued eating the bread, saying separate blessings over each different part of the meal.

"Rabbi," said Abram.

"Yes?" they both said at once, the son smiling and nodding in deference to the father.

"Yes, Abram, what is it?" asked Rabbi Shimon as he stuffed another piece of sheep's cheese into his mouth.

"There's talk of another uprising against the Romans. Another Zealot uprising. If there is one, should I join in?"

Rabbi Shimon reeled in horror. "God forbid, my child. Don't talk that way. Don't think that way. The last time there was an uprising against the Romans, they crucified Zealots by the thousands, called our land Judea, and even then took away our name, Israel, the name that our forefather was given when he changed his name from Jacob. It means triumphant with God, but God's home has now been destroyed. And to further humiliate us, the devils now call our beloved nation Philistia, mocking us by calling us after King David's mortal enemies, the Philistines. And Jerusalem, our precious Jerusalem, was destroyed. And look at it now. A foul Roman city they call Aelia Capitolina with pigs roaming the street and with temples and idols where their gods Jupiter and Mars and Venus are worshipped.

"No, Abram, God's eyes are closed when He looks at the Israel of King David and the prophets. He smiles on our brothers, who have been exiled to distant lands, but He doesn't smile on us, and if we do anything to further anger the Romans, they'll bring legion after legion to our hills and valleys and then there will be nobody left. We'll be crucified or exiled. And only God Almighty knows which is the worse fate for the Jews."

Abram shook his head. He was only fourteen years of age, a man by Jewish custom and tradition, but he was still loath to argue with such a renowned figure as Rabbi Shimon. "But, Rabbi, when the emperor Hadrian visited Jerusalem a few years ago, he promised to rebuild the temple. Isn't that good?"

Rabbi Eleazar interrupted. "He will rebuild the temple, but he's announced that the new building will be dedicated to their god Jupiter. And don't forget Hadrian's ban on circumcision, the act of commitment of Jews to our Lord God. No, Abram, we are a defeated people, and you must not—"

"But what about Simon bar Kokhba? Even Rabbi Akiva has called him a messiah. He will rise up and defeat the Romans and save us all. Won't he?" the boy said plaintively.

The two rabbis looked at Abram's eager face, a young Jewish boy hoping for an end to the misery of the Romans, a boy just wanting to be free of the chains that bound him into servitude.

Rabbi Shimon sighed, smiled at the lad, and nodded. "Perhaps Bar Kokhba will gather our people together and fight the Romans. And please God Almighty that if he does rise up, that he wins, because if he loses, then the Romans will be merciless. They'll exile every Jew and the land will be empty and desolate of people, our fields sowed with salt, our woods burned. Then where will we go?"

Abram looked at Rabbi Shimon, his face creased with a frown.

"But these things probably won't happen, my dear. God will protect us. Those who were sent into exile will return. It may take a hundred years, a thousand years, maybe more, but they will return. Meanwhile, those of us who remain in Israel will keep the flame of Judaism alive, just like the Maccabees kept their flame alive in the time of the Greeks. Who knows what plans the Almighty has in store for us?"

Now the father and son looked at each other. Abram wondered what they were thinking.

"Abram, my child. As you know, my son and I are unable to leave this cave. And it is very likely that most of the Jews who live in Israel will be expelled should there be another onslaught by the Romans. Many will tell you that it is not going to happen, but God has spoken to us and has told us to prepare the Jewish people for a long and sorry separation from our land."

Abram began to argue, but the elderly rabbi held up his hand. He reached into his robes and took out a piece of stone. It was beautiful, made perhaps of alabaster or white onyx. Looking at it closely, it had very odd Hebrew writing on it, writing such as Abram hadn't seen before.

"My child, this tablet was put inside a tunnel that runs from the floor of the Kidron Valley to the top of the mountain, where the Romans now live. The top of this tunnel comes out at the very foot of the temple. It was placed there in the time of King Solomon and was removed by those Jews who were exiled to Babylon in the time of King Nebuchadnezzar. They returned it and replaced it, Abram, but when we were forced to leave Jerusalem, my son, Rabbi Eleazar, though but a child, risked his life to retrieve it. We didn't know then what would happen to us Jews, but it now looks as though there will be no Jews living here when the Romans are done with us."

The old rabbi didn't know how to make the request he had in mind, and he looked at his son, tears filling his eyes. But suddenly Abram said, "Why don't I go to Jerusalem and put it back? Then, if all the Jews leave Israel, at least the Lord God Adonai Elohim will know that we used to be here."

The boy's eager and innocent face, completely unaware of the dangers that faced him on the incredible journey he was offering to undertake, made the old rabbi cry. He hugged the boy and kissed his head.

"And," said Abram excitedly, "when I get to Jerusalem, I'll hide the tablet in a crack in the wall and cover it with mud so that no Roman will find it. Of course, Adonai will know where it is, because He sees everything."

Rabbi Eleazar said softly, "Let us pray, Abram, for God's love and mercy to save our people, Israel. Let us pray that we are not exiled as we were in the time of the Babylonians. Let us pray for your safe return from this journey."

They walked to the precipitous edge, surveyed the village of Peki'in far below them, and prayed together. In the center of the village was the square, populated by many people walking about on a Sabbath afternoon, sitting on stools shaded by cloths from the midday sun, and enjoying the weekly luxury of not working. In the middle of the village square, a spring, which slaked the thirst of the rabbis in the cave before it descended back into the mountain, ran out and cascaded down the ruts it had cut into the rock over countless millennia. Not far from the square was the roof of the synagogue where the villagers had just been praying, a prayer house built by Abram's grandfather to the memory of a good doctor, long forgotten.

It was a building of love and peace and harmony, where the Jews gathered every evening and many mornings before work to pray to the Lord God Almighty.

Rabbi Shimon sighed as he looked down at the amity and accord of the village. Perhaps this is what God wanted for His people Israel. Jerusalem had been nothing but a thousand-year dream, one that would be inhabited by the Romans for another thousand years. And when their empire came to an end and died, as had the Egyptian, Babylonian, and Greek empires, Jerusalem would be inhabited by another invader. Or maybe the Jews who had been exiled would return and rebuild the temple. Who knew?

But in the meantime the Jews of Peki'in, and those Jews adjusting to their new lives in distant lands, would carry the Temple of Jerusalem in their hearts. And a part of the Temple of Jerusalem would be in every synagogue where they gathered: to pray, to do, to be.

November 17, 2007

YANIV FELT HIDEOUSLY uncomfortable in the synagogue. He didn't want to return to Peki'in, to relive the horror, to remember the smell of bullets and hatred and death. But Yael had insisted. She had to reclaim her memory of that terrible day, and no matter how much Yaniv told her of what had happened, no matter that he related the incidents minute by minute, it didn't satisfy her. She had to return to recall, to re-create, to reexperience, to fix the day in her mind: the time between arriving in Peki'in and waking up in the hospital to the sound of beeping monitors and the expectant faces of nurses and doctors.

They walked into the synagogue and Yael's gaze was immediately drawn to the blood on the floor. After the police and forensic experts had departed the place and the synagogue was no longer a crime scene, attempts by caretakers and cleaners to remove the stains had been valiant but ultimately unsuccessful. Where once bright red blood had pumped from the still-beating hearts of three men mortally wounded, now the luminous sheen had become a dark brown ominous stain. It was as though the lives of three vital men had oozed through the floorboards and drained into the ground, invisible, veiled, and eternal.

She looked at the stains and wondered whether the good or the evil had leached out of their bodies into the ground. Troubled, Yael reached for Yaniv's hand and their fingers intertwined not in affection but for protection.

"Bilal was there." He nodded toward a stain on the floor where once a congregant's bench had sat. "Over there"—he nodded to a spot nearby—"was where Hassan fell. And there"—he nodded again, this time toward the front of the synagogue—"was where the imam's body ended up. For some reason, when he fell, he seemed to fall furthest from you."

She couldn't take her eyes off the stains, knowing that once they were parts of human beings. She felt absolutely no emotion. She was a doctor and very used to blood, and in the years since she'd become a surgeon, she'd trained herself not to feel revulsion, empathy, or compassion. She would just get on with her job of saving lives. But this was different. This was a wooden floor, blemished and inanimate, and despite what her intellect told her, she couldn't feel any association with pain or grief or loss.

Yet, she couldn't take her eyes off the stain on the wooden floor where Bilal's blood had been spilled. His blood; her blood. They'd come from the same bloodline. Perhaps their lines had been joined when the Muslims were exiled from Circassia in the middle of the nineteenth century; perhaps when the Jews were expelled from Israel by the Romans in the first century. It was a history she'd never be able to uncover. But in the end, what did it matter? What difference did it make that she was a Jew living in Israel and Bilal had been an Arab living in the same country but wanted to call it Palestine. What did it matter? They were all human beings. And trace everybody's ancestry back a couple of million years and they all had the same mother, a four-foot-nothing apelike creature living in the Great Rift Valley of Africa. What did it all matter in the end?

She turned to Yaniv and said softly, "Let's go."

Half an hour later, they were standing on the ledge outside the cave, high above the village of Peki'in, where legend had it that a famous rabbi and his son had hidden for fourteen years from the Roman invaders. In that time they were supposed to have eaten from the fruit of the massive carob tree that had spread over the entire hillside, and drunk water from a spring inside the cave; but a landslide sometime in history had closed off the cave and all that remained was the entrance.

Yael and Yaniv sat on a bench that the local authorities had placed nearby for the thousands of religious tourists who came to say prayers at Rabbi Shimon bar Yochai's cave.

"Well?" said Yaniv. He sounded diffident, almost reluctant to ask.

She shook her head. "Nothing. There's no memory. I just can't picture a thing. I remember the synagogue because I've been there before, but I have no memory at all of Bilal and Hassan and the imam being there. It's as if my mind is a slate and somebody has rubbed out the words."

Yaniv nodded and, deep in thought, continued to look over the town. The terra-cotta roofs, the bright café awnings, the cars negotiating the narrow lanes—it was like a picture postcard. Yet, just weeks ago, half a mile away, a murderer called

Eliahu Spitzer, a willing servant of a crazed ultra-religious Jewish sect called Neturei Karta, had killed three people and almost succeeded in killing Yael and him. And, of course, it had all been hushed up by the government, who'd told him that if he had hard, concrete evidence to show them of Neturei Karta's involvement in the murders or the plots to bring down the government, then show them; if not, keep *schtum* and don't cause trouble between the secular and the religious communities. And in return for them not making waves, no charges would be brought against either Yael or him for abducting Bilal from lawful custody.

So Eliahu's suicide had been put down to grief. The murders of the imam, Bilal, and Hassan, for want of evidence, had been earmarked as the work of a new and violent Islamic terrorist group. And the wounding of Yael had been an accident of proximity: wrong place at the wrong time. A senior executive of Shin Bet had visited the mosque in Bayt al Gizah and spoken to the community leaders, telling them that the imam's coterie of young terrorists would be disbanded immediately or certain young people would be arrested. It was all so neat.

Yaniv felt Yael's closeness, her warmth, and thanked God that she was alive and well and that her wound would heal and leave her with only a small scar on her chest. He reached over and kissed her on the neck, then the cheek. With a shock, he realized that he'd never kissed her before. Not properly. She had beautiful skin.

But she didn't seem to notice. She was miles away in thought. He heard her exhale long and hard, as if she were venting her body of the last evil breath, the last evil thought, before returning to her peaceful world of trauma surgery, where she was in charge and nobody except for the fortunes of nature was ordering her about.

As though she were talking to herself, she asked softly, "One thing I still don't understand. How did Spitzer know that we'd be in the synagogue? Why did he come up from Jerusalem? Who told him?"

Yaniv thought hard how to respond. Just as softly as Yael had asked, he replied, "Perhaps the imam, and Spitzer used it as an opportunity to take him out. Perhaps it was Hassan playing a double game. Or perhaps he followed one of us using satellite tracking and blew away the only people who could connect him to the attempt to destroy the temple and expose him as a member of Neturei Karta."

He instantly regretted saying it. Her mind was dazed, and he knew he shouldn't be specific. He held his breath, hoping that his answer would be the end of her questions.

She rested her head on his shoulder. He put his arm protectively around her waist. It was so peaceful up here. Below her in the valley was laid out a history of people wrought in the landscape, in the streams and rivers, in caves and villages. A history of rulers and religion, of power and corruption. Of love and loss and hope.

People had survived here when war, disaster, and persecution were bent on destroying them. People had been trapped here when their neighbors refused to harbor them. People had fled here when they had nowhere else to go.

And yet, despite all the blood that had stained the soil in the valley below her, to Yael it seemed so very peaceful.

"This is the only country in the world that has more trees at the end of the year than it does at the beginning," Yael said softly, almost to herself. Yaniv's only response was to smile and draw her closer.

Looking down at the peaceful village of Peki'in, she thought for a moment how pleasant it would be to live in a tiny community and do menial work close to nature and to whatever passed in her mind for a deity.

Just weeks ago evil had visited that village, pierced the

sanctity of its synagogue with bullet holes, and spilled blood in the place where men, women, and children worshipped an invisible deity. An imam corrupting a boy to strap a bomb to his body; a rabbi manipulating the pain of a soldier to make him a weapon.

To some, such acts would encourage and inspire; to others they would create outrage, fear, and distrust. As for Yael, she might never remember how Bilal shielded her from the bullets, never remember the sacrifice she would not be able to repay. But she remembered Bilal, his face and the bloodline connection she was yet to understand. Rather than despair, she felt a strange kind of calm. That bloodline was a part of the country in which she stood.

When she was a child, Yael's family had taken a vacation to America. They had traveled through the great national parks and in South Dakota she had visited the huge carved mountain memorial of the Native American chief Crazy Horse. His immortal words had stayed with her all these years: "My lands are where my dead lie buried." Yet, it was only now, as she gazed out over the valley, that she understood what they meant. The country wasn't hers; she didn't own it. She belonged to it. The land owned her and all who lived here—it always had and always would. And it would never let her go.

She turned to Yaniv and said quietly, "I wonder when . . . when in our family history Bilal and I became joined?"

He didn't answer. It would always remain one of the hidden secrets of human history. Just like the seal that Bilal had discovered when he accidentally blew the detonator in the tunnel and brought a small part of the roof down. Her late grandfather Shalman had been thrilled by the discovery, but for Yael and for Yaniv it was one of the mysteries of a life that other people had once lived. Unknowable, undiscoverable, and eternal. And now, regardless of the fate of the people who had made it and then discovered it millennia later, the seal would sit for all time on a museum shelf, behind glass, looked at by countless generations of people. And in the end, what did it all matter?

She nuzzled further into his neck, feeling warm and secure. As the sun began to set over the distant Mediterranean, they stood and slowly walked back to their car.

And then they drove back to Jerusalem.

ACKNOWLEDGMENTS

In the time of Austen, Fielding, and Dickens, authors invariably worked alone, isolated until the sunlight of publication. Today this is no longer the case. Authors work with a team of unseen but hugely talented people to turn their ideas into the reality of a book.

Without Harold Finger and his eagle-eyed wife, Rebecca, there would have been no Heritage Trilogy. Their support, contacts, and advice in every facet of the work's creation has brought it to life. It was Harold who instigated this project, and to him go special thanks. And to my coauthor, Mike Jones, whose innate understanding of plotting, structure, and characters is extraordinary, my admiration and gratitude.

My wife, Eva, and my son, Raffe, were instrumental in helping me edit this work, and to them go my deepest gratitude.

My most sincere appreciation and admiration go to the team at Simon & Schuster in Australia and the USA. Lou Johnson, managing director of Simon & Schuster in Australia, has an incisive understanding of how books today have had to change to meet the challenges of a digital world, and her brilliance puts her head and shoulders above the rest. Larissa Edwards, head of publishing, is the bedrock of its publication, the ideal colleague in such an enterprise, tough but always understanding; Roberta Ivers brought a wonderfully perceptive and critical eye to this manuscript and her advice and suggestions were invaluable, as were those of Jo Butler and Jo Jarrah. No book will be a success unless marketed and sold professionally, and there is no more professional group in the Australian book industry than the wonderful Anabel Pandiella, Greg Tilney, and Kate Cubitt and her remarkable team. In America, my thanks go to the president and publisher of the Atria imprint of Simon & Schuster, Judith Curr, and my editor, Daniel Loedel.

And to Abraham, Isaac, and Jacob goes my reverence, because without them, where would I (or Western civilization) be? The world's three great Abrahamic religions have an intimate, if strained, alliance in Israel. Judaism, Christianity, and Islam—father, son, and grandson—live there in the closest proximity; yet, tragically, at times they could not be further apart. From this benighted land has sprung the most profound philosophies, literature, and poetry; yet for thousands of years its peoples have been torn apart by hatred, jealousy, and violence.

So will there ever be peace among these three faiths? God knows!

Alan Gold

A book is no easy thing to write. It's a titanic wrestle of words and endurance. And it's not an endeavor one can face on his own. To that end there are many to thank.

First and foremost, to my collaborator, Alan Gold, whose energy and enthusiasm know no bounds. Thank you for having me along for the ride. Thanks also to our producer, Harold Finger, who saw the vision and wanted to back it.

We could not have wished for a more engaged, insightful, or forward-thinking publisher than Simon & Schuster Australia. Endless thanks go to Lou Johnson, Larissa Edwards, Roberta Ivers, Anabel Pandiella, Greg Tilney, Kate Cubitt, and all the S&S team.

Of course, the greatest thanks of all go to my family for putting up with me, loving me, and catching me when I fall.

Mike Jones

ABOUT THE AUTHORS

ALAN GOLD is an internationally published and translated author of fifteen novels, his most recent being *Bell of the Desert*, published in 2012 in the USA.

He speaks regularly to national and international conferences on a range of subjects, most notably the recent growth of anti-Semitism. He was a delegate at the United Nations World Conference on Racism and Xenophobia held in Durban, South Africa, in 2001, and has addressed UN conferences and meetings throughout the world as well as universities and community groups.

Alan is a regular contributor to the *Australian*, the *Spectator*, and other media as an opinion columnist and literary critic, and a lecturer and mentor at the master's and doctoral degree level in creative writing at the Universities of Sydney and Western Australia and the Australian National University.

MIKE JONES is a writer and creative producer working across screen, page, and digital media. His work has received numerous accolades, including an Australian Writers Guild AWGIE Award. He has lectured internationally on interactive and multi-platform storytelling and is currently commissioned to write a three-volume series of gothic horror novels to be published in 2015.

VISIT BOTH AUTHORS AT
HeritageTrilogy.com.